Praise for

THE ONLY SUSPECT

'The best Louise Candlish novel yet' **Lisa Jewell**

'I couldn't put it down' **Shari Lapena**

'I'm blown away by how good it is. A gripping tale of love, secrets and deception – it's the best psychological thriller I've read in a long time' **Mark Edwards**

'An incredible page-turner . . . An absolute must-read. Get this on your 2023 wish list' **BA Paris**

'Incredibly tense. Louise Candlish is one of my favourite writers and this is her best book yet' **Clare Mackintosh**

'A compelling, nerve-tingling treat' **Nicci French**

'A twisting, seductive, ingenious thriller from the consistently brilliant Louise Candlish. I'm a huge fan' **Chris Whitaker**

'Took me straight back to the heady days of 1995 – brilliant stuff' **Harriet Tyce**

'Completely addictive and devilishly clever - the queen of the killer twist strikes again!' **T. M. Logan**

'The Only Suspect is a heady pleasure from the very first page. It's both a page-tearing mystery and a pitch-perfect 90s period piece. Shimmers with mystery, tension, and dirty glamour' **Abigail Dean**

'Such a vivid sense of place, a gripping plot . . . The Only Suspect is the book version of a Rubik's Cube with so many unexpected twists and turns. An adrenaline burner for sure!' **Liz Nugent**

LOUISE CANDLISH

THE ONLY SUSPECT

SIMON &
SCHUSTER

London · New York · Sydney · Toronto · New Delhi

First published in Great Britain by Simon & Schuster UK Ltd, 2023
This paperback edition first published 2023

1 3 5 7 9 10 8 6 4 2

Simon & Schuster UK Ltd
1st Floor
222 Gray's Inn Road
London WC1X 8HB

Simon & Schuster Australia, Sydney
Simon & Schuster India, New Delhi

www.simonandschuster.co.uk
www.simonandschuster.com.au
www.simonandschuster.co.in

A CIP catalogue record for this book
is available from the British Library

Paperback ISBN: 978-1-3985-0982-5
eBook ISBN: 978-1-3985-0981-8
Audio ISBN: 978-1-3985-0973-3

Typeset in Sabon by M Rules
Printed and Bound in the UK using 100% Renewable
Electricity at CPI Group (UK) Ltd

*To one of the UK's keenest consumers of
crime fiction: my dad.*

1

Alex

Black skies would have made a more fitting backdrop, some monstrous winter storm that tore the house from its foundations, but as it transpired the moment he'd been dreading for twenty-five years came on a still, gentle morning in May.

Well, not the moment *exactly*, but the precursor of it. The beginning of the end.

It was the weekend and he and Beth were at the kitchen table in their pyjamas, drinking coffee and scrolling through the news on their phones, when she exclaimed: 'Yay, the council's finally given the go-ahead for the trail! Dulcie's *literally* just got the email. Isn't that fabulous?'

'The trail. Right.' This was as much as he could muster before his body went into a kind of arrest, a frankly terrifying sensation, as if he might look down and see his limbs crumble to dust in front of him.

Get a grip, Alex. You knew this would happen.

Ever since that damn campaign was launched two years ago, it had only ever been a matter of time, for Beth's compadres – Dulcie and Samira and the rest of them – were typical thirty- and forty-something Silver Vale women and mostly mums, which was to say committed to the point of psychotic.

'Persistence beat resistance in the end then,' he said with an approximation of good cheer.

'Always does, Alex. Always does.'

That had been one of the slogans of the trail committee: 'Persistence Beats Resistance'. There'd been something different to begin with – 'Take Back the Track', maybe – but once it became clear that the council were playing silly buggers, fighting talk prevailed and suddenly they were all Churchill.

We shall never surrender!

'Can you let Olive out, babe,' Beth said, and thankfully he'd recovered sufficient bodily function to get to his feet and open the door for their collie cross, who promptly pivoted and skittered straight back inside. Alex slipped her a treat before settling back in his seat. He was experiencing a weird cartoonish spasm in his jaw that he knew must be visible, but Beth was too busy thumbing through her messages to notice.

'You know, the more I think about it, the more I think how bloody criminal it's been to keep it blocked off all these years. Everyone knows how easy it is to climb over the barriers – it's been *way* more dangerous closed than open. I mean, the kind of people who've been hanging out up there . . . Druggies, winos, all the rest of it. It's been a security risk this whole time.'

These were comments she'd made a hundred times before and that he'd routinely nodded along with. He'd stopped short of participating in the campaign, however, intent on keeping his local profile limbo-dancer low. The last thing he wanted was for Silver Vale to come under the spotlight a second time; it would only resurrect interest in the first.

Not that he could say this to Beth.

Sometimes when he looked at her, at that enviably sharp jawline, those bright, busy eyes the exact same shade of burnt umber as her hair, he caught himself wondering how he had come to have *this* wife and not the one he'd once fantasized about. How he'd come to find himself here, in Silver Vale, of all places, resident now for over a decade and passing for the most part as a contented suburban husband and homeowner.

He'd never told Beth he knew the area from before. When she'd first invited him back, almost twelve years ago now, they'd only known each other a few hours and he hadn't heard the address she'd given to the taxi driver. He wasn't exactly paying attention to the route, either – it was late at night and tipping down with rain, and in any case they were kissing – and he'd only twigged where they were when they passed the parade of shops on Surrey Road and took an abrupt left uphill. That was what made him break away from her and peer for a street name – *Exmoor Gardens* – at which point his lungs tightened with a horrible asthmatic panic he hadn't felt for years.

'This is . . . This is your street?'

'No, but we're almost there,' she said, mistaking his urgency for lust and clutching him again, and it was then that he glimpsed, through flyaway strands of her hair, the Stanleys' old place. The driveway had the same layout as before, smartly landscaped now and with a huge people carrier parked where Drew's BMW used to be. Moments later, the taxi turned right into a street of old railway cottages he'd forgotten all about – Long Lane, that was it. Beth's place was in the middle, directly opposite the steps to the track.

The second they stumbled inside, he excused himself and went straight to her bathroom, where he vomited into the toilet bowl and sluiced his mouth with the Listerine he found in the cabinet. Amazing he'd got away with it, when you thought about it, for he must have been obviously agitated when he rejoined her, but she was giggly, boozed up, all over him.

He remembered waking up next to her in the morning with horror in his heart, and how, after dressing, he'd been irresistibly drawn to the bedroom window, which had a view across the road of steel barriers at the top of the steps, the tangled wilderness beyond.

'Sneaking out before I can get your number?' she drawled from the bed, and he thought, *If only* that *were my biggest problem.*

Since she asked, he *had* assumed it was a one-night thing, but, well, she'd insisted on pursuing him and eventually he'd thought, *Let her have me if it means that much to her.* (He didn't say that in his wedding speech, of course, which had been barely a speech, in keeping with the discreet mood of the occasion; he'd kept the whole photos thing to a minimum, too.)

'Let's have a look,' he said, returning to the present, and she passed him her phone, a WhatsApp thread named 'Trailblazers' growing in front of his eyes. Christ, how he'd preferred life before you were subjected to these streams of other people's consciousness; he had enough on his plate wrangling his own.

Go, Team Persistence!
Full steam ahead now – pun totally intended!
Philip says the builders can start the week after next!

The week after next? *Fuck*.

'Apparently a journalist from the *South London News* has already been in touch,' Beth said, taking back the phone. 'Did you read that bit?'

'No. What for?'

'To report on our triumph, of course. They'll want to follow the progress of the project, you know, document the *journey*.' She pulled a face. 'I know, don't say it, you hate that word. Everything's a journey now, even putting out the bins.'

Alex just sipped his coffee, unable to smile at his own line.

'It's not like we don't have a juicy back story, though, is it? Dulcie's told them they should talk to Cordelia on Pleasance Road – she was here when it all happened and had a lot of contact with the police. Apparently, it was right behind her garden where the body was found.'

The coffee turned sour in his mouth. *Juicy back story . . . when it all happened . . .* All this time there'd been barely a murmur and now, suddenly, here it was at full tilt, sirens wailing. Who the fuck was Cordelia when she was at home? Surely she couldn't be the old biddy they'd met that time, the one in the gardening gloves? Well, not really an old biddy, back then she'd probably only been about fifty, but to men in their twenties she'd seemed ancient. She'd be in her seventies now and he was pretty sure that in all these years of being dragged by Beth for Aperol Spritzes in neighbours' gardens he'd never run into her. But what did that mean? He'd been lucky, that was all, and luck had a habit of running out.

'What body?' he said, and Beth looked at him in disbelief.

'I *told* you, don't you remember? A woman was killed on Exmoor Gardens, back in the Nineties. She lived at number fifty-four, where Tim and Frankie are? The couple with three young boys, all blond and feral, like snow wolves.' She paused, as he'd noticed she often did when speaking of large families, as if it were necessary to mark the injustice of their postcode's fertility lottery. How did *that* couple get three when *they* weren't allowed even one? 'Google it. The murder, I mean, not Tim and Frankie.'

'I will,' he agreed, as if he hadn't a hundred times already. There was nothing to find, of that he was confident, not even on Wikipedia. To read reports of a local crime story that pre-dated the online news era, you had to go to the British Library and look at microfiche of the original newspaper pages. Would Beth's reporter bother doing that?

Hopefully they'd be too young to even know what microfiche was.

Beth picked up the cafetière and drained the last inch of slurry into their cups. 'Anyway, by the time I bought this place in ninety-nine it had all died down, otherwise I'd have made sure I got some money knocked off the asking price.'

'Then why let a journalist stir it all up again now if there's a risk of it affecting house prices?'

'Oh, if anything, this will help. A cool new nature trail? Prices will go up.' A flicker of irritation crossed her face. 'Honestly, Alex, you're being very weird about this. You're not interested in the trail, you've made that clear from the start, but there's no need to put a dampener on it for the rest of us.'

'Sorry.' She was right, his attitude *was* weird, even for him, and it jolted him that she'd noticed early on. He thought he'd been more careful than that. 'I'm just, I don't know, a bit cynical about the whole eco-community thing.'

'You, cynical? Surely not.' There was more than a trace of indulgence in her tone and he grinned roguishly at her, finally finding the right mode, the one he'd perfected, the one she was used to.

I could tell her now, he thought. It might be his last opportunity to reveal his connection. What was that line from the police caution? *It may harm your defence if you do not mention when questioned something you later rely on in court . . .*

But, God, it was far too late for that, wasn't it? She'd only want to know why he hadn't said anything before.

Why he'd chosen this entire time to hide in plain sight.

2

Rick

May 1995

He noticed her before she noticed him – you could even say he'd been watching her (okay, that sounded creepy). Every lunchtime that week, she'd been in Annie's, the lobby café of their office building on Victoria Street, ordering frozen yoghurt from the new gizmo behind the counter. She'd buy nothing else, not even a drink, each time taking the little polystyrene dish to the same pedestal table and perching on a stool, lost in thought.

Rick had never tasted the stuff himself but, thanks to this sudden propensity to stalk young women, he was up to speed on its production: deposit the chosen frozen fruit into one compartment, slot a small carton of yoghurt into another, pull a lever and out it came from the nozzle in a neat soft-scoop spiral.

The girl was soft scoop too (again, yes, creepy): pale

golden hair and creamy skin, wide-set eyes and small curved chin – one of those classic faces shaped like a love heart. She was petite, maybe five three, and younger than he was, which was twenty-five, almost twenty-six, and ancient enough for him to wake every morning with the urgent desire to make it happen – whatever 'it' was. Success, money, love, *life*.

By the Thursday, he thought she might have noticed him back, because her gaze rested on him for a second or two before flicking away. Then, on the Friday, he *knew* she'd seen him, because that was when he joined her in the queue. When everything changed.

'What's your poison this time?' Annie asked her. 'Raspberry? Banana?'

'Blueberry,' the girl said, with a conviction he wouldn't have expected from the fragility of her. *(Have a word with yourself, Rick, it's only a yoghurt flavour!)*

Annie spotted him lurking. 'You going to try it as well, Rick?'

'Maybe I will.' He spoke to the girl directly before he could bottle it: 'Is that good then, blueberry?'

She turned and looked at him. Her eyes were only a tone darker than her hair and very clear, kind of like, what was it? Sea glass. He wanted to ask if she was of Nordic extraction, but decided that might sound strange, like he was an anthropologist or geneticist or something. Besides, she hadn't answered his first question yet.

'Yeah, it's delish. My favourite so far and I've tried them all.' Her voice was low-pitched, with a cute estuary rasp.

'Then I'll have the same,' he said, handing over the coins.

'I've seen you around,' she remarked, and licked the peak of the yoghurt spiral. Her upper lip was plumper than the lower, he noted.

'I work on the fourth floor at B&F. The auditors?' That drew a blank, justifiably. He could count on one finger the number of people who'd said, I've always wondered, what does an auditor actually do? 'You're in the building as well, are you?' Though there was nothing to stop outsiders using Annie's, there were better places to get lunch.

'I'm temping at Culkins, just started a couple of weeks ago.'

Culkins was an insurance firm, no less dry a line of business than his own. 'Which floor's that again?'

'Eighth. It's horrible up there, really stuffy, and it's not even summer yet.' She sent a bleak glance past him to the bank of lifts. 'I never go back up till the last minute.'

His own yoghurt now in his possession, he summoned his courage. 'Well, I was going to walk up to the park if you fancy it? It's the first time we've had sun in ages.'

Her spoon was in her mouth and there was a moment while she bit down on it that made him fear humiliation, but then she smiled and said, 'Yeah, okay, why not.'

They emerged into the sunshine and he held her yoghurt pot for her as she fished in her bag for her sunglasses. The lenses were large and round, with two dark brown stripes across the top of the frame.

'I got them from a charity shop for next to nothing,' she said. 'They're Dior, from the Seventies. No one's interested in the Seventies now, but I reckon they'll come back in soon.' He saw now that the standard requirements of secretarial uniform – knee-length skirt, blouse, heeled court shoes – had been embellished with a woven belt at her slender waist and a silver fish pendant on her breastbone. His suit and shirt were both Marks & Spencer and entirely without embellishment. His shoes could do with a shine, he noticed.

'They look great. My name's Rick, by the way.'

'I know, I heard the lady say.'

There was something sweet and provincial about the way she said that – *the lady* – and he already knew he was going to find every one of these idiosyncrasies charming.

'Do *you* have a name? Wait, don't tell me. Give me three days to guess, like in "Rumpelstiltskin".'

'What's Rumpel . . . ?' Her sunglasses had slipped down her nose and she pushed them up again. Her fingers were slender and prone to graceful little flutters. 'What is it?'

'"Rumpelstiltskin", you know, the fairy tale? I can't believe you don't know it. Which fairy tales *do* you know?'

'"Cinderella",' she conceded. '"Snow White". "Red Riding Hood". All the female victims.' She chuckled at her own comment. They were breezing along now, inches from speeding cabs, he could feel the fumes scratching his throat as he told her the story of the miller's daughter and the imp who helped her spin straw into gold.

'He'll only agree to do it if he gets something in return. His approach is very transactional. Maybe it's an imp thing.'

She giggled. 'Oh, I think it's a human thing, too. Marina,' she added, as they waited for a van to pull out on Caxton Street. 'My name, I mean.'

Marina. A name that suggested sailors doing deft things

with ropes; striped tops and deck shoes; loud, confident voices. On the other hand, he *had* thought of sea glass, hadn't he?

Outside the pub on Buckingham Gate, a coven had gathered, the kind of young women who both scared and fascinated Rick. Swearing and cackling and sizing up the passers-by, lining up their beers like blokes and tipping them back, their smooth throats glowing white in the sunshine. He was relieved when he and Marina passed without attracting mockery about his punching above his weight.

At the gates to St James's Park, they tipped their pots into the bin and took the path anticlockwise around the lake. 'Not the coolest part of town,' he said, gesturing to the tourists with their maps spread out on the grass, the guidebooks with the classic shot of Buckingham Palace. Royal London.

'I think it's beautiful,' Marina said, and she touched the leaves of the willow they were passing, as if caressing the hair of a child. 'Where do you live?'

'Camden.'

'Okay. Well, that *is* cool.'

'How about you?'

'Oh, I'm miles down south.'

'Where?'

'Right out in the burbs.'

It wasn't hard to guess why she kept this vague. Every young person Rick knew who lived in the sticks did so with their parents and preferred not to admit to it. In the capital, if you couldn't afford rent, you slept on a friend's floor or even squatted. Living at home was a soft option.

He realized the conversation had dried up. 'Oasis or Blur?' he asked, joking.

She shrugged. 'I'm not that into either of them.'

'Who d'you like then? Pulp?'

'No, old stuff mainly. Dusty Springfield's my favourite.'

Spellbound as he was, he couldn't for the life of him think what the singer's big hits were, felt the opportunity for true connection slipping through his fingers.

'She's amazing,' Marina continued. 'My dad got me into her when I was little.'

The note of grief in her tone made him blurt out, 'He's still alive, is he, your dad?'

'I think so,' she said, her expression impassive.

'You *think* so?'

'Well, I haven't seen my parents since I was seventeen.'

'Why not?'

She dug in her handbag for a pack of Silk Cut and a gold Zippo, which had a picture of Minnie Mouse stamped on the side. Exhaling smoke, she snapped the lighter shut. 'Because they threw me out,' she said.

'Oh, Marina!' The way he discharged her name was as if he couldn't wait a second longer to use it. 'That's really sad. What happened?'

She stepped closer to him and gently bumped her shoulder against his. 'I'm not going to tell *you* that. I barely know you.'

'Sometimes that's the best kind of person to tell.'

She drew on her cigarette, angling it upwards, dangerously close to a strand of her hair lifted by the breeze. 'Yeah, you say that, but then they get to know you and start using it against you.'

'Wow,' Rick said. 'So cynical for one so young.' And it seemed to him it was taking shape in front of his eyes, the uncommon contradictory allure of her. The heart-stopping beauty hiding behind shades as big as safety goggles; the free spirit tussling the sad girl.

'What about your family?' She swerved to avoid a clutch of pigeons on the path. To their left, sunlight sparkled on the lake.

'They're all right. Mum, Dad, older sister. They live in Horsham, where I grew up. Just a normal family.'

'Sounds wonderful.'

'More like boring. They don't understand why I want to be in London. They have no, you know, *vision*.' Or too much realism – one of the two. If his father was to be believed, the capital existed for the sole purpose of chewing up and spitting out foolish young people, every single one of whom expected to be the exception to the rule. '*You'll learn*, my dad always says. I mean, what kind of a motto is that?'

'Maybe he's right,' Marina said. 'Maybe it's only when you've learned that you can survive.'

Unable to decide if this were bitter or optimistic, Rick said nothing, just gave a cautious chuckle.

They completed their leisurely circuit of the lake, looking at the geese and ducks and pelicans, and all too soon they were strolling back down Buckingham Gate and into the lobby of their building.

'Thank you,' he said, watching her put her sunglasses back in her bag. 'I enjoyed that.'

'So did I.'

'How about a drink after work and you can fill me in on this misspent youth of yours?'

She blinked. 'Oh, I can't. Sorry. I'm busy.'

Of course, it was Friday. He'd only succeeded in advertising his own lack of popularity. 'Meeting your boyfriend?'

'Not really,' she said, then, sweetly rueful, 'No.'

'Well, look, here's my card, if you'd like to do this again next week.'

She slipped it into her bag, entirely noncommittal.

'Do *you* have a card? Sorry, you said, didn't you? You're just a temp.'

'*Just?*' Though her tone was teasing, somehow the mood had altered between them. As she raised a hand in farewell and darted into a waiting lift, he felt a lurch of panic. Why had he not at least asked how long her contract lasted? If she even had one, for she might be being renewed on a weekly – or daily – basis. They came and went, the girls in the building.

The lift doors closed. As if to prolong his connection with her, he picked up a second frozen yoghurt before going back up to the office. He chose cranberry, which came out a jewel pink, clotted with bits of fruit. It looked a bit bodily, if he was honest, and at the team desk Jake and Si and the others gathered around making a big fuss.

'What the hell is that red shit, Rick?'

'Frozen yoghurt. From the new machine Annie's got

downstairs. Try it.' He thrust the pot at Si, who reacted like a child, spitting his mouthful into his hand.

'Ice cream gone sour. On the turn.'

'You are such a fuckwit, Si,' Jake said.

'Takes one to know one, shortarse.'

Though it was only the usual trading of insults (their desk mantra: 'Nothing personal, mate'), it occurred to Rick as the team gathered for their 2.30pm meeting, at least two of them smelling of a lunchtime pint, that a correction seemed to have taken place inside him. He looked at his colleagues slightly differently now – Si, a blond beanpole with unexpectedly dark eyebrows; Jake, no shorter than Rick, but with the solid frame of a bulldog – as if, in the course of a single lunch hour, they'd slipped a notch in importance.

After work, he stopped by Virgin Records and bought a CD of Dusty Springfield's greatest hits. *Oh*, he thought, scanning the track list: 'You Don't Have to Say You Love Me'.

Now I remember.

3

Alex

May, present

Christ, he thought, as he left the house on the first Saturday since work had begun on the track. *What a total fucking nightmare.*

The workers had knocked off for the weekend, of course, but any hope that this thing was going to be low key was dispelled with a single glance, for the scene on Long Lane was like a fête. A row of trestle tables had been set up, with residents handing out leaflets and collecting donations and even serving cups of tea from one of those catering kettles, while kids skidded down the ramp the builders had installed for getting their machinery up to the site or dangled idly from the hoardings.

'Quite a bit of kit they've got up there,' Alex said to the woman with the tea urn, as if it were a casual observation and he had not arranged to work from home two mornings this week expressly to watch the arrival of said kit. (For a so-called Head of Change, his boss Janice had been surprisingly reluctant to allow the adjustment, but, hey, persistence beat resistance.) So far, he'd noted a digger, a loader and a compressor, along with tonnes of gravel, sand and wood chips. 'I thought they were trying to keep a light touch so as not to disturb the wildlife? That's what my wife said, anyway.'

'She's absolutely right, there'll only be construction work at this end.' The woman was half-familiar, with glossy dark hair and immaculate dental work, her floral midi dress, denim jacket and kitsch bluebird earrings the nearest the Silver Vale mums had to a uniform. 'For most of the site, they're just taking up what's left of the rail tracks to make it safe, and going up and down with a strimmer, I think, to cut back any tripping hazards.'

'So they're not re-laying the path or anything?' he asked.

'Oh no, we don't want to dig anything up that doesn't *need* digging up. This is a conservation project, not a full-on redevelopment.'

The relief he felt at this almost lifted him off his feet. Turning his attention to another trestle a little way off, clumps of dirt laid out in a display, he said, very cheerfully, 'What's going on there then?'

'Penny's daughter Bronwen's doing archaeology at UCL, have you met her? She's showing some of the things they've found so far and explaining them to the kids. She's been out investigating the path all week.'

This was rather less encouraging. Shuffling over, Alex caught the student's eye and smiled. She was slight, thick-haired, fresh-faced, which made him feel very conscious of his own heaviness, baldness, and whatever the opposite of fresh-faced was. Jaded. Dead-eyed. 'Investigating?'

'Only a little surface exploration with hand tools,' she explained. 'We're not using GPR or anything hardcore like that.'

'What's GPR?' Alex asked.

'Ground Penetrating Radar. You know, like they use on the detective shows? But we wouldn't risk disturbing the wildlife, not when we know there's unlikely to be remnants of an old industrial site or anything significant.' She motioned to her trays. 'Please, feel free to pick anything up.'

It was immediately clear there were only bits of old pottery and tools, the kind of thing people got excited about because they didn't realize they were two a penny. 'Not exactly Sutton Hoo, is it?'

The girl turned pink. 'True, but even everyday objects have fascinating human stories behind them.'

They were joined just then by a small boy with his mother. Neither was known to Alex, though he had no doubt they'd be on Beth's radar. 'Have you found any dinosaur bones?' the kid asked the student.

'Not yet, but fingers crossed,' she said, playing along. 'The builders are creating a pond, you know, so they'll probably come across the remains of birds and small mammals when they're digging.'

'It's a natural cycle,' the mother said. 'Creatures will have died on the trail over the years and then their bodies will have helped nourish the earth.'

'What's nourish?' asked the kid and the mother began to explain in that performative way parents did now, as if the point of the exercise were not to educate your child but to demonstrate to onlookers that you were educating your child better than they were theirs.

Alex ignored her. 'Where's the pond going to be?' he asked the student.

'Right here, at this end, in the original clearing.'

Excellent. He began to move away, but she called after him, 'There's more back here, if you're interested.'

Thank God she did, because that was how he came to spot it, in a plastic container on the ground: the pager. It was a little dented, but clearly recognizable, with its three buttons and Zap logo, even the little hook where the cord had once been attached. As he reached out to touch it, it came back to him with a ghastly whoosh of terror, that night two and a half decades ago: the *thwack* of metal on bone, the agony in his knuckles and shins, and that low intermittent buzzing that his brain had been too jumbled to identify.

'I think that was part of a stoneware bottle used by one of the original railway workers,' said the student, thinking he was interested in the chunk of pottery lying in front of the pager. 'The navvies drank small beer, pints and pints of it every shift, like water.'

'Those were the days,' he replied, passably jovial. 'What are you going to do with it all?'

'The plan is to do some kind of roadshow with the local primary schools, get the children to help us clean and label everything, just like on a real dig.' She turned to look for

20

the young boy, but he and his mother were now chatting to the glossy-haired woman, which was a shame, because Alex couldn't possibly snaffle the pager with her focusing on him the way she was. She was almost unbearably sincere.

He imagined remarking on how bizarre it was to see it displayed in this way, a worthless bit of ephemera from a disused suburban railway track, when it was in fact a vital piece of evidence from a crime scene. 'You're not leaving your artefacts out here overnight, are you?'

'No, no. They're stored in the not at all climate-controlled stock room of my mum and dad's garden shed.'

He added a little eye twinkle to his answering smile. 'I don't suppose they'll come to much harm there.'

*

He mulled the situation over a beer later while Beth was upstairs having a bath. In short order, he had become the kind of man who couldn't wait for his wife to leave the room so he could apply himself to the maintenance of a double life. Even better, she was going out, so he had hours to ponder the problem of the pager without interruption.

Did it have some sort of serial number on it? And, if so, did that mean there was a chance it could be cross-referenced against historic sales receipts or even security footage from Carphone Warehouse or whichever other retailer they'd used for their communications needs back in the mid-Nineties? Wasn't this exactly the sort of lead they followed on *Unforgotten*, one of Beth's favourite TV shows?

But no, he was fairly sure the item must have been part of

a bulk order, the individual end users never recorded in any permanent way. He couldn't let such rabbit holes distract him from the larger concern that something far more dangerous might be discovered on the track, in which case the police would requisition every bit of the student's tat in a flash.

He tried to let the beer distract him, to focus on his non-pager thoughts. It was good, one of the new breed Beth added to their weekly Ocado order, and tasted of—

Screw the beer, what about the pager's chip? Was it in a sealed unit, protected from the elements? Might some genius forensics whizz be able to coax it back to life?

He had to get it back, there were no two ways about it. With any luck, the student wouldn't notice it was gone or, if she did, wouldn't sweat its loss. Plenty more junk where that came from. He checked the time: just past six. He didn't need to look out of the window to know she'd have packed up and gone home by now. Was she going to set up shop again tomorrow?

No matter. He couldn't tolerate an overnight wait; he needed to do something now. Locating Beth's phone in the kitchen, he tapped in the passcode she happily shared because that's what trusting spouses did, and found the 'Trailblazers' thread in WhatsApp. He trawled through the tedious back and forth before finding the comment he was looking for:

> Hi everyone! My daughter Bronwen is an archaeology student and wants to offer her services to the cause. What do we think?

No need to read all the '*Fab idea!*' responses (not least from his own wife); the only important detail was that the author of the comment was 'Penny at number 32'. He replaced the phone where he'd found it and cracked open a second beer. Minutes later, Beth came down, dressed in a black boilersuit with a silver midsection and perilous-looking platform ankle boots. Her hair was curled and she had something glittery on her skin. The whole look was straight out of Studio 54, but he knew better than to presume there was some sort of intentional theme.

'You look nice,' he said. 'Where're you going again?'

'Shoreditch. Drinks with the girls from Food Focus.'

This was the charity she'd worked for before he'd known her, which meant well over ten years ago. She held on to old connections, did Beth – indiscriminate wasn't quite the right word, open-hearted was better – whereas he could count on two fingers the people he'd actively remained close to, and she was one of them.

'What are you going to do tonight?' she asked.

'Takeaway and telly, I thought.'

'The two Ts,' she said, with the affectionate dismay of the mother who has finally accepted that her child is not gifted and talented.

After she'd left, he remained where he was, Olive next to him, her head resting on his thigh. He cast regular glances through the window at the darkening sky and, when it was properly night, put on his trainers and strolled into the street. The neighbours on both sides had their curtains closed.

Since it was impossible to enter the track at their end,

he strolled the length of Exmoor Gardens, taking a surreptitious photo of the roof of number 32 on his phone en route, to the northern entrance on Surrey Road. As he'd hoped, the original barriers had not been replaced and were easily breached.

He turned on his phone's torch function. Eleven years he'd lived here and in all that time the old embankment had barely changed, what remained of the original chain fencing that divided it from the gardens still broken, even flattened, in places. He wondered if there were plans to repair or replace it: he'd need to be alert to news on that. As for the path itself, just as the Trailblazer had promised the work was purely cosmetic, the foliage chopped back in such a way as to give a pleasing sense of undulation, along with the sweet, ripe smell of cut vegetation.

He counted the houses up to what he calculated to be number 32 and checked that the roofline matched the one in his photo. The shed was right at the end of the garden and once he'd slipped through a broken section of the chain fencing, there was only a hip-high picket fence to navigate to reach it. The door was unlocked and he opened it silently. A bare bulb hung from the ceiling but there was no question of turning it on and alerting someone in the house. Instead, he used his phone torch, keeping the beam low.

There they were, on the floor, a set of plastic trays, including the larger one that had contained the pager. He rummaged, finding it easily and shoving it in his pocket. On Monday, he'd dispose of it in Central London on the way to work.

As he returned to the track, intending to turn right and retrace his steps, to get the hell back home before anyone spotted him, he found himself pausing. Then, as if mesmerized, he turned left, counting the houses until he was at the right place.

He settled behind a silver birch and turned off the torch.

Lit up like a drive-in cinema, the back of the Stanleys' old house was easily identifiable over the top of a new lattice fence (the stretch of chain fencing here had been removed long ago). The ground floor was different now, having suffered the addition of one of those identikit glass-box extensions designed to combine all household functions in one: cooking, eating, TV watching, office work, supervising children. (What did these people do with their other rooms?)

The three blond children Beth had mentioned sat slouched on a sofa in front of a TV screen, while the woman he assumed was their mum stood at her kitchen island, phone in one hand, a glass of wine in the other. Sofa, screen, island and wine glass were all massive; this was oversized living at its best. Alex knew there was no possible way the mum could see him, but to be quite safe he waited till she left the room before turning his torch back on and casting its beam over the section of bank nearest her fence. It was thickly carpeted with vegetation, clearly untouched by the landscapers, with only a narrow route through the undergrowth from a corner gate; desire paths, they were called, weren't they? Created by human feet – the kids', he guessed. He picked his way down it and tried the gate – locked – before returning to the top and to the spot where, if memory served, the body had been found.

Don't you remember? Beth had said, with the dismissiveness of someone for whom a quarter of a century was just as it should be, a substantial chunk of time separating them from a half-forgotten era, with no pressing need to revisit it. How he loved her for that innocence – and hated himself for putting it at risk.

The woman had reappeared in the glass room, so he shut off the torchlight once more and watched her gently dislodge the kids from the sofa. The TV screen went black – it must be their bedtime – and, soon after, the main lights dimmed to a sunset glow.

He stood there for a further silent minute, his throat sore and eyes starting to glisten, before he turned and retraced his steps home.

4

Rick

May 1995

It escalated a lot more quickly than he expected. Not escalate, that wasn't the right word: *deepen*. It deepened quickly (yeah, like quicksand, his friend Eddie would say; a notorious commitment-phobe, Eddie had *literally* left the country to escape a girlfriend).

She rang him at his desk on the Monday at twelve thirty. All morning, as the working week at B&F got underway exactly like any other, Rick had felt a prickling excitement just to know she was in the same building as him, that he and this beautiful, bewitching girl occupied the same footprint of SW1. He'd thought about her all weekend, of course, working through a whole battery of tactics as to how he might resume relations and, typically, coming to no conclusion. And yet, when his extension let out a double ring, he had such an overwhelming certainty that it was her that he fumbled to answer it and knocked over a mugful of coffee. Its sickly aroma filled his nostrils as he said his name into the receiver.

'This is Marina from upstairs. We met on Friday?'

He snickered silently at the inflection of doubt in her voice. Did a girl this attractive *really* think a man wouldn't remember? 'Of course. How are you? How was your weekend?'

'Oh, fine, I suppose. I wondered if you fancied one of our walks again?'

Our walks, as if it were already an established habit! He felt his heart buck inside his chest. 'Absolutely.'

'Absolutely,' Si mimicked from the next desk as Rick hung up. 'Who is she, then? Come on, spill. Oh wait, you just did.'

'Fuck off,' Rick said cheerfully, and used the mopping of the coffee with paper towels to avoid further interrogation. For fear of tempting fate, he already knew he would be keeping this budding friendship from his colleagues. It was all too easy to imagine them heckling and goading, frightening her off.

This time, they skipped the frozen yoghurt – she was broke, she said, and wouldn't let him treat her – and walked down to the river to sit on the steps of the Tate, a rather less pastoral spot than the park, what with traffic tearing along Millbank and vans clogging the bridge, horns blasting. The sun was veiled by thick yarns of cloud and a gull or two plunged heedlessly towards them, but beyond that he couldn't register the details, had eyes only for her, like an absolute dope.

'I was worried I'd offended you. What I said about you being just a temp?' He thought, too late, why repeat himself then? *Idiot.*

Her eyes widened a fraction and he was able to assess their shade at close quarters: palest sea green, with a thread or two of gold. She seemed to have a naturally flamboyant sense of colour, her yellow blouse contrasting with her oxblood-red lipstick, bringing to mind a tropical bird. 'No, you were right. It *is* "just". For any normal person, anyway. But for me, it's a lot. It's hard to explain, but it really means something.'

'What did you do before?'

'Casual shifts in bars and clubs. I didn't go to college, I didn't even do A-levels, so I'm not really qualified for an office job, but a friend got me the gig at Culkins. I totally lied about my words per minute, but luckily, it turns out to be more filing than typing.' This was said with an air of polite finality and a half-turn of her head, which gave Rick the opportunity to admire her profile, the loveliest he'd seen outside the pages of a magazine, with its high-bridged nose, that full upper lip, the fine angle of the jawline leading to a dainty earlobe.

'Did you go to university?' she asked.

'Yes. King's, here in London.'

'Was it fun?'

He considered. You were supposed to say you'd had a ball, made friends for life, but other than the absent Eddie, he wasn't so sure. 'Sometimes. Maybe. I don't know.'

'You sound as lost as I am,' she said, and her fingers brushed his upper arm very lightly. Even through the layers of his shirt and jacket, her touch caused a crackle of heat.

'You're lost? You mean because of falling out with your parents?'

'I suppose.' She dropped her gaze. 'Sometimes, I actually think it's easier to be disowned. You're not letting anyone down but yourself, you know?'

Disowned: that was an interesting word. 'That's quite hardcore, Marina.'

'If you say so, Rick.' Sighing, she lifted her arms in the air and stretched, tipping back her head, effortlessly graceful. 'Filing makes your shoulders so stiff.'

A group was settling next to them, bearing carrier bags from the gallery shop, and Rick saw one of the men glance at Marina, then look again, harder, longer. He wasn't surprised, he'd done the same himself, after all; you scanned idly and every so often you paused. Marina was a pause. And yet it made her uneasy, he could tell, because she shifted slightly under the stranger's scrutiny, angling herself away from him.

'So where in the burbs are you based?' he asked. 'I don't think you said.'

'Silver Vale, it's called. You've probably never heard of it.'

'I don't think I have. Hang on, is that out by Putney?'

'Further than that. Beyond Wimbledon, almost Surrey.'

'Bet there's some nice country pubs down there, though.' He saw himself stepping into the walled garden of a medieval coaching inn and scanning the tables for her, finding her in front of ... what? A rhododendron bush or something. Then she was springing to her feet and he was taking her in his arms like in a movie, and they were kissing, completely oblivious to—

Stop it! Stop fantasizing about her when she's sitting right here beside you!

Re-entering, he found she was asking him about his flat, about the famous Camden music scene, and he was telling her all about the bands he knew she didn't like, while internally debating whether to mention having bought the Dusty Springfield CD. He decided against, in case it sounded weird and obsessive.

'Same again tomorrow?' she said, when they returned to the office.

'Yeah, definitely.'

'These are nice, these lunchtime walks,' she said, and she touched his arm again, the pressure more significant this time. The way she was looking at him, it was ... well, it was as though she was thinking how pleased she was to have met him.

More than that: to have *found* him.

*

The next day, he asked for her home number and, seeing her hesitate, gave her his instead. It was a surprise when she phoned on the Thursday evening – late-ish, just before nine – and asked if she could come over. He said yes, of course, though it entailed a speed-clean of the flat and a trip to the off licence for wine.

His flat was at the upper end of Albert Street, near the junction with Delancey Street, the second and attic floors of a narrow Victorian terrace, with outside space in the form of a flat roof reached by stepping through the kitchen window. It wasn't the Savoy, but if he ever felt frustrated by the dodgy wiring, semi-functioning heating or curling carpets, he reminded himself that he lived smack bang in the middle of one of the trendiest parts of the city without having had a rent increase in three years.

'The less said about flatmates the better,' he told Marina, as they toured the place and she marvelled at the vacant second bedroom. 'Let's just say, when my last one moved out, I decided I deserved a sabbatical.' A decent salary, plus a natural ability – some might call it a talent, given the cost of living in London – to save meant he had been able to gift himself a whole month of solo living.

'Was he a nightmare then?'

'She,' Rick corrected.

'Ah.' Marina raised her chin, as if catching the scent of a rival. It was impossible to know if she'd come to seduce, not least because her choice of clothing – ankle-length skirt and high-necked shirt – was so prim as to make her office wear seem louche. On the plus side, her lipstick was pinker and glossier than the rather Gothic oxblood, and her hair had been released from its clasps, falling to her shoulders in sexy twists.

'Yes, "Ah". If you ever meet a girl called Vicky who says *I'm* the nightmare, don't believe it.'

'What happened?' she asked.

'Let's just say we should have left things on a roommate basis,' Rick said smoothly.

'Understood.' She regarded him through narrowed eyes and he wondered aloud if green-eyed women got tired of being described as feline.

'You do say strange things,' she said, but she was edging

closer now, so she obviously didn't mind. 'Will you get a new flatmate soon, d'you think?'

'I'll have to.' Already halfway through his month-long reprieve, he should really have got the process underway by now, but he didn't want to think about that. He didn't want to think about anything but her, especially now she was closing those last inches between them, tilting her head, and kissing him.

*

She stayed the night. It was so exactly the blend of tender and erotic he'd imagined he half-wondered if he was controlling her by telepathy – or she him. More likely the latter.

When he woke in the early morning, there was enough dawn light for him to see her dressing. As she hooked her hair behind her ears and buttoned her shirt, her expression was peaceful, almost empty. He glanced at the alarm clock: 6am. Outside, the street was silent.

'You have to go?'

'Sorry, I was going to leave you a note.' She plucked the fabric of her shirt. 'I need to go home and change for work. I wasn't expecting to stay out.' She perched on the edge of the bed, her bottom pressed against his legs, and swivelled towards him. 'Happy?'

He grinned. 'I can't believe my luck, to be honest with you.'

Her giggle stayed with him as she left the flat and descended the stairs. She opened and closed the main door so gently he wasn't convinced – until he went down to check – that she'd actually left.

*

Over the next few days, a stream of mates of mates came to view the second bedroom and, associating it now with Marina and one of the greatest moments of his life, he found fault with every one of them. It was only when Rollo, an old college friend, turned up that Rick recognized what it was he'd been holding out for: an upgrade. Someone whose charisma would rub off on him, whose lifestyle might elevate his.

Okay, so 'friend' wasn't quite the truth. Though they'd been on the same course at King's, Rollo and his privately educated tribe had mixed separately from the herd, naturally endowed with more of everything – confidence, funds, sex, drugs – except academic application (if Rollo had attended a morning lecture even once in three years, Rick had not witnessed it). But they'd both been close to Eddie, whose independent senior school and state sixth form meant he had a foot in both camps.

When Rollo arrived for a viewing, Rick was playing early Roxy Music, telling himself it just happened to be the album he had reached for while knowing full well he wanted to impress his visitor with some declaration of cool.

'Fantastic location,' Rollo said, in his well-polished drawl. 'I was just at the Underworld the other night.' He had a classic pretty-boy look to go with the accent: silky dark hair, wide-set eyes, the gentle rosebud mouth of a Little Lord Fauntleroy, the effect roughened by careless styling and the general sense that he could do with a shower. As he strolled about, he kept up a steady stream of updates on his college circle, as if he and Rick had been much closer than they actually had. 'You been out to see Eddie in New York yet?'

'Not yet. You?'

'I went over New Year. It was complete carnage. I mean, *debauched*.'

'I can imagine.'

Upstairs, peering into Rick's bedroom, with its neatly tucked navy duvet and perfectly aligned blinds at the windows, Rollo asked, 'You going out with anyone, Rick?'

'No,' Rick said. 'Yes.'

Rollo smirked. 'Which is it?'

'Yes. But we've just started, so she's not here all the time is what I'm trying to say.' They returned to the landing. 'How about you?'

'I'm seeing this girl I met through work, she's in music PR. Lives in Ladbroke Grove, that's where I've been shacked up the last few months.' Rollo pulled a face. 'But it was doing my head in. I need my own space.'

'I get that. Yeah. So this is the second bedroom. As you can see, there's only a skylight and the wardrobe's small, but it's pretty decent.'

'I can always trick you into swapping.' Rollo threw him a look of theatrical intensity. 'Don't worry, this isn't a *Single White Female* situation. Or male, unless we're *both* into cross-dressing.'

Rick laughed. The odd thing was they *were* kind of alike, both dark-haired and of similar height and build, but Rollo was better looking, a couple of points out of ten higher than he was. And even from a distance an individual was distinct, it was a question of bearing. *Mien* was the word, and Rollo's mien involved a self-assurance that Rick's lacked, evident in the way he now drifted back down the stairs as if he were the incumbent and Rick the grateful applicant.

In the kitchen, spying the flat roof, with its pair of wrecked old deckchairs, Rollo slid up the sash and stuck his neck out. 'I like *this*.'

'Cool, isn't it. I usually smoke out there. I mean, it's not officially ours, it's undemised.'

'Undemised,' Rollo repeated. 'I like the sound of that. Fancy one now?'

They stepped out onto the roof, so close to the neighbouring houses you could have batted a ball back and forth, and Rollo produced a pack of Marlboro Lights, rattling with laughter when Rick used his inhaler before lighting up. 'No way. You're asthmatic and you smoke? A man of dangerous contradictions.'

'I only really need the inhaler in hay-fever season,' Rick said.

'So we're not allowed to smoke inside then?'

'In our rooms, sure, but we're not meant to in the shared parts.'

Since they were already talking as if the room was his, Rick now offered it formally. They agreed the rent and a moving-in date and Rollo wrote him a cheque for the first month, joking about Rick banking it quickly before it could bounce. After he'd gone, Rick grabbed a beer and went back out, enjoying the soundcheck that had just started up in the pub on the corner. It was impossible not to feel a bit smug about the week's developments: first his drop-dead-gorgeous new girlfriend – if he could be so bold as to call her that – and now his cool new flatmate. *Put that in your pipe and smoke it, Dad*, he thought.

A police helicopter clattered overhead, briefly obliterating the band's guitars, and he glugged his lager with a new contentment. What a time to be alive, he thought. What a city. What a *life*.

5

Alex

June, present

'I need to ask you a favour,' said Beth. She'd come to bed pensive, even a little nervous, and Alex put down his phone, happy to close his latest, and mercifully fruitless, news search on 'Silver Vale Trail' and pet Olive's ears instead.

Don't worry, he felt like saying, *I'll agree to almost anything,* and not because he was a selfless and doting spouse but because it had never seemed more likely that he'd need a favour in return. A *Will you stand by me when I'm in prison* kind of favour. For breaking into his neighbour's property to steal the pager – and subsequently dropping it from one of the Waterloo footbridges into the river – had granted him only temporary respite from the ghastly new dread he'd carried in his bowels since news of the trail project had broken.

That missing section of chain fencing behind the Stanleys'

old place: what if there were plans to restore it? To strip out the undergrowth and replace the original posts with new ones driven deep into the ground?

Beth got herself settled, patting the duvet around her legs and hips the way she always did, and said, 'You remember me talking about my friend Zara?'

'Not sure I do,' Alex said.

'From Food Focus? We went out last week? I'm sure you've met her, maybe at my fortieth? The thing is, she needs somewhere to stay for a few weeks and I've offered her our spare room.'

Alex wasn't sure he liked the sound of this. With the construction work on the track occupying the deepest reaches of his brain's fear network, he could do without variables of any kind.

'I know I should have asked you first,' Beth continued, 'but it was one of those vague, off-the-cuff things. I didn't think she'd say yes, but she almost took my arm off. She's just left a voicemail to check that I still mean it.'

In other words, she'd made the offer when drunk. She'd staggered in that night off her face, he recalled, completely incoherent; he envied her that simple sense of abandon, her one and only fear that someone might take her up on a proposal she'd never meant.

Beth sighed, the type of sigh that typically preceded a long exposition of a girlfriend's calamities. 'It turns out she's desperate. She's split up with this guy and he's cut off all contact. I don't think—'

'Fine,' he said. 'Yeah, no problem.'

'Really? That's so brilliant. I was dreading having to go back to her and say I'd changed my mind. I mean, she's *literally* about to be homeless.' She reached for her Kindle. 'She's a great character, I'm sure you'll love her.'

'I'm sure I will.' But already his mind was returning to its central fixation. 'Beth, I was thinking, maybe we should take advantage of the buzz around this new nature trail and get the house valued.'

He couldn't remember when he'd last raised the idea of their moving, but he'd certainly done so several times in the early days of their relationship. Having initially moved in on a temporary basis, he'd lobbied to relocate closer to town, but finances had scuppered that: what little spare cash there was had to be set aside for the wedding. Once married and, at his new wife's gift, legal co-owner of the cottage, he'd tried again, citing their need for more space – surely, if they were to have kids, they'd need another bedroom? But as Beth's fertile years receded the argument had carried less and less weight: their home was, for a child-free couple, ideal.

'Where would we go?' Beth said.

'I thought maybe Barnes or Putney? A flat on the river?'

'In your dreams, babe. We'd need at least twice as much money to get even half as much space. And we have a garden here, we'd never get that in town.'

'I can do without a garden,' he said. 'A balcony would be okay, a few pots.'

'A few pots?' She looked at him more closely. 'What about Olive?'

40

'We'd walk her along the tow path.'

You'd think he'd proposed throwing her in and leaving her to drown the way Beth reacted. 'No way! If we were going to move, I think she'd prefer the country to some shoe-box in town.'

'Fine, somewhere further out then,' he said, hasty to agree, almost despairing. At the change in emotional register, Olive was on her feet, licking his face, her tail whipping Beth's face. Beth steered her aside to peer at Alex.

'But we have friends here, a community. We might not have kids of our own, but I like having other people's around, I like hearing them playing in their gardens. I want to be around to see them enjoy the new trail.'

Alex knew better than to press. The last thing he needed was to rake over the tragedy that was their failure to conceive, not when he remained unsure if that failure had bonded them or simply eroded what bond had originally existed. At least, for Beth, the emotions were deep and distinct: sorrow, yes, but also a determined optimism, an eagerness to be useful in other ways. For him, they were muddied – even he couldn't distinguish the suffering from the relief – and, if he was honest, less intense.

Events (or non-events) in this department had come to a head soon after his mother died, almost five years ago and barely a year after his father's death, and it came to light that what family wealth there was would pass directly to the grandchildren, with no provision for future additions. Though he had not given two hoots – only hoping his sister might be willing to advance funds in the event of his needing a good barrister – Beth had been devastated to be written off so conclusively. Then tests revealed that their fertility problem lay with her, not him, and she admitted defeat – declared it, actually, with the decisiveness of a general. All at once, their private loss was the community's gain as she threw herself into local causes: sustainable fashion this, guerilla gardening that; she, Samira, Dulcie and the others were constantly cooking up something and it definitely wasn't a delicious meal for their husbands.

No, they were activists, environmentalists. Trailblazers.

'Okay,' Alex said now, scratching behind his ear. 'It's just an idea.'

Perhaps remembering his easy acquiescence to her own favour just minutes earlier, Beth issued a sudden concession: 'Why don't we review the situation in a year's time? If you still feel the same, there'd be no harm in scoping out some new areas.'

A year? Anything could happen in that time. But it was a perfectly reasonable compromise and he had no choice but to nod his assent.

As Beth settled down to read, he wondered what prevented him from telling her that if she didn't agree to move, he'd leave on his own. Why had he always stopped short of ultimatums or anything too forceful? Was it because, deep down, he *wanted* to stay? Had he come to appreciate being on the spot for an early tip-off, an advantage he'd sacrificed all too readily in those preceding years of strict avoidance? If he kept a bag packed, he could leave with five minutes' notice, whereas if they lived anywhere else . . . Well, even with his constant news refreshes, he'd only know the game was up when it was too late.

Yes, now, of all times, perhaps it was smarter to stay close.

*

What with one thing and another, he didn't meet their house guest till the day she arrived. She was younger than them – late thirties, forty at most – and heavy-set, her short blonde hair not so much cropped as slashed, her smile unsettlingly rectangular, and it took less than five minutes to decide she was going to irritate him (life had taught him that these instincts were usually mutual). For starters, she was an over-stater, volubly expressing her gratitude even before she'd unloaded her possessions from the taxi.

'Can I just say how completely *amazing* this is? You are my total hero, Beth!' She had one of those slightly strangulated voices that sounded whiny even when not complaining. 'There aren't many people in the world who would do this.' Met with Beth's embarrassed protests, she spun to address Alex. 'You're a lucky man. I mean, this woman? Wow. Just wow.'

'Yes,' he replied agreeably. 'She's a lot nicer than I am – be warned.' As the taxi disgorged bag after bag, he couldn't avoid the suspicion that this was everything Zara owned. Okay, Beth had said she was pretty much homeless, but there was such a thing as a storage facility, wasn't there? Or a friend's loft? And yet, here came boxes of books and shoes and kitchen equipment, even a microwave, and, most alarm-ingly, a Moses basket filled with baby clothes.

Not heavy-set then, but pregnant. He was no expert, but it was somewhere in the early to mid-region. Four months, perhaps?

'You didn't tell me she's preggers,' he said to Beth in an undertone, as their guest set about installing herself in the spare room. At his feet, a year's supply of toiletries strained the sides of a large cardboard box. They'd all be sharing a bathroom, since the cottage had only one and space was already restricted. (There was, at least, a downstairs loo.)

'I'm sure I did,' Beth said, frowning. 'Olive, stop barking.'

'She's just confused,' he said, sharing the dog's disquiet. 'I'm sure you *didn't* say. Where's the father?'

'That's kind of the point, babe. They've split up and he wants nothing to do with it. He says she tricked him, I mean, what a *bastard*. She's completely on her own.'

'But she does have somewhere to go next? This is just for a couple of weeks, right?'

'She's only just got here, Alex!'

No, then. Great. 'When's it due? The baby?'

'I think November-ish? She'll tell us all about it at dinner, I'm sure.'

Beth had cooked for the new arrival, a vegetarian curry since Zara was a flexitarian who by her own definition 'preferred not to flex', whatever that meant. As they shared their first meal, he made an effort to please his wife with a stab at welcoming small talk.

'So you're going the single mum route, then, are you, Zara?'

'Alex,' Beth said.

'What? It's just a question.'

44

'It's fine, Beth,' Zara said. 'There's no conventional way to parent anymore, Alex.'

This clearly wasn't true, but he resisted saying so. 'So is it a boy or a girl?'

'Oh, I'm leaving that to the gods.'

'What, the gods of genetics?'

Zara pulled a humble, 'who am I to say?' kind of face.

'Are you still at Food Focus?' he asked.

'I am, for my sins.'

He disliked that saying, invariably uttered by people thrilled with their own virtue.

'What do you do, Alex? Beth said you work for the civil service?'

'That's right, the Home Office. I'm a Business Change Manager. What that means is I develop the business readiness criteria by identifying, qualifying and updating before implementation.'

'You're making it sound absurdly dull,' Beth protested.

'No, that is literally my job description.'

'Updating what before implementation?' Zara asked.

'Numbers, Zara. I stare at numbers on a screen and decide how the fuck I'm going to explain the overspend to the ever-multiplying stakeholders.'

'He trained as an auditor,' Beth said, passing Zara the rice. 'More?'

'Started,' Alex said. 'I didn't ever finish.'

'Well, if you hate your job this much, leave,' Zara said, tipping the rest of the rice onto her plate. 'Maybe it's time to, you know, shift the narrative. Pivot.'

Pivot on this, he thought, his middle finger twitching. She was going to get on his nerves, there was no doubt about it, but he mustn't let it distract him. Estranged couples expecting a baby had a habit of reuniting, so he figured he need only sit tight and she'd be reclaimed soon enough. And while she was here, she could at least absorb some of Beth's bottomless enthusiasm for the trail, a role that, Lord knew, he was struggling to fulfil himself.

Yes, he thought, watching her respond to his wife's account of the trail's proposed new log pile as if hearing the emperor's plans for the Great Wall of China, there could be advantages to this arrangement.

6

Rick

June 1995

How long was it before it occurred to him that Marina was never going to invite him to her place? Weeks, it must have been, maybe even a whole month. The superior central location of his flat, not to mention the temporary luxury of his living alone, had made the preference automatic.

Somehow, in the early stupor of sex and infatuation, he'd failed to ask obvious questions about her home situation. Questions like, how could a young woman in a low-wage job afford to rent on her own? Money was demonstrably tight – those frozen yoghurts were not supplementary to lunch, it transpired, but a replacement for it; sometimes, she couldn't even afford a round in the pub – so why not find a flat-share and split the bills?

It was time to see these living arrangements for himself, he decided, and the perfect opportunity arose in the form of his first gift to her: a beautiful silk wall hanging with a sunflower motif that he'd spied in an artist's studio near the market.

'I know sunflowers are your favourite,' he said as she unwrapped it. They were in Ruby in the Dust on the High Street, drinks and a plate of deep-fried mushrooms between them.

'It's lovely, Rick.' She handled it with care, admiring the design. 'But why? It's not my birthday.'

He took a glug of lager. 'There doesn't have to be a reason.'

'Well, that makes it even nicer.' Her tone was warm with the pleasure of the unexpected treat, her eyes glowing. 'You're so sweet.'

'Where will you hang it?' he asked, selecting a mushroom and dipping it in mayonnaise.

'I don't know.' She rewrapped the gift and hung the bag over the back of her chair, before resuming the sucking of her Bloody Mary through a paper straw.

He finished chewing. 'Rollo moves in next week, so let's go back to yours next time, shall we? Then I can help you find the perfect place for it.'

Instantly, her gaze turned opaque. 'It's too much of a trek, Rick.'

'You do it every day, so it can't be that bad.'

'Do you mind if we don't?' she said, and he hesitated. As a rule, he found it hard to resist any appeal she cared to make and it didn't help that she looked so intoxicating this evening. She'd changed her work blouse for a baby-pink knitted vest, and her pale, slender arms were arranged in perfectly symmetrical acute angles, a silver and turquoise bangle on her left wrist. Her eyelids were smudged a deep smoky brown, accentuating the eerie paleness of her eyes.

'I do mind, yes,' he said, firmly.

'It's just . . .' She chewed the end of her straw. 'I don't want you to see where I live.'

'Why not? I mean, I couldn't care less that it's a boring area. We can't all have the bohemian street life of Camden Town on our doorstep.'

But she failed to smile at his air quotes around 'bohemian', his ironic nod towards the drunk guy who'd just slammed against the window before staggering into the gutter to an outbreak of car horns and yells. 'It's not that. Seriously, I wish it was.'

'What then?'

Her voice dropped, scratchy with new emotion. 'I have a housemate who's a bit tricky.'

Rick inhaled in surprise. A *housemate*? *This* had never been mentioned before. 'I thought you lived on your own?'

She gave a helpless gesture with her free hand. 'If only.'

'How've you not told me this before?' This was met with an imploring look. 'Okay, well, you've come to the right person for advice, I've had a revolving door of tricky flat-mates. Give it a few weeks and my new one will turn out to be a pain as well. Wait, unless . . .' He grinned at her. 'Unless *I'm* the problem.' When even this failed to raise a smile, he gave up. 'So yours, she's tricky in what way?'

The straw destroyed, Marina gulped straight from the glass, her grip a little shaky. 'Not she, he.'

'He,' Rick repeated. The conversation was becoming more

perplexing by the second, not least because it echoed the one they'd had weeks ago about Vicky. It seemed incredible that they'd discussed his flatmates, both past and future, and yet Marina had not once thought to disclose the existence of her own. 'What's his problem, then?'

'He's a bit . . .' Her despair was palpable; it was as if she were willing him to guess for himself and save her the horror of having to explain. 'He's just a bit controlling.'

Rick recalled the day he'd met her, when he'd asked her if she was seeing her boyfriend in the evening; *Not really*, she'd said, and he began now to see how the pieces might fit together. 'Let me guess, he's your ex, is he? Your lease isn't up for a while and you're stuck together until it is? That's a bummer, for sure. Why don't I come down and meet him? If he knows you've got protection, he might back off. What's his name?'

Her mouth opened as if to dispute some element of this – which? Rick's offer of protection when he was almost as flyweight as she was, or the idea that the other guy might back off? – but she evidently thought better of it. 'Drew. He's called Drew.'

'How long have you lived together?'

'A long time.' On the table, where the straw had been discarded, watery tomato juice pooled and she placed her index finger in it, began circling. When she looked up again, he was horrified to see her eyes brimming with tears. 'Do you mind if we don't talk about it anymore? It's really depressing me.'

'Of course. I shouldn't have brought it up.'

'You're so lovely, Ricky,' she said, and at exactly the same time the opening bars of Edwin Collins' 'A Girl Like You' poured out of the bar's speakers. Like every other bloke in love, no doubt, Rick had privately adopted it as *his* song.

'Look, if you really have a problem with this guy, you could move in with me,' he said, then, seeing her look of shock, backtracked. 'Only joking. Last resort, that's all.'

She laid a hand on his wrist, thumb pressing gently. 'No, no, you're not a last resort. Please don't think that.'

He affected a casual air. 'Anyway, I'd have to consult Rollo. I get the feeling he's up for more of a bachelor experience.'

'Really?' Her expression darkened. 'What does he do, this Rollo?'

'Something to do with covermounts. You know, those promotions when you get free CDs with music magazines. He said he gets loads of invites to gigs, so I doubt I'll see him from one day to the next. You can still stay as often as you like.'

Her face cleared. 'Good. It might still feel like it's just us.'

He didn't mention the housemate again; she'd tell him when she was ready. If he was honest, he already had an inkling that it was going to be bad, that it was the cowardice that allowed him to keep the truth at bay – for however long she cared to dictate.

Denial, in other words.

*

By the time Marina met Rollo, he was well established at Albert Street, if not in time served then certainly in force of presence. From the first hour of his residence, the flat operated as a party pad and Rick soon lost count of the visitors passing through, of the six packs and bottles of vodka and cartons of cigarettes that fuelled them all. Rollo's circle was a mix of the moneyed and hedonistic he'd run with at King's and the street-smart kids he'd picked up through work. A blonde called Flavia was soon identified as the girlfriend in Ladbroke Grove who'd sought – and failed – to shackle her man. She wore long dresses with low necklines that revealed a tanned bony chest and had the self-possession of the trust fund set in such spades she made Rollo look insecure.

'What kind of a name is Flavia?' Rick wanted to know.

'Roman, from the Latin *flavus*. Did they teach you nothing at your school, Rich?'

'It's Rick. And no, I don't suppose they did, not compared to Cheltenham Ladies' College, anyway.'

'St Paul's, please,' she corrected him.

'Don't be such a name-dropping cow,' Rollo said, laughing. 'Rick couldn't give a toss which school for posh slags you went to.'

Rick couldn't imagine being so rude to a girlfriend, even one as irritating as this.

On the same visit, he overheard her telling Rollo the flat was a 'complete hole'. 'I don't know why you're here,' she added.

'It's all I can afford,' Rollo replied. 'I told you my old man's pulled the plug. The job's a laugh, but I earn fuck all. We can't all live in palatial grandeur like you.' There was no hint of shame in any of these statements, rather of defiance.

'Well, you know where I am if it doesn't work out.'

'Says the prophetess of doom,' Rollo said. 'For fuck's sake, Flave.'

'I take it she's not impressed with your new digs?' Rick said, when she'd gone.

'You heard that, did you? Nothing personal, she just thought she had me tamed. Mind you, it's gorgeous, her place. Massive. That presenter from "The Big Breakfast" lives in the flat above. You'll have to come to one of her parties there.'

'Sounds amazing. Why *did* you move out?'

'Like I said, it was starting to feel a bit claustrophobic, a bit *permanent*.' Rollo grimaced. 'It doesn't help that her mates are all getting engaged. What the fuck is wrong with these people? They're way too young!'

Rick pretended to agree. He knew it was foolish, not to mention totally uncool, but he'd already begun fantasizing about proposing to Marina. He wouldn't, of course. If she wasn't ready to open up to him about her family history or her 'tricky' ex, then she was hardly likely to want to join him in matrimony. Like Rollo, she was not to be leashed. The best people never were.

'When am I going to meet *your* missus?' Rollo demanded, on cue.

'I'm not sure. Soon.' Many times, as the evening kicked off, Rick had wished Marina were here to show Rollo's crowd he could hold his own, and yet, if she *were* present, well, one of them might make a play for her or 'Flave' might humiliate her.

'Give her a buzz, get her over now.'

'I can't,' Rick said. 'Her phone's been cut off.'

'Why? She's brassic, is she?'

'No, I mean yes, she *is*, but this is to do with BT slicing through cables or something.'

'She needs to get herself one of these.' Rollo displayed the pager his employer had supplied, not because his cover-mount negotiations warranted emergency communication but because a client had done them a deal. He'd twice been mistaken for a drug dealer, which amused him.

'She'd still have to go out to the phone box to call,' Rick pointed out.

'Yeah, but *you* could contact *her*. Or maybe she should get a mobile?'

'The contracts are pricey, prohibitively so.'

'"Prohibitively so"?' Rollo mocked. 'Spoken like the true boring fucking auditor you are.'

'Get lost, mate,' Rick said.

In the end, it was at least a couple of weeks before girl-friend and flatmate broke bread (or shared a bag of Doritos and jar of salsa, as was the standard dinner at Albert Street), especially as Marina tended to stay over on Thursdays, a night Rollo was usually out at a gig. Then, one week the guestlist inexplicably let him down and the three of them assembled on the roof with vodka and cigarettes. The punky guitars and petulant drawl of Elastica vibrated from the stereo inside.

'How're you getting on in the flat?' Marina asked him. She and Rick were in the deckchairs, Rollo on the ground with his back to the wall, vodka bottle within reaching distance.

Though it was dusk, he wore sunglasses, the kind with hexagonal frames and bluish lenses Rick had seen Liam Gallagher wear in the *GQ*s and *Arena*s that now covered his coffee table.

'Loving it,' Rollo said.

'He enjoys slumming it,' Rick said, smiling. 'His girlfriend thinks this place is – and I quote – a complete hole.'

'Yeah, well,' Rollo said. 'Let's just say she may not be my girlfriend for much longer.'

'Why not?' Marina asked, re-crossing her legs and somehow making the unfashionable tan office tights she wore incredibly sexy. She'd kicked off her shoes and when she flexed her toes Rick could see the dark polish on her toenails.

'She's way too much like the girls I grew up with,' Rollo said. 'I need someone with a bit more edge.'

'You're from some rich family then, are you? Rick says you've got *two* middle names. I haven't even got *one*.' She raised her eyebrows, as if there were mischief to be had from this oversight.

Rollo shrugged. 'I don't know about rich, but a complete nightmare, definitely.'

'You two have that in common,' Rick said, casually, knowing all too well he was fishing. Marina might reveal something new to Rollo in the interests of impressing him.

'You don't get on with your folks either?' Rollo unscrewed the vodka, splashed more into their glasses.

Marina took a glug. 'I don't see them at all. Haven't for years.'

'Why not?'

'You don't want to know.'

Yes we do, Rick thought.

'Like that, is it? So how did you wind up in the South London wilderness?'

'Through a friend.'

'But now he's not so much of a friend,' Rick prompted.

'Just the two of you, is it?' Rollo peeked over the top of his shades at her, eyebrows raised. 'If you want to know what I think, a bloke and a girl can't be just roommates. Look what happened to Rick. As a flatmate, Vicky was normal, but after they shagged, she turned completely psycho.'

It gave Rick a warm feeling to hear Rollo speak of this so familiarly. He'd never even met Vicky and yet it was as if he'd been there with Rick, shoulder to shoulder, through the ordeal.

'The police were called, you said, didn't you, mate?' Rollo added.

'Don't remind me,' Rick said.

'Anyway, don't say I didn't warn you,' Rollo told Marina, his wink discernible through the coloured lens.

'You have my word I won't move in,' she laughed, and just as Rick was thinking how remarkably relaxed she was about a subject that normally caused tension and resistance, he understood that she was acting. He felt a lurch of tenderness for her, as well as guilt for having manipulated the conversation as he had.

Rollo turned her Minnie Mouse Zippo over in his hand and peered at the engraving. '"*To my Minnie, love D*".'

'D' for the housemate – and almost certainly former love interest – Drew, Rick thought. 'Are you Minnie?'

'No. I got that from Portobello Market. I like things that other people have had.' Marina's tone grew wistful. 'I wonder who she was.'

'Just some random bint who died of lung cancer, I expect,' Rollo said, and they laughed at his callousness, at the way he grabbed Rick's inhaler and issued a series of puffs, made his eyes go mad like he was high.

'You're a nutter, you are,' Marina said, and he mimicked her, his accent exaggeratedly Essex. Next thing he was chanting 'Common People', out of tune, and she was saying how totally predictable he was, he'd have to do better than that, and then they were finishing the vodka and playing truth or dare. Rick braved the gale of Rollo's laughter when he gave his total of sexual conquests as nine, while Rollo claimed that he literally didn't know his own tally (Rick believed him – already long hairs that were not Flavia's clogged the drain of their shower). But Marina chose dare every time, including having to climb down the drainpipe from the roof to the ground and beg their downstairs neighbours to let her in.

It was hard not to note that she'd rather risk breaking her ankle than share a truth about herself.

*

In the morning, she headed off early as she always did, preferring to shower and change at home. When Rick surfaced, Rollo was already downstairs, stretched out on the sofa in just his boxers, a pint glass of orange juice in his hand.

'You been up long?'

'A little while. Couldn't sleep. You'll be pleased to know

I was the host with the most and made the goddess Marina her morning brew with only slightly sour milk.'

Rick opened the fridge and sniffed the carton. 'Urgh. More than slightly. What do you mean, goddess?'

'You worship at her altar, that's all.'

Rick hit the kettle switch and readied his mug and teabag. 'She's my girlfriend, Rollo, it would be a bit sad if I treated her like dirt. I thought you got on okay last night. Did I miss something?'

Rollo sat up, set the glass on the table, and yawned. 'Don't get me wrong, I think she's gorgeous. *And* she's a good laugh.'

'But?'

Rollo's gaze narrowed as he passed a hand through his hair, exposing a clear, unlined forehead. For someone so unhealthy, he had an excellent complexion. 'I dunno, she's maybe a bit damaged.'

Rick was taken aback. 'Damaged?'

'Needy, you know?'

'How did you get that?'

'What can I say, I've had a bit of experience with high-maintenance women.'

'Marina's not high maintenance,' Rick protested, raising his voice over the roar of the kettle, and he saw Rollo regard him with pity. 'All this stuff you complain about with Flavia, her being too intense and all that, there's none of that.'

Rollo shrugged. 'It's just a different kind of aggro, isn't it? The way she keeps you dangling.'

'Dangling?'

'Yeah, look at yourself, you're sitting by the phone the whole time, waiting for her to tell you the date of her next official visit.'

Rick felt annoyance burn as he poked his teabag with a spoon. 'I told you she has to call me because—'

'I know, I know, her phone got cut off. BT can't sort it out. Is it right out in the country then, this Silver Vale?'

'It's just a suburb, I think. I've never actually been down there,' Rick admitted.

'You've never been to her place?' Rollo's surprise was overblown, the way he jolted upright as if startled, but nonetheless genuine, Rick could tell. As he brought his tea over and perched on the arm of the sofa, he could feel a horrible drumming in his chest as if he were heading into serious danger.

'She's having a laugh, mate.' Rollo chinked his pint glass against Rick's mug. 'But cheer up. It won't take long to find out what she's hiding.'

7

Rick

He might have dismissed Rollo's speculation had it not been for the incident in the Lamb & Flag a week later. (Equally, he might have dismissed the incident had it not been for the speculation.)

He and Marina had just started their second round when she excused herself for the loo, leaving Rick to scan the *Evening Standard*: Greenpeace were getting a slagging off again and it was Ladies' Day at Ascot – cue photos of women in dusty heels and outlandish headgear. He pushed the paper aside in time to see Marina, just emerged from the loos, being flagged down by a young woman standing on her own at the bar. Marina looked quite stricken by the intervention, her body language tense the entire time they chatted.

Next thing, she was striding off, not back towards their table but out of the pub door. Confused, Rick thought she must have left to pick up cash or cigarettes – maybe the machine was out of her Silk Cuts – but then he heard a rap on the window behind him; it was her, in the street, gesturing for him to join her. By the time he'd emerged, her work jacket over his arm and a glass in either hand, she'd moved to the mouth of the passageway that led to Floral Street, evidently keen to keep herself out of sight. It was midsummer, as light as day.

'What's going on?' he said.

She took her blazer from him and slipped it on. 'I had to get away from someone.'

'That girl at the bar? Why?'

'In case she decided to join us. The bloke she was meeting hadn't turned up.'

'I don't get it,' Rick said. 'Why would that be a problem? I'd like to meet your friends. Let's go back in.'

'She does my head in, Rick. Can we please just get out of here.'

Clearly it wasn't a request: he'd never known her be so curt. 'Let's at least finish our drinks.' He slurped his pint, tried to give Marina her white wine spritzer, but she refused it and he lost his patience. 'It's a waste, Marina. Money doesn't grow on trees, you know.'

'Believe me, I know,' she snapped. 'There's no need to patronize me.'

He watched, mystified, as she marched off through the passageway. Such histrionics were completely unmerited by the need to shake off some random third wheel, but he had no choice but to ditch the drinks and chase after her. 'Marina, wait! Who is she?'

Back in the light, she swung to face him, eyes burning, spots of pink on her cheeks. '*What?*'

'That girl. You said she does your head in, tell me why.'

'It really doesn't matter, Rick. It's too hard to explain.'

Frustrated, Rick caught her by the wrist. 'No more. I'm sick of this. You need to tell me what's going on.'

'Don't grab me like that!' She wrenched her hand from his grip and glared at him with an awful alien hostility. Then, noticing a passing couple cast curious looks their way, she recovered herself. 'Sorry. Look, can we just go somewhere else?'

Barely speaking, they cut through to Long Acre and up Upper St Martin's Lane towards an evening sky with streaks of gold and pink in it, tauntingly romantic. Every pub was heaving, but by some miracle there was a table going spare in the window of Beaujolais wine bar on Litchfield Street. Rick ordered two large glasses of red and watched as she glugged hers so fiercely a drop ran down her chin. Between them a candle struggled to stay alight, glued to its holder with gnarled layers of wax.

'Come on,' he urged, 'who was she?'

She lowered her glass to the table with a sharp crack. 'Who she is isn't the problem.'

Rick frowned, tapped a cigarette out of his pack. He felt as if he were going to spontaneously combust. 'Then what *is* the problem?'

Her gaze held a new balefulness. 'She knows something about me that I haven't told you.'

'Which is what?'

'I'm married, Rick.'

He gaped at her. The cigarette remained clamped between his fingers, unlit.

'That's why I ran out of the pub. I didn't want to have to introduce you and risk her saying something when I haven't told you yet myself. Drew isn't my ex. He's my husband.'

Oh, God. How obvious it was now she'd said it – blindingly, laughably obvious. Only a fool could have blocked the possibility, a fool in love. The refusal to let him visit her home, the possessive 'housemate', the disconnected phone line. Rollo had been right: of course she had a working phone line, this was 1995. She just couldn't have Rick calling it in case her husband picked up.

'Fucking hell.' He gazed at his drink as if willing the burgundy liquid to offer up a solution (it did, in its own way), but all he could see were his dreams in tatters. He'd characterized their connection as love at first sight, the real thing, his reward for suffering all that torment with Vicky, and instead here was more suffering, more torment.

He lit the cigarette, holding the smoke in his throat like punishment, feeling its burn on the tender skin. What a prize idiot he'd been.

'I'm so sorry,' Marina said. And she *did* look sorry. Her mouth trembled and, when she raised her glass again, there was that shake in her wrist he'd noticed before.

'Why didn't you just tell me in the beginning?' he said.

'Because I liked you and it was obvious you were the kind of person who'd just walk away if you knew.'

His mind was filled with such commotion he could not say

categorically if this were true. *Would* he have walked away? As she gazed at him with a childlike hope for forgiveness, he understood just how much of a red herring her youthful looks had been. She was twenty-five, but looked years younger, far too young to be hitched. His gaze lowered to her left hand. A stack of three silver rings on her middle finger, but nothing on her ring finger.

'What do you do with your wedding ring? Take it off five minutes before you meet me?' Like the middle-aged philanderers in the movies. He pictured her in the office lift coming down from the eighth floor, hands meeting behind her back as she discreetly slipped it off. What if the doors opened at the fourth and he got in before she remembered? Would he have noticed? Again, he couldn't be sure.

'I don't wear one,' she said. 'Not every wife does.'

Wife. Jesus.

'You do live in this place, Silver Vale? *That* wasn't a lie?'

She looked hurt by the accusation, but answered 'no' in a steady voice. 'Please, Rick, don't be—'

He interrupted her. 'What's the exact address?'

'Why?'

'Just tell me, for fuck's sake!'

A trio of women at the next table turned as one, obviously concerned that he was getting belligerent with the sweet girl in tears. He huddled closer. 'Go on.'

'Fifty-four Exmoor Gardens,' she said, barely audibly over the clamour of music and conversation. Rick committed the address to memory.

'And Drew, your husband. What does he do for a living?'

She began picking off bits of dried wax from the candle, her fingers nervous. 'He runs his own business selling flooring, but it's struggling at the moment. He's really stressed out about it. He has a shop in Wimbledon and another one in Manchester. He stays up there every Thursday night, that's how I've been able to stay at yours. So far, at least.'

Rick drew on his cigarette. The women at the next table, no longer concerned, were howling with laughter at something. 'How old is he? What does he look like? I want to know everything, Marina.'

'Be careful what you wish for,' she groaned, with an attempt at a conciliatory smile, but Rick didn't return it. There was a clutch of nausea in his stomach that he already feared would never ease.

'I wish for a bit of honesty, that's what I wish for.'

'Okay.' She sucked in her breath as if about to plunge underwater. 'He's older than me, mid-thirties. He's about six two, built pretty big, strong and really competitive, he used to play football professionally. Or semi-professionally, but he had a trial somewhere big. He likes to flash the cash. He wants people to think he's wonderful, but he's really not. Like I say, he likes to win.'

'Is that why you're having an affair? To beat him in some fucked-up game?'

'What?' Her surprised, almost offended look irritated him; it was as if she'd never questioned her own motives.

'Come on, you must know why you got involved. What is this, if there's no chance of it leading anywhere? A bit of a laugh?'

'No! It's love, Rick. I love you, don't you realize that?'

Rick inhaled sharply. This was the first time either had made the declaration – he'd held himself back for fear of smothering her too hard, too soon. Far from being the joyous emotional breakthrough he'd dreamed of, it struck him as possibly the most defensive, fatalistic utterance he'd ever heard.

Met with silence, Marina placed her bag on her lap with the air of someone who accepted she'd come to the end of the line. 'I know you won't want to see me anymore and that's fine, I get it.'

'I didn't say *that*,' he said, and her shoulders relaxed. Her gaze not leaving his face for a second, she returned her bag to its spot by her side.

Rick caught the eye of the waitress. 'Same again,' he told her, though he might just as well have been speaking to Marina.

*

They parted in agreement that they were still together, even if she wasn't coming back to the flat as she usually did. And it was probably just as well that they missed their usual lunch-time meet the next day – his call, not hers; he had team drinks at the Cask & Glass for Si's birthday, an old man at twenty-seven.

He was glum company – how could he not be in the sober light of day?

'You all right?' his colleagues asked, but there was no way he was going to confide his new troubles to any of them – and not only because Marina worked in the same building. They would take the piss, as they had when Jake had had a one-night stand with a married woman. A bit of extracurricular, Si called it, and, God, his own name was in there – extracu-RICK-ular. Wordplay of that calibre would not be passed up.

His best bet was Rollo, who'd come home last night hours after Rick had gone to bed and hadn't been up when he left that morning (he was given a certain leeway with his start times at work, or took it at any rate). Rick picked up a six pack on the way home, hoping for a session on the roof, some advice from the resident cynic, but it turned out his flatmate was on his way out to a dinner party at Flavia's. He'd made an effort for once, smelling expensive and looking almost wholesome in properly ironed clothes, hair damp from the shower.

'She's married,' Rick announced, flatly, waylaying him by the front door. 'She told me last night.'

'Shit.' Rollo regarded him with exactly the unruffled camaraderie he'd hoped for; he didn't think he could bear pity. 'So she's come clean, has she?'

'Wait, you knew?'

'I didn't *know*, but when you said she was still living with her ex . . . I thought it was a bit of a cliché to be honest, plus she seems way too young, but it was one of my theories, yeah.'

'*One* of your theories?' Rick repeated. 'What were the others?'

Rollo slouched against the wall, cheerfully resigned to the delay. 'Well, I actually thought she might have a kid or something. Didn't want to tell you because she was worried you wouldn't be interested if you knew.'

'It wouldn't have made any difference to me,' Rick said. 'I've got nothing against kids.'

'Yeah, but they're a bit of a pain if you're competing with them for their mum's attention, right? I'm not sure *I'd* be up for getting involved with some single mother. Anyway, it wasn't that.'

'No.' Rick bit down on his resentment. 'It was the cliché all along.'

'Don't beat yourself up, you were blinded by lust, she's fucking sexy, anyone can see that.' Rollo injected a note of optimism: 'But at least you know now. I take it you've kicked her into touch?'

Rick said nothing.

'For fuck's sake, Rick.'

'I can't turn myself off just because I now have some unwelcome information,' Rick protested. 'What? You've never slept with someone who's going out with someone else? A player like you.'

'A *player*?' Rollo smirked. 'Sure I have, but not some drawn-out thing. Not an affair. Wait, they're not in some kind of open relationship, are they? She sees you and then goes back and describes every sordid act. He does the same and they get off on it.'

'No,' Rick said. 'Definitely not.'

'Okay. Well, it's your call, obviously. But listen, you know I've got your back either way, yeah?'

The sentiment, kindly voiced — certainly kindlier than

Rollo's normally were – was just as overwhelming as Rick had feared and he felt his eyes fill. He stepped aside to let his friend pass. 'You go or you'll be late.'

'You want to come with?' Rollo offered. 'Get shitfaced to take your mind off it?'

'No, I'm not in the mood. But thanks.'

After Rollo had gone, he used the shower himself. The hot water had run out, but he turned the flow to the maximum, battering himself with cold, groaning in the tiny tiled capsule as he gave vent for the first time to his humiliation. How could he have been so easily tricked, when Rollo clearly had not? What Rick had taken to be enigmatic had been the oldest deception in the world, albeit practised typically by men and for far longer than the month or so Marina had managed.

The words she'd used to describe her husband swarmed his mind: *big, strong, competitive . . . He likes to win.* The very opposite of her, of Rick himself.

It was only as he towelled himself with an already-slick towel that it struck him there'd been something else in her manner as she'd painted that picture, something besides embarrassment and apology, something more troubling. One line he'd paid no attention to at the time now reverberated with a sinister energy: *He wants people to think he's wonderful, but he's really not . . .*

She'd not just been critical of her husband; she'd also been afraid.

8

Alex

June, present

'You stay here,' he told Olive, as if entrusting the animal with a very important duty, and shut the front door gently in her face.

One development he was grateful for regarding the new nature trail – correction: Community Eco Trail, complete with self-important capitals – was that it was to be a dog-free zone. Not that any responsible dog owner had previously encouraged their pooch to snuffle among the barbed wire and faecal matter on the old track, but now signs had gone up to make it official, punishable with a fine.

It had become a habit of his whenever Beth was out – usually, these days, with Zara – to go and have a little nose around up there, see how the project was progressing. He'd enter, as he had on the night of his foray to the young archae-ologist's shed, at the Surrey Road end and stroll as far as the new internal barriers that prevented access to the excavations at the Long Lane end, before doubling back. Again, exactly as he had the first time, he'd come to a pause directly behind 54 Exmoor Gardens.

This evening, as before, he was chiefly concerned to see that this mid-section of the path remained only superficially improved, the banks on either side still the overgrown wilderness they'd always been. Yesterday, Beth had reported that the surviving stretches of chain fencing were to be repaired where practicable, but none added where previously removed, and all original fence posts were to be left untouched to avoid the embankment becoming destabilized. He'd been so pleased to hear this that she and Zara had remarked on his good mood.

Smirking at the memory, he startled at the sudden sharpness of a woman's voice from down the bank on the Pleasance Road side.

'You're not supposed to be up there, you know!'

Though he couldn't see who he was talking to, he replied in a friendly tone: 'Don't worry, I'm a local. Just checking out how it's all looking.'

There was the sound of gentle panting as a woman came into view. She looked to be in her seventies, her hair a sleek helmet of striped silver and blonde. She wore a crumpled peach-coloured dress, with a zone of reddened skin above the square neckline and sunglasses hanging on a chain around her neck. It was a warm evening and he guessed she'd been sitting in her garden when she'd heard a suspicious rustling.

Apparently satisfied by his benign appearance, she

softened her manner. 'You do know the path's still closed? Careful you don't injure yourself.'

'Of course.' He ran the sole of his trainer over an exposed root as if to demonstrate his awareness of the hazards. 'It's nice and neat now, isn't it?'

'Yes,' she said. 'At least all the syringes have been cleared up.'

'The junkies must have moved on,' he agreed and a snatch of dialogue burst into his mind out of nowhere, causing that almost erotic sense of nostalgia that memories from that fraught period of his life often did: Marina in the Albert Street flat, talking about the trail.

'*He* calls it a mud bath for junkies. Well, *I* call it an escape route.'

'Oh, darling.'

How sincere that endearment had been, how youthful!

His insides clenched. 'It'll be good to see it in use after all these years,' he added, and though his tone was bland, his remark seemed to trigger some kind of connection in her and before he knew it, she was right up next to him, inspecting him with narrow suspicion.

'We've met before, haven't we?'

'We probably have,' he said smoothly. 'I've lived here for over ten years, how about you?'

She frowned. 'No, I mean from back when we had all the trouble. I know your voice. You were with that other boy.'

And just like that, his heart went berserk, pumping his blood with an emergency fury, bringing fire to his face. Was it . . . was it *her*? She was the right sort of age and her cool, interfering gaze was the same. It *had* to be, in which case any doubt that she was the woman Beth had mentioned as being lined up to talk to journalists could be dismissed once and for all. How easily she could redirect reporters his way: *He says he wasn't around then, but I'd know his voice anywhere.*

Jesus.

'Trouble?' he repeated. 'Oh, wait, my wife said something about a woman being killed up here, back in the Nineties, was it?'

'Ninety-five.' She stared at him with the intensity of someone who knew everything but could prove nothing. 'She lived just there, the garden that lines up with mine.'

Alex swallowed painfully, tried to think how a normal person would take this discussion forward. With curiosity, surely. With questions. 'What was she like? Did you know her well?'

Her tone softened. 'She was a lovely girl. Sweet as anything. We actually moved in the same month as them. We were empty nesters, they were young, hadn't started a family yet.'

'Were you the one who discovered the body?'

Distaste crossed her face (*too* curious, Alex). 'No, we were out that evening. Came back and found police swarming all over the place, just like on the telly. They found her right where you're standing.'

He took a deep pace back, almost as if stepping over a corpse. He longed to turn tail and end this encounter, but it would be too peculiar to leave a sensational story like this midway. And yet . . . and yet he couldn't bring himself to ask outright about the killer. 'Were the police around for long then? There must have been a lot of disruption?'

'That's one way of putting it.' Her jaw tightened and he saw he'd hit a nerve. 'They dug this whole section up, pulled up a couple of trees and all sorts. Kids were coming from all over to look at the crime scene, they tore the police tape to shreds, destroyed the flowers the neighbours left there. So disrespectful. I was furious.'

'I can imagine.' And as he was manufacturing some matching indignation, another unsolicited line surfaced, spoken in a familiar insolent tone: *Fucking rozzers, you know how they twist stuff you say . . .*

'It must have been a very distressing time.' Discreetly adjusting his eyeline, he scanned the house behind her for any features that might be identifiable from the street. It looked pretty standard except for an unusually tall side gate with an ornate set of spikes.

'I should head back,' he said. 'Do you need help getting down to your garden?'

She declined this offer and he didn't look back to see if she was watching him as he walked away. At the Surrey Road exit, he turned left, looping home via Pleasance Road. There was only one side gate in the central section of the street topped with those distinctive spikes and, Googling as he walked, he quickly discovered the occupant's identity: Cordelia Smyth, aged seventy-six. He was fairly sure this was the same name Beth had mentioned. It rang a more distant bell, too; likely it had cropped up in the news coverage of the murder.

Fuck.

*

Beth and Zara were in when he got back, settled in the living room with foul-smelling chamomile tea. It had not passed him by that his wife had drunk virtually no alcohol since Zara had moved in – sympathy abstinence (would she get contractions too, when the time came? No, that was months away, Zara would be long gone by then, surely). Zara was recounting a story of how she'd had to slap away someone's hands on the train to work that morning.

'She doesn't like people touching her bump,' Beth explained to Alex.

'Just because you're pregnant doesn't mean you're fair game for anyone who fancies a grope,' Zara clarified, crossly, as if admonishing him personally. Her face was a flushed shiny moon.

'I would imagine it's a fairly niche fetish,' he said, then, to Beth: 'I just met a strange old trout from Pleasance Road.'

'Who?'

'You can't call women "old trouts"!' Zara objected. 'I *assume* it was a woman?'

He ignored the interjection and addressed Beth. 'She's in her seventies, Cordelia something. I thought she might be the one you said was involved in the trail, who was going to talk to the reporter about the Nineties?'

'You've got a good memory,' Beth said. 'Yes, Cordelia's been really helpful actually. She knows someone at the council.'

'Cordelia, I *love* that name,' Zara exclaimed, and her fingers plucked at Beth's sleeve. 'Shall I add it to the list of baby names?'

Alex glanced at her. Was it him or was this a bit peculiar, as if Beth were a stakeholder? 'It's *your* list,' he pointed out, reasonably. 'You can add whatever names you like.'

'Or is it a bit Shakespearean?' Zara continued, as if he'd not spoken, which he guessed was payback for his having ignored her comment about trouts. '*King Lear*, wasn't it?'

'Yes. Maybe. Oh, but I did love Cordelia in *Brideshead*,' Beth said.

'Really? I found her the most annoying character in the book,' Alex said.

'He's such a grump, isn't he?' Zara said. 'Has he always been like this?'

'I'd say it's a fairly recent development,' Beth said, more candidly than Alex had expected and to Zara's evident relish.

'Come on then,' she baited. 'What's his hidden talent?'

As Beth joined her in laughter, he felt a flare of violent resentment. 'I suppose I must be amazing in bed,' he said, looking Zara hard in the eye. 'No, wait, it could be my longsuffering tolerance of her girlfriends?'

'Alex, that's rude,' Beth said. 'She was only joking, weren't you, Za?'

'Course I was,' Zara said. 'Let me make a note before I forget . . .' And she took out her phone, presumably to add to her list of baby names – and not to one of collected grievances against *him*.

*

In bed that night, he considered his ugly new problem. Not Zara – she was merely an irritant, any clash between them purely personality-based – but Cordelia, confirmed now as the official spokesperson for Silver Vale's dark past. One dangerous word from her and he'd need to be on his way. Better if *she* went, of course, taking her inconvenient memories of him with her. Could he . . . could he try to silence her somehow?

What did he even mean, 'silence'? Threaten? That would only strengthen her conviction that they'd met before and he had reason to deny the fact.

What if she had some kind of accident?

He jerked an inch off the mattress. *Shut the fuck up.* If he was going to get through this, he needed to keep a lid on the catastrophizing. What was the worst this pensioner could do, after all? Insist to a reporter that she'd recognized another neighbour from a quarter of a century ago? Even if she remembered what Alex and 'that other boy' had been doing that day, he would simply deny it. Such was England now, a savage ageist place, no one would believe an old person over a middle-aged one. Her memory would be dismissed as faulty.

No, now he'd ditched the pager, there was nothing to link him to the Stanley scandal. And the only person with any real substance to such a claim was long gone.

9

Rick

June 1995

Rollo said it was the act of a madman, going down to Silver Vale behind Marina's back. That was how he put it when they next overlapped, on the Sunday morning in the kitchen, pouring milk on cornflakes and waiting for toast to brown, adding with an evil laugh, 'All the more reason to do it.'

That was the great thing about Rollo: he applauded the mad, he celebrated the reckless, the rogue, the absurd. 'I'd come with you, mate, I'd be a pretty decent Dr Watson, don't you think? But I'm a bit the worse for wear, know what I mean?'

Rick did. His flatmate had wangled himself onto the guestlist at Blow Up the previous night, then on to a house party in Primrose Hill, not getting home till four in the morning and only drawn from his room by the urgent need for tea and toast. Rick, meanwhile, had stayed in, drinking alone and playing his Dusty Springfield tracks, dwelling on 'I Just Don't Know What To Do With Myself' as if it had been recorded expressly for him. He'd woken early, still brooding about Marina, hardly knowing which had derailed him more, her bombshell news about being married or that sudden instinct that the marriage was unsafe. By the time he'd recalled an earlier damning remark – that her 'house-mate' was 'controlling' – he'd convinced himself she was spending *her* weekend chained to a radiator.

He'd go down there, he decided. Check that she was safe, see this Drew for himself – since it was a Sunday, he presumably wouldn't be in his shop. (Flooring, of all things? A bland, utilitarian kind of product that offered no clues as to how this psychodrama was to play out.)

'Best of luck, Rickster.' Mug and plate in hand, Rollo turned to head back up to bed. 'Don't forget your binoculars.'

'Drat, I knew there was something.' Rick did, however, dig out his camera, which had a couple of exposures left on the roll, and his *A to Z*. Silver Vale was on the periphery of southwest London, Marina's street just an inch from the edge of the page where the guide cut off. As for how to get there, he was familiar with the route from her descriptions: Northern line to Waterloo and then an overland train via Clapham Junction that was slow but at least direct.

He was there by a quarter to one. First impressions were uninspired: low skies the colour of oyster shells lent a drabness to the tree-lined streets and the few people in evidence were middle-aged at best. The station was a good twenty-minute walk from Marina's street, the route taking him past an old geezer pub and along the main road towards a short parade of shops – nothing special, a newsagent and a betting shop; a chippie pumping out deep-fat odours; plus the famous phone kiosk from which she'd occasionally phoned him – and then uphill onto Exmoor Gardens.

Well, this is a turn-up for the books, he thought. For, if not a millionaire's row of gated mansions, Exmoor Gardens was undeniably affluent, with big detached and semi-detached houses, some with in-and-out drives showcasing the usual rich people's wheels, high-end BMWs and Golf GTIs. Others had been converted into flats and the gardens paved for parking.

Maples lined the street, as immaculately spaced as soldiers on parade.

Rick drew to a halt opposite number 54, mouth agape. It was one of the detached single residences, big enough for a family of six, with picturesque old chimney stacks, glossy black drainpipes, and half a dozen windows at the front, including an enormous one that belonged, presumably, to the sitting room. Blinds, made of bamboo or something similar, were drawn low. There was a tall bush out front that he was pretty sure was a rhododendron, which took him aback a bit because that was how he'd initially pictured Marina in Silver Vale, sitting in front of a rhododendron bush, like a girl in an oil portrait. That aside, it was a long, long way from the abode he'd envisaged for his cash-strapped girlfriend. Even out here, the rent on a place this size must be huge. She'd said nothing about Drew being wealthy – in fact, she'd described his business as struggling – and she herself earned a pittance, so how could they afford it?

Not to mention the blue BMW parked in the drive, she'd never mentioned *that*, but if it did belong to the Stanleys then it suggested they were home. His heartrate quickened at the thought. En route, he'd visualized himself marching up the path and rapping on the door, with any ensuing confrontation improvised, but now he was here he saw that this would be an act of pure self-sabotage. It had taken over a month to gain Marina's trust even to this extent; he'd blow it in an instant if he presented himself unannounced, unscripted.

No, this trip would need to be reconnaissance only.

He trained his camera on the door, willing it to open – *Let me see you, Drew Stanley. Let me at least get a look at what I'm up against* – but of course it did not and he took his photo anyway.

As he considered his next move, a voice from behind roused him: 'Looking for Drew and Marina?'

He turned to find a man in his forties, mug of tea in his hand; behind him, a coiled green hose pipe dripped onto the tarmac near the wheels of a silver Mondeo. Washing the car – pure suburbia. If Rick weren't so unnerved, he'd probably laugh. 'Er, yes. I was trying to remember which number they were. It *is* fifty-four, isn't it?'

'It is, but I think they're out. I saw them going off in a taxi about an hour ago.'

'Ah, okay. Thank you. I'm . . . I'm a friend of theirs. I was in the area and thought I'd drop in. Actually, maybe you can remind me . . .' Aware that it was unwise even as he spoke, Rick heard himself voice the doubt that had lodged in his heart the moment Rollo had aired it: 'They haven't got a kid, the Stanleys, have they?'

'A kid? No, it's just the two of them.' But it was not something a friend needed to ask and the man was no longer smiling. It was obvious he was thinking *You don't know them at all,* and Rick could only pray he hadn't seen him take the photo. The camera was still in his hand, lowered by his side.

'Right. Okay. Well, not to worry. I'll head off then. No need to mention I came by.'

The man turned back to his hose. 'If you say so.'

*

At Albert Street, the phone was ringing as he stepped through the door and he snatched it up, eager to hear Marina's voice.

'Rick?' Bugger. It was only his sister, Stacey.

'All right?' he said, without enthusiasm. They weren't close, partly owing to a six-year age gap and partly to the fact of her being the kind of person who only ever rang to have a go at him about something.

'Why are you so totally rubbish, Rick?'

Bullseye. 'That's your opening gambit? Nice to speak to you, too, Stace.'

'You missed Mum's birthday yesterday!'

'Really? I'll put a card in the post tomorrow.'

'Yeah, but she'll know it's only because I've rung you.' Unprompted, she updated him on her life: a pay rise for her husband, Rick's niece starting nursery, his nephew showing signs of genius at infant school. Finally, her attention returned to him. 'I hear you've found a new flatmate. I hope you remembered my advice: no more girls?'

Rick sighed. 'Last time I looked, Rollo was not a girl, no.'

'What kind of a name is Rollo?' she scoffed.

'He was a Viking, actually. The first ruler of Normandy.'

'Can't be home much, then,' Stacey said, with a cackle. 'So, no real news?'

'Real' meant relationships in her worldview and until Rick brought word of marriage and ankle-biters he was a second-class citizen. 'Actually,' he blurted, 'I'm seeing someone new. Someone special.'

'Ooh! What's she like?'

'She's . . .' He savoured the question, challenging himself to define Marina by a single adjective. 'Ethereal. She's ethereal.'

'Ethereal? For God's sake, Rick, what does that even mean? Like she's a ghost or something? What's her name?'

'Marina.'

'Marina? *Rollo* and *Marina*, is this some sort of posh people's cult?'

'There's Flavia as well,' he said, starting to enjoy himself, 'though I'm not sure she's allowed in the cult. She's maybe a bit *too* posh.'

'You've lost your mind in London.'

'Thanks for letting me know. Look, I've got to go now. I'll send Mum a card, cheers for reminding me.'

As he hung up, he was amazed with himself for having confided in her the way he had, especially given Marina's marital status and what he'd just gleaned of the lifestyle she enjoyed with her husband. No matter how it was being funded, she was hardly likely to want to give it up for Rick, so by the time he and his sister next spoke he'd doubtless have to report their having parted ways.

But, after a little reflection, he saw he'd disclosed his news precisely to elicit her mockery – more than that, her rejection. Because the more convinced he was by his sense of otherness to his family, to his origins in general, the more urgent was his desire to cement the bonds with those he *did* connect with: Rollo, the lads at work, the hedonistic hordes of Camden Town.

And, front and centre, at least for now, Marina.

10

Rick

June 1995

The next morning, Monday, she called him at his desk. 'Are you still speaking to me?'

'Yup.'

'Can we meet for lunch?'

'Sure.'

'One-word answers only, okay. I'll be in the lobby at one.' And she hung up without a goodbye, like a secret agent.

Or a married woman having an affair and not wanting her colleagues to know.

They picked up sandwiches from the café opposite and, without even discussing it, headed up to St James's Park, settling on the grass near the children's playground. She positioned herself close to him, close enough for him to feel her breath on his cheek, register the stirrings of his own desire, and yet he couldn't bring himself to look at her for more than a second at a time.

'Please don't go all silent on me, Rick. Come on, call me whatever you like, ask me any question – anything but this sulking.'

'I'm eating.' He concentrated on his sandwich, trying to gauge his own mood. *Was* he sulking? It was true that overnight an element of self-pity had set in, countering his concern for her. While he'd spent his Sunday crossing town to check she was safe, she'd been out for a boozy lunch with her husband, likely not giving *him* a second thought.

Only when he'd finished chewing did he look at her properly. She was wan, her usual bold make-up absent. She could have been eighteen or nineteen. He felt his heart reopen. 'Did you mean it when you said what you said?'

'About being married? I'm afraid so.'

'No. The bit about love.'

'Ah. Yes, I did mean it.' Her smile was nervous. 'Is it enough? I mean, now you know the truth?'

'Oh, Marina, I don't think I know the truth at all.'

She drew back a fraction. 'What do you mean?'

He balled up his sandwich wrapper and squeezed it in his fist. 'I mean your other secrets. Like, when were you going to tell me you're loaded?'

'I'm not,' she said, shocked, almost offended.

'Please stop screwing with me. I've seen your house. It's massive. I couldn't believe it when I walked up the street. You've got an L-reg Beamer, for God's sake, how much did *that* cost? And if you can afford that, why can't you afford your own lunch? I don't get it.'

She gaped at him in alarm, patches of red sprouting on her cheeks. 'You went to my house? In Silver Vale?'

'How many have you got? Don't tell me there's a holiday home as well? What, a flat in Paris?'

She shook her head. 'Why did you do that? You didn't knock on the door, did you?' Her fists were clenched so tightly the knuckles shone white. She was terrified, he realized, presumably at the thought of her husband having answered and Rick having identified himself as her lover.

'No, don't worry,' he said, more gently. Whatever his own hurt, he had no wish to torture her. 'Your neighbour across the road told me you'd gone out.'

Her eyes moved from him to the park beyond, as if searching for a solution to this breach of trust. 'What day was this?'

'Yesterday. Early afternoon. One-ish. The guy said you'd left in a cab?'

'Oh. That's right, yes. We had lunch with some customers of Drew's. We took a minicab so we could both drink. Drew works on Saturdays, so Sunday is one of the only times he can socialize.'

It was clear that one of the unwelcome consequences of her speaking openly about her marital status was going to be her frequent use of her husband's name. Drew Stanley was in their relationship now – or, rather, Rick was in *his*. As absurd as it was for him to be jealous, he was.

'Look, I know it sounds a bit stalkerish, and to be honest with you, that was how it *felt*, but I just needed to be able to visualize where you are when we're not together. I assume the money comes from his side, does it?'

She nodded, eyes downcast.

'Tell me the truth, Marina. You can trust me. Why aren't you happy, what's wrong? Are you scared of him?'

She blanched. 'What makes you say that?'

'You said he was controlling.'

'Did I? Oh, God.'

'Controlling in what way? What's going on?'

For a moment she said nothing, just stared hard, assessing him. Assessing *them*, perhaps, the incorruptibility of their bond. Finally, she spoke. 'He's a monster, Rick.'

'A *monster*?' In this sparkling green park, it was a brutal word, like gunfire.

'I don't know what other way to say it. You asked me when I was going to tell you I'm rich, well, the answer is never, because I'm not. If I was, don't you think I'd have been picking up the bills all this time? Buying *your* sandwich, not the other way around? But I don't because he takes every penny I earn. It's his house, in his name.'

'He *owns* it?'

'Yes. The car, as well. I can't even drive.'

Rick was astounded. 'But this is the 1990s, not Victorian times. You have rights. If you divorced him, you'd be entitled to some of the cash, probably half.'

'I wouldn't get that far,' Marina said.

'I don't understand.'

'I was very young when we met, only nineteen. You know I told you I was thrown out by my parents? Well, I had a friend in London, living in a squat in Clapham with a bunch of people, and I stayed with them. We moved from place to place and every time we left somewhere we had a big party.

Anyone could come, it was a free-for-all. I met Drew at one of those. We started seeing each other and then he asked me to move in with him.' She paused, as if gathering her nerve. 'It was great at first, just living in a normal flat with hot water and heating, it was like paradise. Then we moved to Silver Vale, just before we got married.'

'Were you working?' Rick asked. 'You said you used to work in clubs and bars?'

'I did. Hostessing, that kind of thing.' She swallowed. Her fingers picked at the wrapper of her untouched sandwich. 'But not after we got married. He didn't want me working at night or talking to other men and moving further out made it harder anyway. I wasn't allowed to do evening classes or anything like that, it suited him that I had no qualifications. He wanted me at home being the little wife.' The words were tumbling from her now. 'This job at Culkins, I had to beg him to let me do it. He rings me at my desk, you know, just to check I'm there. He works whatever hours he likes, but I have to be on the right train home every night, through the door at the right time.'

Rick felt himself flush with horror. 'How would he know what train you got? Wait, he rings you to check you're back home?'

'If he's not already there, yes. Thursdays, when he's away and I stay at yours, I have to go home first for his call. That's why I always come over quite late. Before you ask, yes, I could just say I was running late or I could leave the phone off the hook – I've tried all of that, believe me. But he's clever. He's started keeping tabs on the log for the burglar alarm. So I have to get home at the right time, turn the alarm off, then I go up to your place. When I leave you in the morning, I go back to the house, turn the alarm back on, leave for work. That's why I have to leave your place so early.'

Rick listened in astonishment. 'What about last week when we went straight from work to the pub?'

'I told him I was with my manager, that we had compulsory team drinks. I had to phone him from the pub to check in. I did that when I went to the loo, just before I saw Jessie.'

This is insane, Rick thought. *Completely insane*. And explaining it was clearly distressing for her. She was nudging tears from the corner of her eyes, wiping her nose with the paper napkin that came with their sandwiches.

'He keeps saying he's going to get me a mobile phone and that will be the next problem. He'll go completely nuts if I don't answer. Or he'll put a tracker on it. I honestly think that will be the end of what little freedom I have.'

Rick couldn't believe the sentences coming out of her mouth: burglar alarm logs, trackers, paranoid husbands 'going nuts'. He'd wanted the truth, well, here it was, and as she began outlining their financial arrangements – Drew collected her earnings, limited her expenses, checked her spending – he felt his brain overloading, disbelief turning to despair. It seemed preposterous that children played and birds chirruped while she laid bare the secrets of this horrendous marriage.

'This is awful. Have you spoken to your family about it?'

She grimaced. 'We're not in touch. I told you that.'

'Then maybe you should get back in touch? Whatever you

say, there's no way they won't still care about you and want to help you.'

'That's the one thing I can be sure they *won't* do.' She glared at him, with fresh emotion. 'I was raped, Rick. By a friend of my parents. Because I was, I don't know, quite wild, they said I was making the whole thing up, like I was some Lolita. Oh God, this is too much to take in, isn't it? You're revolted.' As he frowned, horrified afresh, she groaned. 'This is exactly why I haven't told you. But it's all connected, that's what I'm trying to say. The situation at home made me desperate enough to say yes to Drew. To feel grateful for what I know is wrong.'

'Oh, Marina.' Rick drew her to him, feeling her anguish ripple through her. The pieces fitted with the sickening truth of a parable: bully meets vulnerable young girl, cut off from her family, presents himself as a saviour, a protector. But she was beautiful and he was jealous. If *he* wanted to protect her, other men might too.

And he was right.

Pulling back, he took her hands in his. 'Has there been no one you could ask for help all these years? What about the neighbours? The one I met yesterday seemed like a decent guy.'

'There's no point, they all think he's great. They think we're the perfect couple.' She gestured to their surroundings. 'All of this, everything that's happened with you ... I just wanted to feel normal, just for a little while. Be like every other girl. You know, go to the pub, sit in the park with a man I like. Feel safe.'

'You *are* safe,' he said. 'You have me now.'

Further gentle questioning about the teenage assault was rejected; clearly, she already regretted that particular confidence. He urged her to eat something and she took a few bites of her sandwich.

'Marina, has Drew ever been violent towards you? Please be honest, I need to know.'

'No. It's more . . . the threat of it. It's like . . . it's like an open prison. But that doesn't mean it isn't still a prison, you know?'

'We'll sort this out. We'll get you free, I promise.' How he might deliver on this, he had no idea. 'Whatever we do, it's going to take some planning. The first thing is you need to start siphoning off whatever cash you can. I know it won't be much, he controls what you have, but a pound here, pennies there, it's a start. I'll help you. Everything I've got spare you can have towards your escape fund.'

But she was shaking her head, eyes brimming once more. 'You don't understand, I threatened to leave once before, when we had this big argument, but . . .' Her voice faded and dread swelled in his stomach.

'But what? What happened?'

'He said if I left, he would come after me and kill me.'

Fucking hell. No wonder she was terrified.

'So, you see, Rick. I can't escape. It's safer for me to stay.'

11

Alex

June, present

Eight hundred grand really wasn't bad for such a prime Camden location, the agent said, and it was exactly the sort of Emperor's New Clothes remark you were expected to swallow without question in London these days.

Over three quarters of a million for this dump? Do me a favour!

Except it wasn't so much of a dump these days, he had to admit. The brickwork had been repointed, the front door and woodwork painted a trendy teal blue. Inside, the common parts were plushly carpeted and the walls replastered.

'I'm down south now but I used to live here back in my youth,' Alex told the agent. No need to clarify that by 'here' he meant this very property.

He'd seen the listing on Rightmove that morning over the shoulder of a colleague flat-hunting in North London (was it any wonder the staff costs for the immigration reporting project were wildly over budget?), and without quite knowing why had got straight on the phone to the agent to arrange a viewing. It was the kind of rogue impulse he'd conditioned himself not to indulge and yet, well, here he was.

'In we go.' The agent had got the flat door open and was ushering him into a space he'd not set foot in since the end of the weird hedonistic summer of '95, an official heatwave, if he remembered. The brief, euphoric era of Rick and Rollo, or R&R as they'd referred to themselves, their 'offering'. *Want to come over for a bit of R&R?* It was the vibe he remembered best, the obliteration of life's complications with the kind of drinking sprees Nero would have been proud of, the soundtrack old Bowie and Roxy Music, plus the Britpop of the day and, oh, who was it again that Marina had been obsessed with? Dusty Springfield, that was it, how could he forget?

He surveyed the space in front of him with a hunger bordering on nausea, only to find that it was almost unrecognizable. The removal of dividing walls meant the living space was now cavernous, with room for an eight-seater dining table, and the kitchen sash had been replaced by French doors, the flat roof beyond a glamorous decked space with sleek furniture and planters. 'That belongs to the flat, does it?' he asked the agent, pointing.

'It does. Fantastic, isn't it?'

They used to smoke out there, he remembered, thinking suddenly of Marina's lighter, the Zippo with Minnie Mouse on it. She'd left it in the flat once during one of their more fraught periods and the act of lighting a cigarette had felt like a connection to her.

There'd been alterations upstairs, too, the bathroom hilariously deluxe, with a state-of-the-art rain shower and claw-foot tub. When he thought of how it had been back in the day, with its dripping cistern and black mould around the plastic bath (had they *ever* put the bath mat in the washing machine? He didn't think so), honestly, it turned his stomach. The bedrooms were the most recognizable spaces. The skylight at the back had been upgraded, the walls papered with a pattern involving birds – swallows, maybe – and the floors covered in sisal, but otherwise they were the same.

'Any thoughts?' the agent asked, just as he was having another memory, this one more guttural, more disturbing. Sex with Marina in the heatwave, the hair at the nape of her neck damp, her breath burning, their skin sticking and pulling. He could hear his own groans as if he was making them now – and half-feared he was.

'It's great, yeah,' he managed, and took the stairs back down two at a time, the agent in pursuit. He promised to phone once he'd 'had a think' and, pleading lateness for another viewing, strode off to the tube.

The mood the revisit had cast was so powerful, so addictive, he remained enveloped in it as he travelled south, listening to old Manics. Richey Edwards had gone missing that year, he recalled, and they'd played the band constantly in the flat, as if their devotion would bring him back. Alighting at Silver Vale, it was almost as if he'd never set foot there before; his legs took him to Long Lane by muscle memory rather than any conscious effort of his own and it was something of a surprise that his key turned in the lock.

There was a further moment of disorientation when he saw the stack of post on the hallway table, the top item addressed to Zara Lloyd. Astoundingly, he'd forgotten about her; in the post-traumatic fugue of the viewing, his mind had reset to pre-date the arrival of their house guest – if that label even applied anymore. The letter hadn't been redirected, he noted, which meant she was now issuing this address as her permanent one. He needed to talk to Beth about this.

'Beth?'

'She's not back yet,' Zara called from the kitchen, and as he approached, she swivelled in her seat, putting her bump between the two of them. It seemed to have grown since he'd seen her last night and yet the way she moved, lightly, as if unburdened, launched an idea that was both fantastic and treacherous: *Was this pregnancy even real?* Was it possible that she was scamming them in some way? Taking advantage of Beth's good nature (if not his own) and collecting confidential information until in a position to siphon off their bank accounts and get the hell out? In a book or film, you'd see her in the back of a taxi, unstrapping her prosthetic bump, checking her bank balance on her phone.

He couldn't bring to mind a single occasion when he'd seen the bare skin. Beth must have, though, surely? They spent so much time hanging out together, and had recently started doing yoga together. Would it be weird to ask if Zara's top had ever ridden up and exposed a sliver of skin?

'You okay, Alex? *Alex?*'

Coming to, he took a seat opposite her. 'What's going on, Zara?'

She glanced at her phone; her email was open, he saw. 'Oh, you know, just a bad day. *Really* bad. I left work early and I'm just waiting for this mail—'

'No,' he interrupted. 'I don't care about that. I mean, what's going on *here*? Why are you still in our house?'

Flushing, she laid a palm on the possibly fake bump, fingers splayed. 'Well, that's a bit aggressive, don't you think?'

'Not aggressive, no. Direct. What do you want from us?'

She stared at him with wide disbelieving eyes. 'I don't want anything. You've already been incredibly generous.'

A new and even more alarming thought now struck him, no doubt influenced by his revisit to Albert Street: did they ... Did they know each other from before?

'I don't know what you're talking about,' Zara said.

Fuck, he must have said it out loud!

'Beth did say you're ...' She abandoned the rest of the thought, giving a light shake of the head.

'I'm what?' Alex asked.

'Just, well, that you're a bit on edge at the moment.' Her expression grew concerned. 'Anything you want to talk about? I might be able to help.'

He glared at her, damned if he was going to be taken in by this Good Samaritan act. 'I wouldn't come to you for help if you were the last man on earth.'

'*Woman*, Alex, in case you haven't noticed.' She scowled, all pretence of concern gone. 'I'm not sure you like us females, do you?'

'I'm not sure you like us males.'

'You know, there's a reason everyone knows the word misogynist but no one knows the male equivalent,' she said, with a sigh.

'Misandrist,' he said, childishly thrilled to be able to prove her wrong. 'We all know one, Zara.'

She raised herself from her seat and transported her cup and saucer to the sink. Then she stood with her back to the sink and regarded him with an almost scientific fascination. 'What is it you're so worried about? You just asked if we knew each other before, when did you mean? Back when you used a different name, maybe?'

He froze in his seat. '*What?*'

She smirked, her natural sense of superiority reasserting itself. 'Beth said you changed it in your twenties.'

'I have no interest in explaining my private decisions to you,' he said.

Her voice grew soft, sly. 'She said she only found out when you got married.'

He remembered it well. *Anything else you need to tell me before we close the deal?* Beth had joked. *A first wife you've forgotten to divorce?*

'You're barking up the wrong tree,' he told Zara curtly.

'So you admit there *is* a tree to bark up?'

Not trusting himself to say any more, he got to his feet and turned to leave the room.

'I'm here if you *do* want to talk,' Zara called after him, faux-cheerful. 'In your own time, there's no hurry.'

No hurry? Clearly, the confrontation had not shamed her

into agreeing to move on. Shutting himself in the living room, he took out his phone and Googled her name. It wasn't the first time he'd done this and he'd clicked on most of the links before, including her profile on the Food Focus website (Zara Lloyd, Citizen Engagement Manager, followed by a load of bullshit about creating peer-to-peer learning environments) and an old JustGiving page for a Jurassic Coast walking challenge.

Nothing new. Nonetheless, he closed down with the sense that he'd not been paying proper attention to this situation and it was about time he started.

*

Frustratingly, a whole week passed without his having the house to himself for a single half hour. Certain that Zara was now eyeing him with an insidious new sense of authority, he withdrew, temporarily, into near silence.

'You okay, babe?' Beth asked, one night, in bed. 'You hardly said a word at dinner.'

'Just missing it being the two of us,' he said. 'Three, obviously, with Olive.'

'Aw, that's sweet.'

Olive had chosen to join Zara in bed that evening, entirely trusting of the cuckoo in the nest, but he couldn't bring himself to complain about this in case he choked up. 'Beth, she is moving out soon, isn't she?'

'Of course she is. There's a problem at work, it sounds as if her boss is giving her a hard time about maternity stuff, but once that's resolved she'll have a lot more head space for flat-hunting.'

He'd stopped asking about the father, his initial presumption of a reunion long overturned. If *he'd* been the one to accidentally impregnate Zara, you wouldn't have seen him for dust either.

In the end, he had to make himself late for a work meeting to get time on his own, waiting at the window for a good ten minutes after Beth and Zara had left. Across the road, the now-familiar grinding and shrieking of machinery had started up and the beep of a lorry reversing into position heralded the arrival of the footbridge for the pond. He could see Dulcie up by the ramp, taking pictures for her daily social media updates.

Satisfied no one was coming back, he scurried up to Zara's room. It resembled the quarters of a hoarder, her possessions piled high against the walls and bursting out of the drawers and wardrobe. Where might she have secreted old prosthetics? They were surely too expensive to discard (plus, this could be a serial scam, her props reusable). He began rummaging through her clothes, then through the shallow baskets under the bed where Beth once kept spare bed linen and Zara now stored a whole jumble of crap.

Nothing.

It crossed his mind that, following that exchange at the kitchen table, she might now take it upon herself to search *his* things, and he spent a further twenty minutes downstairs in the cupboard next to the loo. Their one decent bit of storage in the cottage, it was a free-for-all of cleaning equipment, paint pots, suitcases, as well as more personal items, and he was sweating by the time he'd unearthed the box he was searching for.

holiday with him; not every girl was, as Rollo insisted, like Flavia, eager to snare her man.

And, now he took stock, there'd been inconsistencies about money, too. She'd been too broke to afford lunch or drinks and yet there'd recently been a new hairstyle, an immaculate bob that she said a student had done but that swished and shone in that way only money could buy. She now admitted that Drew had paid for it at a prestigious West End salon. Rick, who had prefered her looser style, was glad now he'd never said as much since that would only have made him a variation on the critical male she had at home. All that mattered was that *she* liked her hair.

Now there was to be a spa treat the following weekend, she reported, booked for her by Drew and to be taken with her sister-in-law.

'What's his game?' Rick asked. 'Why's he suddenly spoiling you like this?'

'He does it when he knows he's gone too far,' she said, heartbreakingly matter-of-fact. 'He can tell I'm losing it and he doesn't want people to start noticing. He wants it to look like I'm living the dream, thanks to *him*. But it's good news for us because I'll come back early and we can have some time together on Sunday afternoon.'

'How did you explain the wall hanging?' he said, remembering. 'Did he ask how you paid for it?'

'I kept it at work,' Marina confessed. 'It's on the wall by my desk. Sorry, Rick, I couldn't take it home. Promise me you won't repeat any of this,' she added with sudden passion. 'It's so *humiliating*.'

It was a request he was well-positioned to honour. He'd been secretive with his colleagues about the relationship from the beginning, at first not wishing to tempt fate (for what *that* was worth) and latterly for fear of mockery over her being married. As for his family, following that naïve blurting to his sister, he'd rebuffed enquiries about the new romance.

But Rollo was different. He knew Marina was married and, feeding off high spirits as he did, he'd intuited that Rick's were steadily worsening. The next time the flatmates had an overlapping free night, he suggested a pint and an update.

'Come on, it's obviously bird trouble. You still feeling down about her little bombshell?'

'No. Well, yes, but there's more. I'm really worried about her.' Though there were no other drinkers within earshot and in any case an old Eagles track thundered from the pub's speakers, Rick lowered his voice. 'She doesn't want me to talk about it, but the husband is bad news.'

Rollo smirked. 'Well, he was never *good* news, was he?'

'No, I mean more than that. He doesn't treat her well.'

'What, you don't mean he knocks her about?'

'No, it's more psychological.' Rick wiped beer foam from his mouth with the back of his hand. 'I don't know much more than that, but she needs to get away from him before it does turn physical.'

'Wow,' Rollo said, with rare solemnity. 'Okay.'

They fell silent. Outside, the wind blew bits of litter across the pavements and turned the umbrella of a passer-by inside out. The papers said there was a heatwave coming, but you'd never guess.

'So what's he like then?' Rollo said presently. 'I mean, what are you dealing with in terms of physical strength?'

In case it came to a fight, he meant. 'He sounds pretty fit. Apparently, he was almost a professional footballer. I've never actually seen him, mind.'

'Not even when you went down to the house?'

'I told you, they were out.' It galled Rick how little information he'd gathered on his expedition to Silver Vale. He'd gone on a whim, unprepared, noticing little beyond a BMW and a rhododendron bush. At least he'd been dynamic enough to take the film in to be developed, even if the photo of the house offered nothing but basic visual reference. (The early part of the roll included two pictures of him with Vicky; it was like looking at a couple he'd never met.)

'Go back then,' Rollo said. He had a knack for making solutions sound simple. 'Go when you know she'll be out, then you can knock on the door and pretend to be a Jehovah's Witness or whatever.'

'She *is* away this weekend,' Rick said, wondering.

'Result. Shame I'm down at the parentals on Saturday.' Rollo was, Rick knew, making a rare visit to the family home in hopes of getting his allowance restarted, the bank having refused to extend his overdraft (he may have taken Rick for this pint, but it had been Rick who'd paid for it). 'But I could come back early and we could go on Sunday?'

'Really?'

'Really. You're obviously bloody useless on your own.' Rollo's eyes glowed, his grin stretched wide, and two girls who'd just walked in checked him out with flirtatious

interest. He was always at his most magnetic when proposing mischief.

'Deal,' Rick said.

*

And so, for the second Sunday in a row, he found himself
clattering down the Northern line to Waterloo, this time
with Rollo in tow. A slightly sulky Rollo, for he'd returned
to Albert Street the night before with his begging bowl empty
('Why are parents such fucking tightwads?'). It was therefore the least Rick could do to pay for his train ticket and
McMuffin and coffee.

As Rollo flicked through the *News of the World*, Rick re-
examined his *A to Z*, hoping to plot a different approach to
the Stanleys' house for fear of encountering the car-washing
neighbour again. Just beyond the left turn from Surrey Road
onto Exmoor Gardens, there looked to be some sort of short
cut between that and the next street down, Pleasance Road; a
strip of woodland or gardens, perhaps a disused railway track.

This was quickly confirmed when they reached the
entrance and, taking no notice of the 'No Entry' sign, hopped
over the ineffectual metal barrier: among the bed of rotting
foliage and litter were sections of broken track. These, along
with low-hanging boughs and overgrown bushes, even a
whole fallen tree, created regular obstacles as they made
their way along. The smell of rot mingled with smoke from
a nearby bonfire to create an ungodly aroma.

'This is rancid,' Rollo complained. 'Why don't they clear
this shit up?'

'Grim,' Rick agreed. 'The houses are pretty posh, as well. They've obviously decided just to abandon it and pretend it's not here.' Personally, he thought the approach pretty promising, the track high enough to give a direct view into the gardens. It was late morning, the weather dry and mild, and people had their barbecues and garden furniture out, even a couple of those swinging canopied seats Rick's own parents had in their back garden. Children were out playing on climbing frames and see-saws, unaware of the two figures picking their way past, though twice dogs dashed in their direction, barking.

A few minutes in, they paused to examine Rick's photo of the Stanleys' house for clues to identify it – the roofline, the height of the chimney stacks compared to neighbouring properties, the position of the satellite dish – and were fairly certain they'd reached the right one. The chain fencing at the foot of the bank was in poor repair, even sliced apart in places, and the Stanleys had no separate fence, only low hedging. Beyond was one of the more pristine gardens, with weed-free flowerbeds and a trimmed lawn. Expensive-looking rattan furniture was arranged on a patio by the kitchen door and Rick imagined Marina sitting here on sunny weekends with her coffee and cigarettes, to all the world an adored wife, while inside slowly dying.

The kitchen door and all the windows were shut, no signs of life within.

'Looks like he's out again,' Rick said. 'Bugger.'

'Let's get a bit closer,' Rollo said, and before Rick could protest, he was easing through a break in the fence and skirt-ing the hedging. Re-emerging on the other side, he gestured to Rick to follow him across the lawn. There were kids in the garden next door, just a few feet from where Rollo now stood, and as Rick navigated the brambles to reach the lawn, he could hardly believe his own brazenness. Rollo, yes, he was a natural rule breaker, but Rick, a prowler in broad daylight?

Then again, he *was* the one sleeping with someone else's wife, not Rollo.

He caught up with his friend at the kitchen door, where he was peering through the glass panel.

'He *is* in,' Rollo whispered. 'Or someone is. Look, the TV's on. Fuck, *move*!'

Rick's gaze jerked from the wall-mounted TV, which was showing football, to the open doorway, just in time to see the entry of a dark-haired man dressed only in a pair of faded denim cut-offs. He was tall and powerful-looking, with a rough coating of hair on his chest and forearms. Drew – it had to be. Marina had described his alpha male look vividly, and here it was in all its glory, not only the muscular strength, but the air of self-satisfaction, of being in charge, unchallengeable.

The shock was physical, immobilizing Rick for a split second before he swerved out of sight after Rollo. After a few tense seconds of breath-holding, he edged back and watched Drew take a carton of orange juice from the fridge and drain it, crushing the empty package into a bin. Then he flicked the switch on the kettle, calling through the open doorway loudly enough for the intruders to hear from outside: 'You want a coffee, babe?'

Aware of Rollo frowning at him, Rick put a finger to his lips. His heart was drumming painfully. *Babe?* Had Marina lied to him? Told him she was away when she was in fact at home? But why would she do that? He never saw her on Sundays, that was Drew's only day off. This evening would be an exception to the rule, thanks to her plan to fib about the time of her return from the spa hotel.

And then, in a ghastly sequence that seemed to unroll in slow motion, he saw why: a woman appeared in the kitchen, a woman who was not Marina, wrapped in a pink bath robe, hair twisted into a turban, and Drew was taking hold of her and kissing her, sliding his hands inside her robe. As he groped her, the robe opened, and the kissing grew more aggressive. Oh God, were they going to have sex right there in the kitchen, almost touching distance from where Rick and Rollo watched?

'Fucking hell,' Rollo murmured. 'This is like a porno. Who is she?'

As Rick mouthed for him to shush, there was a sudden blood-curdling wail from one of the kids next door, causing Drew and the woman to break apart and turn. Rick squeezed his eyes shut, face burning, feeling like a child caught in the act of something shameful. When he opened his eyes again, the couple was gone, the kettle steaming and the mugs untouched on the counter. Motioning to Rollo, he hared back across the lawn, through the hedge – scratching his hands in the process – and up to the track. Rollo came scrambling after and the two peered back at the house. From this elevation, they were almost level with the first-floor windows and it was at one of these that Drew and the woman now reappeared. A curtain was pulled across half the window, though not before the woman had crossed, naked now, and laughing.

So *this* was why Drew had sent Marina away for the weekend. Pampering, she'd said, and Rick had thought he caught the note of pride in her voice because her husband was treating her well – for once. Well, hardly. He had another woman and he didn't even have the decency to take his dirty deed off site.

'Looks like Marina's not the only one playing away,' Rollo said, amused.

Rick swallowed his protests. Yes, Marina was also being unfaithful, but she wasn't the one trying to control her partner's life. She wasn't the one withholding his earnings and checking burglar alarm logs.

'Can I help you there?' called a commanding voice, and, turning, Rick was startled to see a woman on the Pleasance Road side of the track, poised midway between the chain fence and the panel fencing to what was presumably her own garden. She was middle-aged, with that busy-body manner and flossy hairstyle all women that age had (his mother, anyway), and wore dirt-encrusted gardening gloves. 'What are you doing watching that house? Are you peeping Toms?'

Rollo sniggered under his breath, before addressing the woman in an insolent tone: 'Right first time, love. Peep, peep, peep, can't get enough of it.'

'He's joking, we weren't watching anyone,' Rick said, hastily.

'I just saw you climbing back up the bank. Were you trying to break in?' Her gaze found his hands, red with scratches. 'I think I'd better go in and call the police, had I?'

'If you want to be done for wasting their time, feel free,' Rollo said, winking at Rick. 'Shall we go?'

'Wait!' called the woman as he paced off. 'What's your name, young man?'

'*Young man! Young man!*' Rollo parroted over his shoulder, picking up speed.

Rick sent a last placating look the woman's way before taking off himself. Rollo had gone the opposite way from the one they'd come, which proved a longer stretch and quickly defeated Rick's fitness. The pollen count was high, too, and he didn't have his inhaler on him, so he was breathing in audible rasps by the time he joined his friend. The barrier at this end was as easily vaulted as the other, with a short run of steps down to a quiet residential road. Long Lane, the street was called, a row of pretty stone cottages with rose bushes and wisteria. They followed it west before turning right onto the street beyond Pleasance Road and rejoining the main road that way.

'I hope she doesn't say anything to Drew,' Rick fretted.

'Oh, she'll be too busy with the next Neighbourhood Watch scandal,' Rollo said. 'Someone taking a piss up there or dropping a crisp packet. Can you *imagine* living somewhere like this? No wonder they're all having affairs, they must be off their heads with boredom.'

Rick had to agree.

Dodging the traffic, they crossed to the station. 'Well, at least we saw him,' Rollo said. 'Good-looking bastard, isn't he?'

'Yeah.'

'You going to tell Marina what he's up to?'

'I don't know,' Rick said, truthfully. It was absurd to feel betrayed on her behalf, given his own role in her private life, but he did.

At least they were lucky with the trains, arriving on the platform just as one was due and soon leaving those inscrutable suburban streets behind and re-entering the grimier quarters of the city.

Rollo stretched across three seats, his feet up. 'I was thinking, shall I ask Sonia to get some background on him?'

'Who's Sonia?' Rick said.

'A mate from college. She works at News International now. She could ask their cuttings service to sort us out.'

'Cuttings? What, like old newspaper articles?'

'Exactly. You know what they say: know thine enemy.'

'But would there be anything? It's not like he's famous.'

'No, but he's a business owner, so there might be some puff piece or other in the locals. And you said he's dodgy, didn't you? Well, if he's been up in court on any kind of charge, then it might have made the papers.'

'Marina might not even know about it herself,' Rick said, which was a sobering thought.

'What's his full name? Is Drew short for anything?'

'I don't think so. He has flooring shops in Wimbledon and Manchester, if that helps.'

'Cool. Leave it with me.'

Rick nodded, gratitude assuaging his unease, if only briefly. 'Please don't mention any of this to her.'

''Course not.' Rollo made a zipping motion across his mouth. 'A bloke's entitled to a few secrets of his own – just ask your man Drew.'

112

13

Rick

July 1995

By the time Marina arrived at the flat in the late afternoon, Rick had spent a fretful couple of hours alone, Rollo having gone to meet Flavia and friends in Portobello Road, and he felt close to combustion. She, by contrast, was mellow, dropping a gift of a bottle of posh cologne into his hands and saying, 'I put it on the old man's credit card.'

'Right,' Rick said. 'Thanks.' Her air of playing the rich wife treating her lover to a trinket riled him. Though he'd never seen her look so beautiful – in a white cotton dress with silver ribbon threaded along the neckline, that usually smooth bob tousled – he was determined not to let that sway him. 'I need to talk to you, Marina.'

She protested, good-naturedly. 'Oh, not another serious talk. Can't we just have a laugh? I'm free as a bird this evening, he's not expecting me home for hours. Let's just get wasted.'

'I'm really sorry, but it's important,' Rick said. 'Come and sit on the sofa.'

'Fine.' There was a slightly sour set to her mouth as she took her seat, a child whose fun was being spoiled by an adult.

'I've been to your house again.' His left knee was twitching and he placed a hand on it, pressing it still.

'What?' She stared at him. 'When?'

'Earlier today, when you were still at the hotel. Don't look at me like that – after everything you've told me, I *had* to see him with my own eyes.' His rival, his *enemy*. 'Which I did.'

'You went to the door?'

'No, I was up on that track at the back.' He was loath to admit to having crept right up to her window. 'I saw him from there.' Best not to divulge Rollo's part in the episode either, given that he'd promised to keep her troubles private. 'The thing is, Marina, I saw him with another woman.'

'What other woman?' she said, her gaze glassy, unfocused.

'I don't know who, I was hardly going to walk in and ask, was I? The point is, when I say he was with her, I mean *with*. They were kissing, right there in your kitchen. They were obviously more than friends. It looked like she'd stayed the night.'

Marina put her thumb to her mouth, let the nail scrape along her teeth. 'But they didn't see you?'

'No one saw me. It's all hidden by trees and bushes up there.' He left it there; he wasn't about to alarm her further by confessing to the encounter with the neighbour. 'I'm really sorry,' he added.

The apology at least seemed to provoke an emotional reaction in her, even if the emotion was fury – with him. 'You *have* to stop sneaking around like this, Rick! The last thing we need is him seeing you and connecting you with me.'

'Why would he do that?' He frowned. 'You're not more bothered by the fact that he's been shagging another woman the moment your back's turned?'

But the crude choice of words only made her defensive. 'Well, I'm doing exactly the same myself, aren't I?' Her theatrical shrug suggested she was convincing herself, not him. She *was* upset by his revelation, but she adapted quickly – and was there any wonder in a dysfunctional marriage like hers?

'You don't have to pretend,' he said, tenderly. 'Not with me. It's got to be horrible hearing something like this on top of everything else he's put you through.' Having had most of the afternoon to reflect on the matter, Rick now strongly suspected that Drew's business trips up north had been facilitating his affair – or affairs. 'I wasn't sure whether to even tell you, to be honest.'

'Then why *did* you?' she snapped.

'What? You make it sound like I *wanted* to upset you.' He gazed at her, hurt and unsettled. 'I just thought it might affect the choices you make. Think about it. If you leave, maybe he won't be as difficult about it as you imagine. If he's got someone else on the go, he might not come after you like you seem to think he will.'

Seem to think: he regretted the phrasing, as if he doubted her instincts, her experience. He'd kill her, that was what Drew had told her, wasn't it? That was a lot more than 'difficult'.

'It might suit him now if you left,' he clarified.

115

'Please can we not discuss it,' Marina said. 'I mean it, Rick, not every time. Don't you get it? Coming here is my escape! If I want to spend the evening feeling like shit, I can do it at home.'

It was a low blow, but not without justification. She had every right to question why he'd gone marching off like that, why he 'had' to see Drew for himself. He had a sudden flash of Vicky sitting right where Marina was now, an outburst of anger.

This is not how people behave!

And nor was this. Rollo, he thought, irritable and in need of a target, it had been Rollo's idea to go down there. He always turned everything into a joke, a stunt. But he knew in his gut that this was grossly unfair. He jumped to his feet. 'Look, I've got something to show you.' He'd been going to wait, but he'd got this wrong and what she needed from him now was evidence of constructive support. He went up to his bedroom and retrieved an old biscuit tin from his bedside cabinet, brought it back to show her.

She'd lit a cigarette (rules about smoking indoors had been ditched the day Rollo moved in) and peered at its contents through a grey haze. 'What is this?'

'Cash. I've started a fund for you.' He'd already assembled a stack of tens and twenties, plus assorted coins. He always kept a decent amount of cash in his wallet and he'd withdrawn more after making his promise in the park that he would help her. 'I know it's just a start, but I'll build it up. You can take it whenever you need it.'

'Oh, God ...' Emotions crossed her face that he could

not track, but at least they were no longer rooted in anger. 'I know you mean well, but I . . . This is all a bit overwhelming.' She stubbed out the cigarette, though it wasn't even half-smoked. 'Look, I think I'd better go.'

'You just got here!' Rick cried, but she stumbled to her feet, knocking the tin to the floor, and looped the canvas handles of her weekend bag over her arm. Next thing she'd gone, making her usual soft-footed descent to the ground floor. He knew he should hold his nerve and let her go, but his resolve lasted twenty seconds before he found himself running out into the street after her.

'Marina, wait!'

She spun, her bag swinging heavily.

'I'm sorry. You're right, I shouldn't have gone to your house. I shouldn't be spying and forcing the issue like this.'

But the apology backfired, unleashing in her a defiance even more intense than earlier. 'You *really* think I don't already know what he gets up to? I'm not a fucking idiot, Rick!'

'No one said you were an idiot!' he yelled back.

The traffic was backed up at the junction with Delancey Street and people were looking at them through open car windows. 'You all right, love?' a man called to Marina, craning out of the passenger window from the driver's seat.

'She's fine,' Rick fired back. He put a hand on her shoulder and felt the blade of her clavicle through her dress. 'Please, let's not fall out over this. I'm not the one trying to hurt you. The opposite, I want to help you. You must see that?'

She dropped her gaze. 'I do.'

'Then come back up?'

'No. I can't relax now. I need to get home.'

'But we can see each other again, yeah?' He tried not to make a question of it, a plea, but this was exactly what it sounded like and she gave him a quick look of pity before turning away.

'Marina?'

'I'll phone you at work tomorrow,' she threw back.

Their mingled despair echoed in his ears as she walked away – stalked, really, as if the only reason she wasn't running was the overnight bag weighing her down. Standing there, he had the unwelcome idea that her haste might not be entirely owing to his latest misstep, but also to her hope of getting home early enough to catch Drew with his lover. And if she succeeded, he wondered if all the cheating bastard had to do was swear that he'd change and she'd believe him, forgive him.

Casting Rick to the wayside, his purpose served.

*

It was clear that their row had had a serious impact when, the following morning, she didn't call him as promised. Temps at Culkins weren't supposed to take personal calls, but he rang anyway and her extension was engaged for so long he suspected she'd taken the phone off the hook. At lunchtime, he hung about in the lobby café, but she'd either been and gone or wasn't intending coming down at all.

'Looking for your girl?' Annie asked him.

'Yes, has she been down yet?'

'I haven't seen her. Working through lunch? Or off sick, maybe?'

At 3pm, on impulse – Lord knew he hadn't learned his lesson on this score – he got up from his desk and took the lift to the eighth floor. There was a large group surrounding the Culkins reception desk, signing in one by one, and, as he waited, he stole glimpses of corridors and offices, his first sense of where Marina spent her working hours, away from Drew, away from all of them.

Seeing a sign for the gents, he headed towards it, turning an extra corner to peer into a work space with a layout similar to his own: individual outer offices with windows for the managers, smart nameplates on their doors, and a large open-plan inner zone for the rest of the staff. Unable to identify Marina among the dozens of workers, he had the sudden wild notion that he was losing his mind, that she was not his real girlfriend, but an imaginary one. The breathless sensation this caused made him reach for his inhaler and take a couple of puffs.

Returning to reception past a room marked Conference 2, he pulled up as the door swung open and a man in his fifties stepped out, revealing a meeting table occupied by other middle-aged men and, just off to the side, the slight, subservient figure of Marina. She was dressed in the rose-pink blouse and grey skirt Rick had seen many times, notebook and pen on her lap – taking minutes, he guessed. The air was very warm and her cheeks were flushed, but otherwise she looked fine. If any scene had unfolded when she'd gone home to Drew the previous evening, she'd emerged from it unharmed.

She didn't sense him looking, unlike one of the other attendees, who got to his feet and pushed the door to, eyebrows raised.

When Rick re-entered the reception area, he found it had emptied, and the receptionist apologized for having made him wait. 'Who are you here to see?'

But the thought of having Marina plucked out of her meeting, or even presented with a message afterwards, was excruciating. She wouldn't take kindly to it, a second attempt in two days to encroach on her turf. 'It's okay,' he said. 'I'll catch up with her later.'

*

That evening, as he sat in mindless apathy in front of a soap, Rollo came into the living room and slapped a large manila envelope onto the coffee table, knocking aside the ashtray. It still held Marina's lipsticked cigarette from yesterday's brief and troubled encounter, her Zippo lying forgotten beside it.

'*Voilà*. Everything there is to know about your love rival. As far as the fourth estate is concerned, anyway.'

'That was quick,' Rick said.

'Sonia biked it over just before I left. Don't get excited, mind, he's strictly small fry. There's nothing in the nationals, just a few bits from local freebies.'

'You've looked through it already?'

'Just a quick glance to see if his name came up in any court reports, which it didn't. Anything more than this, we'll have to hire a private detective.'

'I don't think we need go that far,' Rick said. It was a relief to hear that Drew Stanley had no record of assault. He would almost certainly have withheld the information from his wife if he had, and Rick had no wish to be the one to have to tell her, not now she'd made it clear his interference was to be punished with silence. 'Thanks, this is great. I owe you one.'

Rollo brightened. 'I'll take payment in kind. You're coming to The Engineer for Adam's birthday? I'm heading up there now.'

'I'll follow you up,' Rick promised.

As soon as Rollo had left, he turned off the TV and spread the cuttings out on the table. Five of the pages were taken up with two profiles in South London magazines, both with a slant that suggested the interiors sections. *PRINCE OF PARQUET*: it made him sound like a ballroom dancer. The images were too crude in the photocopies to be able to see much of the interiors, but in one Drew had been photographed at home and Rick recognized the tall, elegant window as the one to the left of the Stanleys' front door. As for the copy, maybe Rick was influenced by what Marina had told him, but it seemed to him that the man liked to speak of himself in somewhat heroic terms:

> The recession hit the business hard, but Stanley insists
> he is 'just about' out of the woods. 'My proudest
> accomplishment is not having to lay anyone off. I'd
> pay my fitters before I paid myself...'

As he read, Rick realized that what he most wanted to find were references to Marina. Clues about her other life – the domestic detail she would not share with him and for which he'd developed a masochistic craving. But other than a mention that Drew was married and 'shared his airy home with his younger wife, Marina', there was nothing about her. Her name was given just once more, when he was asked if he'd supplied the flooring used for his own home.

> 'I supplied it, yes, but I didn't choose it,' he says, laughing. 'That's Marina's department. Call me old-fashioned, but women just have better taste.'

A third article was a brother/sister profile, the sister being Gillian, Marina's companion at the spa.

> 'She's got a much better business brain than me,' Stanley raves. 'I'll always trust her judgement over mine.'

He certainly laid it on thick, this idea that he operated with the utmost respect, if not devotion, to the women around him. And these feature writers lapped it up (all bylines were female), not knowing they were interviewing an abuser, the kind of man who threatened to kill his wife.

Feeling more powerless than ever and eager to pre-empt any further disastrous urges, Rick slipped the Zippo in his pocket – he'd return it to Marina when he next saw her – before grabbing his jacket and setting off for the pub.

14

Alex

July, present

'We need to help,' Beth said. She was known to be cool in a crisis, though you could – if you were being churlish – argue that she'd never actually faced one, not by *his* definition of the word, anyway.

It wasn't as if the little girl was blundering about or screaming hysterically, as you might expect of an infant who'd lost her family on Wimbledon Common, but only wept silently, eyes closed in some primitive instinct to minimize the horror.

For a strange moment, Alex envied her that quiet solitude.

'What's the matter, sweetie?' Beth asked her in her gentlest voice. 'Can you not find your mummy?'

As she crouched next to her, Alex kept his distance. At least this humanitarian mission put an end to the conversation they'd just been having about his birthday, which was a callous and self-interested way of viewing a child's distress, but, come on, *of course* the parents were going to turn up again.

He and Beth had driven to the common for a walk with Olive, delightfully *à deux* since it was too strenuous for the normally inescapable Zara. Far from having moved out, she was now at home 24/7, having resigned from her job following 'pregnancy-related bullying' by her director and now bringing a claim of constructive dismissal against her employer. As Beth had sympathized, Alex had thought only, *Great. First no home and now no job.* The idea that an operator like Zara could be bullied was preposterous.

And, while they were on the subject, he'd still yet to see evidence that the pregnancy was real.

He'd been permitted a good twenty minutes of private reflection in the car, plus a further twenty on the ground, before Beth dropped the news that she was throwing a party for him for his fiftieth birthday – 'whether you like it or not'.

'A *party*?'

She chuckled. 'You make it sound like an execution.'

'Sorry, it's just . . . Who've you invited?'

Dulcie and Jon, Samira and Philip, plus two other sets of neighbours and Trailblazers; Eddie, Alex's only remaining friend from university days, and his wife Suki; a few old friends of Beth's who they'd been on holiday with over the years. Zara, naturally.

'Please say you haven't told my sister,' he said, groaning. 'I can do without some surprise reunion.'

Beth tugged him out of the path of a mountain biker. 'Of course not. The idea is that you have a good time.'

'And I can tell you now that Eddie and Suki won't come.' Having returned from New York only five years ago, Eddie had been late to marriage, Suki fifteen years younger, and, as night followed day, the guy was now saddled with two pre-schoolers, with a third on the way. 'They'll have some sort of babysitting calamity, they always do.'

'There's no need to sound so hopeful,' Beth said. 'Honestly, this is the whole reason I've organized it – you're getting really anti-social. It's not natural.'

'I don't mean to be. I've got a lot on my mind. Work stuff.' All at once he was felled by the sheer exhaustion of having perpetually to defend himself – *protect* himself. Even sleep afforded little respite; only last night he'd had a grotesque dream in which Cordelia Smyth had arrived at his door to blackmail him about forensic evidence.

'You'll never match any fibres,' he'd told her. 'I destroyed my clothes a long time ago.'

'Not fibres, Alex,' she'd crowed. 'Blood. *Your* blood.'

Beth took a deft diagonal step as Olive shot in front of her. 'All the more reason to have a bit of fun when you're *not* working,' she said. 'What's been your best party ever? Come on, what springs to mind when you think of a classic birthday party?'

Her sincerity was almost painful, her desire to please him, *celebrate* him, when he considered his utter lack of worthiness. What was the harm in having a stab at answering her truthfully? When *had* he last enjoyed a party? 'There was a good one in the flat when I lived up in Camden. Twenty-five or -six, we must have been. We thought we were so old.'

Marina had been at the party. She'd arrived late – she always arrived late. She'd done that wild dance, hadn't she? Shimmying in and out of the window in the most erotic way, like pole dancing or something. She'd worked in dodgy clubs, she probably *had* done it for a living, though she'd never admitted to it outright. Right from the start she'd been someone who'd led previous lives. Right from the start, she'd been unlike the other girls.

Suddenly he had a lump in his throat as hard as a golf ball.

'What kind of vibe,' Beth pressed.

'Oh, you know, typical Nineties. Cigarettes and alcohol. Music, drugs. You know what they say, if you remember it, you weren't really there.'

'That was the Sixties.'

'Yeah, whatever.'

Just then, Olive went rigid as a succession of ponies passed on the bridle path, and they decided to branch off down a narrower trail.

'Look,' Beth said, 'if you really don't fancy celebrating, I can cancel everyone. It's not my aim to *torture* you.'

He was just considering the best way to respond to this, to salvage something from the ruins of his own ingratitude, when they noticed the lost girl. She was further down the path, in a gulley, knee-deep in brambles, a tiny thing in a yellow summer dress. She was three or four years old, scared and struggling to remember basic stuff like her mum's name.

'They can't be far away,' Beth told her. 'Let's stay still for a minute and see if we can hear them calling? It's hard to know how far she's drifted,' she whispered to Alex. 'If they went looking in the opposite direction, that's a lot of trees between us.'

They waited in silence for a minute or two, but couldn't pick up any shouts or cries. Beth consulted Google Maps. 'We're not far from the Windmill Café. Let's take her there. The staff will know what to do.'

They chose the most direct route, which involved overgrown paths that scratched the kid's bare legs and made her cry. Though they were unquestionably doing the right thing, Alex couldn't help seeing events in a different light, perhaps as a witness might following the news of an abduction. *They were leading her down this narrow path. I could tell she wasn't theirs, the way she was crying and looking so scared . . .*

That was the problem now, people glimpsed something for half a second, guesswork became fact, and two minutes later it was all over social media. It was a brainless, kneejerk world and even if falsehoods were retracted or corrected, no one was interested. This was why he avoided drama like this; he had no intention of going viral.

As the car park came into view, he calmed. Once the situation was explained to a member of café staff and procedure discussed, a hot chocolate was produced for the kid and a name extracted: Amelia.

'When I was your age, my favourite story was about a girl called Amelia,' Beth told her. 'Amelia Jane. She was a doll.' She left it there, remembering perhaps that the character was less than pleasant and therefore likely on the banned list of any millennial parent. 'You drink your hot chocolate, darling. We're here as long as you need us.'

It was an odd way to phrase it. Shouldn't they say *until your mum and dad get here*? Reinforce the message that she'd be reunited with them soon. He could almost see it in his wife's eyes, the fantasy that this little creature would not be claimed and she'd be asked to take her.

But, of course, Amelia was still blowing on her hot chocolate to cool it when the parents came dashing in, the dad bouncing a toddler in his arms, the mum as tear-stained as the lost girl.

'Oh my God, sweetheart, we thought you'd fallen in the pond! We were about to call nine-nine-nine!'

'I *knew* she'd be safe,' the dad said, but he looked shaken. He had a lavish head of dark hair, which made Alex feel absurdly miserable. What a crap outing this had turned out to be.

'She was chasing butterflies,' the mum told Beth. 'She must have wandered down the hill after one and got lost.'

It was a classic case of turning your back for a moment and unleashing a nightmare. There was nothing to be gained from further reconstruction and the parents' thanks were heartfelt. The dad got a lid for the hot chocolate to take it away, while the mum instructed Amelia to thank her saviours.

'Thank you,' she said, bolder now. 'I was fine!' Her natural personality was emerging and it seemed to Alex that she might be a bit of a brat.

With a faintly supervisory air, Beth went out to the car park to watch her being strapped into the back of a fifty-grand Range Rover. The younger sibling looked awed by events, while the parents spoke with barely moving lips, sniping at each other under their breath.

As the car passed, crushing the gravel under its huge frame, the woman noticed Beth and put up a hand. Beth waved until they were out of sight.

'What a horrible scare,' she said. 'They won't let it happen again, that's for sure.'

Alex was intrigued by this. 'Or maybe now they've got away with it once, they'll assume they will again the next time?'

'What a bizarre way to look at it, "getting away with it",' she said, irritably, as if he were criticizing her. He sensed the adrenaline draining from her system, the gloom approaching. And now they'd return to their childless home, the home in which he was refusing to throw a party. She must think she had the worst of both worlds, neither the children she wanted nor the rip-roaring social life parents envied of the child-free.

And her new best friend Zara would be waiting both to stoke her discontent and demonstrate all that she lacked.

'You know what?' he said, opening the boot of their car and urging Olive in. 'Let's have this party for my birthday. As many people as you like.'

Beth brightened. 'Really?'

'Absolutely. You're only fifty once.'

And, when you thought about it, it was pretty fucking miraculous that he'd made it this far at all.

15

Rick

July 1995

'What's this, babe?'

Rick snapped on the bedside lamp. They'd undressed with the lights off, but the moment he'd felt her flinch at his touch he'd drawn back and reached for the switch. 'Oh, Jesus, this isn't . . . Is this a *handprint*?'

His voice – the whole of him – was throttled with horror at the sight of a thick cuff of bruising on her upper left arm, the patterning clearly suggesting a man's grip. He was no medic, but he knew it had to have been an act of vice-like restraint to damage the tissue like this.

'I didn't want you to see it,' Marina said, and she wouldn't look at him as she wriggled upright.

'When did he do this?'

'Sunday, after I got home from seeing you. We had a bit of an argument.'

'Is this why you didn't want to meet this week?' To his shame, his alarm at her injury was tempered by relief that he wasn't as personally at fault as he'd feared when, after that Monday of silence, there'd been a further twenty-four hours of no contact. Until this, their regular Thursday night, she'd been unwilling to meet and he'd naturally assumed it was owing to *their* row. 'Tell me what happened. Did you confront him about the other woman?'

She shook her head. 'Even if I wanted to, how could I explain how I knew without him guessing someone was spying for me?'

This was a very generous interpretation of the episode, Rick noted. He couldn't take his eyes off the bruising, its brutal rainbow of discoloration. She must have been in pain, he realized, that afternoon when he'd glimpsed her in the Culkins conference room, not to mention emotional distress. Work must have been unbearable. 'What then?' he asked.

'He'd spoken with Gillian and she obviously said something about what time we left the hotel. He figured out I didn't go straight home.'

They were close, Drew and the sister, that was obvious from the interview Rick had read, but he knew better than to reference this.

'I told you, Rick, he likes every hour accounted for.'

Appalled though he was, he kept his voice level. 'He has no right to get angry with you like this.'

Her fingers found the bruise and rubbed it gently. 'It looks worse than it feels. It really doesn't hurt. I'm sure it won't happen again.'

'Marina—'

'Forget it, Rick. I don't want to talk about it.' She rose from the bed, her back to him, and hunted for a T-shirt of his to put on.

'Okay.' It was the same as always, this denial that Drew's cruelty warranted acting on. At least she came back to bed and didn't announce she was going home, her standard move in shutting down unwanted discussion. Turning off the lamp, feeling her roll towards him, her conciliatory touch on his stomach, he willed her not to make him promise to forget this, to not act – *react* – in his customary kneejerk way. He already knew that if she did, he would not be able to keep his word.

Because all bets were off now – even if he did risk another round of stand-offs and reunions. No decent man could bear witness to these bruises and not confront the attacker; it was only a question of when. Not tomorrow, since Drew would be in Manchester until the evening, nor the weekend, since there was no guarantee of Marina being out of range. No, it had to be when she was safely at work, which meant Monday. Rick would sacrifice his lunch break with her to meet – finally – the monster she'd married.

*

Floors Galore, the business was called (how cheesy was that?), a ten-minute walk from Wimbledon Station. The show room, a large strip-lit space with a sharp chemical odour and discount signs at every turn, was on the ground floor and, Rick quickly ascertained from the girl at the counter, the office situated directly above. Stairs were visible through a glass door directly behind her.

He took a step towards the door. 'Is the boss in?'

'Wait up.' She held out a hand to stop him and multiple rows of bead bracelets clattered towards the elbow. 'Let me check he's not on the phone. What's your name?'

'Timothy. I'm a friend of his wife's.'

'You know Marina? Okay, great.' More obliging now, she made the call, reporting back, 'He just has to finish something urgent, then you can go on up.'

As he waited, Rick gazed blindly at samples of hardwood. Over the sound system, M People played 'Search For The Hero', and he found himself – as he often did now with music, so heightened were his emotions – making a personal soundtrack of it.

At last, the phone rang and he was admitted through to the stairs. At the top, an open doorway revealed a light-filled office with two high windows onto the street. The top deck of a bus was a reassuring sight – it meant he was close to other people – plus there was the girl downstairs, of course, and any customers that might come in. Witnesses.

Drew, at a desk between the windows, stood to greet him. He wore laundered blue jeans and a brilliant white shirt, his impressive musculature evident through the cotton, face and hands tanned. His good looks were blander than Rick remembered; his expression was quizzical, untroubled, as he offered the chair opposite his.

'How can I help you? Timothy, was it? I didn't catch a surname?'

Rick faltered at the sound of his voice, which was not the masculine rumble he'd expected but something milder, almost silky, with a Mancunian accent. 'Foster,' he said. 'I'm a colleague of your wife. Marina.'

Drew raised an eyebrow, a curl of amusement on his lips at the notion that he should need a reminder of his own wife's name. He had a touch of Rollo about him, the unerring self-assurance. 'Colleague? Emma said friend.'

'I'm both.' Rick inhaled deeply. Adrenaline had got him this far – that and moral outrage – but squaring up to a man of such physical confidence was more intimidating than he'd imagined. Why had he said colleague? Now he risked Drew pressuring Marina to leave her job, the only bit of agency she'd managed to acquire.

He cleared his throat. 'The thing is, a few of us have noticed she's got some bruises on her arm. It looks like someone's hurt her quite badly.'

Drew's gaze narrowed. 'And you think that someone is me, do you?'

'I didn't say that.' Rick was taken aback, not expecting so combative a response. He chose his next words with care. 'We just want to know if there's anything you can do to help make sure it doesn't happen again.'

Contempt flickered in Drew's eyes. 'What's your real name, mate?'

The street outside was suddenly very quiet.

'I told you, Timothy Foster.'

'Show me some ID.'

Rick felt his face reddening. 'I don't have any on me.'

'You don't have a driver's licence or a credit card?'

'Not on me,' Rick repeated.

'Well, *Timothy Foster*, why don't we start this little inter-action again. My wife said she had some weirdo hanging around at work and I assume that's you, is it? Looking to stir up a bit of trouble, are you? Got some sick fantasy about her being a damsel in distress?'

The arrogance of the man was astounding. Clearly, he was one of those narcissistic bullies for whom an admission of guilt was impossible. 'I'm not the one with the sick fantasy,' Rick said, a charge of indignation giving him fresh courage. 'Just know that if you hurt her again, you'll have me to answer to.'

'Will I? *Really?* I think you've got your wires crossed, mate, and it's making you say things I find extremely offensive.' Abruptly, Drew pulled open a desk drawer and for a horrible moment Rick thought he was going to pull out a weapon. But no, it was a photograph, which he passed across the desk. Rick could feel the animal heat of him as their hands met.

'Tell me what you see,' Drew instructed.

Rick examined the picture. It was of the Stanleys, seated at an outdoor café table somewhere by the sea. Marina looked happy, blissfully, dreamily so.

'Well?' Drew said.

'It's you and Marina. On holiday, maybe.'

'Right first time. And does she look like a battered wife to you?'

She did not, though it might have been taken in happier times, Rick reasoned, searching for details that might date the image. It was Marina's old hairstyle, before she'd had the bob, and the dress she was wearing was not one he'd ever seen, black and lacy, with a plunging neckline, her fish pendant sitting on the smooth skin of her sternum. But wait, that pendant . . . Hadn't she said she'd bought it on her holiday in Nice? In April, she'd said. Had this photo been taken on that trip?

Doubts swarmed his mind. Was it possible that Marina had been happy with her husband only a few months ago? If so, the Stanleys' marriage was clearly not the crude 'Beauty and the Beast' story he'd allowed himself to believe, but had complex emotions, nuance. But there was no nuance to those bruises, he reminded himself, and felt fury rip through him once more.

'This is just one picture,' he said, placing it on the desk. He heard the petulance in his own voice.

'You're right, it is. One of many. And I have no intention of showing some lying random arsehole the rest.' With this, Drew sprang from the desk, paced towards the door and flung it open. 'Now get the fuck out of my office and don't come back.'

16

Rick

July 1995

Later, he had no memory of the journey back to Central London – nor of much of the rest of the working day – only of the words in his head, chanted over and over: *What have I done?*

Also, *How am I going to tell Marina?*

For he could no longer deny the pattern of behaviour here: three times he'd flounced off on an ill-advised expedition to South London, three times he'd agonized over whether to report it to her. This time, though, he'd not only shown himself to the enemy but also opened fire, and only a fool could believe Drew wouldn't raise it with his wife, even blame her for it.

If Rick carried on like this, she'd need a new lover in whom to confide the trouble *he* was causing her.

Wracked with confusion, he rang Rollo at work.

'Rollo's no longer with us.' The voice was a stranger's, not one of the work gang Rick had met at the flat.

'What d'you mean?' he said. 'When did he leave?'

'The week before last. Who's calling?'

'It doesn't matter. I'll ring him at home.'

It took several tries before Rollo picked up. 'Yup?'

'Why didn't you say you'd left your job?' Rick said, and heard his friend sigh heavily. 'What happened, Rollo?'

'Nothing spectacular. Just a load of warnings about lateness. Anyway, it's my problem, nothing to worry about. You've got enough on your plate.'

This was true, even if Rick's mind did venture temporarily to the minor matter of rent and bills. 'You're looking for something else, though?'

'Give me a chance, Rickster. I thought I'd have a couple of weeks catching up on kip first.' Rollo fell silent, as if embarking on this aim there and then.

'I've just done something stupid,' Rick blurted, and, with a quick check that none of his colleagues was earwigging, summarized his confrontation with Drew. 'What d'you think I should do?'

Rollo groaned. 'Don't take this the wrong way, but have you considered dumping her? This is all getting a bit intense.'

'I'm not going to dump her.' Rick glanced around again, aware that his emotions were in danger of exploding, and noted Si and Jake safely on their phones. 'I *love* her.'

There was another pause during which he pictured Rollo's nauseated expression. At least he didn't go so far as to make any gagging sounds. 'The words glutton and punishment spring to mind, my friend. Fine, then I would just keep shtum for now. Chances are, even if he does tell her about it, she won't say anything to you – I mean, given your tendency to *escalate*. In which case, result.'

Rick considered this. 'Yeah, I reckon you're right.'

'You're not going to do that, though, are you?' Rollo guffawed. 'Why do you ask for advice, when you never take it?'

Another question Rick didn't know how to answer. Easier just to say goodbye and leave his flatmate to his newly acquired life of leisure.

*

To be fair, he did *try* to do as instructed. When he and Marina next met – Tuesday lunchtime, St James's Park, the beginnings of what was being touted as a once-in-a-generation heatwave – he waited, tense and skittish, for her to bring up the matter of his latest transgression. She was subdued, but in a way that was content rather than sullen, quick to lie on her back on the grass with her eyes closed.

Don't say anything. Like Rollo said, keep shtum.

'Marina? Did Drew tell you what happened yesterday?'

Eyes snapping open, she propped herself up on her elbow. 'No, what?'

'You mean he was completely normal last night?'

'I think so, yes.'

Was this good or bad news? Typical of Drew or not? Rick's immediate thought was that he must be banking the incident to use at a later date, one that served him better.

From the lake, the sudden squawk of a goose was followed by a spray of laughter – both sounded otherworldly to him.

Marina, now upright, pushed her sunglasses into her hair and fixed him with her green gaze. 'What have you done now?'

Just as Rollo had predicted, he confessed. There was no disguising the momentousness of it and, if anything, it sounded worse in the telling than it had felt in the doing.

'Oh, God,' Marina said, in a horrible desolate tone. On her lap, her hands clutched and squeezed.

'I didn't accuse him directly,' he said feebly.

'It sounds as if you did. You shouldn't have done that, Rick. I mean, after everything I've said. You *really* think this is how people help victims? By going to the abuser's place of work and telling them they probably shouldn't do it anymore or else everyone'll be really, really cross?'

It chilled him, her use of the term 'abuser', the first time she'd overtly applied the word to her husband. 'I know,' he said. 'But someone needs to stand up to him, on your behalf. Okay, I admit it backfired, but—'

'You bet it backfired! Let me guess: he made you feel like *you* were the one in the wrong? He probably got you thinking *you* gave me those bruises. This is what he does, Rick. He convinces people, he makes them think he's the big man.' There was a raw honesty to her response that Rick hadn't seen before. He could tell she was genuinely worried on *his* behalf and this reversal of their established roles gave him an illicit flare of pleasure.

'No, he didn't convince me and it's obvious to me he's a very small man. Bullies always are.'

She shook her head. 'You're out of your depth. Trust me, you've made this so much worse for yourself.'

'How? I didn't give my name. I said I was called Timothy Foster.'

'Well, *that* sounds made up.'

'Only because you know it is.' He didn't add that Drew Stanley had dismissed it as fictitious at the first utterance.

'The point is, he saw your face, he heard your voice. He knows you know me. All he has to do is have me followed and he knows where you live. Then he can get your real name from the electoral roll or whatever. Easier than that,' she exclaimed, more fearful. 'He can get just someone to buzz him in and look at the names on the mail downstairs.'

Rick felt self-loathing creep through his body as he understood the full implications of his latest idiocy. Might Drew really have Marina followed? And, since he already knew Rick as a 'colleague', mightn't he identify him without even having to tail them up to Camden? 'He said you had a creepy admirer at work. Did he mean me? What have you said about me?'

'I haven't said anything! I've been doing everything in my power to keep you a secret from him – whereas you've been hellbent on making yourself known. This can't go on,' she said, with a terrible finality. 'It's just getting too complicated now. You know what?' With this question, her voice grew more certain, as if she were at last resolving a longstanding dilemma. 'You should walk away from this, from me. Do it, Rick. Do it today. I'm serious.'

Rick felt a clutch of panic. Coming so soon after Rollo's

advice to do the same, it felt like an attack on his loyalty, his character, and to his shame he felt his eyes swim with tears. He responded by straightening his spine and injecting new resolution into his voice. 'No. Absolutely not. I'm not someone who just walks away, I'm not a coward.'

'They're not always the same thing,' Marina said.

'I said no.' As she gazed at him with dismay, he sensed the discussion was going to end with the familiar shared dejection. 'I'm still saving cash,' he said, brightly. 'I want you to know that. Whatever we do, we'll need money.'

To his surprise, she leaned forward to kiss him, a long, hard kiss, a welcome reprieve. When she broke off, she said, 'Give me a bit of time to think about this, okay? Let's skip this week and I'll see you next Thursday, after work.'

Next Thursday? That was nine days away, an eternity! But he was in no position to object.

'Whatever you think is right,' he said.

*

For those nine days Rick was like a man on probation – or the road to hell, one of the two. Other than in meetings in which he was required to contribute, he worked in near silence, unapproachable to his colleagues. 'What's up with him?' they murmured to one another, before remembering their own adage, 'Nothing personal, mate'. Maybe he just didn't get on with the heat that had finally invaded the city. Scorcher after scorcher, as the tabloids put it, everywhere you looked there were sweaty faces and stains at armpits, tourists in flip-flops, their toenails grimy, growling bus engines and black, grainy exhaust fumes that had him reaching for his inhaler.

It was a period of too much R&R on the Camden roof. He'd get home from work and the newly unemployed Rollo would already have cracked open the lagers, sometimes having been boozing all afternoon. They soon had enough empties to construct a low wall inside their railing and Rollo countered complaints of falling cans from their downstairs neighbours – Matt and Julie, a couple in their late twenties – by summoning them to the party. Six hours later, they were still there.

Saturday, Rick slept, only to spend Sunday in a ten-pint challenge with three of Rollo's mates that resulted in a toilet bowl streaked with vomit and the rare pulling of a Monday sickie. Tuesday brought a trip to the GP, who prescribed antibiotics for something sexually transmitted – he could blame *that* on Drew Stanley, too. Complicated, Marina had said, and it was hard not to notice that it was also getting a bit sordid.

Then, on the Thursday, as promised, she got back in touch, waiting for him in the lobby after work. 'Let's go to yours,' she said.

'You don't need to go home for the burglar alarm?'

'Don't worry, I've sorted it. Let's walk up to Camden.'

'Walk? It's miles – and way too hot.'

'I don't care, I just want to move my body, to get from A to B, you know? Look, I'm sorry I reacted the way I did,' she added, as they set off. 'I know you meant well. It was brave of you to take him on.' She sent him a sheepish look. 'To be honest, I can't believe you haven't gone off me.'

That made him smile. 'There's actually something I need to tell you, Marina. It might be you who goes off me.' Then, seeing her fearful expression, 'No, nothing to do with Drew.'

'What then?'

As they crossed traffic, he pulled her safe from a suddenly accelerating messenger bike. On this side of the road, there was the overpowering stink of drains. 'It's about Vicky. I haven't been completely honest about what happened with her. She wasn't the bunny boiler I've let you and Rollo and everyone think. It was ... It was kind of the other way around.'

Marina sent him a dubious sideways look. 'You're saying *you* were the bunny boiler?'

'Not exactly, but she thought I was a bit intense.' Rick's face grew hot. Ten minutes into their ninety-minute walk and sweat was already drenching his shirt. 'Our neighbours even called the police one time.'

'Rollo said that, I remember. What happened?'

'We were arguing – I mean really shouting. She wanted to end things between us and I, well, I didn't want that. I didn't ever hurt her, though. I'm nothing like Drew, I swear.'

'Of course you're not.' Marina linked her arm through his, oblivious to the tuts of a woman walking towards them who was forced to divert. 'Don't worry about it.'

'Really?'

'Yeah. Relationships are hard. It's her loss, totally.'

After that, they spoke little. The route took them past Buckingham Palace and through Green Park, a fiesta of deckchairs and picknickers, then up through Mayfair and

Marylebone and into Regent's Park, where the ground was parched and cracked, a dirt mosaic. They arrived at the flat with burnt skin and stinging lips. Marina's feet were swollen, she'd walked the whole way in work heels, and he rubbed them for her on the sofa, drawing rare irritation from Rollo, who came into the room and snapped, 'Could you two stop pawing each other for one fucking minute.'

Sensitive as they were, the criticism felt harsh, dismantling – Rick could see the hurt in Marina's face and feel it in his own. But he knew Rollo was stressed about being out of work. A party for his birthday was planned for the weekend and their rent was due on the first of the month, neither of which obligation he was in any position to meet.

'Sorry,' Rollo said. 'It's just some of us aren't quite so loved-up, yeah?'

Rick didn't point out that it was his own preference to keep relations with Flavia or any other woman on so strictly casual a basis. He only had to snap his fingers and he could have what Rick did – minus the anguish.

'Fancy going to the pub?' Rollo said, in one of his signature gear changes (he was not one to hold a grudge). 'It *is* my birthday today.'

'I thought that was Saturday?' Rick said.

'The party, yeah, but the day itself is right here, right now.'

'Well, in that case, we're going out. Okay, Marina?'

'Sure,' she said, with just the subtlest note of self-sacrifice, and slipped her feet back into her shoes. 'Sorry I haven't got you a card, Rollo.'

'Oh, I'll forgive you,' Rollo said in a sarcastic drawl, and

Rick, looking from girlfriend to flatmate, got the distinct impression of mutual dislike.

When did *that* happen?

He sighed and fetched his wallet. Neither of them would have a penny to put towards the bar bill, that much he knew for a fact.

17

Alex

August, present

He had to hand it to Beth, the party was pretty decent, and not least because they happened to get one of those lustrous cobalt-skied evenings that made you think you were in Happy Valley in the 1920s – or maybe Central London in the summer of 1995. Catered by the posh deli on the parade, it involved delicious things stuffed in mini cones and wrapped in chicory, all washed down with English wine.

'It's my new thing,' Beth told Dulcie and Jon, the first to arrive. 'Everything English. Positive patriotism.'

'I feel exactly the same,' Dulcie agreed and Alex hoped for her sake the cotton palm-print dress she wore hadn't been run up in a sweatshop in Bangladesh. (He had a feeling his own shirt had.) 'Flowers, as well. And cheese. Let's get Cool Britannia going again.'

'If you can do that, I really will be impressed,' he said,

sipping his flute of native fizz with restraint. Booze was one of his reasons for not having wanted this party in the first place: if he drank enough to relax, he risked saying something he shouldn't, but if he didn't drink enough, he risked saying nothing at all – and what kind of a weasel birthday boy was *that*?

He tried not to startle as he felt a grip on his shoulder from behind – Samira's husband Philip – and a boxed bottle of champagne was thrust at him.

'Well, Alex, your half-century. Quite a feat.'

'Not really a *feat*,' Alex said. 'Millions manage it every day. Like childbirth.'

'Only a man could compare turning fifty with going through labour,' Zara said, treating him to her letterbox smile. 'I *never* want to be fifty,' she added, with a theatrical shudder.

'I think you'll find it's better than the only alternative,' Alex said.

'Have you had any close calls, Alex?' Dulcie asked.

'What d'you mean?'

'Near-death experiences? I had one in Rome once. This bus came up on the kerb and missed me by a millimetre. The driver didn't even care, either, he'd have been happy to mow me down.'

'I've had two,' Zara said.

Third time lucky, Alex thought, as the episodes were regaled, beginning with a lump of concrete smashing through an office window and missing her by inches. He let his mind wander. *A half-century*: the same phrase had been used in every one of his birthday cards, and yet, with Eddie absent (he and Suki had cited a whooping cough outbreak in Stoke Newington, as if this were the nineteenth century), there wasn't a single person here from the first three decades of his life.

Which was just how he liked it.

As more guests arrived, armfuls of Prosecco and flowers hot-housed in South America or wherever because they didn't know about Beth's new English-only edict, talk turned, inevitably, to the progress on the trail site.

'When will it open to the public?' asked Beth's university friend Charlotte, one of the few non-locals in attendance.

'They're still on schedule for mid-September,' Samira said.

'You're lucky the archaeologists didn't get involved and slow the whole thing down. We had a section of our local woods cordoned off with zero warning. Turns out it was once a major coppicing site.'

Alex thought of the student with the pager, her face seamlessly morphing into that of some CID technician as she took the thing apart and identified its last received messages.

'God, what a nightmare,' Dulcie said. 'We've had nothing like that, it's just an old railway line, so it's all quite straightforward.'

'As you'd expect railway lines to be,' Beth said. She was on tremendous form. Local teens had been hired to serve the drinks so she could concentrate on getting hammered – disregarding Zara's abstemious influence for once. Personally, Alex would have liked to see their non-paying guest lend a hand, but instead she stood next to Beth, glass of sparkling elderflower in her fist, every inch the expectant woman – expectant of service. The bump, perfectly, symmetrically rounded, had never looked more fake. At any moment, someone else would notice, surely?

'Apparently there are ring-necked parakeets in there,' Philip said.

'So we'll all be twitchers,' Zara said. 'I'll have to dig out my binoculars.'

Was it his imagination or did she glance his way when she said this? He didn't care for the way she spoke as if she'd still be here when the trail opened. A serious talk with Beth was long overdue.

As friends and neighbours blathered on about woodpeckers and stag beetles, he became aware of a mounting sense of something new and terrifying in his response to talk of the trail. If the latter stages of the build *did* result in terrible discoveries at the back of the Stanleys' old house, and if he *didn't* get wind and disappear in time, then at least it would be over. His part in it all would be revealed and he'd be punished, but he'd be able to live the rest of his days with nothing to hide.

Because prison time, horrific though it must be, at least came with a release date. All the criminals of the mid-Nineties – O. J., those peculiar brothers in California who wiped out their parents, the nanny who shook the baby to death – were historical figures now, citizens of the foreign country that was the past.

(Actually, maybe the brothers were still in jail.)

As he tuned back in, with a slight fogging at the periphery

of his vision, he found that Beth was being quizzed on her birthday gift to him.

'Oh, it hasn't arrived yet,' she said. 'It's a big surprise.'

'Give us a clue,' Charlotte insisted.

'I *demand* to know now!' Samira cried.

How childish grown women got after a few drinks.

Beth made a 'calm down' gesture with her hand. 'It's not a *thing* as such, it's more like the results of something. They won't come for a few weeks yet.'

'So not a pregnancy test then,' Dulcie said.

'No, that would be a bit more immediate,' Samira said, with a chuckle.

'I'm a bit old for that now, anyway,' Beth said.

'I don't see why. Who's that actress who's just had a kid at forty-eight? No, wait, is that only if you've already had them? You can't have a first one at that age.'

'What if you're perimenopausal?'

'What about surrogacy? Or are your eggs, like, lower grade by then?'

As a free-for-all regarding geriatric fertility ensued, Alex registered how upsetting this must be for his wife and was about to shut it down when Zara said, 'I'm sure you'll be really close to *this* little one, Beth. Like a second mother. We can share,' and Beth was hugging her and everyone was saying, 'Aw, that's so sweet!'

Everyone except him. 'I guess that depends where you'll be living,' he said.

'Alex!' Beth protested.

'What? I'm just saying, property around here doesn't come

up very often, we all know that. Or she might decide to move out of town altogether.'

'Who's "she", the cat's mother? You're making it sound like I'm a right freeloader,' Zara said with a giggle, which was rich since she *was* a freeloader – and at his own insistence. When, a few weeks ago, Beth had suggested she start paying rent, he'd said no, because guests didn't pay. If she paid, it would formalize the arrangement, she'd have a tenant's rights.

'You know he doesn't mean it,' Beth told Zara, and the subject moved on to Frankie and her husband Tim, who had just left her and their three sons for a twenty-eight-year-old gold-digger in Client Services. As the scandalized women rallied afresh, Alex asked Philip if he happened to know the score in the cricket.

*

It was, in the end, a middle-aged affair, and by one o'clock they were all gone. Zara having retired to bed, Alex joined Beth in the kitchen, where she was scraping the collapsed remains of a birthday cake into the bin. Both dishwasher and washing machine whirred, low and soothing.

He kissed her on the mouth. 'Thank you,' he said.

'I told you it would be fun,' she said.

'You did and it was.'

Beth edged away, poured herself a glass of water from the tap. 'What you said to Zara,' she began.

'Oh, I think she can stand up for herself,' Alex said.

'It's just, you know she has her antenatal appointments at St Helier hospital?'

'Does she?'

'Well, it makes sense for her to have the birth there too.'

'Entirely up to her,' he said.

'Alex,' Beth said, a touch warily. 'I'd really like to resolve this bad feeling that seems to have sprung up between you.'

He drew breath. He'd have preferred not to get into this now, not after such a successful party – not to mention the rare skinful he'd had – but since she'd brought it up, he supposed he ought to roll up his sleeves and fight his corner. 'I'll tell you what we can resolve. That bump of hers, have you seen it properly? Is it even real?'

Beth stared at him, taken aback. 'What else could it be?'

'A prosthetic. I've seen them on TV. Women use them to trick men into paying child maintenance – or in her case to get this constructive dismissal claim through. Oh, and to manipulate her friend into letting her intrude on her marriage for months on end.'

'You're joking, right?' Beth said, with an astonished smile.

'I'm totally serious. All this talk of hospital appointments, I bet she's not even registered. I bet it's all made up.'

'Made up?' Beth's smile faded. 'Do you even hear how this sounds?'

'It sounds completely plausible. Fraudsters are everywhere now, you can't move for them. Think about it, Beth, right from the start she's known your weak spot and played on it.'

Beth flinched. 'My *weak spot*?'

'Yes. There's no way you'd be this accommodating, this generous, if she wasn't claiming to do exactly what you wish you were doing yourself.'

A heartbroken flicker crossed Beth's eyes, before she hardened her glare. 'To answer your question, the pregnancy *is* real, she's not "claiming" anything. Quite apart from the fact that I *have* seen the bump, yes, I hardly think an employment tribunal could take place without her being asked to submit proper medical documentation.' She gave an exasperated sigh. 'You know, it's very unattractive to harass a pregnant woman like this.'

'Harass?' Alex let out a yelp of bitter laughter. 'I think I've been more than patient about this. If you can't understand that *she's* the aggressor . . .'

'Alex, this is deranged!'

He reached for Olive's lead, hooked on the back of the door. 'A happy birthday to you too,' he said, and, deaf to any further entreaties, clipped the dog's lead on and left.

They circled the block clockwise, down Pleasance Road and right onto Surrey Road, then right again onto Exmoor Gardens. In spite of the row, he felt the night streets suppressing his anxiety as they always did, with their splashes of light from the streetlamps and silhouettes of foxes slinking from gate to gate. Only at this silent hour could he be seduced into believing that the calm he experienced belonged *after* the storm and not before it.

He circled a second time; Olive couldn't believe her luck.

Back home, Beth had gone up and turned off the lights. Sending the dog up to join her, he shut himself in the living room in the dark and had a quick look at the cricket scores on his phone, before remembering the murderous brothers in LA. *Menendez, that was their name!* Lyle and Erik.

Wikipedia confirmed that they were indeed still in prison, having been convicted in 1996. Poor buggers.

He knew he should put the phone down and go up to bed, but was aware of a craving for something dangerous, something reckless, and, in an act akin to uncapping the vodka after a period of hard-fought sobriety, he now keyed in a name he had not searched for in a very long time:

Rollo Farnworth.

18

Rick

August 1995

'Surprise!'

No effort had been made to mute either music or chatter as Rick put his key in the lock and stepped into the flat, but that didn't stop Rollo shushing those assembled with the flourish of a conductor at the Royal Philharmonic when he finally noticed the birthday boy hovering, open-mouthed, in the doorway. As the stereo blared Rick's favourite Oasis track, 'Columbia', everyone dropped like boa constrictors behind the nearest piece of furniture, before rising up again and screaming 'Happy birthday!'

Bobbing on the carpet and being idly batted about were children's birthday balloons stamped with '2's and '6's.

'Oh, wow!' Maybe it was the emotional escalation of recent weeks, but Rick felt the overwhelming urge to sob. 'I thought you were broke?' he said to Rollo.

Rollo pulled a face. 'It's only a bit of booze and a few grams of charlie. The usual.'

The usual crowd, too, which was to say Rollo's crowd, mostly, but he'd made the effort to ring Rick's office and invite Si and Jake, and Matt and Julie from downstairs were also here. Julie worked from home and she and Rollo had been hanging out recently, drinking coffee and developing an addiction to daytime soaps, apparently (best not to ask). Flavia had not been seen at the flat for some time.

'You two dress like that on purpose?' Julie asked Rick. By coincidence, he and Rollo were in exactly the same shade of blue, his a work shirt and Rollo's a Fred Perry polo shirt. 'Wait, are you actually brothers?' Her eyes, ringed with black liner, were disconcertingly large, like billiard balls. Rick almost expected to see a '2' and '6' in them, too.

'Only brothers in arms,' he said, nicely swaddled by the heat of his first shot of vodka. He surveyed the crush beyond: boys with mop-top haircuts and hot Friday-night faces, girls with silver clips in their hair, spaghetti straps on bare shoulders; freckles and sunburn and the occasional insect bite. All of this for him. *I have everything I need,* he thought. *Job, social life, girlfriend.*

Ah, there it was. The defect no brain scanner would miss, the doubt that would never stop niggling. More than doubt, fear – that his relationship with Marina was doomed. That he might lose her. That she'd never been his to lose in the first place.

Whether or not she was right about Drew Stanley tracking him down and learning his true identity, Rick had discovered all too quickly the effects of his shortsightedness in confronting the man. Since the night of Rollo's birthday, Marina had been kept on the shortest of leashes, unable to see Rick at all outside of her lunch hour.

'Is Marina coming?' he asked Rollo, though they'd never met on a Friday night. That had always been Drew's night, back from Manchester, expecting her home.

'I'd say that was your department, mate.' Rollo gave a Sid James cackle, echoed by the already rat-arsed Matt.

'Did you ask her, though?'

''Course I did. But you know what she's like, last to arrive, first to leave. I mean, is that *really* what we want from our women?'

Rick sighed, lowered his voice. 'Come on, you know why she has to sneak around.'

There was a silent moment of shared knowledge and, overcome with gratitude for the simple dependability of their friendship, Rick clutched his flatmate in an embrace. 'Thanks for organizing this, mate. Shame Eddie's not here, isn't it?'

'Our matchmaker, you mean?' Rollo mocked. 'I don't think he's ever coming back. Do yourself a favour and get a flight out there and see him – might take your mind off affairs of the heart, you know what I mean?'

But plans to visit New York belonged to a different era. Rick simply could not visualize himself checking in at the airport and flying across the Atlantic, not as long as Marina was his primary concern. Standing there, at the first surprise party anyone had ever thrown for him, he had the sudden gut-twisting realization that his life might have continued really quite happily, painlessly, had he never met her.

The feeling passed as quickly as it had arrived.

*

She arrived after ten dressed in a short silver slip dress, a glittery mesh bolero camouflaging any residual bruising on her arm. On her feet were pink sandals with huge plastic daisies on the toe bar. She'd curled her hair and done her make-up in a Fifties style, a waiflike Marilyn.

On the stereo, Björk wailed.

'How did you get away on a Friday?' he asked.

'Don't worry about that. I'm here now, aren't I? Happy birthday, darling.' She presented him with a bunch of sunflowers.

'Did you know sunflower buds turn east to be ready for the first drop of sunrise?' Rollo said, threading towards them with a plastic cup of wine for her.

'How poetic,' she said.

'Heliotropism, it's called. Bit of a big word for you, Marina. I know you went to the university of life.'

'Rollo,' Rick objected, but Rollo held none of the terrors of men like her husband and she fixed the joker with a frigid gaze.

'Whereas you're more of a vampire, aren't you? At the first drop of sun, you put a pillow over your head. If only someone would hold it there.' There was the faintest pause before she laughed, pleased with her retort.

'Don't you two fall out,' Rick said and he remembered

that sense he'd had the last time they'd been together, that they'd somehow developed a mutual antipathy. 'Things are fucked-up enough around here.'

'We're not going to fall out,' Rollo said. 'Are we, Marina?'

The way he said her name, with a touch of warning, made Rick think they'd been talking privately. When he'd phoned her about the party, Rollo must have emphasized that tonight was Rick's night and there was to be no drama, no angst.

Marina ignored him. 'Come on,' she told Rick. 'Time to dance.'

*

Later, Rick climbed onto the roof for a blast of fresh air. All day, the sky had been an eerie hypnotic white, but this evening it had cleared, taking the humidity with it. He longed, for a second, to lie on the cool tarmac and close his eyes.

'Can I ponce a ciggie?' Si asked, joining him.

''Course.'

'Great party.'

'It really is.'

'Smile, boys!' someone called out, on cue, from the window, and they pulled daft faces for the disposable camera flashing their way.

Inside, 'Spooky' by Dusty Springfield was playing, one of Marina's favourites, and Rich and Si watched as she used the long, curved stand of a lamp as a pole to dance, swinging and spinning, her hair thrown back, throat stretched tight. Spotting Rick, she began snaking in and out of the open window, possibly the most erotic thing Rick had ever seen – and Si too, judging by the size of his eyes. In the room beyond, whooping started up and even Rollo paused his conversation to watch.

'Who is she?' Si asked Rick, when she'd shimmied back in and disappeared from view.

'Marina. You don't recognize her? She works in our building.'

'She's spectacular. Going out with anyone, is she?'

Rick burst out laughing. 'Yes, me!'

'*You?*'

He'd kept his secret all this time, but it was worth letting it go to see the look of unadulterated envy on Si's face.

'Well, well, well. You're a lucky man, Rick. A lucky man.'

And even as it was happening, he had a sense that this was a defining moment in his life, one that he would always remember. Albert Street, Camden Town, August 1995, the lights of this particular patch of the earth's surface burning bright as, briefly, intoxicatingly, jeopardy was paused and hedonism reigned.

*

She stayed the night, promising, for once, not to run off early. Evidently, she'd spun Drew some yarn about a workmate needing someone to stay after dental surgery, which meant they could laze in bed all morning or go out for brunch, whatever Rick liked. It was the best birthday treat he could have asked for: to wake up late and find her still there, sleeping quite angelically. You'd imagine the hunted would frown in their sleep, cry out at the nightmares, but evidently it was

161

the opposite. Maybe it was their only opportunity for peace.

The alarm clock said 9am. Needing to empty his bladder, he crept from the bedroom and used the loo. Rollo's door was closed and he heard a giggle from within – God knew who he'd taken to bed last night; Flavia had been absent, Julie back in her flat with Matt, but attractive girls had circled Rollo till late, as they always did.

He'd bring Marina a cup of tea in bed, he decided. Downstairs, he was grateful not to find any guests passed out on the sofa or floor, which had been known to happen, not that it wasn't carnage, of course, a disaster zone of smears and spillages, of cans, bottles, cigarette ends, bits of burst balloon rubber. Others, still inflated, hovered on the carpet. It was going to take half the day to clean up, but it was worth it. He was pretty sure it was the best birthday he'd ever had.

In the kitchen, he turned on the kettle and rinsed the residue of alcohol from two mugs. Every last vessel, including the jug he'd put Marina's sunflowers in, had been used last night for drinking. He located the flowers and reinstated them. His head boomed like a struck gong and he searched in vain for paracetamol. He didn't do drugs often, well, at least not as often as Rollo did, and he hoped he hadn't said anything he was going to regret.

He made the tea, thinking a cigarette would be nice. There were empty packs on every surface, but he had to get on his hands and knees for a sweep of the floor before he found a discarded pack of Marlboro Lights with two still in it. No sign of matches or a lighter, so when he went back up to the bedroom with Marina's tea, he grabbed her handbag and brought it down to the sofa. Rummaging for her Zippo, he was intrigued by the mix of expensive and cheap items, the expensive ones no doubt gifts of remorse from Drew – a bottle of Gucci perfume, his favourite, she'd said, and Rick had come to find it heavy and cloying – and the cheap, the Boots lipsticks and eyeliners, bought for herself.

He located the Zippo and lit the fag, enjoying the brief obliteration of head pain. He wondered what his landlord would say if he saw the flat right now. There was not a wall in the place that was not marked or discoloured, not a soft furnishing that didn't reek. When he moved out, he'd have to get a professional clean done, maybe even a paint job, or he'd never get his deposit back.

The thought snagged: *when*, not *if*. Why was he having thoughts of leaving?

He knew exactly why. Marina might ask him to. She didn't want his help now, but she would. Her presence at the party, that dangerous lie she'd told Drew, it proved her commitment. He'd felt it when they'd had sex, too, a new sense of need, of faith.

He closed his eyes and saw thousands of tiny white stars, watched them sink and fade as he reopened them again. There was a sizzle between his fingers as a tuft of tobacco caught light. His gaze fell on the gaping bag on the sofa next to him, the zipped inner pocket that bulged a little. Without hesitating, he tugged the zip open, expecting to find tampons or perhaps the contraceptive pills he'd seen once or twice – she kept them on her person, she said, because Drew thought they were trying for a baby (that was a *whole* other concern) – but what he actually found was a small brown packet, the flap tucked in but not sealed.

He slid it out and opened the flap. Inside, there was a newish-looking passport. Wow, he thought, she even carried her passport with her – who did that? Stupid question. A woman who hid her contraceptive pills from her husband, that was who. A woman who lived with secrets, who might need to abscond at a moment's notice.

Idly, spilling ash, he opened it to the photo page and studied the image. She was make-up-free, her lips slightly parted and eyes surprised, and the effect was curiously intimate, almost intrusive, as if she'd been caught off guard by a paparazzo. Perhaps she didn't like having her photo taken, he thought. Certainly she'd never let *him* take one of her; it was too much of a risk, she said. (He dismissed the undesirable memory of that holiday snap Drew had forced him to examine.)

Then, taking in the details printed alongside the photo, he exclaimed in surprise. *What on earth . . . ?*

The name in the passport wasn't hers.

19

Rick

August 1995

Frowning so deeply he felt his eyebrows meet, Rick studied the print: *Kirsten McKenzie*. He was fairly sure he'd never heard the name before – who was she? But before his hangover-addled brain could register anything beyond basic confusion, a cold tone rang out behind him:

'What are you doing with that?'

He spun, startled. Marina was standing in the doorway, barefoot, dressed in one of his shirts, its tails pointing down her pale thighs. Last night's curls had drooped and she looked boyish, more street urchin than sex bomb. The mug she held tipped slightly and a drip of tea ran down the side and dropped to the carpet.

'Why've you got my bag down here?'

'I was looking for your lighter,' he said, aware of how guilty he sounded. 'I didn't want to wake you by scrabbling around in the dark. Come and sit down.'

This she did, her gaze not leaving the passport in his hand. Her breathing was audible as she tucked her legs under her and watched as he slipped it back into its envelope and handed it to her.

'I unzipped that side pocket. I'm sorry, I shouldn't have.'

'No, you shouldn't.' Her voice was wintry, unyielding.

'Whose is it, Marina? Why's it got your photo in it?'

She hesitated, looked towards the window and then reluctantly back at the package in her hands, as if the fib she sought had fluttered out of reach, leaving her with only the truth. 'It's mine,' she said, finally.

'But it's not your name.'

'I know that. Obviously.' She spoke with a quiet fury, but whether this was directed at him or at herself he couldn't tell because she was looking at the passport and not him.

'Why isn't it?'

Only when she'd zipped it back into its compartment in her bag did she meet his eye properly. 'Why do you think, Rick? It's a fake. My real passport is locked away in Drew's desk drawer at home. It's been there ever since we came back from Nice.'

Rick's heart reared violently against his sternum. 'He's taken your passport? You never told me that. That's got to be illegal, keeping it against your will?'

'I'm sure it is.' She shrugged. 'But even if I could get it back, it wouldn't be any use to me, at least not at first.'

'I don't understand,' he said, though he suspected he was beginning to. Her gaze had grown baleful; there was a sense of withdrawal, a shutter coming down.

'I'm getting the fuck out of my marriage, aren't I? I'm

starting again. But I can hardly do that with my real name. He'd find me in five minutes.' She hugged her bag to her with a tender, almost maternal possession. 'Whoever this Kirsten woman is or was, we're about the same age and I'll be using her name and her date of birth. At least until I know I'm safe.'

Rick felt his thoughts spiralling. 'That's ... that's great news that you're leaving him. Really great. But why ...' *Why didn't you tell me?* But he couldn't put himself at the centre of this, not when he'd so recently vowed to step back. 'Don't forget the cash, will you? I've been adding to it and there's nearly a grand now.'

'Thank you.'

This was the first time she'd accepted his offer of financial help. Clearly matters had moved on quite significantly. Likely, thanks to Rick's own unhelpful interventions, Drew had tightened his grip on her finances, just as he had on her freedom outside of office hours.

She reached for her tea, less shaky now, and drank a mouthful. 'Plus, in the drawer where he keeps the passports, I think there's some money. I don't know how much, but I thought if I could break in, I'd take that too.'

'Right. Good idea.' Already Rick could feel his resolve weakening. 'So if I hadn't found the passport, when would you have told me all this?'

At the sound of the choke in his voice, her gaze softened. 'I'm not sure I would have. It's not really anything to do with you, Rick.'

'Nothing to do with me? We love each other, Marina! *Don't* we?'

His cry was interrupted by sudden pain: his cigarette had burned down to his fingers and singed the skin. At once Marina took his hand and kissed the wound. There was a message in that kiss, he thought, an apology.

'I'll see if there's any ice,' she said, and got to her feet. She reappeared with ice cubes wrapped in a tea towel and applied it to the burn. 'I didn't mean it like that. It *is* to do with you, of course it is. You've helped me so much, you've been amazing. But I can't draw anyone else into it. Any more mistakes and it's over.'

His mistakes, presumably. It occurred to him that Drew might have confronted her about their set-to after all; he'd hurt and threatened her again and that had led to her getting this passport. And yet it couldn't have been bought so quickly, could it? No, she must have cut Rick out earlier, after one of his previous errors of judgement. Avoiding her pitying gaze, he looked at the ashtray, nauseatingly overflowing from last night. 'How did you get the passport? I wouldn't know where to start.'

Another shrug. 'I know a guy.'

'Who?'

'From where I worked years ago, a club in Soho. Not all of the friends I've had in my life are law-abiding auditors, you know.'

If this was a dig, he ignored it. 'How did you pay for it? It must have cost thousands.'

She inhaled deeply, her chest rising. 'I sold one of Drew's watches. He never wears it.'

'You're sure he won't miss it?' Drew struck Rick as the kind of man who kept an inventory of his valuables.

'I had to take the risk. If I didn't, I'd never get out of there.'

How well she'd done on her own, strategizing like this, measuring risk, and yet, shameful though he knew it was, he couldn't help feeling obstructive. 'Even with the passport, it's not so easy to change your identity.'

'How do you know? Have you ever tried?'

'It's just common sense, Marina. For starters, that passport's probably been reported stolen and cancelled, so you'll need to be careful how you use it. And you'll need a national insurance number to go on the pay roll of a new employer. Same for a new GP, anything official.'

'I'll say I've lost it,' she said.

'How long is that going to work for?'

'Fine, I'll apply for a new one or I'll work cash in hand.' She lost her cool. 'Why are you saying these things, Rick? You're the one who's been telling me to leave! Are you saying I shouldn't now, that I've got no chance on my own?'

'No, of course not!'

'What, then?'

There was a simple explanation to his mixed messages, of course, one he couldn't bring himself to voice: he wanted her to leave Drew, but he didn't want her to leave *him*. She sighed, guessing. 'Look, now he knows who you are, it's safer for you not to know my plans.'

'But we have no reason to believe he *does* know who I am,' he protested. 'And even if he did, what's he going to do? Come into my office and put a bullet through my brain? He's not a gangster. Forget about *my* safety, that's not the issue.'

Upstairs, the loo flushed. Rollo or his bedmate had

surfaced; soon they'd be down to make tea or scavenge for breakfast. Rick lowered his voice, speaking urgently, impulsively: 'Move in here, Marina. Move in with us. Rollo won't mind.'

'What?' She looked at him with disbelief. 'People come and go here all the time, it's party central. When I leave, I need to be completely out of sight, disconnected from my old life. That's the whole reason I got the passport.'

She was right, it wasn't realistic. Rick couldn't even name half of the guests at his own birthday party. 'Then why don't we get advice from one of those women's refuges? Have you ever spoken to anyone like that?'

'No.'

'Then will you at least let me do it, on your behalf? Or I could find some sort of safe house? I could even come with you?'

As one proposal followed the next, she lapsed into silence and it took every ounce of his strength to back off. 'This is a great step, Marina. I'm proud of you. Whatever you choose, I support you.'

'So do I, darlin', so do I,' drawled a rough, hungover voice from the hall, and they turned to find Rollo in the doorway, half-naked, a pair of threadbare black pyjama bottoms hanging from his hipbones. 'You were the star of the show last night, you know. Can I book you for our next party?' He strolled in, picking up the nearest cigarette pack, shaking it, dropping it, looking for the next. 'Don't worry,' he said at the sight of their stricken faces. 'I didn't hear anything. What? What's wrong now?'

'Nothing,' Rick said. 'There's one left in here, take it.' He passed Rollo the last cigarette and lit it for him with the Zippo.

'Cheers.' Rollo strolled towards the kitchen, humming the melody of 'Spooky'.

Using the lighter had aggravated the burn and Rick returned his hand to the dripping tea towel, noticing for the first time the food stains from meals eaten days, maybe weeks, ago. Watching his flatmate toe balloons and empties aside as he waited for the kettle to boil, he realized Marina was right to refuse his offer. This squalid chaotic bachelor pad was no place to harbour a victim of domestic violence, even if they did manage to keep one step ahead of Drew.

Rollo reappeared in the doorway with two mugs. 'Room service,' he said and, when Rick asked the name of his conquest, gave a wicked laugh. 'I'll get back to you on that, yeah.'

When he was out of earshot, Rick turned back to Marina. 'Will you at least let me know when?'

'When what?' Her tone had changed, as it often did when they'd been discussing Drew and been interrupted. Rick knew that when they dressed and went out for brunch, she'd be back to how she always was when he wasn't ramming her marital problems down her throat. Even-tempered, self-effacing, kind. A flick of the 'act normal' switch by a seasoned dissembler.

'When you go. Will you let me know when it's really goodbye?'

'Yes,' she said, solemnly. 'If I have that luxury.'

20

Alex

August, present

Crammed so savagely against the bar that he was in danger
of cracking a rib, Alex sank pints with Eddie in the French
House while waiting for their table in the restaurant upstairs.
Whenever he drank in West End pubs now, particularly in old
haunts like Soho or Covent Garden, he had an overwhelming
sense of excommunication – or, to be precise, self-exile.

Eddie, meanwhile, appeared to be experiencing the opposite phenomenon. He gazed around the bar as if readmitted to
paradise following an extensive ban, the colours lusher than
he'd remembered, the scents more intoxicating. 'You know
we're dry now in my house?' he said, handling his pint like a
priceless piece of Ming.

'I assume that's Suki's doing?'

''Course. Wants me to lose the flab.'

'You look fine, mate.' And he did. Even as a student he'd

liked his threads and he was dressed tonight in £200 jeans and a cashmere polo shirt. Sure, his hair was silvering, but he still had most of it, which would have been enough for Alex. 'How are the brats?'

'Bratty. I have *literally* no anecdotes that don't involve sick and snot and fluids I don't even know the name of. Parenthood is exactly like everyone warned, *The Exorcist* on repeat. Sorry about missing your birthday, by the way. Hope you weren't too pissed off with us?'

'Not at all,' Alex said, meaning it. Since Eddie's return from New York, he'd operated a policy of compartmentalization and the party would have been the worst possible time to bring church and state together, what with the trail under constant discussion. All it would have taken was some passing reference to the historic murder investigation and Eddie might have been caught off guard.

'You still got Beth's mate staying?' Eddie asked.

'Yep. She's a nightmare. I honestly have no idea how to get rid of her.'

'Just give it to her straight, tell her to sling her hook. That's what I did with Suki's sister. She was supposed to be helping with the kids, but she was more like an extra kid herself.'

'Yeah, but she wasn't pregnant, abandoned by the father?'

'Er, no.'

'Well, that's what I'm dealing with. She's very manipulative, but I seem to be the only one who can see it.'

'Hmm,' Eddie chuckled. 'Evil pregnant homeless woman, I can see that would be a hard sell.'

Had Alex been in any doubt before that Zara had an

agenda beyond simply outstaying her welcome, he wasn't any longer – and that agenda involved the ousting of *him*. That morning, he'd been out walking Olive, having left his mobile at home, when Zara had taken a call on it from the estate agent who'd shown him the flat. Was Alex still in the market for the two-bedder in Camden Town? If so, could she let him know an asking-price offer had just been accepted.

She'd had a clear choice to pass on the message discreetly or not and had chosen not to. Instead, fully versed, Beth had confronted him the moment he got back. 'What's going on? Either you were going to surprise me with the news that we're moving into town or you're planning on a secret second home for yourself.'

He'd barely had the energy to argue. 'Don't be ridiculous, it's neither. It's the flat where I used to live, I wanted to check it out, that's all, out of curiosity. Zara should never have given you the message – can't you see she's stirring up shit?'

'Why would you waste an estate agent's time like that?' Beth demanded. 'It wouldn't occur to me to do that.'

He lost his patience then. 'Well, newsflash, Beth, not everyone is exactly like you! Who cares about some agent, they deal with time wasters every day of the week.'

Beth glared at him and, muttering that he could at least load the dishwasher while he still 'deigned to live here', took herself off to the living room. Olive scuttled between them, unsettled by the tension.

Zara, naturally, had made herself scarce. Her role was merely to plant the landmines.

Alex loaded the dishwasher, all the clichés of marital disharmony swirling in his head: he could do nothing right, there were three in this marriage, enough was enough, and so on. He kicked shut the dishwasher door and went to find his wife.

'I want to know when she's moving out. It's about time she gave us a date, don't you think?'

Beth frowned in disapproval. 'Shh, she'll hear you! Come in and close the door.'

He stayed where he was. '*When*, Beth?'

'We can't turn someone out who's about to have a baby,' she said, her voice a hiss. 'And please don't start that nonsense again about it being fake.'

Alex said nothing. Perhaps he *had* let his imagination run away with him on that score. Somehow, it was more problematic to know that the pregnancy was real.

'She has nowhere else to go, Alex.'

'Which in itself should be a red flag! Why's she fallen out with everyone? Even if the father's refusing to support her, why can't her family help her out? She's not an orphan.'

'*You* don't get on with *your* family,' Beth pointed out, reasonably. 'It's not that uncommon.'

'Maybe I *should* be flat-hunting,' he grumbled. 'Leave the two of you to it. She'd love that.'

The argument had concluded with his remarking that a visiting alien would think Beth and Zara were the couple and he the problem lodger and Beth calling him childish and resting her case.

'Mate?'

He came to, realizing that Eddie was looking at him, waiting for a response.

'Thought you'd gone into a trance there. C'mon, our table's ready.'

Upstairs, in the dimly lit restaurant, they could barely read the menu with their half-century-old eyesight, but it didn't matter because they knew they were ordering steak, contraband in both households, such were these pussy-whipped times.

At least the music was from their heyday, some kind of Nineties mix. All Saints' 'Never Ever' came on and Alex had a sudden overpowering image of Marina singing it in the Albert Street flat – *I'm not CRA-zy!* – but he knew he must be wrong because the song had come out a few years later, he remembered seeing the new girl band on *Top of the Pops* in his next flat in East London. By then, Marina was history of course. This was a first, his mind placing her in a memory where she didn't belong, as if her presence mattered more than chronology. More than truth.

Their steaks arrived. By now Eddie was so deep into his nostalgia trip as to be in a hypnotic state himself. The vibe, the freedom, the licentiousness that could never be recovered. 'None of this puritanical nonsense, it was easy come easy go back then.'

He spoke with his mouth full and the gloss of pink juice on his teeth made Alex feel sick.

'Can we change the subject? There's a hell of a lot about the Nineties I wouldn't relive if you paid me.'

Eddie looked briefly confused, before getting it. 'Oh yeah,

there was all that business, wasn't there? Sorry, I forgot. I missed all that in New York.'

All that business. For once, Alex couldn't bear speaking in euphemisms like this. 'It was completely horrific, Eddie,' he blurted. 'The police put the fear of God in me. I was shitting myself at the interview, and even when I signed the statement, I felt like they were suddenly going to turn around and read me my rights.'

Eddie nodded, respectful of the altered mood. 'Must've been terrifying.' Then, with rather more caution: 'He got life, didn't he?'

'Yes.'

They didn't utter his name as if by prior agreement.

'Life doesn't mean life, though, does it? Which prison was it?'

'Belmarsh, I think,' Alex said. 'At least it was early on.'

Eddie put down his cutlery. 'Let's Google him. See if he's out yet.' And in a trice he had his phone in his hand, the screen aglow with the toothless smiles of his kids.

'He is,' Alex said. 'He served over twenty years in the end.'

The release day had been in early 2016, heralding a brief, exhausting period during which a strung-out Alex had taken to scanning tube carriages and pubs as he entered, pausing on the threshold of crowded lobbies, even peering out of the front window at home before answering the doorbell.

Eddie put away the phone and picked up his knife and fork again. 'Twenty years is fucking *brutal*,' he said, with the arrogant relish of the lifelong innocent.

'I suppose,' Alex said. But then it *had* been pre-meditated. It *had* been, as the judge described it, 'wicked and repugnant'.

'Doesn't bear thinking about,' Eddie said. 'Maybe our domestic failures aren't so bad after all, huh?' He spoke – had spoken all evening – as if having relinquished all control over his own destiny. Perhaps that was the key to managing this current phase of heightened anxiety, Alex thought, to embrace the *qué será será*. To try to take a perverse pleasure in the uncertainty – after all, he might step out onto Surrey Road one morning and be flattened by a lorry.

Meanwhile, drink through it, as they used to say. Used to believe. He signalled to the waitress for another bottle of red.

21

Rick

August 1995

We have no reason to believe he does *know who I am ...*
Why in Christ's name had he allowed himself to utter those
words, to tempt fate so brazenly?

For it was only a few days after the party, as Rick came
home from work, that he became aware of a man watching
their flat from the driver's seat of a red Vauxhall Astra parked
directly across the street. He was an individual of immense
bulk, with butterball arms and a belly that strained the buttons of his beige shirt; all Rick could see of his head was a
greasy sweep of sandy hair.

Initially, he dismissed his fears as paranoia and said nothing to Rollo, but when the guy was there a third evening in a
row, he knew he had a duty to alert his flatmate. 'Have you
noticed that Astra across the road? There's a really mean-
looking bloke just sitting there, eyeballing our front door.

Every time he sees me, he gives me the evils, but he never gets off his arse to say anything.'

'I haven't looked,' Rollo said. Having come down with the flu after the party, he'd mostly remained in bed, sleeping. As the heatwave continued to liquefy their brains, the rattling of a desk fan could be heard from his room at all hours; Rick tried not to think about the electricity bill. 'Show me,' he added, and tailed Rick to the living-room window.

'Maybe I should just go back down and bite the bullet, put an end to the intimidation even if I do end up getting a smack in the teeth.' Rick pulled the curtain aside. 'Oh! He's gone. That's good, I suppose.'

'Who is he, d'you think?' Rollo pressed alongside him and Rick stepped discreetly back. The last thing he needed was to catch his flu.

'I'm pretty sure someone to do with Drew Stanley. He's found out who I am and he's looking to scare me off.' It was becoming necessary to remind himself frequently what he'd told Rollo and what he hadn't: the ill-advised confrontation in Drew's office, yes, but of Marina's passport and her nascent plot to leave, he'd promised not to breathe a word. 'Well, at least we know it's not twenty-four-hour surveillance. I was starting to think he was going to sit there literally until she turns up. He's a real heavyweight, looks like a bailiff or something.'

'But if he wants to scare you off, why doesn't he just grab you when you walk by?' Rollo said, his voice a little hoarse. He was more rattled by this development than Rick had anticipated.

'All I can think is maybe he doesn't want any witnesses. Maybe he's waiting for you to go out, then he'll barge in and attack me.' For all his bravado, Rick was terrified by the thought of being roughed up by such a man mountain. Tomorrow, if he was back again, he'd challenge him, tell him he was reporting him to the police, and, if it got nasty, run; fast-moving pedestrians could outpace motorists in the Camden rush hour. 'Rollo? What's wrong?'

'I can't breathe.'

Well, he *was* breathing, Rick could see and hear evidence of that, but in scarily rapid, shallow mouthfuls. His face was flushed, eyes intense and darting, like a spooked dog. 'Sit down, mate. Here, use my puffer, it'll open the airways . . .' He pressed down on the canister, talking Rollo through the process, then found a paper bag for him to breathe in and out of. Within moments, he had steadied and was brushing the episode off as insignificant.

'It's just this flu. It must have spread to my lungs.'

'That looked like a panic attack, Rollo. I'm really sorry, I didn't mean to scare you. Honestly, there'll be no case of mistaken identity. It's me Drew Stanley wants to warn off, he doesn't know you exist.'

Of this he was a hundred per cent certain, but that didn't mean Rollo couldn't get caught in the crossfire, and when Rick came home from work the next day, he found his flatmate nursing a badly bruised eye. There'd been a confrontation in the street with the fat bloke and they'd got into a scuffle, he admitted.

'It was like being punched by Frank fucking Bruno.'

'This is terrible!' As Rick examined the ugly swelling on Rollo's face – the white of the affected eye was entirely bloodshot and a demonic red – he was engulfed by guilt. 'He obviously got us mixed up, which explains why he was letting me go in and out. Did he admit he's been hired by Drew?'

'I didn't ask,' Rollo said. 'I just said "What the fuck do you want?", and he decked me.'

'I'm so sorry, Rollo. Do you need more ice?'

'That would be great. And I've finished the Nurofen.'

'I'll nip out and get some more.' Rick paused. 'You're not . . . you're not thinking of going to the police, are you?'

''Course not.' Rollo exhaled. 'But this can't go on, Rick. We don't want our legs broken, just because . . .'

Just because I've fallen in love with someone else's woman.

He tried to make amends by cooking Rollo dinner. Roast chicken, decent wine, even a pudding. By now, the damaged eye had closed completely, the skin bloated and angry like a monster insect bite.

'I don't blame you if you'd rather move out,' he said, serving up. 'You didn't sign up for this shit.'

Rollo shrugged. 'Where am I going to get the deposit for a new place? Speaking of which, there's no way I can go to job interviews looking like this.'

'You'll have to wait for it to heal,' Rick agreed. 'Don't worry about the rent, you can owe me it.' Given that his friend's shiner had been intended for him, it was the least he could do.

'Thanks,' Rollo said, scooping mashed potato into his

mouth. 'Unless ... you couldn't bung me a few quid, could you? Just five hundred, maybe a grand?'

'I don't think I can, sorry.' A grand? That was more than a few quid. And Rick needed every spare penny for Marina's escape fund. 'Forget about money,' he advised. 'Just concentrate on getting better.'

*

They both stayed in on the Saturday, Rick making regular trips to the window to check for the Astra. It was gone, the brute having evidently moved on, his warning satisfactorily delivered – except ... it *was* the weekend, wasn't it? Marina was at home and presumably Drew could keep a close eye on her personally.

But all assumptions were blown apart on Sunday morning, when the buzzer went mid-morning; not the normal short alert, but a sustained blare, a distress signal.

Both still in bed, they emerged onto the landing at the same time.

'What the fuck?' Rollo groaned. 'It's not even midday.'

Rick took the stairs, slipping slightly in his haste. 'He must have found out he got the wrong man and come back. Now it's my turn.'

Rollo followed him down more cautiously, his impeded vision causing him to rely on the banister. 'On a Sunday morning?'

'Well, I'm guessing he's not a churchgoer.' As Rick moved towards the intercom, Rollo sped up and put a hand out to stop him.

'Wait. Can't we just pretend we're not in?'

Looking at his eye, it was certainly tempting to avoid a manhandling of his own. 'We can't stay imprisoned another day, Roll. We've run out of food, I need to go to Sainsbury's and—' He stopped at the sudden silence from the intercom, sent a more hopeful look Rollo's way. But a second later it was back, only fainter. 'Fuck, he's trying Matt and Julie. D'you want to phone them and warn them not to buzz him in?'

But it was too late: the main door was opening and shutting. Then came the sound of feet pounding up the stairs.

Rollo seized his arm. 'Let's get out of here via the roof. We can climb down by the drainpipe, hide downstairs.'

'I'm not even dressed,' Rick protested.

'Just put some shoes on! Come on!'

At a violent smacking on the other side of the door, they sprang apart. Then, as if at the starter's gun, Rollo made a dash for the kitchen, while Rick dithered long enough to hear the cry of a familiar voice: 'Rick! Are you in? Please, please be in!'

'Marina?'

'Thank God. Open the door.'

As Rick drew the door towards him, Rollo slunk back into view and watched Marina throw herself into Rick's arms, dishevelled and sobbing, totally incoherent.

'What's happened?' Rick cried, squeezing her tightly, one hand cupping the back of her head.

'Can we go in your room?' she said, eyeing Rollo through her tears. In other words, not in front of *him*.

'Okay?' Rick mouthed over her head to Rollo, who nodded, plainly relieved their intruder wasn't his assailant from a few days ago, and Rick steered her upstairs and into his room. They sat side by side on the bed and Marina collapsed backwards with relief.

'What's going on, babe? You're scaring me.'

'*I'm* scared,' she said simply, wide eyes staring at the ceiling. 'If I stay with him much longer, I don't think I'll make it.'

'Has he hurt you again?'

'You could say that. He . . .'

'He what? What is it, darling? Show me, please.'

Still prostrate, she unbuttoned her top and lifted her bra. There was an ugly bite mark on her left breast. Teeth had broken the skin and left it purple and blistered.

'Jesus Christ, this is nasty!' Rick flushed with shock and anger. 'I can't believe he's attacked you like this. We need to report this to the police. I'll go with you. I'll be there every step of the way, I promise.'

'No, no, no.' Instantly, she began covering herself up, sliding from range. 'No way.'

'Marina—'

'The police don't listen. Take my word for it, I've been to them before about a bloke.'

'You have?' Aware of his open-mouthed horror, he adjusted his face. He needed to learn to react with more composure. 'Why did he do this?'

'He knows I'm seeing you. He threatened to kill us both if I didn't end it right now.'

Kill us both? Rick assumed that meant Marina and him,

not Marina and Drew. There was a painful jabbing in his chest. 'But how did you get away from him this morning?'

'That's what I'm trying to say, Rick. He brought me here, he's parked outside right now!'

'What? Where?' The jabbing increased to a hammering, jolting him to his feet. Checking the window, he saw the Stanleys' blue BMW below, a male figure at the wheel. 'I don't understand. Why's he just sitting there?'

'I begged him to give me a few minutes. I'm supposed to be finishing with you.' She hurried on, almost as if blurting it out before she could change her mind: 'Did you mean it about finding a safe house? Did you mean it about coming with me?'

'Yes!' In spite of her distress, he felt hope awaken. 'Of course I meant it. We'll hide out together.'

She was on her feet now, charged, spirited 'Maybe if you came for the first few weeks, if you can take time off work. Do you have any holiday left this year?'

'A week, maybe ten days.' Which wouldn't be long enough. He supposed he could fake an illness – given his recent moodiness, they'd probably believe he had depression. 'I think the easiest thing would be for me to leave.'

'I can't ask you to do that,' Marina said, aghast.

'You're not asking. I'm offering. It doesn't have to be for ever, does it?' Now he'd said it, it was obvious it was the only solution. If he remained here, Drew would come raging back the moment he knew she'd gone, and he wouldn't sit waiting in the car either. No, if Rick wanted to be with her, he had to start from scratch too. He could pick up another job easily enough, but she was in bodily danger here, perhaps even mortal danger. 'We'll play it by ear, maybe get one of those restraining orders. The main thing is to be somewhere safe while we do all of that. And together.'

Marina fell against him, thanking him, telling him she loved him. He could feel the beat of her heart, as violent as his own. 'I have to go. He said ten minutes, no more.'

'Go,' Rick urged. 'Tell him I've got the message, job done. We'll start planning tomorrow. One o'clock in the lobby?'

'One o'clock in the lobby.' She was on her feet, tear-stained, but brighter now. 'And please, don't say anything to Rollo.'

'I won't.'

'What happened to his face?'

Rick hesitated. She was already terrified by the prospect of returning to Drew, she didn't need to know a wider campaign of violence was already underway. 'Just a bit of argy-bargy at the pub,' he said. 'You know how he winds people up.'

He watched from the window as she left, pulling the door as gently as ever, conditioned, he supposed, by a life lived on eggshells. As she emerged into the street, the driver's door of the BMW opened and Drew stepped out. Expecting him to address Marina, even grip her arm and yank her into the car, Rick was caught off guard when he barely acknowledged her and instead swept his eyes upwards, coming to rest on Rick at his bedroom window. Even as Marina got into the passenger seat and closed the door, he remained where he was, fixing Rick with a narrow, malignant gaze for a good thirty seconds, before finally, almost nonchalantly, returning to the car.

'Jesus,' Rollo said. 'That look.'

Rick turned. 'You saw?'

'He's so fucking menacing. He makes the bloke who smacked me look like a pussy cat.'

'I know.'

The BMW nosed from its space and accelerated off.

'Is she all right?'

'Just about. But this is why I'm worried, Rollo. He's capable of anything.'

They stood for a moment in silence, just looking down at the space where Drew's car had been parked.

'I feel like we're in a movie.' Rollo touched his swollen eye and winced with a campy flourish. 'And it's nowhere near as great as you'd think.'

'I know. It's bloody terrifying,' Rick said.

22

Rick

August–September 1995

It was more than a little awe-inspiring – ironic, even, given his own previous misplaced impatience – how Marina now switched from stall mode to overdrive. By the time they'd returned to their desks the next day, each having stretched their lunch hour by thirty minutes and to hell with the consequences, a plan was already in place.

The date she had in mind for her departure was Friday, 15 September, when Drew would be away on a stag weekend in Canterbury. Owing to his Saturday hours in the Wimbledon shop, he rarely left town for the weekend, and it was too good an opportunity to pass up.

Finding somewhere safe for them to stay was Rick's chief contribution. In books and films, victims fled to remote locations, but instinct told him this classic escape was flawed. How could a pair of Londoners *not* stand out in a rural village where everyone had known each other from birth? And if they were to hide away for weeks on end, they'd need to go out for supplies and exercise, and work of some sort too, eventually. Much better to do that among the multitudes of a big city, where no one would give them a second glance.

There was a defiance to it, too, a pride: London was his city and he trusted it to protect them.

For the rest of the week, he sacrificed their lunch hours together to phone the helplines of various domestic violence charities, quickly wishing he'd done this sooner as he learned that his own 'support' to date had been less than helpful. Confrontations with the perpetrator, for example, were not recommended by the experts – the anger they generated was all too often taken out on the victim. Rick had done everything wrong, albeit with the best intentions, and now he had to do it right.

The charity supplied him with a list of shelters, all of which proved full, but once it was established that there was money to pay for a private rental, a short trail of informal recommendations led him to the manager of a building in the West End who had been known on occasion to turn a blind eye to the usual onerous references required for a short-term let. He had a furnished studio unit coming free the week of 11 September and would not require references or formal ID.

'Can I take a name?' the manager asked.

Rick had not prepared a false one and, absurdly, Timothy Foster floated into his mind. *Definitely* not that. 'Gary,' he said, firmly. 'Gary Smith.'

'Gary, great. We'll just say plus friend. I'm Sam. Ask for me when you come.'

Rick went to view the place after work. Populated chiefly by postgrad students from overseas, it was a reassuringly anonymous-looking building on Newman Street, just off the eastern end of Oxford Street, with no reception or, that he could see, security cameras. The unit was on the top floor, the farthest from the lift and closest to the stairs. It was clean and featureless, with grey carpet and magnolia walls, one wall taken up with kitchen cupboards and appliances – microwave, kettle, a small fridge – with a small window over the sink; furniture consisted of a double bed, a table and two chairs. The adjoining shower room was poky but functional. Crucially, he could pay up front in cash – £650 for the first month, with the verbal commitment of a further one.

'I'll just need an emergency contact,' Sam said, taking care of the paperwork, which was as minimal as promised. He was low-key to the point of deadpan, very tall, and skinny for his age, which Rick estimated to be about fifty.

Giving the Camden flat number and Rollo's name, he arranged to return to collect the key the day before he and Marina moved in.

'Don't tell me where it is,' Marina warned, when they next met at Albert Street to update each other on their progress. 'Not even the street name. If I don't know it, then I can't be forced to give it up.'

Forced to give it up: the implications were too chilling to contemplate.

As for her possessions, the obvious solution was for her

to smuggle luggage out in advance and store it at work or at Rick's, but since it now transpired that Drew drove her to the station every morning and had announced there'd be no Manchester trip ahead of his weekend away, they had run out of time. There was also the question of her passport and – she was fairly sure – her birth certificate, under lock and key in his desk drawer, plus that suspected extra cash, which could end up making the difference between their holding their nerve longer term or having to re-emerge in surrender.

They settled on a solution. She'd secrete a bag in the cupboard under the stairs; then, on the Friday morning, she would leave for work as usual with Drew, returning at the end of the day as expected to deactivate the alarm. Safe in the knowledge that he would be on his way to Canterbury, she'd break into the desk drawer for the documents – Rick would teach her how to use a nail file to open the drawer lock. ('Just call me Simon Templar,' he joked, but, like Rumpelstiltskin, *The Saint* wasn't known to her.) She'd then retrieve her luggage and leave.

'Take a taxi straight to the safe house,' he said. 'Is there a local firm you trust?'

'I'm not sure,' Marina said. 'It might be too obvious. I'm worried he'd be able to trace me. I was thinking, could we hire a car, maybe? Then we've got it if we need to move on.' She chewed her lip; fear chased her every rational thought, he realized. She *wanted* to believe they'd be safe, but she *actually* believed Drew would find them. Perhaps it was because she was in Rick's flat for the first time since that drama-filled Sunday morning; she no longer felt secure here.

'We won't need to move on,' he assured her. 'But a car's not a bad idea. Between us, we'll have a fair bit of kit.'

'And that way, you could collect me from work and come with me to the house?' she proposed, hopeful.

'I'd better not come in, in case I'm seen. I'll wait in the car.' But there remained the problem of neighbours seeing her get into it, complete with the memorable detail of her luggage. 'Maybe come back out via that track at the back? No one will see you, it's completely overgrown. I'll wait on that side road by the steps.'

Again, she looked doubtful, but then her face cleared. 'I completely forgot about the track. Drew doesn't like me going up there. He calls it a mud bath for junkies.' She gave Rick a brave smile. 'Well, *I* call it an escape route.'

'Oh, darling.'

The sound of Rollo on the stairs brought home to Rick just how surreal this discussion was. Here they were plotting a spell in hiding and his own flatmate had no idea he was about to vanish. 'What should I say to Rollo? I mean, I have to say something or he'll report me missing.'

'Tell him you've been transferred overseas for a bit,' she suggested. 'Does B&F have any offices outside the UK?'

'No, but he doesn't know that. Good idea. I'll say India. Loads of companies are opening branches out there. Mumbai.'

'Perfect.' She exhaled, relaxing at last. 'So now we just need to resign.'

'We'll have a joint leaving party,' he joked. 'Ask accounts if you can have your final week's wages in cash,' he added. 'By the time Drew notices it hasn't been paid into his account, it'll be too late.'

*

He handed in his notice almost at once, using holiday owed to facilitate an exit on Thursday, 14 September. He told his workmates he was off travelling, reasoning that it was simpler to stick with the India theme than to come up with a whole new story. A *Rough Guide* was procured, left on his desk for anyone who fancied leafing through.

'Bit old for backpacking, aren't you?' Si said.

'I'm only twenty-six,' Rick said.

'Yeah, but they'll all be students. You don't wanna be sleeping in hostels, cockroaches crawling into your ears, do you?'

'Absolutely not,' Rick agreed, thinking of the unit that awaited Marina and him, as spartan as any hostel. But secret, completely secret.

'Your dancing girl going with you, is she?' Si had checked in regularly on the subject since the party, always with a gratifying awe that Rick should have pulled so spectacularly out of his league.

'No,' he said. 'It's a solo thing.'

'Say no more.' He gave Rick a look of commiseration. 'These things don't last, mate.'

'What things?'

'Y'know, affairs with married chicks.' Si shrugged. 'Come on, we're not stupid. How was one of *us* going to get a girl like that? There had to be a catch.'

Clearly, the assumption among Rick's colleagues was that

he'd been dumped, his travel plans merely the time-honoured means of healing a broken heart. 'Tell me about it,' he agreed, and Si was more than happy to drop the sensitive stuff and focus on practicalities.

'You got all the visas and jabs sorted?'

'Yep, all in hand. I just need to pick up my malaria tablets and order some currency and I'm all set.' When he spoke like this, he almost believed he actually was going to India. Perhaps, if Marina's real passport was successfully reclaimed, they might go together.

'Don't go swallowing any water from the Ganges,' Si advised. 'Swimming with human shit, I read.'

'You should think about retraining as a travel agent,' Rick said. 'You're wasted here.'

*

He broke the news to Rollo about the short-term transfer to Mumbai, saying, by way of explanation, 'It's good for the CV.'

'Yeah, sure, I get it.' Rollo being Rollo, he switched smoothly to the impact the change might have on his own creature comforts. 'Wait, you're not giving notice on this place, are you?'

'No.' Rick shared the good news that he intended paying his rent in advance, so Rollo could have the flat to himself for two months. His bank savings would cover this, while the £2,000 he'd stashed in the biscuit tin would pay for his and Marina's essentials in hiding. He didn't add that he hoped to return with Marina, a restraining order against her husband in place. 'You can sublet my room if you like? That would cover your half and you could start going out again.' He'd seen Rollo's latest bank statement, left abandoned on the coffee table, and knew the alarming extent of his overdraft.

'Yeah, I probably will, if you're sure,' Rollo said, cheering.

Choose your toughest, roughest mate, Rick longed to say. Someone who could take on a hardman like Drew Stanley (not to mention *his* hardman), should he come calling again. But however horrible the thought of Rollo being exposed to more violence, he had to be ruthless about this. Marina was right. No holes, no leaks. It was safer for Rollo not to know.

'You having a leaving do?' Rollo asked.

'Nah. It's not like I'm leaving the company.'

'Still, we've got to have *some* kind of a send-off for you.'

'Please, my heart can't take another surprise party. I'm serious, Rollo. I'm leaving on a Thursday, no one will want to get wrecked.'

Rollo scoffed. 'Well, we both know *that's* not in the R&R rulebook. Fine. I'll book the curry house, at least. How's Marina taking the news of your transfer?'

'She's okay about it,' Rick said, truthfully. 'It's only a short secondment.'

'Gives her a bit of time to get her own house in order,' Rollo said.

*

He put off dealing with his family till the last minute. He'd hoped simply to leave a message on his parents' answer-phone: 'I'm just off on a work trip for a few months, be

196

in touch!' Then he'd thought, if something did go wrong and he had to get himself a fake passport like Marina, the two of them living under false identities for the rest of their lives ... well, maybe it was kinder to bid a more formal farewell.

'*India?* Can they not ask someone else to go?' his mother said. 'Just be careful who you trust out there, Rick.'

'For God's sake, it's a perfectly civilized country,' Rick protested. He was starting to wish he'd said Paris or Milan.

'I'm just worried. Maybe you'll know how it feels one day.' The melancholic note in her voice was unexpectedly touching and he replied, as if in a sacred pledge, 'I'll be back before you know it, Mum. Don't worry. Give my love to Dad and Stacey and the kids.'

He wondered if it should concern him more than it did how readily he was sacrificing them all for a woman they'd never even been introduced to.

*

By the time he and Rollo went for their farewell curry, he was nervous, almost too nervous to tackle the multiple dishes ordered, though he had no problem downing the pints of lager.

'Dig in,' Rollo urged, slopping spoonfuls of chicken Madras onto his plate and leaving a trail of red on the white tablecloth. His mood was carefree – he had a job interview the next day, he reported; a role that needed to be filled in a hurry, which meant he could be earning again very soon. He was also newly free of girl trouble, Flavia having taken a job in Edinburgh and told him she wanted no further contact with him.

'Said I was a fuckwit and a loser,' he reported, mouth full. Then, swallowing, 'Isn't that your mate from work?'

Rick followed his line of vision and arrived at the familiar broad, squat shape of Jake. 'Oh yeah.' *What the fuck?* All the years he'd worked at B&F and there'd never been an accidental meeting between colleague and outside friend until now.

He pushed back his chair with the aim of intercepting him, but it was too late, Jake was approaching and he had no choice but to deal with it. 'Jakester! What're you doing in this neck of the woods?'

'Seeing this girl up here,' Jake said. 'Just doing the honours with the takeaway.'

'She's got you well trained.'

'Takes one to know one,' Rollo said, and for a second Rick found himself floundering, unable to remember which of the two of them thought he'd split up with Marina and which that they were still together.

'You remember Rollo from our party?'

'Just wishing our mutual friend bon voyage,' Rollo told him, gesturing to their many dishes, everything artificially red and yellow and a little unappetizing. 'Coals to Newcastle, eh? There'll be nothing but curry where he's going.'

'All right for some,' Jake said.

Thank God for meaningless male banter, Rick thought, frantically willing Jake to step away. But Rollo, ever desirous of new stimulation, was looking to prolong this.

'You want to join us while you wait?'

No, no, no! And screw him if Jake wasn't about to say yes, when – a gift from the gods – a kitchen worker appeared at the counter with his takeaway.

'If I don't see you, have a great time,' Jake said. 'Keep in touch.'

'Like I won't be faxing him ten times a day,' Rick scoffed for Rollo's benefit, turning his head slightly to be sure Jake was out of earshot.

'If they've even got fax machines in India,' Rollo said.

*

Rick had drunk more than he'd intended, so when, back at the flat, Rollo collected a bottle of cheap white from the fridge and slid up the kitchen window, he knew he should demur, keep a clear head for the morning. 'Think I'll get a good night's sleep before the flight,' he told Rollo, yawning. He longed to be able to phone Marina and quell the last-minute nerves he knew she'd be suffering, but that was out of the question. The thought of her quelled *his*, at least. 'I'll see you in the morning though.'

But seeing his friend in the deckchair, alone, bottle in hand, smoke streaming from his nostrils, he was overcome by the recognition of how precariously *his* world had tipped, too. Rollo had moved in at the beginning of the summer with a job and a girlfriend, his handsome face unbruised, and now, just three months later, look at him. He'd been sacked, beaten up, insulted by his girlfriend, and now sat drinking straight from the bottle like a wino. *And* he was about to be thrown to the wolves by Rick.

He stepped out onto the roof. 'You've been a good mate, Rollo. I won't forget it.'

Rollo jeered at him affectionately. 'For God's sake, you're not on death row. You'll be back in a few months.' He lifted the wine bottle in the air like a trophy. 'Sure you don't want some of this?'

'All right,' Rick said. 'Why not. One for the road.'

23

Alex

September, present

And so, the great day had dawned at last. Arcadia unlocked its gates and the Silver Vale Eco Trail was declared open.

'Isn't it *glorious*?' Beth exclaimed, as they climbed the repaired stone steps from Long Lane and beheld the trail's entrance, all shiny new signage draped with bunting and shrubs decorated with paper flowers and lanterns.

'It's like that Singer Sargent in the Tate, you know?' Zara said. 'The girl with the lanterns.'

Hardly, Alex thought. There was a solitude to that work, a silence, whereas this was the predictable pandemonium of undisciplined children stomping about in their novelty animal wellies and Breton stripes and yelling, always yelling. Was it any wonder that their parents swarmed the stall from which Samira and others dispensed Prosecco in paper cups (plastic was to the new trail what broken syringes had been to the old, but what the two had in common was a need to self-medicate while obliged to contemplate nature).

He imagined saying this aloud to Beth and Zara and watching their mouths fall open in dismay. Enough is enough, Beth would say, later, if not on the spot. I can't be married to you any longer. You've turned into a miserable killjoy.

'Quite the transformation,' he said, brightly. 'They've done a great job with these information boards.' And he made a decent show of studying the text about the amphibians and mammals expected to inhabit the new log pile, the dragonflies that might come to lay their eggs on the aquatic plants in the new pond. Then he, Beth and Zara set off down the trail, which, as far as he could see, had exactly the same eco elements as before – and there was no need to fake his celebration of *that*.

Every so often, locals clustered to admire the elevated views of their own gardens, debating whether the trail made their homes less safe and whether it even mattered when Rachel-from-number-16's sister was an estate agent and had said the owners of all adjoining properties could expect an overnight uplift in value of at least ten per cent. 'That will include Long Lane,' Zara said to Beth and they exchanged satisfied smiles.

What Alex wanted to know was whether Cordelia Smyth was up here somewhere or spectating from the comfort of her garden. He was careful to avoid eye contact with the older women he passed, expecting at any moment to be scolded by Zara for treating them as invisible.

'Guys, this way!' It was Dulcie with her phone, angling

it self-importantly as she got her shot of their dysfunctional little trio, berating Alex for turning his face away.

'Just crop me out,' he told her. God, there were phones aloft everywhere you looked – not just parents videoing their kids, but younger adults too, taking artful shots of a single leaf or a terrified beetle. It was going to take all his concentration to avoid edging into an Instagram square or a Facebook montage.

At least the fast-moving woman with a real camera, who was surely the reporter Beth had spoken of, seemed interested only in the kids.

'Just imagine moving in and having this at the back of your house,' Beth said to him, as Dulcie admired Zara's growing bump. 'We used to play in the street growing up, not a tree in sight!'

Her earnest positivity cut through Alex's paranoia for a moment and he saw the scene through her eyes: the good intentions of the project, its obvious and well-deserved success. Let people trail along it, blissfully ignorant, he thought. Their footsteps would compact the earth, not churn it up. He reached for Beth's hand and gave it a squeeze; she responded with a surprised, pleased glance his way.

At the Surrey Road end, more pilgrims traipsed in, many greeting Beth with triumphant cries. 'I'm just nipping home to the loo,' he told her, knowing she wouldn't mind if he didn't return. He'd shown his face. 'I'll pop to the shop after.'

'Bye, Alex,' Zara said. 'Don't forget we need dog food.'

We need. Like she had a share in Olive now. The sad truth was that she did: at home every day, as she now was, she'd been promoted by Olive to man's best friend status. (*Woman's* best friend, Alex!) It was hard not to see it as a betrayal.

Reaching the section behind number 54 once more, he saw that a pair of children were climbing the larger of the silver birches, violently bending its outer boughs. He looked around for a parent to haul them down – everyone knew you weren't allowed to lay a finger on other people's kids these days, the parent would have you for paedophilia, but watching the rough way they were treating the tree, he couldn't just stand by.

'Hey, careful,' he called. 'You don't want to break the branches. That's like breaking a person's arms.'

Two identical faces peered down at him in surprise. They couldn't be older than six or seven.

He addressed them kindly. 'Don't you want to explore the trail? I think I saw chocolate cake at the entrance.' He congratulated himself when they dropped from the tree and tore off.

Seconds later, a blonde in jeans came striding out of the glass box of number 54 and across the lawn, a toddler by her side. She wore a grey hoodie and baby-pink Hunters over white jeans. As she gestured to Alex, an oversized Fitbit slid down her slender forearm and over her wrist bone, and he thought, involuntarily, of Marina and the silver and turquoise bangle she'd always worn.

'You haven't seen my kids, have you?' she asked.

'What flavour?' he said, squeezing every last drop of charm from his fraudulent smile.

'Boys. Seven and five. They look a bit like this one.'

The young kid scowled up at him.

'Ah, I think they went that way. There was talk of treats at the trail entrance, I believe.'

'I bet there was,' she said.

She looked sanguine enough, but Alex remembered the little girl lost on Wimbledon Common, her distraught parents, and adjusted his tone to something more reassuring. 'It was just a minute ago, I'm sure they've come to no harm.'

She chuckled. 'It's more the harm they might be *causing* that concerns me.'

He seconded *that*. He offered a hand to help both her and the kid up to join him on the path.

'Thanks,' she said. 'Frankie.'

'Alex. I live on Long Lane. I'm walking back up that way if you need an extra pair of eyes?'

'Great. Thanks, Alex.'

They fell into step, almost immediately having to revert to single file when the woman with the camera bore down from the opposite direction. Alex tried to ignore the awful shudder that passed through him.

'Well, everyone seems very pleased with the new trail,' Frankie remarked.

'Pleased with the trail or pleased with themselves?' he asked.

'Oh my God, you speak Cynic,' she said, with a cry of delight. 'I thought I was the only one.'

He smirked at her. 'Absolutely not. I've been fluent for years.'

'Then maybe we can improve our vocabulary together?'

She was fun, this woman in Marina's house, and he was sorry to say goodbye when her tearaways were located, a cupcake in either hand, and she set about herding them back home. He vaguely remembered Beth and her gang gossiping about her – hadn't her husband left her recently?

Another male idiot who wouldn't know a good thing if it was dropped on his head from a great height.

24

Rick

September 1995

His schedule for Friday was plotted to the minute and he was damned if he was going to let a hangover disrupt it. He set his alarm for 7am and, with Rollo still slumbering, finished his packing unobserved. Having already assembled the clothes, shoes, toiletries and books he would need, he now added a few days' worth of snacks and a litre of vodka he'd kept hidden, cramming the whole lot into the rucksack he hadn't used since he was a student. The thing was almost unliftable.

Next came the anticipated eleventh-hour call from his mother, who had advice to share about Tums and keeping his traveller's cheques out of sight of slum-dwelling knaves. Talk of traveller's cheques reminded him to split the biscuit-tin cash between rucksack and wallet, and there was a brief shock when he took out the tin and found it empty.

He phoned Marina at work. 'Did you already take the cash?'

'Yes, I thought I told you, I took it last week. It's in my bag at home.'

'I thought I was bringing it?'

He heard the bristling of her nerves as she struggled to explain. 'I just thought, you know, just in case.'

'Just in case what?'

'You change your mind. At the last minute.' There was rawness in her voice, an admission of shame. 'I wouldn't blame you if you did.'

'Marina,' he said, firmly. 'I'm not Drew or anyone else you've known who says one thing and means another. I'm not going to change my mind – ever.'

'Okay.' Now he heard the smile in her voice.

'Good. So, I'm just going to organize the car and finish up here and then I'll see you at five. Go get a final frozen yoghurt and stop worrying.'

Hearing her chuckle, he was pleased he'd helped assuage her last-minute jitters. It didn't quite banish his own, how-ever, and he decided to walk to the car-hire place – the nearest one was down near Euston Station – in the hope of burning off some nervous energy. It was a fine day; the street cleaners must have been out because the tarmac gleamed, and it seemed to him as he bounded along that the passing drivers and pedestrians were connected to him in a new way, that they too knew this was an auspicious day.

At the rental office, he had no choice but to present his driver's licence and documents confirming his ID, which meant there was now a paper trail in place, but he was confident he'd have returned the car by the time any investigations on Drew's part made it this far (he hadn't said as much to Marina, but he had a strong suspicion that Drew would hire a private detective to track her down). The car was a white Fiesta and, as he drove the short distance to Albert Street, he enjoyed the comforting aroma of its recent valet clean. He was careful to park a good way from their door to avoid being seen by Rollo, who would question why someone leaving the country for two months should need to hire a car. Back in the flat, however, there were signs that his flatmate had showered and left for his job interview.

It would take thirty minutes to get from Camden Town to Victoria Street, but he aimed to leave an hour, in case of Friday gridlock. The idea of Marina exiting the building and finding he wasn't there, their escape bungled before it was even underway, was unthinkable. He spent the rest of his time packing his room up into boxes so Rollo would be able to sublet it as urgently as he wished. By the time he was ready to leave, Rollo still hadn't returned – perhaps he'd been offered the job on the spot and found a spare playmate to celebrate with in the pub – so Rick scribbled a note to leave on the kitchen table:

Off to airport – look after the flat! I'll drop you a line as soon as I'm settled, R

That should buy him a bit of time. Hopefully, by the time Rollo noticed he'd not heard a dicky bird from India, Rick would be in a position to phone him and explain.

He closed the door to the flat behind him with a sudden instinct that he might never set foot in there again.

*

He reached their block on Victoria Street ten minutes early and circled a few times, addressing his last-minute fears. Marina's confession that she worried he'd change his mind had, inevitably, stirred the question, what if *she'd* changed *hers*? Taken the money and holed up in a B&B or somewhere, reverting to her original instinct that she was safer alone?

But no, here she came, right on the dot of five o'clock, carrying her handbag, a can of Coke and a balloon. She was dressed not in her usual jacket and skirt, but a summer dress.

'I like the blue,' he said, when she climbed in.

'Not blue, Rick, indigo.' She slotted her can in the cup holder and set her bag by her feet. 'I bought it at lunch, got it cheap in the sales.'

'I thought Culkins had strict rules about office attire?'

She buckled her seatbelt. 'It's my last day, what were they going to do? Report me to the Minister of Temps?'

'You were there a while in the end,' he remarked, pulling into a gap between a white van and a taxi.

'Almost four months.'

A long time for a temp; less so for a relationship.

But these were not the normal circumstances of romance. For one of them, if not both, this was life or death. Not for the first time, he wondered if they were doing the right thing going back to Silver Vale. What if Drew had forgotten something he needed for his stag weekend and returned to the house? He was only going to Canterbury, it would be easy enough for him to follow his mates on a later train.

'Did he phone you?' he asked, as they cut through a side road to Vauxhall Bridge Road. Like any getaway driver worth his salt, he'd memorized the route.

'Drew? Only at the usual time,' Marina said, 'nothing different.'

'Which station's he going from on this stag?'

'Victoria, I think.'

'*Victoria?* Jesus, Marina, what if he sees us?'

She placed a hand on his thigh. 'He won't. He'll come on the tube and I think he's meeting the guys at the pub in the station.'

If he was coming at all, Rick thought, for it struck him now that this stag weekend might be fictitious, Drew's real trip being with the other woman he was seeing – they might at this very moment be on a plane to Paris or somewhere far more romantic than Kent. Well, anywhere but here was fine with him. He allowed himself to relax a fraction.

The balloon bobbed against the roof of the car. It had the words 'Bon Voyage' on it in a pink scrawl.

'Where do the Culkins crew think you're going?'

'Nowhere. Just off to the rest of my life.'

'Which is true. Did they get you a cake?'

'Actually yes. There was cava as well and I think they were up for a session, but I made it clear I was leaving on the dot. I stuck to this.' Marina raised the Coke in a mock toast, before returning it to its slot. 'This is so surreal, Rick. We're okay for time?'

'Perfect. You'll turn off the alarm at exactly the same time you do every day. To him, everything will be just as he's expecting.'

Fucking monster, he thought, for the hundredth time.

They were already at the last set of lights before the river. The traffic was heavy but flowing; he'd seen a lot worse on Friday afternoons. All these weekend getaways, he thought; was anyone else's as fraught as theirs?

'I like the car,' Marina said. 'We've got it for a week, right?'

'Yep. If everything goes according to plan, I'll drop it off at the rental place this time next week. Out of hours, keys through the door.'

She knew all this, of course. They'd perfected their timeline and both knew it by heart. At this stage, questions and answers were purely for reassurance.

She fiddled with the radio, quickly finding something she liked. Massive Attack, 'Unfinished Sympathy'.

'*Hey-ey-ey-ey-ey*,' she sang, as they crossed the river, and she rolled her window down to release the balloon, leaving her arm outstretched after she'd let go, fingers twisting with a ballerina's flourish.

*

They pulled up on the corner of Exmoor Gardens and Long Lane on a late summer's evening so perfect Rick felt an emotion oddly like nostalgia. Suddenly – now of all times! – he could imagine settling here himself, with Marina and a couple of kids maybe, in one of these golden-brick houses that were so square and solid and inviolable. Among all the well-stocked gardens and wooded paths that made the sub-urban neighbourhood feel rural.

'I think I'm going to be sick,' Marina said.

'Stay strong,' he told her. 'It's almost over. Then you'll never have to see him again.'

Exmoor Gardens had acres of empty kerb but, as agreed, it was on Long Lane that he tucked the hire car away, right at the foot of the steps to the track. A combination of nerves and rustiness threatened to sabotage his parking skills, but he managed it without too much crunching of gears. There was a spray of cigarette ends on the steps — teenagers hung out here at night, perhaps, or up in the clearing beyond, ignoring the barrier at the mouth of the track, with its red-and-white 'No Entry' sign. Marina would ignore it too, when she used this route to return with her luggage.

And when Drew Stanley came home and started knocking on neighbours' doors, he'd hardly be likely to come all the way up here.

Rick turned off the ignition. 'Ready?'

'I think so. I just ... Thank you, Rick.' And she leaned across to kiss him, not a peck, but a long, open-mouthed kiss in which he could taste her fear.

He pulled back. 'Someone might see. Go, while there's no one about. And if you do meet anyone, remember you're just walking home from the station like any other Friday.'

'If I'm not back in half an hour, come down the track and meet me. Promise?'

'Promise.'

With no further word, she climbed out of the car. As

she hurried to the corner, she used her palms to subdue the swirling skirt of her new blue dress ('not blue, Rick, indigo'), before shooting him a backwards look of excitement and disbelief. *It's happening, it's finally happening!* A blink later and she was out of sight. He followed her in his mind in real time as she hurried down Exmoor Gardens, turning at last into her drive, past the BMW (she'd be expecting to see it, Drew having told her he'd be dropping it home mid-afternoon before taking the train into town), and letting herself into the house. She'd tap in the alarm code, maybe check the post for anything worth bringing, and then dip into Drew's study to crack the lock of the desk drawer.

He checked his watch: 6.17pm. In five minutes – ten if the desk drawer proved tricky – she'd retrieve her bag from its hiding place under the stairs and leave by the kitchen door, crossing the lawn and easing through the gap in the hedge to access the track, just as he and Rollo had done that Sunday in July. He waited, hands folded on his lap, sweat prickling his armpits. He considered turning the engine back on for the fan, but decided against it and wound down his window instead. The air was still and dry and smelled slightly putrid, like garden waste starting to decompose.

Fifteen minutes passed, during which he smoked two Marlboro Lights, elbow sticking out of the window, and tossed the butts to join the others by the steps, watching the fiery ends turn grey. Finally, he rolled up the window, checked for pedestrians and got out of the car. Time to meet her on the path – she must be struggling with her bag, probably overpacked like his own. Seconds later, he was at the top of the steps and inching his hips through a gap between the barrier and the post it had once been chained to.

He moved at speed. Though he'd been up here twice before, he'd not appreciated how thickly veiled it was overhead, and with a screen of foliage on either side and a tangle of brambles underfoot the effect was of an ivy-green tunnel, like something out of a fairy tale. She'd be as spooked by it as he was and at every moment he expected her to appear in front of him, breathless fear giving way to relief: *Thank God it's you! It's so creepy back here!* They'd exchange nervous smiles, he'd take her bag, staggering a little under its weight, and they'd continue through the green tunnel in single file.

Back on track, back on schedule.

It was when he was two or three houses away – the screen of trees was too dense to keep precise count – that he glimpsed it, on the ground just ahead, beyond the twisting, low-hanging bough of a silver birch.

A bolt of indigo blue.

25

Rick

September 1995

She was lying on her front, legs straight, with one arm bent protectively over her head and the other at full stretch. He could see straight away that her upper body was not rising and falling as it should be, that the only movement was the flicker of the fabric of her dress as the breeze lifted it from her legs. There were dark coppery smears on the blue.

As he took a small step closer, there was a noise between his ears like the boom he imagined when you jumped from a plane, right before the parachute released, for what he saw now was too shocking to comprehend: the back of her head was broken open, her fair hair stained and glued to the tissue and the hand touching it swollen, streaked with brown and red. The earth below was drenched black.

For a moment or two he just stood there, rejecting the evidence point-blank, until he experienced an overpowering need to retch and swallowed just in time to force it back down. His thoughts were reduced to chants, basic and repetitive – *swallow, breathe, swallow, breathe* – until, at last, the ungodly roar receded and other sounds registered: children's voices, one bossing, others protesting; birdsong; road traffic – peripheral, but present. He could no longer deny that this experience was real. He was on the track behind Marina's house and someone had attacked her and left her for dead.

Not dead, you don't know that!

He squatted, touched her neck with his fingers, searching for a pulse. Nothing. He touched the wrist of the outstretched arm: again, nothing. His palm on her back registered utter stillness. He was too late: the beat of life was gone. He saw he'd smeared the pale skin of her forearm with her own blood and the sight paralysed him anew. He couldn't straighten his legs.

Get help. Get help.

Do it, you fucking idiot, do it!

At last, he staggered upright. There wasn't a soul in sight. The kids he'd heard were several gardens away, he judged, on the Pleasance Road side. Turning to the Stanleys' garden, he saw that the kitchen door was wide open, so he stumbled down the bank, through the hedge and across the lawn and into the house, where he moved through the unfamiliar space in search of the phone. Where was it? In a house this size you'd expect an extension in the kitchen, but he couldn't see one and hurried through to the hallway. Notes of Marina's Gucci perfume hung in the air – she hadn't been wearing it in the car, but the scent was achingly familiar. The urge to vomit was still so powerful he wasn't sure he would be able to speak when he found the phone.

At least no alarm blared. What looked like the keypad for it was by the front door. *OFF*, it read, in angular red-lit letters. That much of the plan had been achieved, then, but what had happened next? How the hell had Drew come to be here?

Because it was Drew who had done this to her, of that Rick was in no doubt. No doubt at all.

Where the fuck was the phone? He found the entry point of the cable near the front door and traced its passage down the wall and along the skirting board. There! A sleek black handset, on a table just inside the living room. Registering only a layout of dark leather furniture and pale rugs, he picked up the receiver and, with a shaking hand, dialled 999.

'You need to send an ambulance straight away. A woman's been attacked, I think she's dead. It's fifty-four Exmoor Gardens, Silver Vale, I don't know the exact postcode.'

It was only as he made this statement that his brain began functioning fully, allowing him to see with sudden appalling clarity how all of this might look to arriving personnel. The stranger in the house, vouched for by no one – no one except her, the silenced victim. Footprints in the dirt and bloody fingerprints on the kitchen door and the phone. A hire car parked at the steps of the track, the luggage of a runaway in its boot . . .

He was being asked for his name, but panic tightened his throat. Should he invent something? If so, what? *Think*.

'It doesn't matter,' he said, finally. 'But *her* name's Marina

Stanley. Her husband is Drew Stanley and he's the one who's done this to her. Please, write that down. It's important. He's killed his wife.'

He must have been lying in wait, Rick thought. He must have watched her arrive and collect her things for her escape, before following her out to the track and attacking her. But where was her bag? Rick was certain he hadn't seen it anywhere near her. And he hadn't noticed her handbag either, unless she'd fallen onto it and it was trapped under her body.

Had she managed to get the drawer open for her documents and cash? Stretching the phone cord, he scanned the open doors across the hallway. In a room next to the kitchen, the drawers of a wooden desk were open, papers heaped on top. So she'd got that far, it seemed. He could only imagine the exhilaration as she succeeded, the innocent, unsuspecting pride.

'Sir? Can you still hear me? I'm dispatching help right away, but while that's happening, I need you to go back and give me a bit more information about her injuries. Will the phone cable reach that far?'

'What?' Rick jerked back to the present. 'No, she's not in the house, she's out the back. They'll need to go out the kitchen door and up onto the old railway track behind the garden, have you got that?'

'All right, then leave the line open . . .' The voice started saying what they wanted him to do with Marina while he waited for help. As he thought of the grotesque soupy mess he'd seen, a spasm started up in his neck.

He interrupted the operator: 'There's nothing more I can

do. I've told you where she is and who's responsible. Please, just get here as soon as you can. I'll leave the front door open.'

Even as he hung up, he experienced a heightened awareness of the mistake he was making. Opting out of normal behaviour like this, defying authority. He snatched a tissue from the box by the phone and wiped both the receiver and keypad with it, before returning to the front door and unlocking the latch. Leaving by the kitchen door, he left it open, just as he'd found it.

Back on the track, he half-expected a crowd to have gathered around Marina, but the woman he loved remained alone, her skin daubed with that sticky, stomach-turning claret. Casting about, he saw he'd been right about her luggage not being here. She must not even have had the chance to take it from its hiding place. The police would find it, though; they'd work out for themselves what had taken place. A wife with a bag packed and about to leave, a husband stopping her in the most ferocious and final way.

Rick's gaze dropped to her sandals, tan leather, with a flat heel. He hadn't noticed her footwear when she'd got in the car. They looked brand new, bought perhaps at the same time as the dress, and the thought that she had worn new clothes for her escape caused a lurch of tenderness that made him want to sink to his knees and cradle her, to watch over her dead body until forcibly parted from her.

But he couldn't be found here. There would be evidence connecting him to her, to this crime scene. Hairs and fibres; microscopic bits of him on her lips from their last kiss. DNA. He thought of his rucksack in the car, and of the safe house, the address of which only he knew, and, acting now on that rogue decision he'd made in the house, he took off. His heart protested at the sprint as if rupturing, splitting in two, but he kept going. Reaching the car, he groped for the key, bashing his knee on the door in his haste to get in. There was blood on his fingers and he spat on them, wiped them on his jeans, before turning the key in the ignition.

Drive normally! Don't draw attention to yourself!

He pulled away and crawled down Long Lane at a cautious pace, passing Pleasance Road and taking the next right onto a road that snaked agonizingly before it joined Surrey Road. There was only one other car at the junction and it turned left almost at once. After that, the flow of traffic was constant and he had to wait a full minute before he was able to pull out for his right turn, back towards the city.

A minute later, an ambulance tore by on the opposite carriageway, siren on.

Then, just behind it, a police car.

*

He retraced his route back into Central London, aiming mindlessly for the West End and the stretch of Goodge Street that he'd originally earmarked for parking. But, sailing up Grosvenor Place and onto Park Lane, he grew paranoid about the spot being too close to the hideout. What if someone had seen him waiting on Long Lane or driving off just as Silver Vale was locked into emergency? Police had that new numberplate recognition thing, didn't they? How quickly could they access cameras, put out a call? They might already be scouring for the registration, the registration he couldn't even quote himself, before hitting up the rental people for his address. Then, discovering his absence at the Albert Street flat, they might stake out the car in the expectation of his return.

He wouldn't risk it. He headed instead for the streets north of Marble Arch, circling until he found a quiet mews without parking meters. He was careful not to block access to a garage; he didn't want the car clamped and towed. Opening the boot, he took a towel from his luggage and began wiping the parts Marina had touched: seatbelt, door handle, window winder. Remembering the blood on his fingers, he wiped the steering wheel, gear stick and handbrake.

At the last moment, he caught a glimpse of something metallic wedged into the back of the passenger seat. It was her Zippo, used to light her last ever cigarette, and the memory of her blowing smoke through the open window, freedom in her head as the radio played, made him want to scream out with grief. He pocketed it and locked up. Lugging his deadweight of a rucksack all the way to Newman Street was going to be torture and so it proved: within five minutes, his back ached and his shoulder joints burned red hot. He limped from that bash to the knee.

It was almost eight thirty by the time he reached the building. The lift was in use so he took the stairs, passing no one, and let himself into the unit. The first thing he did was drink a gallon of water from the tap, before using the loo and washing his hands and face. The room felt suffocatingly hot and he opened the window, hearing the grinding gears and accelerating engines of the black cabs below. Then, noticing the washing machine, he tore off his clothes and shoved them, along with the towel he'd used to wipe down the car, into the drum. He added detergent, turned the dial for the hottest wash, and headed for the shower.

He was acting like a murderer, but he didn't know what else to do. Until he processed what he'd seen and grew calm enough to make a plan, he had only instinct to guide him.

Scrubbed clean and clothed in fresh jeans and T-shirt, he dug once more into his backpack. Having known the unit had no TV set, he'd packed a portable radio with fresh batteries. He tuned it to Capital, sat on the edge of the bed, and waited for the news on the hour.

Two songs, some Friday night party patter, and then it came:

'News is coming in that a woman has been fatally injured this evening in an attack in Silver Vale, southwest London. Police have yet to confirm if the body has been identified.'

Fatally injured. A body. He'd known it, of course he had, but still, it destroyed him to hear it reported as fact. As the music resumed, he dropped to the floor, arms crossed over his face, and allowed himself to sob. The wringing sensation inside his ribcage was so painful he brought his knees up to his chest in a pre-natal curl and squeezed his eyes closed.

In the background, the washing machine spun, erasing traces of Marina's blood.

26

Alex

'Your birthday present's arrived – *finally*.' Beth dropped an envelope onto the pillow next to him, before settling herself back in bed in readiness for his thrilled reaction. 'I had it sent by post. Email is so unromantic.'

'Why not by TikTok,' he said, though he had little idea what that particular medium entailed. He'd never opened social media accounts, conducting any necessary viewing of photos – such as those from the opening of the trail – over Beth's shoulder. Amid continued unwelcome speculation about the promised coverage in the *South London Press*, which Beth, Dulcie and co hoped would be 'picked up by the nationals' (sweet Jesus), he'd completely forgotten about the mystery gift. As he set aside his phone and reached for the envelope, he felt unusually receptive to the simple pleasures of civilian life. A holiday would be good. Just Beth and him.

A pool. The shade of a swaying palm. Very strong cocktails –
Hemingway strong. Sex. Maybe he could even . . .

Maybe he could even have that last perfect holiday, being
sure to lavish her with the love and attention that had been
sorely lacking of late, and then end it all. Maybe the location
would provide the perfect method: a high cliff he could leap
from, a dangerous riptide to surrender to.

It was, he noted, his first thought of suicide.

'"An ancestry investigation",' he read aloud.

Beth grinned. 'I suppose they call it that because "DNA
test" makes it sound like something police forensics would
order from the lab in the hope of nailing a rapist.'

'What?' He felt a rush of blood to his face.

She grimaced. 'Sorry, was that a bit brutal?'

'Wait, you've sent off my DNA to be tested? What the
hell for?' In the turmoil, he wondered if this was something
to do with fertility, some last-ditch bid to conceive. Then he
remembered the word 'ancestry'.

'For fun, darling,' she said, as if placating a belligerent
teenager. 'Come on, read it. You have to admit you're a little
intrigued to know what your genetic mix is.'

Battling a terrible urge to spring out of bed and punch
the wall, he forced himself to calm down. Beth was guilty of
nothing but using her imagination to buy a present for her
husband that differed from the standard socks and wine. It
had probably been costly too, this 'investigation'. He tried to
take in the words in front of him, but his vision had blurred,
and he held the document to her, wordless, childlike.

'You want me to read it for you? You *are* funny. There's

nothing to worry about, they're not going to say you're an Inca or anything. Not that that would be a problem, you might have hidden talents for, I don't know, stonework.' Giggling at her own joke, Beth scanned the information. 'Right, so your ancestry is eighty per cent England and Wales, fifteen per cent Scotland and Ireland and five per cent Scandinavia.'

He reached for an appropriate response to what should be nothing more than mildly interesting information. 'Is that it?'

'What do you mean?'

He had no choice but to simulate his own worst traits. 'I'm just saying, it does slightly whiff of Emperor's New Clothes. I'm a bog-standard British blend, we knew that already.'

'I suppose it is a bit of an anti-climax.' Beth sighed. 'Maybe there'll be more information to come. They do say they send regular updates as they increase their database.'

The word 'database' unnerved him afresh. 'Just promise me you ticked all the data protection boxes, yeah? Nothing they've tested is available to the authorities?'

'I don't think so.' Beth chuckled, infuriatingly casual. She didn't *think* so. 'Why, what have you done?'

'Nothing,' he said. 'It's just a privacy issue.'

She accepted this. It was, after all, consistent with his long-term eschewal of Facebook and the rest. 'Don't take this the wrong way, but I don't think anyone's interested. Except me, of course.'

And Zara. That remark she'd made returned to him with fresh menace – *Back when you used a different name* – just as the sound of creaking floorboards outside raised the suspicion that she was listening at the door. 'Hang on,' he said, 'was this *her* idea?'

Beth frowned. 'Whose? You mean Zara's? Why d'you say that?'

He gripped her wrist. 'Just tell me, Beth, was she involved?'

'No! And get off, you're hurting me.' Their voices were more strident now and, inevitably, Zara's called out from the other side of the door.

'You okay in there, Beth?'

'Yes,' Beth replied, 'fine. With you in a minute, Za!' And she was on her feet, pulling on tracksuit bottoms, glowering at him. 'Talk about how *not* to accept a gift. Honestly, you're so ungracious.'

'Wait, Beth!' His blood pumping, Alex was filled with a crazy urgency. 'We need to talk about this. About *her*. Can't you see she's trying to get rid of me?'

Beth's head emerged from the neck of a grey ribbed sweater. 'I thought you were the one who wanted to get rid of *her*?'

'I did, I *do*, but she's already won that battle, hasn't she? Now she wants me out.'

Beth scoffed. 'Which she achieves by being thoughtful enough to suggest a birthday present for you?'

'So it *was* her idea!' As his wife gaped, he thundered on. 'What's the endgame? Come on, tell me. A world without men? Freeze their sperm and then exterminate the lot of them? Raise all future generations on tofu and jackfruit?'

'Stop this,' Beth said. 'Do you have any idea how ridiculous you sound?'

'Just because it's ridiculous doesn't mean it not's true!' he cried.

Beth was at the door. 'I'm going downstairs and when you've calmed down, let's just have a normal day, okay? No conspiracy theories, no smearing our friend, just *normal*.'

'Beth, *please*.' But she'd gone, door clapped shut behind her, and, defeated, he looked again at the offending ancestry report, trying to make sense of the small print about privacy. That a time bomb had been set off, he was in no doubt; the only question was how long he had.

And, as he stuffed the pages back into the envelope, it seemed to him that he could feel the ache in his hands from a set of wounds long-healed.

27

Rick

He thought he'd never be able to sleep, that adrenaline would keep him awake and wired for ever, but by 2am his nervous system was overcome and he surrendered as if anaesthetized for the next six and a half hours.

Waking, the disorientation lasted several seconds: where was he? Above, the walls joined the ceiling in smooth modern angles – *this* wasn't his bedroom in Albert Street. He heard the slam of a fire door below: was he in a hotel room? Why was his knee throbbing? Had he fallen, drunk?

Until the events of the previous day rolled heavily into place.

Their escape had failed. Marina had not returned to the car. He'd found her on the track with her head smashed in and then, in an irrational, nightmarish sequence, he'd abandoned her, fled the scene and come here, into hiding, alone.

The woman he loved was dead – and yet, every last fibre of

him resisted this knowledge. As he raised his body from the bed, his chest ached not with grief but with the rejection of it. He'd been hallucinating, he told himself, or at least misunderstanding. He'd misjudged what he'd seen, misheard that news report. He fumbled for the radio, making a deal with himself: if it wasn't mentioned on the next news bulletin, then he'd imagined it. It hadn't happened. But if it was . . .

Almost at once, the time was given: 8.45am. Fifteen minutes to wait. After emptying his bladder, he registered how ravenous he was, having not eaten anything since a sandwich at lunchtime yesterday. He unpacked the food items from his backpack and wolfed a couple of cereal bars while the kettle boiled for a cup of black Nescafé. His knee had swollen and he took a couple of Nurofen with the coffee. Still hungry, he peeled an orange. As his fingers dug through the pith to the juice, he recoiled at the scent, rich and sickening, thinking of the blood he'd seen – not just seen, *touched*. This prompted him to pull his damp clothes from the washing machine and drape them over the radiator to dry. Good, he could see no spots or stains. Then he remembered his shoes and, with a stutter of panic in his chest, took them to the sink to scrub them.

It was at this point that the news came on:

'Police have launched a murder inquiry following the discovery of a woman's body yesterday near her home in Silver Vale, South London. We have this from Lydia Timpson at the scene . . .'

Rick dropped the shoe in his hand and sat down at the table, his whole body trembling. The reporter came on, urgent and grave:

'Emergency services were in attendance in this normally peaceful street from seven o'clock last night and there remains a visible police presence this morning. The name of the victim has not been released and we think this may be because her family have not yet been notified. What police have said is that they've launched a murder inquiry and believe they have a very clear lead to pursue.'

As the newscaster moved on to the next item, Rick turned off the radio, his palms damp. He had to accept this now, denial would achieve nothing. A murder inquiry – already? But of course, injuries like the ones Marina had suffered, they couldn't have been self-inflicted or caused by an accident. And he had to assume the police knew she *was* Marina Stanley, even if they weren't yet naming her. Not only had he identified her himself, but there would also have been mail and other documents in the house, perhaps even the passport and birth certificate she had been in the process of retrieving.

Family not yet notified ... Did that mean her parents? If the latter, it might explain the delay, since they'd been estranged from their daughter for almost a decade. Did Drew know where to reach them? Had he even met them? Despite her having cut herself off, wouldn't a husband be curious to meet his in-laws at least once, if only to confront them about their mistreatment of their daughter?

As for the police's 'clear lead', even without Rick's allegation, there could surely be no doubt in their minds that Drew was responsible for this horrific crime. They'd have taken one look at her, consulted their stats about domestic violence, and thought, *Where's the husband?*

Already in a cell, if there was any justice in the world, but just as likely at large, the police on his tail.

Rick hungered for more detail, but it had happened too late for the story to have made the morning papers – doubtful, in any case, that it would be covered by the nationals – and the next radio bulletin simply replayed the earlier segment. But as the caffeine and painkiller flooded his system, he began to feel clear-headed enough to reconstruct events for himself.

As he'd half-suspected, Drew's stag weekend must have been a ruse, not to cover up his philandering but because, either owing to a leak of some sort on her part or to his own sinister surveillance, he had been fully aware of his wife's plot to leave. He'd come home before her and concealed himself as she came through the door.

What next? If he was already there, then the alarm must have been off: had she paused at that anomaly, perhaps convincing herself that they'd forgotten to turn it on that morning? Or had she panicked and raced to the study, begun tearing things out of the desk drawers, sticking to the agreed plan but with none of the rehearsed methodical cool?

About then, Drew must have made himself known. They'd argued and, at some point, she'd made a run for it, abandoning all thoughts of luggage and instinctively choosing the escape route of their original plans (if only she'd used the front door instead!). Somehow, she'd got the kitchen door open without harm – Rick could not remember seeing any signs of disturbance in the kitchen – but Drew was close behind, pursuing her, grabbing something as he went, something heavy and lethal enough to break a person's skull. Had she screamed? How could it be that no one had come to her aid as a violent abuser chased her across her lawn and up the bank? The injuries Rick had seen could not have been the result of a single strike and it was his guess that Drew had brought her down with the first blow, then added to it when she was defenceless, even unconscious, charged with a savage anger, unable to stop.

He'd then left by the track himself, taking his weapon with him, out of sight of housewives and returning commuters. He must have gone towards the Surrey Road end, because Rick would not have missed him exiting the Long Lane way – he might even have encountered him on the path.

Which delivered him to a harrowing realization: if he'd gone with Marina, rather than waiting in the car, or if he'd waited on the track behind her house, or simply mobilized a few minutes earlier than he did, he might have saved her life.

Or wound up dead next to her.

Feeling nausea rise once more, he dashed to the bathroom and threw up in the toilet. The burn in his throat from the acid momentarily distracted his brain from the ache in his chest, and, moments later, the pain caused by his first mouthful of vodka continued the job. It wasn't even 10am, but at least he now knew how he would spend the rest of the day.

*

He woke on Sunday morning to the sound of knuckles rapping on the door. His first thought was it was Marina. This would go on, he suspected, morning after morning, his faith in her kept cruelly alive.

Thanks to the vodka binge, his head felt horrendous, an exploding battery of pain.

'Hello there? Gary?'

'Who is it?' Rick eased the door open a crack to reveal a rangy, long-legged man in tracksuit bottoms and a T-shirt. Of course, the building manager. He must have come to check if they were safely installed. What was his name again?

'Sam,' the guy supplied, offering an empathetic smile that made Rick's heart squeeze. Here was someone who still thought Marina was safe, who viewed himself – and Rick – as being on the side of the angels.

'I'm not normally here on Sundays, but there's been a leak in one of the other flats and I thought I'd just check you arrived okay. I did knock yesterday, but there was no reply.'

Rick tried to look grateful. 'Everything's fine, yes. Thank you.'

'Your friend all right, is she?'

'Yes,' Rick said, 'she's in the bathroom.' It wasn't possible to see from the door that the bathroom door was half-open, the space empty. 'It's really kind of you to stop by. And to rent us the place short-term. I know you usually ask for six months. Thank you.' He was starting to babble, snapped his teeth to shut himself up.

'Well, just come and find me if there's anything you need. You remember where the office is? Basement, by the stairs.'

'Yes. Thank you.' Rick bade him farewell, listening for the opening and closing of the fire door at the end of the corridor before heading to the bathroom to shower.

As the adrenaline of the encounter subsided, he was filled with a sense of hopelessness. All at once, he saw how naïve his thinking had been. Disappearing from a crime scene like that had not removed him from attention: how could the police *not* be interested in locating the witness who'd phoned 999 and declared himself able to identify the killer? And they recorded those calls, didn't they? Even if Drew was on the run and unable to point them towards Rick, plenty of other people might have the tape played to them and recognize his voice. Drew's assistant in the shop, for one. And any colleague of Marina's might offer up his name or, at the very least, mention her closeness to some guy on the fourth floor. *They've been going for lunch together every day for months …*

What would the police do next? If they went to the Camden flat, Rollo would tell them what he thought to be the truth: that Rick had left on Friday afternoon for Heathrow and a flight to India to start a two-month transfer from his London office. Rollo could vouch for this personally, tell them about their farewell curry on Thursday, even show them the note Rick had left. And yet the most cursory of checks with B&F (not to mention the airlines) would contradict this claim and show Rick to be a liar and a deceiver. He'd in fact just split up with Marina, Si might explain, and at *her* behest, not his …

The same man whose previous girlfriend had called the police when they'd argued over their break-up.

Oh, God.

There were fewer news bulletins on the radio on Sundays and, since none included an update from Silver Vale, he realized he was going to have to wait till the following afternoon when the *Evening Standard* came out to see the full horror of the situation.

See if he hadn't unwittingly made every one of his own actions look criminal.

28

Rick

September 1995

By Monday morning, he felt as if he'd been in solitary confinement for three weeks, not three days. When he caught sight of himself in the bathroom mirror, he looked atrocious: hunted, haunted – and still suffering the ravages of that litre of vodka on Saturday. But his isolation had to come to an end, not only for his excursion to buy the *Standard*, but also because he needed food.

And the shopping would have to be low budget, since he couldn't risk advertising his location by using his cashpoint card, which meant he had only the cash in his wallet until he thought of a way of acquiring more. The thought of his and Marina's £2,000 still sitting in her bag – presumably now in the possession of the police – was bad enough, but a new theory had surfaced overnight that was even less palatable: what if Drew had seen her fetch her bag from its hiding place and, after killing her, gone back into the house and taken it with him? Removed all evidence of her having tried to leave and in the process taken Rick's hard-earned cash, cash that might at this very moment be funding the killer's fugitive needs.

But no, if he was going to hold on to his sanity, he had to trust that the police had, or soon would have, Drew in custody, and that the cash would only strengthen an already convincing case against him.

He'd packed a plain black fleece and baseball cap for forays into the outside world and he put these on now. Good, he thought, with another glance in the mirror, he looked nothing like the man he'd been before last Friday.

He locked up and took the stairs to the ground floor, nerves rising with every step of the descent. This was the West End, he reminded himself. So long as he kept a lid on his emotions, he'd be unmemorable, anonymous.

Navigating the slipstream of office workers and tourists, he reached the small Tesco on Goodge Street and took a basket from the stack by the door. Never in his life had he been less interested in what he should eat; it was fuel and he'd take no pleasure in it – unlike the new bottle of vodka he picked up at the till with his cigarettes. Smoking wasn't allowed in the flat, so he lit up in the street using Marina's Zippo, the act creating a brief connection with his old self, with *her*, and bringing hot tears to his eyes.

On Tottenham Court Road, at the entrance to Goodge Street tube, the first edition of the *Evening Standard* was on sale and, almost dizzy with trepidation, he paid the 30p for his copy. Dropping his bag of groceries to his feet, he scanned the pages in the street, grateful, at least, that the murder hadn't made the front page.

He found the report several pages in:

VICTIM NAMED IN
SILVER VALE MURDER

The woman found dead in Silver Vale on Friday evening has been identified as Marina Stanley, 28. Police confirmed she lived with her husband on Exmoor Gardens, close to the spot where her body was discovered. The couple have no children.

Mrs Stanley was the victim of 'a brutal and depraved attack', a police spokesman said.

Rick broke off to examine the single image that accompanied the story. He'd braced himself for the experience of seeing the pixelated face of his lover, perhaps stamped with the word *victim* or *slain*, but was presented instead with a shot of her covered body being removed from the property.

Oh, Marina!

He didn't realize his cry was audible until he became aware of passers-by glancing his way, and, berating himself, he scooped up his shopping and hastened back to Newman Street. As soon as he'd locked the door behind him, he poured himself a half-tumbler of vodka, added a splash of orange, and read the rest of the piece:

At the weekend, locals spoke of their shock at the loss of a well-loved neighbour. 'No one can believe this has happened,' said Louisa Rippon, 36. 'She was so young. Only the other night she dropped everything to babysit my kids for me when I had a family emergency. She was like that, always the first to help out.'

'I spoke to her several times over the summer,' said Cordelia Smyth, 51, of neighbouring Pleasance Road. 'She was always so cheerful. We all thought she was such a beautiful, stylish girl.'

Rick read the descriptions a second time. 'Well-loved', well, of course she was. In spite of her marital troubles, Marina had been kind and fun-loving, a beautiful soul. And twenty-eight? She'd lied about her age then, told him she was twenty-five. Not that that mattered now. The girl he'd been waiting for all his life, who he'd known for so brief a time, had been taken from him, and he would never see her, speak to her, touch her again. All their shared dreams remained just that, sealed in the past.

How could life be this cheap, this easy for a bad man to steal?

As he grew heavy with the alcohol, he found himself staring at the photo until it blurred into something from a newspaper decades ago. He thought of Marilyn Monroe and all the other goddesses who'd left their homes on stretchers, their faces covered.

The men they left behind with blood on their hands.

*

He hadn't intended making a phone call, but coming to from a semi-conscious fugue, he felt that old restlessness, the compulsion to act in some way, to get his thoughts circulating. It was almost dark by now, safer to venture out.

He put the cap back on and took the stairs again. On the ground floor, two Japanese students were waiting for the lift; he avoided eye contact. Outside, the evening traffic was thickening, late workers drifting down Charlotte Street towards Soho. Carefree faces were alien to him now; the thought of going for a drink with colleagues and picking over the injustices of the day felt like an experience deep in the past, never to be revisited.

When he saw the empty phone box, he fished reflexively for change. The first coin he found was a twenty pence piece. He gripped the receiver, greasy from the fist of the previous user, and punched in the number of the Camden flat.

'Hello?' There was an unmistakable wariness to the answering tone.

'Rollo?'

'Rick? Thank fuck! Where are you? You arrived okay, obviously?'

The question threw Rick momentarily, but then he remembered he was supposed to be in Mumbai. 'I . . .' He couldn't form the words. It felt like months since he'd communicated with another human.

'Have you . . . have you seen the news about Marina Stanley?' Rollo said.

'I have.' Rick paused, suffering a fresh punch of pain at the way Rollo used her surname – so formal, as if it were already consigned to a gravestone, her life a statistic. 'I can't believe it,' he choked. 'I honestly can't believe it.'

'I know. It's completely horrific. When did you find out? Is it in the news over there, then?'

'It's . . . I don't know, I just . . .' This incoherence was getting him nowhere and he rallied. 'Drew must have done it, the fucking evil bastard.'

'He's certainly the obvious suspect,' Rollo said. 'But they haven't mentioned any arrest, at least not that I've heard.'

'He must be on the run. He'll be miles away by now, maybe out of the country.'

There was a pause. 'I'm not sure about that, Rick.'

'Why? What's happened?' As his social antennae twitched to life, he sensed his friend holding back. 'Please, tell me.'

'Okay, well, the police phoned here earlier and it seems they've already spoken with him.'

Rick's heartrate began speeding. 'I don't understand. You mean they *have* got him?'

'They've *spoken* to him, definitely, and he's told them she was having an affair with you, which is why they've rung here.'

'But why haven't they arrested him?'

'I don't know.' There was a pause. 'I'm sorry, mate, but I had to confirm that you knew her. Loads of people saw her with you here, so it would just've made it worse to lie. Fucking rozzers, you know how they twist stuff you say.'

Fuck. He'd craved fresh information, but now he had it

his brain couldn't process it. Did the police know that he was the one who'd made the 999 call? That he'd been in the Stanleys' house? At the pips, he fumbled to find more coins. 'What do you mean, "twist"? What else did they say? Think, Rollo, it's important.'

'Just that they want you to contact them as soon as possible.' Rollo made a game attempt to make this sound like an everyday request, no big deal. 'And they want to come round and look through your stuff. I'm not sure I have a choice about that, do I? Is there anything you want me to get rid of?'

'What?' Rick felt a tightening in his chest. 'No! Why?'

'No reason, I don't know, I just thought I'd check. Look, I know you must be devastated, but I think you should phone them right away. They left me a number – have you got a pen?'

'I haven't, I—'

'What time is it there, anyway?'

But Rick couldn't handle any more of this. 'Look, I need to think. I'll call you back, okay? I'll get the number then.'

But as he lifted the receiver from his ear, Rollo continued to speak, his voice more urgent: 'Wait, Rick, don't go. Do you think you ought to come back? Will you be able to change your flight?' Was it his imagination or was there a sense that his friend was firing out questions in the hope of an answer, any answer, so long as he kept him on the line? Rick had seen this in police dramas when they were using equipment to trace calls.

He hung up.

He smoked a cigarette as he paced back to his block. It

couldn't be right, could it? Drew in touch with the police but not under arrest; Rick already identified as Marina's lover, his home to be searched. By the time he'd returned to the flat and sunk more of the vodka, he was absolutely certain Rollo must have misunderstood. Rick's name must have been extracted from Drew in the interview room, his attendance requested as a formality in confirming the husband's guilt.

He decided to wait for the next day's paper. Everything would make sense then.

*

He was already there when the *Standard* guy was setting up. *Union Halts Tube Strike*, screamed the headline. Mindful of his public display of anguish the day before, he waited this time until he was back in his room before studying the coverage. He caught his breath in horror to see it sharing space with the O. J. Simpson trial.

The reporting was more substantial today, the crime team having hit their stride:

HUSBAND 'TORN APART' BY SILVER VALE SLAYING

The husband of the woman found bludgeoned to death in Silver Vale has spoken of his grief following her murder near the house they'd shared throughout their seven-year marriage. Drew Stanley, speaking from his sister's home in Colliers Wood where he is being assisted by victim support officers, gave a

brief statement about the murder that has devastated
a community:

'While my wife's family and I have had our world
torn apart by the death of our beloved Marina, we gain
strength from helping the police with their mission to
bring the killer to justice. We appeal to anyone who
was in Silver Vale last Friday between 6pm and 8pm
and who may have noticed something out of place to
come forward without delay.'

Rick's guts churned. So Rollo had not misunderstood. Far
from languishing in a police cell, Drew Stanley was evidently
talking to reporters, working with the police, which meant
he'd somehow got himself an alibi. How the hell had he
managed that?

He couldn't bring himself to read a sidebar headed 'Very
Much in Love', in which friends of the couple spoke of how
happy the Stanleys had been together. *Yeah, right*. It was
amazing – no, *tragic* – how little the people closest to the
victim knew of her suffering.

He studied the photos: the picture researchers had been
busy and there were no fewer than four of Marina. One
showed her in a holiday snap, a pool in the background,
blonde bob sharp on her chin, black Wayfarers halfway down
her nose; the second pictured her in what Rick recognized as
one of the chairs on the couple's patio, glass of champagne
raised to the camera in celebration; the third was of her and
Drew on their wedding day.

In each of these three, it was hard to see her face clearly, but the fourth was different. It was a photo-booth shot, passport-style, in which she looked heartbreakingly young, her gaze holding that ambiguous quality you often found in the portraits of the departed, a kind of foreshadowing – as if they'd always known they wouldn't live long.

But none of this was the reason why Rick's heart kicked in his ribcage or why terror raged through every cell of him – deep, primal terror.

No, the reason was that the woman pictured, this Marina Stanley who her community mourned so effusively: he'd never seen her before in his life.

29

Alex

September, present

He heard the excitement before he saw what was happening. The sweet, feral chorus of young children, accompanied by the yapping of two Jack Russells on the Pleasance Road side, known thugs who had often tormented Olive in the street. He quickened his step, familiar enough now with the trail to recognize exactly where he was – passing 42 Exmoor Gardens.

He often took the trail route home these days rather than strolling up the street as he used to. Unexpectedly, having spent years behaving as if he'd be electrocuted if he so much as set foot up here, he was now experiencing the opposite, the need to patrol. No, not *patrol*, that was too officious; it was more a sense of confirming to himself on a daily basis that the trail was open, the builders and the archaeologists and the reporters had all come and gone, and yet *nothing bad had happened.*

Not only that, but the ancestry business had also failed to bring the police to his door. Even if they *did* have access to these private companies' data, which, having triple-checked the terms and conditions of the transaction, he wasn't clear they did, it was hardly going to be feasible to cross-reference every participating citizen's DNA with that of every unidentified case in the history of crime. The scale was insane. No, they'd need to be actively seeking a match and all common sense suggested that the only case that mattered to him was not an active one.

So, if these early-evening turns down the trail had become a ritual – okay, an addiction – then what the hell. It was nobody else's business.

Once, he'd been coming down the Long Lane steps when he'd seen Beth in their tiny front garden, trimming their laurel, and there'd been a peculiar moment when they'd looked at each other across the street as if they'd never met before.

'You look like you've seen a ghost,' she said when he reached their gate.

He laughed it off. 'Funny, I was thinking the same.'

'Did you come from the station?'

'Yes, I often cut along the trail. I like it, it's peaceful.'

'I *told* you you'd like it, Alex!'

That was when he'd heard a low groan and Zara had made herself known, seated on their little antique bench behind the hedge. She reached for Beth's hand to help her to her feet.

'Careful people don't think you're some kind of

prowler,' she said, with the playful air she often assumed in front of Beth.

'Alex,' Beth warned, pre-emptively, though it was Zara who was doing the baiting, not him. It must have been after their ancestry row, then, for that was when it had become unequivocal that his wife took her friend's side over his in any altercation.

'I'll prowl wherever and whenever I choose,' he said, eyeballing Zara with what he hoped was a good dash of intimidation.

She did something then that she'd never done before in his presence: slid up her top to reveal a small section of skin, holding his eye as she did. Beth must have told her what he'd said about the prosthetic – or she'd been eavesdropping. It was ages ago now, but clearly this was someone who didn't forget a slight, who took pleasure in the long game.

Reaching now the source of the fun on the trail, he found a whole gaggle of kids, quickly identifying among them the three blond ones who lived in the Stanleys' old house – Frankie's boys. They were petting a dog – wait, not petting, poking, urging. Urging it to dig.

And not just any dog but *his*, Olive. How had she been allowed out of the cottage? They had no side gate, so it had to have been via the front door. Once free, she must have followed old scents of her master up the steps to the trail and gravitated to the spot where he'd stood multiple times, looking down at the garden to number 54. Bloodhounds could scent their owner hours after they'd passed through a place; how did a collie cross score?

'Hey, Olive,' he yelled. '*Stop that!*'

She lifted her head and swung her tail to acknowledge her friend, before returning to the job in hand. He took a grip of her collar and dragged her away. 'What's going on here?' he asked the kids sternly, and they answered in a clamour:

'She won't stop digging!'

'She thinks there's something under there!'

'A bone, we thought!'

'Or gold coins!'

Christ, this was like *Scooby-Doo*.

'Dogs aren't allowed up here and this is the reason why! They want to dig holes to get to old smells, and you could trip in the hole and break your ankle. Come on, everyone, help me stamp the soil back down. You don't want the trail closed because you've made a mess of it, do you?'

They followed his lead in flattening the loose earth until it was compacted to his satisfaction.

'Good job, guys! And remember, if you see a dog up here, shoo it off, okay? We have to stick to the rules if we want to keep enjoying the trail. Well done!'

Their little faces flushed with the glow of his praise – they weren't bad kids – they scattered before he could issue any further orders.

He didn't have Olive's lead, but she trotted by his side as he moved on, regularly glancing up at him the way she did to check she'd understood the directive correctly. Back on Long Lane, he found their front door wide open, Beth and Zara in the kitchen, heads bent over a laptop. They both started slightly at his arrival.

'Did you not notice the front door was open? Olive escaped!'

'Oh, I didn't see,' Beth said. 'I *thought* it was a bit chilly.'

'That must have been me,' Zara said. 'I just came back from Samira's and mustn't have closed the door properly. Sorry. Is Olive okay?'

He bristled at her faux concern. 'Well, obviously. You can see that for yourself. But she *could* have been run over.' Glimpsing the laptop screen on the table between them, he froze: *Silver Vale Murder*. Oh God, what was this? Was that pale-haired woman in the photo Marina Stanley? Then Zara stooped slightly to pet Olive, cooing her apologies, and he saw that what it actually said was *Silver Vale Mothers* and the image was of a pregnant woman.

'I feel terrible,' Zara said. 'Let me give her a treat to—'

'No,' Alex interrupted, sounding more petulant than he'd intended. 'You don't treat animals for breaking rules and putting themselves in danger.'

The women exchanged a look.

'Whatever you say,' Zara said.

'I've got some exciting news, Alex,' Beth said, with the unsinkable cheer of a primary school teacher galvanizing a shy child. Since the ancestry debacle, she'd taken to presenting new information to him like this, ideally with a witness present. 'Zara's asked me to be her partner at her antenatal classes. They start next week.'

'Right,' he said.

'You're very welcome to join us, Alex,' said Zara. 'I wouldn't want you to feel left out.'

'Alex?' Beth prompted.

'Thanks,' he said coolly, 'but I think I'll pass.'

Shaken by his misinterpretation of the web page – God, was he having hallucinations now? – not to mention the scare of the incident on the trail, he left the two of them to their antenatal scheming and shut himself in the living room with a beer.

After a few minutes of profitless contemplation, he got up from the sofa and plucked a book from a high shelf of old novels: Wilkie Collins' *The Woman in White*. He'd owned it since his days in Albert Street and it had accompanied him from address to address in the years since.

For an unstrung moment he thought he might have mislaid the item he kept pressed between its pages – or, far worse, that it had somehow been discovered by Zara, drawn to the classics during her time off work – but, no, here it was, as yellow as old parchment:

The only cutting he'd kept from the Marina Stanley murder coverage.

Private Funeral for Marina Stanley, read the headline to a brief, respectful report of the occasion. Alongside the once-familiar headshot was a picture of her gravestone in the Surrey cemetery where she'd been laid to rest. He'd never visited it, though he'd considered doing so once or twice.

He peered at the image of the engraved words, pale on the new stone:

MARINA LOIS STANLEY
BELOVED SISTER, DAUGHTER
& GRANDDAUGHTER
MAY YOU REST IN GRACE AND LOVE

He thought of all those lives altered by this young woman's terrible and untimely death. One spent in prison; another – his own – in a perpetual, erosive holding pattern; and at least one other taken along with her.

And yet we never even knew you, Marina, did we?

30

Rick

September 1995

It took several minutes for the shaking to subside. For his heart to cease its diabolical pounding and his mind to begin to recalibrate. He had never in his life known discombobulation like this. What the fuck was going on? Who was this woman in the photos? And what had happened to *his* Marina?

On this last, well, the immediate, perverse, euphoria-inducing conclusion was that she must still be alive. The woman he had met in the lobby of their Victoria Street offices and fallen in love with, the woman whose escape he had plotted, who had kissed him goodbye last Friday, *she was alive*! And yet ... and yet the ecstasy of this miracle was counteracted by the bleakest of instincts: for a misunderstanding of this magnitude to have taken place, she must have got caught up in something very dark indeed, something that had put her in almost as much danger as the woman in the photos.

The woman in the *mortuary*.

Feeling an itching sensation in his lungs, he located his inhaler, fetched a glass of water, and returned to the same spot.

Start again, Rick.

Start with the facts.

What do you know that is real and undisputed?

A woman had been killed, *that* was real. He'd seen her poor, mutilated body with his own eyes and she had been formally identified soon after as Marina Stanley of 54 Exmoor Gardens, Silver Vale. There could be no question of mistaken identity on the part of the police, and it was surely impossible for the body to have been substituted, which meant the misconception was Rick's and Rick's alone. The photos made it clear that the victim was of a similar build and colouring to the woman he *did* know, similar enough for him to have assumed it was her. She had the same pale skin and fair hair. She'd worn the same, or at least similar, clothes.

But he had not seen her face. He may have caught the curve of an ear in that horrible bloody mess, but she had been lying face down and he had not moved her head, only gently touching her neck in search of a pulse.

The memory of her blood, slimy on his fingers, brought a convulsion to his throat and he gulped his water in an attempt to subdue it.

Rereading the main report – ambushed as he had been

by those pictures, he'd only skimmed the first paragraphs – he progressed to a passage that offered further facts about the victim:

Daughter of Gerald and Sally Jenkins of Farnham, Surrey, and sister to Tobias, Marina married Drew Stanley in 1990 and worked in a succession of executive jobs before leaving three months ago to focus on starting a family. Granddaughter of Harry Jenkins, founder of the high street stationery chain, she is said to have had considerable personal wealth and one theory the police are considering is that the attack may have been a burglary that went awry.

'We are exploring the possibility that the intruder expected the house to be empty and was disturbed by the presence of Mrs Stanley,' a police spokesman said. 'The fact that Mr Stanley had plans for a weekend break may suggest the killer was privy to this information and had expected Mrs Stanley to be with her husband on the trip.'

Close friend Tilly Lister, 29, who was at Bristol University with Marina and now lives in the capital, spoke today of her heartbreak at the news of her friend's death. 'From the moment we met in our student hall of residence, I knew we were going to be lifelong friends. I'm totally devastated that her life has been cut short, and in such a horrible and violent way.'

Considerable personal wealth. A university education. Old friends and doting relatives, including a brother. Even without the photos, it would have been clear from today's coverage that the victim was a different woman from the one Rick had known. As for the grief-stricken husband . . .

Drew bloody Stanley, he thought, burning with hatred, for the only conviction that had remained unshakeable in the last ten minutes was that Drew was guilty of attacking his wife – even if that wife had been an entirely different woman from the one Rick had been defending. He'd swear on his own life that the man he'd met was capable of killing.

His eye tracked back to the phrase *'burglary that went awry'*. He'd seen no signs of forced entry, but then he hadn't been looking for them, he'd simply rushed in to get to a phone. And while he'd had a general sense that the furniture was undisturbed, he'd never been in the house before and was in no position to judge if anything was missing.

But wait, there was the drawer, the drawer that *his* Marina had been supposed to break into. Of course, her talk of taking back a confiscated passport had now to be treated as fiction, but there'd been that heap of papers, hadn't there – might the drawer have been forced open by someone else? Had it contained valuables of a different sort?

A new thought burst then – something to do with that confrontation with Drew Stanley in his office – but it slithered from his grasp before he could get a fix on it.

Only when he'd put the paper aside did he give full rein to the soaring hope that the woman he loved might still be alive. *Must* be, for it couldn't possibly be the case that *both* women were dead, could it? Squeezing his eyes shut, he strove to recapture her the last time he'd seen her. She'd got out of the car and hurried to the corner, sending a last look his way, then she'd turned from Long Lane onto Exmoor Gardens and vanished from his life.

Had *anyone* seen her as she walked to – or past – the Stanleys' house? He had a mind-bending vision of her knocking at the door of number 54 and it being answered by the real Marina, both women in the same dress, the same shoes.

No, it was too fantastical, like something dreamed up by David Lynch.

But why would a woman say she was someone she was not? Why would she create a whole fictitious story of a marriage and then disappear? Surely her unfathomable actions had nothing to do with the attack on the real Marina Stanley?

And yet, how could they *not*?

Start again. He breathed very deeply and summoned once more the evidence of his own eyes. Not that last time, but all the times before. What had been real about *his* Marina?

The bruises had been real – and the fear. *Someone* had been hurting her, most likely Stanley, who Rick knew for certain she was involved with since he'd seen her get into the man's car that awful Sunday in Albert Street. And her job had been real. He'd seen her in that meeting room at Culkins, impassive as she took notes, every inch the temp counting down to the day she moved on to something better.

Except, she'd told him her work was a lifeline, a big deal for her, a taste of normal life. That had struck him as a genuine sentiment. Had she actually left her job last Friday? Yes, she'd come out of the building with a balloon, talking of a cake, but he understood now that nothing that day had been as it seemed. For all he knew, she might still be there, in her temping job, paid by the hour! Had she used the name Marina Stanley at work? Had *he* ever used it with a third party at Culkins? Thanks to the firm's hard line on personal phone calls, she had always called him, snatching moments when her manager was out of earshot. Well, if she *was* still there and going by that name, then it surely must be attracting remarks about her murdered namesake in the papers.

His heart smacked in his ribcage as it occurred to him what he should do next. He checked his watch – past the end of office hours, but there were always people working overtime, someone who might field a stray late call – and raced out to the phone box. He knew the switchboard number for Culkins by heart and tapped it out at double speed.

'Culkins Insurance, how may I help?'

'Extension 139, please.'

As the ring sounded, he was overpowered by a sense of unreality. Was this really him, right here, right now, in hiding from an enemy he couldn't even define? Or was he some marionette now, his every move choreographed, all free will removed? He counted fifteen rings and then redialled the main number. 'I'm trying to get hold of one of your staff. Her extension's 139, but no one's answering.'

'That's the temps' desk,' came the reply. 'They'll all have left at five. I think the office manager's working late, though, let me try her for you.'

A new voice came on. 'Caroline Pierce, how can I help you?'

'Hi,' Rick said. 'I need to get in touch with one of your temps, Marina. It's quite urgent.'

'Sorry, there's no Marina here.'

'I think she's probably left, but I was hoping you might have a forwarding number for her.'

'A forwarding number?' A note of impatience entered the woman's voice: 'As I said, there's no Marina working here. I've personally hired all the temps we've had in the last two years and I'd definitely know.'

Well, at least that was *one* question answered, for what it was worth. 'Can I ask the names of the temps you *have* had then? This girl I need to contact, she started with you in May, I'm not sure of the exact date.' His mind seized on a detail. 'She had a wall hanging by her desk with sunflowers on it. I gave it to her!'

'Employees aren't allowed to put up their own decorations, so I don't think so. Besides, I can't give you information about members of staff, even those who've left. Personnel details are confidential. Who's calling, please?'

'I'd rather not say,' he said, hearing the desperation in his own voice, and there was an answering sigh, a subtle alteration of mood; she took him for some hapless admirer, he guessed. Calls along these lines were perhaps common when one employed attractive young females, maybe even the use of false names too.

'Sorry I can't be of more help, but it's strict policy,' she said, with a touch of humanity that struck him deep in his core, and though he knew he should be extending the discussion, breaking down her defences to get to some potential names, he found he was too choked with emotion to continue.

He offered a few tight words of thanks and ended the call.

*

Another evening of radio, vodka and regrets, of falling asleep in inebriated denial. Normally he woke up hungover and hopeless, but this time was different, for he had the instant feeling of having secured that elusive but crucial thought from the day before:

The photo.

The photo Drew Stanley had taken from his desk drawer at Floors Galore had been of *Rick's* Marina, not the Marina in the newspaper – there'd been no sunglasses or hair obscuring her eyes to cast doubt on it. Which meant his Marina had been on holiday with him; they'd been, most likely, lovers.

Which led inescapably to the conclusion that Drew Stanley was behind this impersonation of hers and all that had taken place last Friday had been the result of careful planning, as careful as Rick's and Marina's own. Marina Stanley had been murdered in cold blood and there could be only one reason why they'd drawn Rick into it . . .

Oh, God.

A man could bury his head in the sand for only so long before he had to come up for air, and by the time he'd walked to the tube for the day's *Standard*, he could have predicted the headline before he saw it, scrawled in thick black on the board:

LOUISE CANDLISH

'STALKER' SOUGHT IN
SILVER VALE KILLING

Buying his copy, Rick saw at once that the story had made it
to the front page, which displayed a photofit of said suspect.
A photofit that looked an awful lot like him.

31

Rick

September 1995

He'd been set up. *Of course* he had.

And he'd known it from the moment he'd dialled 999 from the Stanleys' phone and refused to give his name – why else but for self-preservation would he have made such a deviant move?

Heart thudding and swooping, frighteningly arrhythmic, he dipped into the nearest alleyway to skim the main article:

MARINA WAS STALKED
SAYS BEREFT HUBBY

Police have today issued a photofit of the suspect they are seeking in the Silver Vale murder. The man, believed to be in his mid-twenties, was seen with Marina Stanley in the vicinity of Exmoor Gardens less than an hour before her body was found.

The announcement comes after her husband told police that an admirer she'd met when working in Central London had turned into a terrifying stalker. 'He worked nearby and always seemed to be passing when she was leaving her building. One time he even followed her into the lift and grabbed her – she had this horrible bruise on her arm. I told her she should report him to security, but she didn't want to. She felt sorry for him and didn't want to get him into trouble.'

Though Mrs Stanley's most recent employer, Ruckus Media, has stated that staff were unaware of any harassment on office premises and no formal complaint was made, Drew Stanley says it was typical of his wife not to make a fuss. 'She would have given this guy the benefit of the doubt,' he claims.

He now fears Marina paid for her kindness with her life. 'He could easily have found out where she lived, he only had to follow her home. She always took the same train from Waterloo.'

'With this new information, we're confident we are getting closer to the truth of what happened to this poor young woman in the hours before her death,' a police spokesman confirmed.

Rick's vision began to fog at the edges. What the hell was happening here? Drew Stanley was merging details from the lives of the real and fake Marinas to create a single fictional history – and evidently had the police and press eating out of his hand.

He read on:

> Distraught Drew says he deeply regrets signing up for his weekend away with pals as he reveals details of the fateful day for the first time. 'It was a crazy busy afternoon, I was overcommitted. I'd arranged to interview a potential new member of staff near Victoria Station at 5.45pm so I could hop straight on the train afterwards, and it was a bit of a mad dash. I made the train by the skin of my teeth.
>
> 'Me and my mates had just got to our hotel and were checking in when my pager went. It was my next-door neighbour, saying I needed to get in touch with the police and come straight home. An officer came to the hotel and I just couldn't accept what she was saying. I was in total shock.'
>
> To the devoted husband's horror, his return to Silver Vale would involve the formal identification of his wife's body. 'I keep thinking if only I'd cancelled the weekend away, I might have been there when this lunatic broke in. I'll never forgive myself for not protecting her.'

Liar. The fact that he had a cast-iron alibi did not impress Rick – and he could only hope the police would blow it apart sooner rather than later. Who was this interviewee he'd met with and who vouched for his presence at 5.45pm? Was it Rick's Marina, lying through her teeth? Was she going to claim she'd gone straight from her office to this job interview? Oh God, if she was, then it would fit perfectly with her having been a temp who'd just that day finished her last gig.

No, the unavoidable truth was that she must have partnered with Drew Stanley to kill his wife, Rick could only suppose for her money, because the idea that *he* was the one with the money in the Stanley marriage was obviously horseshit. Every news report mentioned Marina's family wealth; Rick was in no doubt that, contrary to what his lover had insisted, the house had belonged to Marina, not Drew. Only the flooring business had been his and it had been in trouble.

And, however Drew had pulled it off, the police had bought into his claim of innocence. For him to be interviewed by a reporter like this, it had to be with official blessing. Everyone knew the police fed scraps to the press and public while withholding evidence, otherwise any attention seeker could claim themselves a witness – or even confess to the crime – based on intelligence in the public domain.

Reading the side column, Rick began to get an idea of how the stalker theory had gained traction:

'I MET MARINA'S STALKER'

The grieving widower's theory is sensationally backed up by the statement of a neighbour, who encountered a young stranger hanging around the street just weeks before the grisly killing. 'I was washing my car when I noticed him standing there, right by my gate, directly across from the Stanleys' house.

He was just staring, like he was in a trance. But the moment I tried to get any information out of him, he scarpered. I remember saying to my wife, it was like he was casing the joint. Now I wonder if it might have been more sinister than that.'

Could this *get* any worse?

He supposed at least they hadn't used a photo of him. They knew who he was – Drew had given his name, Rollo had told Rick that days ago – so it couldn't have been difficult to unearth a photograph. To withhold both his name and image like this, they must have *some* doubts. Might they be using a photofit to smoke out further witnesses? There'd be tried and tested method to this media manipulation.

Stuffing the paper under his arm, he strode back to Newman Street, his intestines knotting with anxiety. His new home was possibly the only element in this nightmare he could continue to depend on. For all their conspiring, neither Drew Stanley nor the fake Marina knew his hiding place, because Rick had never told her. They'd agreed – actually, *she'd* suggested – that it was safer for her not to know until the day itself. Well, now it was clear that she hadn't been interested because she'd never intended coming with him in the first place.

Except, wait . . . If he'd been framed, as he was certain he had, wouldn't it have made more sense for her to know the location in order to set the police on his tail? Was it possible that her passivity on this detail had been her way of helping him? Because there *had* been something between them, underneath all the lies and misdirection and subterfuge, something real on *her* part too – hadn't there?

How he despised himself for hoping.

*

Distasteful as it was, he was grateful that by the next day other deaths were more shocking than Marina Stanley's. A schoolgirl had been killed and police had arrested five youths in a dawn raid. It was the main story in all the papers, including the *Standard*.

Coverage of the Stanley case was down to page nine, but there was scant comfort in that demotion given the incendiary new content that ran alongside the now-familiar facial composite:

MARINA'S KILLER DROVE HER HOME

Following the release of a police photofit of the suspect sought for the murder of Marina Stanley, witnesses have come forward with sightings of a man believed to have been her stalker driving a white Ford Fiesta, with Mrs Stanley in the passenger seat. Police are investigating the theory that Marina accepted a lift from him in good faith, but that he later entered her residence via a disused railway track that runs behind the houses. Their search for the car, possibly a rental vehicle, continues and any information from the public is welcomed.

Rick felt his pulse erupt. The car! Somehow, in the bedlam of his mind, he'd managed to let it slip out of reach. Did this mean they'd found it and impounded it, begun scouring the interior for evidence? If not, and it remained where he'd left it in that mews in Marble Arch, the week's rental almost up, had his cursory clean-up been effective enough? The fact that it hadn't been the real Marina Stanley sitting in the passenger seat that Friday afternoon was scant consolation next to the catastrophic reality of his having touched the murder victim before driving away from Silver Vale. He'd literally had her blood on his fingers as he turned the key in the ignition and gripped the wheel. There'd be traces everywhere, surely.

After long deliberation, he decided to go and see for himself if it was there; if it was, he'd move it somewhere more desolate where he could clean it properly. If it wasn't – well, he wouldn't think about what *that* meant.

Studying the *A to Z*, he identified a stretch a mile or so north of King's Cross that he recalled being diverted along in a cab once: industrial buildings mainly, and pretty desolate. He'd aim for that. He slipped out to Oxford Street before the shops closed and bought gloves, disinfectant wipes, a small jiffy bag, pen and paper, and postage. Back in the studio, he addressed the jiffy bag, scribbled a note, and then set about making something to eat.

He'd need energy for the task ahead.

*

He waited till after dark to depart, by which time it was raining heavily. This was easily the farthest he'd roamed since moving to the unit and he was jittery at first, whirling at the sound of splashed footsteps behind, covering his face at every dazzle of oncoming headlights.

He saw the Fiesta from the entrance to the mews, exactly where he had left it, and he lingered for a few minutes to double-check that no one was watching from a parked vehicle or a window before he approached. Rain thundered down on the roof and bonnet as he strapped himself into the driver's seat. He thought he could detect the rusty, metallic smell of blood and rolled down the window, letting the downpour in. As he exited the mews, a light flared above garage doors, causing his foot to stutter on the pedal, but he kept his gaze trained ahead.

Snaking up towards Marylebone Road, he was unsettled by the amount of traffic so late, black cabs and buses backed up at red lights, the closing-time crowd stumbling and screeching on the pavements, but once past Euston towards King's Cross and up York Way into the wastelands near Caledonian Road, he calmed again. The location was ideal: no cameras, no houses, no curious eyes. He pulled up next to an ancient white van with two flat tyres – no one was coming for *that* tonight – before setting to work, using the wet wipes to scrub the interior, including the back seat and other spots he'd neglected the first time.

He'd also overlooked fake Marina's Coke can, he saw; it was still sitting in the cup holder behind the handbrake and, extracting it, he spilled a little of the liquid. Cursing his clumsiness, he was about to mop it up when he spied something glinting in the footwell of the left-hand rear seat and hooked it out: it was a woman's watch, stainless steel, set with what appeared to be diamonds. It took precisely ten seconds to guess that it belonged to the real Marina, planted by Drew's accomplice as evidence that she'd been in Rick's car – or perhaps to make it look as if Rick had stolen it from the house during his murderous spree and mislaid it in the chaos of his getaway. This made him think of the Zippo, which he'd assumed she'd dropped by accident. Had that been planted too? Had it once belonged to the real Marina, taken in and out of the Stanleys' house, her fingerprints all over it? All part of the trail of clues intended to lead to Rick's arrest.

If so, the level of detail in the conspirators' planning surpassed anything he'd feared.

Shaken, he ran a gloved hand under both seats to check for further smoking guns, before pocketing the watch and locking the car. As planned, he sealed the keys in the jiffy bag with the note about the vehicle's location, and posted it in the first postbox he passed. Then it was time for the trek back towards Goodge Street. He retraced his route down York Way to King's Cross, then zigzagged through Bloomsbury, past the university buildings, the dark offices and closed pubs. The entire time, the rain came down like a punishment. Spying a massive catering bin behind a pub, he disposed of the Coke can, gloves and used wipes. Ought he to get rid of the watch too, he wondered? Slip it down a drain or something? If so, now was the time to do so. On the other hand, it *did* look valuable. Could he risk visiting a pawn shop and topping up his rapidly vanishing cash reserves? He decided to keep it.

As he pounded, his damaged knee grinding unpleasantly in its socket, he felt the loosening of another memory to do with his new acquisition: that was right, *his* Marina had mentioned a watch, hadn't she? She'd said she'd sold one of Drew's to pay for her second passport. It was the passport, not the watch, that was the crucial detail for, given that she wasn't Marina after all, wasn't it likely that it hadn't been a fake one at all but her genuine and only version, in her bag that day for any number of reasons? That, when unexpectedly challenged by Rick, she'd simply improvised a story on the spot, one that dovetailed nicely with the rest of her charade?

If the abrupt boom of his heart was any guide, the answer was yes. The name he'd seen in that passport *had* belonged to her and was the key to finding her again.

The problem was, he couldn't for the life of him remember what it was.

32

Alex

September, present

'We got almost everything on the list,' Beth said. 'Honestly, you wouldn't believe all the kit you need for something that weighs about seven and a half pounds. That's the average, apparently,' she added.

'Right. Well, it sounds like you deserve a drink,' Alex said, slipping out of his jacket. The bar in the theatre was uncomfortably hot, its sealed Victorian windows foggy with breath, the staircases clogged with new arrivals, but any feelings of claustrophobia were overridden by the sheer liberation of being away from Silver Vale, from the cottage – from *Zara*. Not that there was much chance of forgetting about her entirely, since Beth was at that very moment detailing the baby shopping that had engaged the two women that afternoon.

'Where's she going to store it all?' he asked.

'We'll work it out. Bronwen's offered her garden shed, she's at number thirty-two Exmoor?'

'I know it, yeah.'

'But, look, I've got something to show you.' Beth reached for her handbag, placing it on the table with a thump, and he slid her wine glass to safety. 'A surprise.'

'Don't tell me. An analysis of my earwax? An X-ray of my genitals?'

'No, you can rest easy on both counts.' She laughed, a proper full-throated response, and he imagined her thinking to herself, This *is why I like you*. This *is why I married you*. She was still chuckling as she produced a magazine from her bag. One of the Harry Potter actors was on the front cover, he noticed, all grown up now and not nearly so appealing. Time was fucking unstoppable. 'It's an article about the opening of the trail.'

Draining his glass in a single swallow, Alex resurfaced with a bogus smile. 'Do we get a good review?'

'Really good. Not that we want a whole load of marauders turning up, but hopefully it will inspire other communities to redevelop wasteland.' She began leafing through the pages. 'She goes on about the Marina Stanley murder a bit, which isn't ideal, but interesting in a way to read it again. I'd completely forgotten about that suspect who went missing. It was in the *Standard* every day for, like, two weeks. It turned into this big man hunt. I wonder what happened to him.'

What the hell? Heat flooded his face. 'Oh, I imagine he's out there somewhere, trying to live a quiet life like the rest of us.' He fiddled with the stem of his empty glass, rolling it between his fingers and thumb. 'You not drinking that?'

She glanced up, saw him eye her full glass. 'Have some. The bell will go in a minute.'

He tipped half into his own glass and felt momentary solace. It was a little late in the game to notice, perhaps, but dangerous conversations always seemed to take place when he had a drink in his hand. Would the events that tyrannized him have unfolded differently if he'd been a lifelong teeto-taller, he wondered? (Who was he kidding, the answer was yes, without a shadow of a doubt. The things he'd done – the worst things – a sober person would have aborted, if not eliminated at the moment of conception.)

'Here it is,' Beth said. 'You look almost as if you're having a good time – that's what I call a talented photographer. I'll have to hire her for our tenth anniversary!'

Tenth anniversary? Jesus, another party. 'Let me see that!'

Distracted initially by the montage of press headlines from 1995 – *Suburb Rocked By Murder*; *Husband 'Torn Apart' by Silver Vale Slaying* – he focused on the image under Beth's finger, in which he was depicted helping Frankie and her son climb up the bank to the trail. *The long and short of it: locals lend a helping hand in their new community back yard*, read the caption, innocuously.

'Pink Hunters,' Beth said, rolling her eyes. 'For goodness' sake, Frankie always has to be so *cute*.'

But Alex had no interest in the colour of her wellies. He peered at the three faces in the picture: Frankie's and her son's were a little out of focus, but *his* was perfectly sharp, featuring a remarkably good-natured smile. Was it recognizable as him? More to the point, as the twenty-something him? A much-receded hairline had lengthened his forehead and weight gain blunted his jawline, but even so, could you tell?

Checking the front of the magazine, he almost had a stroke – it was the *Weekend* section of the *Guardian*. 'This is a national newspaper, Beth!'

'I know, and it's online as well. Amazing, isn't it? It's such a lovely tribute to the Trailblazers and everything we achieved. Dulcie's totally chuffed.'

'Well, I'm not.' He thrust the magazine back at her with more hostility than he'd intended. She was clearly startled, as were other theatre-goers, who frowned and looked away with that air of presumption that this would not escalate – not in a place of *culture*. 'I *expressly* said I didn't want to be in any press. I didn't sign any kind of release. This is a gross invasion of privacy. I'm going to talk to a lawyer.'

There was a beat of surprise before Beth burst out laughing. 'I think that's a bit of an overreaction, don't you? It's not like you're naked or snorting coke or doing anything that might damage your reputation. The opposite, you're being a good citizen, lending a hand. Anyway, we're all fair game now, I don't think signing a release is even a thing anymore.'

'It's a thing for me.'

As her laughter faded, her eyes narrowed. 'What's this about, Alex? Who's going to see it that you'd rather didn't? Come on, most people would be thrilled to see their face in a national newspaper.'

'Most people are narcissistic morons,' Alex snapped, 'like everyone else in this stupid feature.'

Beth raised her eyebrows. 'Well, I won't pass on your view to our neighbours, if that's all right with you. They might be just a *tiny* bit offended.'

He'd gone too far, he saw; he was losing his ability to rein in his anxiety before inciting a falling-out. 'Come on, Beth, I didn't mean you and Dulcie and everyone.'

'Who *did* you mean then?'

The five-minute bell rang then, prompting them to take their seats. Beth stalked ahead of him, almost as if she didn't know him.

Well, she was right about that, he thought.

33

Rick

September 1995

The next morning, fuelled by the mugs of black Nescafé and a multipack of the cereal bars that now constituted his diet, Rick spent a couple of hours scanning the handful of books he'd packed, plus his pile of *Standard*s, for female names that rang a bell. Though he could conjure the fake Marina's passport photo exactly – that sweet, trustful gaze – her name continued to elude him. Thwarted, he put on his cap and walked through the Oxford Street crowds to Books Etc, where he bought a baby name book. He then spent the hours until that day's *Standard* went on sale reading the entries.

It was only on a second rotation that he came to one in the Ks that jolted his memory:

> Of Scandinavian origin and meaning 'follower of Christ', Kirsten is a form of the name Christina and has long been popular in the UK, particularly in Scotland.

Kirsten, that was it! He was certain of it.

The surname he couldn't picture, but at least it was a start.

On his outing to buy the paper, he stopped at the phone box to ring Culkins a second time. Adopting a crisper tone than previously, he asked the receptionist to connect him to a temp named Kirsten.

'I'll need a surname.'

'I don't have it, but she's twenties, about five three, blonde, green eyes. Very pretty.'

'I think I know who you mean, but I'm fairly sure she's left the company. Let me put you through to the office manager and we can check.'

'Thank you.' He kicked himself for not having detailed a physical description last time – he might have saved himself three days.

The familiar voice of the office manager came on the line. 'Caroline Pierce here, you're looking for Kirsten, I hear? She's no longer on our books, I'm afraid. She left us last week.'

So that much was true. It made sense – at least something did – because she'd have guessed that once he understood he'd been scammed, the first place he'd try to find her would be her office. Would she also remember that he'd seen her name on her 'second' passport?

'That's what I thought,' he said, confident that this Caroline had not connected him with the lovelorn caller asking for Marina. 'Do you happen to have a contact number for her? I'm at B&F on the fourth floor and I'd like to offer her some admin work here.'

'I don't, I'm afraid, only an address.'

'Would it be possible to have that? Maybe we could send her a letter.'

'I'm afraid that's strictly confidential. I'm not sure you'd have much joy anyway, because she said she already had something lined up for after her holiday.'

Rick started. 'Holiday?'

'Yes, she was off to India, I think it was.'

India. He remembered the 'Bon Voyage' balloon. Instinct told him she'd simply borrowed for herself the cover story they'd created for him. He had no doubt now that the 'something' she'd lined up was with Drew Stanley; that non-existent job interview at Victoria Station. Or maybe, for authenticity, he'd actually offered her a position, the start date now on hold while he navigated the horrors of a police investigation into his wife's murder.

This manager was right: there was no joy ahead.

'Can I just ask, did she come to you via a temp agency?'

'No, I think she was recommended by a friend.'

Which Kirsten had told him herself, he now recalled; another dead end. 'I don't suppose you could just remind me of her surname? It's slipped my mind?'

He wasn't expecting her to oblige, but it seemed this was one bone she was willing to throw. 'McKenzie.'

Of course! Kirsten McKenzie – he remembered the pleasing alliteration of the Ks. As he ended the call, he thought of Si and his old colleagues at their desks four floors below Culkins. Had they made the connection between their old colleague and the photofit of London's Most Wanted? Or did they continue to picture Rick as carefree and sunburnt, making his odyssey through the subcontinent in a rickshaw?

His mind moved to Rollo, who'd innocently advised him to change his flight and come home. It was now four days since they'd spoken, with critical developments having been reported in the interim. He, surely, was following the story in the *Standard* and had seen from the photos that the Marina who had died was not the same woman Rick had dated. Had he told the police this crucial fact? Had he gone to them and insisted the victim had had nothing whatsoever to do with Rick?

If he had, then they had clearly not allowed it to get in the way of their theory, if today's edition was anything to go by, for Drew Stanley had been at it again. Rick could hardly bring himself to read the latest spin:

HUBBY OF SLAIN MARINA MET KILLER

It emerged today that the man police are searching for in their investigation into the murder of Marina Stanley could be the same person who threatened her husband at his place of work earlier in the summer. 'He was agitated, spouting gibberish about Marina,' Drew Stanley told our special correspondent. 'He had these delusions that she was in trouble and he was protecting her.'

Oh, God. And there'd been, of course, a witness to back his story up, the girl on the shop floor. Customers, too, perhaps, who'd overheard their altercation.

> 'I feel sick at heart. I should have realized she was in trouble and it was because of him. I should have put two and two together.'

You're not the only one, Rick thought. Still the police withheld his name, he noted; they declined to commit fully to their suspect.

But it could be only a matter of time before they did.

*

A second weekend in hiding. No new *Standard*s and no coverage in the national newspapers, at least not so prominently that he noticed it in his quick flick-through in the newsagent (he could not waste money buying every title and edition). Most importantly, he still had no new reason to believe anyone had a chance of unearthing him, which meant a respite of sorts.

And yet, he could never have imagined that the first weekend would compare favourably with this. Then, he'd 'only' had to contend with the discovery of a murder and the consequent unleashing of grief for a love so intense he'd turned his life upside down for it. Now, he was a fugitive, a rodent eluding his predators, his only strategy to stay hidden. And he could see no way of transforming the dynamic; when he tried to visualize himself in another week's time, he could not do it. There was only a depthless blank.

Even his discovery of Kirsten's name led nowhere. Back in the phone box, fast becoming his second home, he learned from Directory Enquiries that there were twenty-five K. McKenzies in London and a further eleven K. MacKenzies. Only one number was issued at a time and every request cost 25p, plus the 20p for the follow-up call.

He worked his way through the list. Not everyone answered, but those who did were plainly not *his* 'K'. He refused to give up, even though he knew it was futile — someone pulling a scam this sophisticated would have made damned sure they were ex-directory.

'I've heard your voice before,' said the final 'K', an elderly woman who was plainly confused and lonely.

'Maybe,' he said, not having the heart to contradict her.

*

Sunday was particularly distressing. Nothing could pierce the seal of his anxiety. He tried to read the novels he'd packed, but he'd chosen them when he'd expected to be holed up with Marina and relatively at peace: they were dense and literary, perfect for filling long days of inactivity, but only if you had the capacity to concentrate. That left only the radio, with its joy-filled anthems and melancholy ballads, the images each evoked of her, always her. Michael Jackson was number one with 'You Are Not Alone', and the song was on permanent rotation on every station, Rick's personal requiem.

He spent hours examining the watch, turning it over in his fingers. It was a Cartier, with a silver face and set with no fewer than forty-four tiny diamonds, entirely different in both style and value from anything *his* Marina would have worn. As for the Zippo, he wondered now about the engraving: *To my Minnie, love D.* Had this been engraved by Drew, after all, using a nickname or endearment? If so, had it been for his wife, Marina, or his lover and partner in crime, Kirsten?

What, if anything, had she told Rick about her relationship with Drew that *had* been true? Had she gone to the spa hotel that tumultuous weekend or just been supplied with the bottle of cologne to present him with? (He'd never used it, even though it was one of the few things she'd given him, because it symbolized bad feeling between them, and he'd left it in the Albert Street bathroom for Rollo.) And had she ever met Drew's sister Gillian or just been given her name to drop?

But every session spent picking at the knots of such questions ended with the same one: why had she chosen *him* as her fall guy? And how had his own very real devotion to her, his genuine love and support, not been enough to gain her trust, to flip her to the light side? The injustice he felt at not having been loved by her as he'd believed was almost as intense as that caused by being wanted for a crime he hadn't committed. The police would eventually get to the truth – a deception on this scale must surely have loose ends all over the place – but a love given and then denied, that was his alone to resolve.

Michael Jackson understood, at least.

*

On Monday morning, he had a splitting headache and stayed in bed until it was time to fetch the paper, sinking in and out of an unpleasant, glutinous sleep. It was, he supposed, depression.

The day's news coverage did little to improve his sense of well-being:

SILVER VALE VICTIM
DRUGGED BEFORE DEATH

Police revealed this morning that Marina Stanley was drugged with a powerful tranquillizer in the hours before being attacked, likely via something she had eaten or drunk.

'What this new evidence tells us is that we are dealing with a calculating and pitiless killer,' commented a spokesman for the police. 'If, as we suspect, he lured her into his car and took her to her home, it is possible he offered her water or a snack that contained the sedative. He then entered her house in the knowledge that she would have been weakened by its effects.

'What took place in the minutes leading to her murder remains conjecture until we find the man in question,' he added.

Rick felt the now-familiar sensation of thick-headedness as he tried to grapple with a new development, to divine why the police should continue to share theories with the public, including details like this drugging, while choosing not to publish the basic facts of their suspect's identity.

The next thought slugged him like a fist: *he'd spilled the Coke and not wiped it up!* What if Kirsten had put something in that can and left it behind intentionally?

The chances were high, very high – and the car that contained traces of it was now back in the possession of the hire company.

He'd been stitched up like a kipper.

34

Rick

September 1995

There was an inevitability to the next day's news. After all, there was only one last piece of information left to release:

SILVER VALE SUSPECT NAMED
AFTER CAR FOUND

The police have sensationally named their prime suspect in the Marina Stanley killing as Rick Ward, a 26-year-old trainee auditor from Camden Town. 'Though he told family and friends he was away travelling, we now believe he is here in the UK, possibly still in the capital,' a spokesman revealed.

The breakthrough comes after a car rented by Mr Ward just hours before Marina Stanley's body was found was returned to the car hire company in Euston.

Police swooped to seize the vehicle and, following intensive forensic examination, found 'convincing and substantive evidence' to link Ward to the crime.

'Mr Ward should come forward as a matter of urgency,' the spokesman added. 'Time's up now, he can't hide from us any longer.'

He confirmed that the police are no longer seeking other suspects in the case.

A photograph had replaced the photofit. It looked several years out of date and it took Rick a moment or two to recognize it as from his security pass at work. The twenty-three-year-old ingenu him. There was no question now that his former colleagues knew he had lied about going to India and would be making their own minds up as to whether or not he was a murderer (if he'd lied about travelling, what else had he lied about?). As for the 'substantive' evidence, it was no surprise that a bit of scrubbing with supermarket wipes had not passed muster. They'd found blood; perhaps also toxins in the Coke spill.

An accompanying piece explored a further unwelcome angle:

STALKER LURED MARINA
TO CAMDEN HOME

In another chilling development, it is now believed the suspect had once lured tragic Marina to his home in Camden Town. A neighbour remembers seeing Ward haranguing the victim in the street just weeks before her tragic death: 'I heard him raise his voice as he called her name – that's what made me look up, it's an unusual name, so it's stuck in my mind. He was pursuing her down the road and she was trying to get away from him. I could tell she was very distressed.'

There was no answer today at the flat, which Ward is thought to have been sharing with a male friend.

The news comes as the victim's husband Drew Stanley announces a 'substantial' cash reward for information leading to Ward's arrest.

Well, of course. The bastard had probably thrown Rick's £2,000 into the pot for the hell of it.

A last twist of the knife came in the form of an 'exclusive insight' into the mind of the stalker's ex, complete with a photo of Rick and Vicky that had plainly been selected for the unpleasant expression he wore on his face:

EX SPEAKS OF 'LUCKY ESCAPE'

The ex-girlfriend of Marina Stanley stalker Rick Ward spoke today of her mixed feelings about the horrific crime he is wanted for. 'On the one hand, my heart breaks for Marina's family and their terrible suffering,' says Vicky, 27, a sales executive from Archway who shared a flat with Ward for almost a year. 'But on the other, I just feel incredibly grateful for my lucky escape.

'Rick was never violent towards me, but he was intense. He wouldn't accept that I didn't want to go out with him anymore.' During one heated argument between the pair, neighbours even called the police, Vicky admits, though no action was taken. 'I didn't feel entirely safe until I moved out.'

Without leaving a forwarding address, she adds, grimly.

This was how it was going to be now: 'Stalker Rick Ward' this, 'Killer Rick Ward' that, the reporter not always careful about prefixing it with 'alleged'.

If he ever came out of this with his innocence intact, he'd need to change his name.

He studied himself in the bathroom mirror. A dodgy photofit was one thing, but a real photo meant a heightened likelihood of being recognized. Was there anything he could do to disguise himself? His hair was getting uncomfortably long: would it help to slick it into a pony tail or buy a cheap dye to change its hue? Or would that only draw attention to him?

He decided to leave well alone – leave *un*well alone. In the hellish event of someone calling out his name, he'd hurry on, not returning to base unless he was a hundred per cent certain he'd shaken them off. He would make one adjustment, however: he'd go down to one of those shops on Oxford Street selling souvenirs and buy a new cap, this one with an 'I Love London' design. From now on, if anyone was interested, he was a tourist, better still, an overseas student like the building's other residents, with limited or no English.

But for how long? His and Marina's – Kirsten's – plans to live off grid had never reached beyond the first month, at which point they'd hoped to get legal advice about court orders and divorce (well, *he* had; *she* must have known she'd need no such thing). A month's rent had been paid up front, which took him to mid-October, after which his only hope for renewing – or indeed, for eating – was to pawn the watch.

Thoughts of rent unleashed a new supplementary fear in the form of Sam, the building manager. Though Rick had used the name Gary, the man had seen his face on two occasions, both at close quarters, and even if he wasn't a daily consumer of the *Standard* it was only a matter of time before he stumbled on a copy bearing a picture of his secret tenant on the top floor. Or thought to himself how odd it was that he'd never laid eyes on the domestic violence victim he'd purported to be harbouring.

On his way out, he ducked into the manager's office in the basement, calling through the half-open door to a seated figure he hadn't seen before. 'Is Sam around?'

The guy barely glanced up. 'Sorry, he's on holiday.'

'When will he be back, d'you know?'

'Not till next week.'

'Gone anywhere nice?' *Please let it be abroad. Anywhere away from the UK media.*

'Yeah, Turkey, I think.'

Result – albeit a temporary one unlikely to have any bearing on the final outcome.

*

Out on Oxford Street, the tourist cap was easily purchased and he made the switch on the spot before picking up cigarettes. Standing with his back to the window of Dixon's, he lit one with the Zippo and surrendered to the street's famous energy, its heartless disregard for the danger any individual might find himself in. His plight was meaningless down here, the pages of the *Standard* mere litter to be toed into the gutter.

Stamping out the end of his cigarette, he glanced through the shop window behind him and almost tripped over his own feet in shock. There, among the electronics on special offer, blown up on multiple TV screens of varying sizes, was the photo of him that had run in the *Standard*, along with the caption: *Mother of Marina Stanley Suspect Tells Son 'Give yourself up!'*

Almost at once, surreally, video footage of his mother began to roll, an interview filmed in the family home in Horsham. Subtitles ran across the bottom of the screen as she spoke:

'We just want Rick to get in touch and explain ... If something happened in the heat of the moment, then it's better to come clean about it ... Running away only makes things worse ...'

How drawn she looked, her despair all too real as she spoke the unspeakable about her own son while still, somehow, letting him know that there was a home where he'd be welcome when this was all over.

When he got out of prison.

This was properly, unequivocally big now. As a clip of Drew Stanley in front of his rhododendron bush now played, with his craven, fraudulent display of loss, Rick accepted for the first time that Stanley was going to get away with this. Husband kills wife for her fortune, while a complete stranger takes the rap.

Winner takes all.

*

The reliable anaesthetic of a vodka binge put paid to the rest of the day, eventually sending him into another wretched, restless slumber. He woke thinking, unexpectedly, of the real Marina. And not just thinking, but *grieving*. It was odd to grieve for someone you'd never known in life, but he'd been the one to find her body and it had left him with a sense of profound connection. Of reverence. It unsettled him that no funeral service had yet been reported, having been delayed, he supposed, by the ongoing police investigation. He would have liked to know she'd been laid to rest.

He would have liked to understand who she'd been in life, too, for beyond the one-note eulogies in the press he knew precious little about her. Had she grown to fear what her husband was capable of or had she experienced their final, deadly conflict as an eruption of fury without precedent or warning? She'd still been attracted to him, Rick knew that much, since it now seemed reasonable to assume she'd been the woman he and Rollo had seen at the Stanleys' house that Sunday back in July and not the illicit lover they'd taken her for. (What a brilliantly nuanced reaction from Kirsten when he'd reported the 'infidelity' that same day. Or perhaps there really had been an element of shock; perhaps she'd been in love with Drew and he'd convinced her he didn't sleep with his wife.)

What else? Remembering the cuttings supplied by Rollo's friend and wedged into his rucksack at the last minute, he kicked off the covers and sprang from the bed. That was right, he'd dithered over whether to bring them: on the one hand, he didn't want Marina to stumble on them and discover his secret research, but on the other, he hadn't felt comfortable leaving them in the flat in his absence – and a rare true instinct *that* had been since the police must have searched the flat days ago and would have filed them under 'Stalker Rick' in a flash.

Had there been anything that had failed to catch his eye when he first read them, but that might now help his understanding of this nightmare?

But reading the pages again, he found no more mentions of her than he'd remembered. Nothing that could have rung alarm bells – he hadn't been quite as stupid as he feared. A photo would have been useful, he thought, wryly, looking once more at the picture of Drew posing at the Exmoor Gardens window; if only she'd been invited to join her husband in the shot. Or even a snap from their wedding day, like the one the *Standard* had run; years old though it was, it might have been enough to alert Rick to the mistaken identity. He'd have been able to confront Kirsten and end their 'romance' then and there.

It was as he refolded the pages that he noticed something odd about the numbering. They were marked 'of 12' and yet there were only ten pages. He double-checked: pages 3 and 11 were missing. Strange. He could think of no reason why the cuttings librarian would have removed pages from the batch.

Which left only Rollo.

35

Alex

September, present

'Okay, please don't freak out,' Beth began and he thought, *Oh God, what now?*

He had come to dread interaction with his wife, seeming as it did these days always to involve a nasty surprise. And what with their omnipresent house guest, private conversations at home took place either in the bedroom or, where they were now, in the bathroom, Beth cleansing her face with some sort of special cloth and he digging at his gums with a too-large TePe.

'I had a very interesting email this afternoon.'

'Hmm?' Instinct told him this might be about said house guest. Did he dare hope that *finally* the scales had fallen from Beth's eyes?

'A message came through from that ancestry service. About your DNA? Someone's been in touch. They've been alerted that they're a close genetic match to you.'

What the fuck? He yanked the brush from his teeth and held his wife's gaze in the mirror. 'Why did this message go to you and not me?'

'I suppose I must've put in my email address when I made the purchase. But isn't that intriguing? I mean, it could be a half-sibling or a cousin you didn't know about?'

He couldn't process what he was hearing. It took every ounce of his willpower to produce a tone closer to curiosity than fury. 'But how were they able to compare their results to mine to know there's a match? I thought you said the data was confidential?'

'I think I must have ticked the box giving permission,' Beth said, and it was the face that did it, the casual regret, like, *Whoops. Oh well, never mind* . . . and his rage exploded.

'That was a fucking great box to tick, Beth! What the hell were you thinking? There's no way I would have consented to that.'

She recoiled, the first time he'd seen her do that, not so much scared as *repulsed* by his anger, his negative force field. 'Why not?'

'Why d'you think? Because I might not want to know about any genetic matches. I might consider it a stinking can of worms that I have no interest whatsoever in opening!'

Her cleansed skin reddened and she pressed the cloth to her left cheek as if staunching a wound. 'I'm sorry, I didn't think anything of it. I didn't think there'd ever *be* any match.'

'Really?' He gave a mirthless chuckle. 'Because I'm constantly seeing news articles about people's lives being ruined because companies like this one tell them their father was a serial philanderer and they've got a bunch of half-brothers they knew nothing about, total deadbeats about to be thrown out of their trailer park and queueing up to move in. In case you've forgotten, we've already got one scrounger in this house.'

'Alex!'

He matched her indignation. 'Beth!'

They glared at each other with deep dislike, as if sworn enemies.

'They're only the horror stories,' she said, cracking first. 'But I'm sure there are lovely ones as well, ones that don't get a headline in the *Daily Mail*.'

What was wrong with her, was she completely mad? 'Okay, so what happens now you've sprung this on me without warning? Am I supposed to just magically forget my father played away? That he died without knowing about some illegitimate—?' Alex broke off, mid-sentence. *Oh. Oh, no. Please, no.* 'Which year was this person born? Did they say?'

Beth turned on the tap and rinsed her cloth. Turned it off again and wrung the thing out. 'Nineteen ninety-six,' she said, finally.

Nineteen ninety-six? His father would have been in his mid-fifties, whereas *he* would have been in his mid-twenties. A 'close genetic match': half-sibling or a cousin, she'd suggested, but she couldn't possibly have missed the third alternative. What was she playing at? If he'd been in any doubt before, he wasn't any longer: he'd boarded a runaway train. He'd fucking *built* the train.

298

He tossed the TePe in the bin and turned.

'What? Where are you going?' Beth said.

'Downstairs. Go to bed without me.'

He went to the kitchen and took a beer from the fridge, wincing at the taste after having just cleaned his teeth. Already there were murmurings upstairs, Zara checking on her and no doubt saying how unacceptable Alex's treatment of her was, how misogynistic. With sudden energy, he wrenched open the door to the storage cupboard and began displacing items until he found his taped-up box. Ignoring the chaos he'd created, he took it to the living room and settled on the sofa to tear off the tape.

It was years since he'd looked at these relics from the predigital age and soon the sofa was strewn with useless old documents – contracts, medical records, even his A-level and degree certificates – and photos of friends he'd thought he'd forgotten but that now grew real once more. Strange how the glossy faces and spiky corners of the prints somehow made the memories they held more precious than their digital successors.

More dangerous, too, perhaps. It struck him that he could separate those photos of himself taken pre-Marina from those taken later not by any details of fashion or location but by the change in his own eyes. There was, post-1995, no sense of his attention having been willingly given, not one smile wholly free of regret.

Ah, *here* it was, the one he was looking for, secreted in an envelope of its own: his only picture of her. It seemed a miracle of self-control that he'd not looked for it, looked at it, in so long. As he stared at her face, his long-lost connection to her oozed through him like morphine. Her gaze was pale and ethereal, mouth captured mid-pout, or mid-speech. *You,* she seemed to be saying. *Only you.*

He imagined their genes merged.

He was fairly sure she'd been the only woman he'd had unprotected sex with that whole year. She'd said she was on the pill, wanted a baby with Drew like a hole in the head, but that could have been a fabrication like everything else that came out of her mouth, and even if she *had* been telling the truth it didn't mean she'd been scrupulous about contraception. They'd been chaotic times.

Had that feature in the *Guardian* prompted this discovery of the DNA match? Had he been, as he'd feared, recognized from the picture or was the timing just another appalling coincidence in a life of appalling coincidences? Either way, he knew he should destroy this photo, but he couldn't bring himself to. He also knew he should think of her as Kirsten, not Marina, but the name was too imprinted, too utterly perfect for her.

'What are you doing, Alex? Have you seen the mess you've made?'

He flinched as if poked. Zara had come into the room and was standing over him, that hideous space hopper of a stomach straining the buttons of a lobster-print pyjama top, face glowering with her usual holier-than-thou outrage (at night, she liked to apply a regenerative facial oil extracted from some rare African nut).

'I think you'll find I'm entitled to make a mess in my own home,' he muttered.

'And are you entitled to shout at your wife?'

'We weren't shouting. We were discussing a serious matter. Go back to bed.'

She didn't move and he placed the photo by his side, face down – the thought of Zara looking at his Marina was diabolical – but nothing escaped her notice and to his intense frustration, she lowered herself into the armchair across from him.

'Who's in the photo?'

'It's none of your business, Zara. For God's sake, is nothing private?'

'You tell me,' she said with satisfaction, as if he'd fed her precisely the line she'd been waiting for. 'Why are you being so weird about this DNA match?'

No need to ask how she was so up to speed when he'd only found out himself ten minutes ago. Beth would have discussed it with her first.

'It's just a shock,' he said. 'News like that, it's sensitive. It needs to be delivered with tact.'

It was hard even for a contrarian like her to argue with this and as she adjusted a cushion behind her, briefly taking her eyes from him, he slipped the photo of Marina into his pocket.

'You know what I think?' she said.

'I'd prefer not to, thanks.' Shovelling items back into the box, his knuckles grazed something hard and metallic and he explored it secretly with his fingertips: a small, smooth square bordered with tiny close-set bumps, a cold ribbed band ... The watch! Heat spread up his body to his face and his heart was a basketball smacking against his ribs. Somehow, he'd forgotten about this treasure.

'I think you're that guy,' Zara said.

'What guy?'

'The guy mentioned in the article. Beth said you completely lost your shit over that as well. Rick Ward, he was called, I read the whole thing. He was suspected of murdering that woman on Exmoor Gardens, but he went missing. Well, I think you're him. I think that's why you changed your name and now you're worried this DNA match is going to expose you.'

Jesus wept. Aware that he'd stopped breathing, he wasn't sure if he was going to be able to speak. 'You have an impressive imagination,' he managed, at last.

She cocked her head, watching his reaction to her next gambit: 'I've seen your driver's licence and I have to say I'm not convinced it's even you in the photo.'

'How the fuck have you seen my driver's licence?'

'Beth had it out the other day to fill in some form. Like I say, it didn't look like you.'

'So I'm a bald cunt now, sue me.' He was regaining his spirit. 'There's not a whole lot I can do about that.'

She edged forward in her seat. 'Is your birth certificate in that box? Show me. *That* will have your original name on it.'

He scowled at her. 'For fuck's sake, who are you, the Gestapo? Anyway, my sister has my birth certificate, it was with all the family stuff when my parents died.'

'Tell me where she lives and I'll get it back for you,' Zara said.

'Why would you do that? Seriously, we are not having this conversation.' He forced the lid back on the box and rose to his feet. 'Leave me alone, you crazy witch.'

She gave a growl of laughter. 'Typical male response to female intuition.'

'Typical human response to complete lunacy, more like.' Clutching the box in his arms, he stood facing her. 'Don't fuck with me, Zara.'

'Is that a threat?'

'It's advice.'

'Well, I don't take advice from you.'

As they faced off, his anger felt kinetic, growing and powering him. 'Why are you still here, anyway? In case you've somehow missed the message, I'd like you to leave. Find somewhere else to live with your devil child.'

But she ignored the slur, returning to the subject she knew had rattled him. 'You know what? If I'm right about this, there has to be a reason why you've gone to such lengths to deceive people. Did you do it, Alex? Or should I say Rick? Were you the guilty one, not this other guy who went to prison? Was he innocent all along?'

He took a pace back. This was getting *way* out of control. The temptation to smash the box over her head was horrifyingly acute. 'Here's a question, Zara. If you *really* think you're living with a murderer, why are you so happy to confront him like this? Why aren't you running for your life?'

There was a flicker of doubt then. Her lips parted, but for once no comeback emerged. She'd been bluffing, he intuited;

defending Beth, looking to get a rise out of him, but basically building castles in the air. She might make a lucky guess or two, but she *knew* nothing.

Unable to look at her for a second longer, he took his box out to the hallway and began the task of clearing up. Only once safely out of Zara's range did he dip his hand back in and retrieve the watch.

*

He went to some lengths to avoid reigniting the discussion with Beth. That first night, he slept on the sofa, using the bathroom in the morning only once she was up, in the kitchen and murmuring with her partner in crime over the vomit-like soaked oats they'd taken to preparing for breakfast. The next night, he crashed at Eddie's in North London. The house, though comfortable and stylish, was under Suki's somewhat inflexible command, which meant that dinner (spaghetti that turned out to be made of edamame beans – she must have a copy of Zara's Food Focus cookbook) was served without wine. And, with sobbing children appearing in the doorway every five minutes, he had no time alone with Eddie even if he did want to discuss his personal crisis, which he did not.

Work was shaping up to be a shitshow of its own kind, with Janice having told him that he and not she would be headlining their forthcoming presentation to the minister about overrunning costs on the immigration reporting project; she even had the audacity to label the manoeuvre an opportunity for him and not the brazen shafting it was. For once, he worked late, and by the time he returned to Silver Vale, Beth was already in bed out cold.

He eased wordlessly between the covers, trying not to wake her, and was lying in the dark, waiting for sleep to claim him, when her voice startled him.

'You think it could be your child, don't you?'

Alex drew his breath, exhaled his reply: 'Yes.'

'Did you know about the pregnancy at the time?'

'No, of course not. And I'd rather not know about it now either.'

There was a silence. It was too much to hope that the discussion would end there and it did not.

'So do you care at all what *I* think?'

He turned his head towards her. 'What?'

'I mean, it might be you who's the biological parent, but since neither of us has ever met this person, we're pretty much in the same boat. Which makes me wonder, don't you care what I think?'

He said nothing.

'You know how much I wanted a family. I wanted it more than anything.' Her voice held an unassailable clarity, the message, perhaps even the phrasing, rehearsed. 'This could be a step-daughter for me.'

A step-*daughter*? He felt his breath sucked from him. His voice, when it returned, was tight with emotion. 'Why do you insist on giving me information I've asked not to know? Do you *want* me to have a nervous breakdown?'

'You mean because I've said she's female?' There was the pull of the duvet, the snap of a switch and Beth's face came into view. She was as fanatical as he'd ever seen her, her umber eyes aflame. 'Look, I'm asking you, for five minutes, *five minutes*, that's all, to talk about my situation, not yours.'

She doesn't know, he reminded himself, she doesn't know why you're being how you are. She really thinks you're bothered about the idea of the girl, not the horrific complications she represents. He exhaled. 'I do care, yes. But I have to sort out what *I* think before I can give what *you* think the attention it deserves.'

'And when will that be?' she demanded.

'I don't know,' he said.

But whenever it is, it's going to be too late.

36

Rick

September 1995

Studying the *A to Z* to plot a back-street route up to Camden, Rick experienced a lurch of horror at how minimal the distance was. Hiding in plain sight had seemed a clever strategy when he'd been known only to a few friends and colleagues, but now that he was London's Most Wanted it was about as dangerously naïve a situation as he could have conceived.

But he had no choice. Whatever his own clumsy deductions, he was making them on the back foot. If he were to obey his own mother's command and hand himself in to the police, he needed something credible with which to challenge the published line, the mounting evidence against him.

Thankfully, it was a Wednesday and not the weekend: there'd be a decent chance Rollo was at home. He set off at 9pm, when it was properly dark and most workers were either long gone home or already settled in their pub or restaurant of choice. The air was sharp, biting his skin through his fleece and canvas jacket, but at least it wasn't tipping it down this time.

Approaching the flat, he darted into the nearest vacant phone kiosk. The phone was picked up after two rings, Rollo's tone louche: 'Changed your mind, have you, darlin'? I had a feeling you might.'

'What? Rollo?' Rick felt a pang of dismay that Rollo had the appetite for chasing girls when *he* was in such horrendous trouble, but now was not the time for self-pity. 'Rollo?' he repeated.

'Rick?' There was a pause, then, 'Is that you?'

He felt another sudden flare of existential horror. When no one else was as you'd thought, how could you be sure *you* were? He was a different creature now, an alien separated from the rest of society. 'Yes,' he said, firmly. 'Listen, I need to see you, but give it to me straight: are the police watching the flat? I mean right now? Or reporters?'

'I don't think so. I've just been out and I didn't see anyone.'

'Good. I'll be up in two minutes.'

Every detail of the approach – the cracks in the paving stones caused by the roots of a tree, the particular way the key scraped an extra notch to the left to release the lock, even the faint creak of the third tread of the stairs – made him sick with regret for what he'd willingly given up for a woman he'd never actually known. When Rollo met him at the flat door and embraced him, the now unfamiliar feeling of someone else's touch almost made him weep.

'You look like shit,' Rollo said. To be fair, he didn't look in peak condition either. Bloodshot and pallid, he'd lost weight and, always slight, was bordering on gaunt. 'Come in, let's have a drink.'

Rick followed him into the kitchen, which was heaped with dirty plates and polystyrene takeaway cartons, and watched his friend tip half a bottle of red wine into two tumblers. He handed one to Rick.

'You were supposed to call me back. You know, for the number for the police?'

'Sorry,' Rick said. 'I wasn't ready to speak to them. Look, as far as you know, they haven't bugged the place, have they?'

Disbelief broke over Rollo's face. '*Bugged* it? 'Course not. I mean, they came last week – I told you that was on the cards, didn't I? But I was here the whole time and I think I'd have seen if they got their toolbox out.'

Rick gulped his wine. If movies were anything to go by, the police didn't need drills to set up surveillance. Everything was miniature, easily affixed to lamps or mirrors or whatever. He slid open the sash and stepped out onto the flat roof. 'Let's talk outside.'

'For fuck's sake, Rick, this isn't *The Firm*. And I haven't got any shoes on.' But Rollo followed without further objection and, once seated in his preferred deckchair, offered Rick a Marlboro Light.

Rick sank into the second chair; it was slightly damp, but he didn't care. He drew the toxins into his lungs, marvelling that the last time he'd sat out here, drinking and smoking with Rollo, he'd been a free man, a man for whom a spell in hiding was an entirely voluntary prospect.

'So come on,' Rollo prompted, 'tell me what the hell's been going on. You're all over the papers, do you realize that?'

'Of course I do. *And* the local TV news.'

'I've been running a switchboard here. I've had your mum, your sister, your old boss, the crazy ex – everyone you've ever met.'

Rick gulped his wine, but after his stint of daily vodka-drinking, it was having no effect whatsoever. 'They all think I'm guilty?'

'Not all of them, no. The worst are the reporters. I mean, if I were secretly in touch with you, I'd hardly be likely to tell *them*, would I?'

'I hope not. What *have* you said?'

'That I haven't heard from you since you left for India.'

This would be the next thing: *Killer's Travel Lies* – evidence of scheming, of malice aforethought. 'I was never going to India. I left my job, it wasn't a transfer. That was just to cover up getting Marina away from Drew and into a safe house.'

'Safe house? Where?'

'Better you don't know, but here, in town.'

Rollo eyed him with perplexity. 'So you've been here this whole time, but you haven't been to the police yet? Why not?'

'Because I've been set up and I have to be able to prove that or they'll nick me on the spot. Before I know it, I'll be confessing to things I haven't done.' Rick lowered his voice to a near whisper. 'I've never even met this woman, Rollo. You must have seen in the paper it isn't her? She isn't *my* Marina.'

'Of course.' Rollo's bafflement mirrored Rick's own. 'I

couldn't believe it. I mean, at first, I thought I wasn't remembering right, but other than the haircut, they actually don't look that alike.'

'Same height as well. I think the woman we saw at the house that time was his wife, the one he killed.'

'Really? Poor cow. She looked happy enough then.' Rollo's tone lifted. 'But this is good, right? For *you*.'

'Not really. A woman's still dead and the police think I'm the one who killed her.'

'That makes no sense to me.'

Rick eased forward in his seat. 'Well, it makes sense to *me*. Drew Stanley wanted to kill his wife – I'm guessing for her money. She had family money, according to the papers, and either she'd threatened to cut him off or he had someone else lined up and wanted out . . .' *Kirsten*. Maybe Kirsten was who he had lined up. The idea was a jab to an open wound. 'I don't know, but either way, I'm the fall guy. He got someone to impersonate her and play the damsel in distress, so that every move I made could be used later to make me look like a stalker. Then all he had to do was get me to the house just after he'd done the deed and, bingo! The stalker did it.'

But it sounded crazy. He could tell from Rollo's frown that he wasn't buying it. If *he* was sceptical, then how would the police react?

'Wait, so you *were* at their house the day it happened?'

Rick regarded him through a veil of cigarette smoke. 'I'm the one who found her. I called for help from her house, my fingerprints will have been there.'

He thought of the watch and the Zippo, still in his

possession. If the police *were* watching the flat and followed him back to his hiding place, they'd find even more evidence to point to his guilt.

'Jeez, Rick.' Rollo dropped the end of his cigarette and went to stamp it out before remembering his feet were bare, so Rick did it for him. 'This whole thing is a mind fuck.'

'You see my problem? They've all fallen for his version of events, hook, line and sinker.'

Rollo scratched behind his ear, clearly at a loss as to what to advise in this perverse, tangled mess. 'Okay, it looks bad, I get that, but once you tell the police you didn't know the woman who died, won't you be off the hook?'

'Only if they believe me. Did they believe *you* when you said you didn't know her?'

Rollo pulled a face. 'Not really, to be honest. It was almost like they didn't trust me to remember who you were going out with, you know? Like I'm some simpleton.'

Rick's spirits plunged. So the police were actively shutting down leads that disproved their preferred theory. 'Did they take anything when they were here? Did you see?'

'I think they had a couple of things, but the only thing I saw for sure was a pack of photos.'

'Photos?' They would hardly be interested in childhood snaps, Rick thought, trying to recall the last batch he'd had developed. Definitely nothing of Marina, who'd refused to have her picture taken, otherwise he'd have kept the print in his wallet. There'd been one or two of Vicky – perhaps they'd soon find their way into the press with more anecdotes about his frightening 'intensity'.

Oh! Now he remembered. The picture he'd taken of the Stanleys' house from across the road. If *that* didn't fit with the profile of a stalker, he didn't know what did. A new hope surfaced. 'You don't have a photo of us, do you, of me and Marina together? We had a disposable camera on the go at my birthday party, didn't we? Was that ever developed?'

Rollo flicked ash over the railing. 'I don't think it was. It must be in my room somewhere.'

'Did the police search your room, as well?'

'No.'

'Then could you find it? If there's a photo of us together and you and Si and Jake, and maybe Matt or Julie, could give a statement saying she was using the name Marina, that might be enough to get the police thinking.'

It would be just his luck that any photo would be blurred or inadmissible in some way. (*Inadmissible*: God, he was already thinking in terms of prosecution, of standing in the dock.)

'I'll find it,' Rollo promised. 'I can get it developed tomorrow, if you like. I know a place that does a two-hour service.'

'Cheers, that's amazing. If I have that and then somehow find an address for Kirsten, I can finally get myself out of this nightmare.'

Rollo glanced up. 'Who's Kirsten?'

'Who d'you think? Marina, of course. My Marina. She's called Kirsten McKenzie.'

Rollo jerked forward, forearms resting on his knees. 'Wait, you know her name? How come?'

'I saw her passport. The day after the party, you remember

you came in when we were talking? I'd just found it. She said it was a fake, she was going to use it to escape from Drew and start a new life, but I'm pretty sure now it was her real one and she came up with the lie on the spot.'

Rollo's eyes widened in disbelief. 'Have you tried to find her?'

''Course I have. Her office said she'd left and gone straight off on holiday, but she probably lied to them about that. I've tried directory enquiries, but it's a dead end. If she wasn't ex-directory then, she will be now.'

'I know I would be after shafting someone like that.' Rollo puffed out his cheeks and exhaled. 'What can I do to help, mate? Other than the photos. You need to hole up here?'

'No, thanks, I've still got the safe house. The reason I came is I wanted to ask you about the cuttings – you know, the ones you got for me about Drew?'

'Oh yeah, from Sonia.'

'The thing is, there were two pages missing. There were supposed to be twelve, but there were only ten in the package.'

'Were there?' Rollo drained his wine. 'I just passed on what she gave me.'

'But you looked through them first, you said. Could you have dropped them somewhere in the flat, maybe? Or at your old work?'

'No way. I had a quick shufti, yes, but I stuffed them all back in. Have you got them with you? Let's have another look.'

Rick produced the envelope and Rollo leafed through the

pages. 'I'm guessing the missing ones were just blank and she chucked them. Sorry, mate.'

Now he said it, it was obvious this was the most likely explanation, and yet the blow at least led to another new hope. 'It was off the record, wasn't it, this job? Would it be possible for us – well, you – to ask Sonia for a search on Kirsten McKenzie? There might be something we can cross-reference with the photo, show the police it's the same person.'

If there was a photo in the first place. The 'if's were amassing, and he could tell Rollo was thinking the same as he handed the package back to him.

'There's no harm in trying, I guess. Leave it with me. I'll ask her to do it first thing and, if there is anything, to bike it over to me. If we meet tomorrow after work maybe, I can give you that and the photos together.'

'You're working again?' Somehow Rick had imagined his flatmate paralysed with the trauma of their predicament, but, evidently, life went on. 'Where?'

'Nothing exciting. Just something at a sales agency. The pay's crap, but the teams's okay.' He stood. 'It's too cold to sit out here, can we go back in?'

'Sure.' Back inside, Rick asked, 'Did you sublet my room?'

Rollo shoved his hands in his pockets, trying to warm up. 'Actually, I'm in yours, but my mate Josh is in my room. You can come back as soon as this is sorted, though, yeah? One of us can sleep on the sofa.'

'He's in right now, is he?' When Rollo nodded, Rick exclaimed at his own recklessness and marched to the door, every inch the fugitive.

'You need to go to the police, Rick,' Rollo said, a pace behind him. 'The longer you leave it, the guiltier you're going to look. It's already been, how long? Two weeks?'

'Twelve days,' Rick said, with a horrible understanding of how long that was, the sheer scale and expense of the police investigation. 'I will go. After tomorrow, after I see how far I've got.'

'Good. So I'll meet you at five. Where?'

'Where's your new office?'

'Leicester Square. I could meet you outside the Hippodrome?'

'Might be a camera out front. I'll see you round the first corner as you go up Charing Cross Road.'

'You're not going to tell me where this safe house of yours is?'

'I can't tell anyone. Not even you.' Rick reached for the latch. 'Wait, you haven't got any cash, have you? Anything will do, even a few pounds.' Could he risk nipping into the chip shop on the High Street? The thought of hot chips with salt and vinegar made him sick with desire.

Rollo fetched his wallet and passed Rick a twenty-pound note.

'This is amazing, thank you.'

The friends hugged and Rick left the flat with a profound, almost childlike sense of relief that he was no longer navigating this nightmare alone.

37

Rick

September 1995

He spent most of the walk back – and the hours afterwards, lying twisting and wakeful in bed – pondering the issue of Kirsten. Tomorrow's haul of photos and cuttings – if they materialized at all – would get him only so far with the police. If they'd refused to believe Rollo, who'd met Kirsten dozens of times, that Rick's association had been with her and not Marina Stanley, then they were unlikely to believe Si or Jake or anyone else who'd met her just once or twice. The only thing guaranteed to persuade the police of his innocence was if Kirsten came with him and confessed to the deception. She was the only person who knew, categorically, that he'd been duped – other than Drew Stanley, of course.

But how to locate her? He didn't have the number of a single one of her friends – again, bar Stanley – much less a family member, and she wasn't registered with a temp agency. Which left only her manager at Culkins, Caroline Pierce, who had explicitly stated that she had an address on file. Kirsten might, of course, have supplied her with a false one, but Rick could see no reason for her to have done that since she hadn't known him when she'd begun the temping gig. Her deception had not yet commenced.

Somehow, Rick needed to find a way to breach Caroline Pierce's filing system and get that address.

*

The next morning, soon after nine, he entered his usual phone box on Goodge Street and rang Si's extension at B&F. 'This is Rick.'

Over the background noises of voices and ringing phones came a low whistle.

'Seriously, Si, please don't let anyone know who you're on the line to, okay? Don't say my name.'

'Mate, do you have *any* idea—?'

'Yes!' Rick groaned. 'Of course I do. But listen to me, whatever you've read, whatever the police have said, it's not true.'

'Right.' Si's nervous snicker suggested it would take more than this to convince him.

But Rick did not have the time. 'I need you to do me a favour. I'll owe you big time if you do it – literally, I'll do anything. Don't laugh, Si, you might not need anything now, but in the future, who knows. You could be the unlucky one next time.'

Mercifully, his plea delivered the intended result. 'Go on then, what do you need?' Si said.

'Go up to Culkins on the eighth floor and find an address for a temp up there called Kirsten McKenzie.'

'Why? And will they just give that out, anyway?'

'I don't mean ask. You'll have to break into the office manager's filing cabinet.'

'Oh, right, nothing too hard then.' Pause. 'Who *is* this Kirsten person?'

'She's the woman I was seeing over the summer.'

Si lowered his voice to a murmur. 'I thought you were seeing Marina Stanley?'

This confirmed Rick's worst fears. Si's memory of her was not clear enough for him to differentiate between her and the woman in the papers. Rick sorely regretted having been so secretive about their romance. About not questioning Kirsten's insistence on secrecy, either. 'She *said* her name was Marina, but it wasn't. It was Kirsten. The whole thing is a massive set-up.' For the second time in twelve hours, he heard how delusional he sounded when he tried to articulate the conspiracy to someone else. 'I can't go into it, but you have to trust me that Kirsten McKenzie is the only person who can get me out of this mess. I'm not joking, Si, that file could be the difference between me going to prison for twenty years and being free. I *have* to get her home address.'

'Okay, okay. So how am going to do it without getting caught?'

Rick had had many sleepless hours to consider this question. 'Go up via the stairs. There's a fire alarm in the corridor to the left of reception, near the staff loos. Set that off and duck out of sight in the loo while they're all evacuated. Then find the right office, they've got names and job titles on the doors, so you're looking for Caroline Pierce, Office Manager. The file will be labelled "Temps", I'm guessing. You'll have a few minutes to hunt around before the fire brigade arrive and check the building.'

'So all totally low-key then.' Though Si scoffed in disbelief, there was also a grain of excitement in his voice. He liked a caper. 'I'll do it at lunchtime when there aren't so many people around.'

'Great idea.'

'If I do manage to find this address, how will I get hold of you?'

'I'll be close by, watching. I'll call you when you're back in the office.'

It occurred to Rick how easy it would be for Si to get straight on the phone to the police, let them know exactly when their suspect would be hanging around his old building. But he had to take some risks, to trust him as he trusted Rollo.

'Good luck,' he said. About to hang up, he snatched up the receiver again. 'Like I say, I won't forget this.'

*

The alarm went off at 1.30pm. He watched from the corner of Victoria Street and Buckingham Gate as the building emptied and workers assembled at the nearby designated meeting point. Annie stood out from the crowd in the blue catering apron she always wore and he tried not to think about her lost revenue this lunchtime – not to mention the abuse of public funds in needlessly mobilizing a fire unit. It was all relative and Drew Stanley was hoodwinking an entire police force, after all.

Soon there came the whoop of the siren and a fire engine pulled up. Some workers stuck around to watch; others dispersed. With a masochistic stab of pain, he pictured himself leaving the building with 'Marina', two office workers in a new romance, slinking off for a bonus half-hour together.

It was almost forty-five minutes before those who'd remained were allowed back in the building and Rick waited a further half-hour before calling Si's extension.

'Mission accomplished!' Si crowed.

'No way, well done, mate! That's amazing. You're sure no one saw you?'

'I didn't say *that*. I was stopped on my way back down by some fire monitor. I said I'd been in the loo and came out a bit late, but twisted my ankle on the stairs. Just had it strapped up by the first aider, even though there's nothing wrong with it. They went, "Does this hurt?", and I went, "Ow, yes, be a bit gentler please!"'

His exhilaration as he relived his triumph was infectious; Rick's spirits were at their highest since this disaster had begun. 'So you found the temp files okay?'

'I did. It's definitely her, there was a photocopy of her passport and a copy of a utility bill from a few months ago. She's down in Tooting. Flat C, 21 Moss Road, SW17.'

Rick memorized it, almost in tears by now as he thanked his old colleague.

'Just keep yourself out of jail, yeah?' Si said.

'I'll try.'

*

There was a spring in his step as he walked to the West End, avoiding the parks and twisting through back streets. Everything had turned – the tide, the worm, Lady Luck – and he was on his way now, on his way back to living his old life, being a regular guy.

He whiled away the time before meeting Rollo with the early edition of the *Standard* on a bench in Leicester Square, pigeons pecking at litter by his feet and tourists conferring over maps. *Judge Backs IRA Prisoners*, screamed the headline, while Brigitte Bardot had met the Pope and Blur had stormed New York. Nothing new on the Silver Vale murder, other than an opinion piece about the proliferation of porn-addicted male loners that the police said was making murders like Marina's 'sickeningly everyday'.

They must have found his pile of *Loaded*s then.

The pavement outside the Hippodrome was mobbed with tourists and he struggled through to get to the turn into Little Newport Street, where Rollo was waiting. He wore a suit and tie, polished leather shoes in place of his usual Adidas.

'Don't say it,' he said, his sheepishness all the more endearing for being so *normal*. 'I don't need to hear from anyone else that I've sold out to the man.' He handed Rick a small yellow packet of photos. '*Voilà.*'

Rick felt his heart contract. 'Seriously? There's one of her in here?'

'There certainly is.'

He sifted through the prints, seeing at once that at least

half were duds, the flash having bleached part or all of the image. Those featuring identifiable faces included one of him and Si out on the flat roof, gurning like lunatics, and another of Rollo with Matt and Julie, their arms around one another, eyes neon red. The single photograph of Kirsten, standing alone against a wall, cigarette between her fingers, was both hauntingly beautiful and pretty much useless.

'What's wrong?' Rollo said.

'I guess I hoped there might be a picture of us together, something that shows we were involved. Otherwise, you could argue that two people at the same party didn't even meet, let alone were in a relationship together.'

'But it was your party,' Rollo said. 'How could she not have met you?'

Rick conceded this. 'It's definitely something. Thank you. Can I take them with me?'

'Of course.'

Rick already knew he would count the number of prints when alone, check them against the negatives. Rollo didn't deserve it, but he'd do it all the same.

'There's this as well,' Rollo said, and a Manila envelope was presented. The cuttings. 'There's not much, I'm afraid. I mean, she's not an axe murderer, but you might wish you'd never got involved with her.'

'Well, I already wish *that*.' Rick scanned the few pages of news items. Each reported the same incident in 1989 involving an attempt to remove squatters from a house in West London; Kirsten McKenzie was one of those arrested for affray and locked in police cells for a night.

'What d'you think?' Rollo asked.

'I think she's had a tough life and that might be why Drew has had such a hold over her.' Rick paused. 'I'm hoping I'll be able to ask her myself in an hour or so.'

Rollo's mouth fell open. 'What d'you mean? I thought you didn't know where she was?'

'I do now. It's been a constructive day. I got her address from her old employer. Don't ask how.'

'Wow. That's brilliant news.' Rollo looked seriously impressed and even in the midst of a crisis, Rick registered satisfaction in the fact. 'But how do you know he hasn't moved her from there?'

This was an excellent point. The possibility that Drew had thought it prudent to hide his accomplice, perhaps even send her out of town, had not passed Rick by. 'He might have. But I think he's using her for his alibi and it would be the kind of thing police notice, a key witness moving in a hurry or ducking out of sight. He'll want her to seem like a regular office girl, solid and dependable, right where she says she is.'

'True. Want me to come with you?' Rollo offered and Rick was more tempted than he might have realized. After all, this wouldn't be the first time in this sorry saga that he'd taken himself off on an ill-advised mission, chasing some perverse high, only to depart deeper in trouble than he'd begun.

'No, it's probably best you don't. Keep your distance now, Rollo. I don't want to get you involved in some conspiracy charge.'

'How will I get in touch with you if anything happens?

Like the police coming round again? Wait, I know, take this.' Rollo extracted something from his trouser pocket and handed it to Rick: his pager. 'So if anything comes up my end, I'll page you. It'll buzz and show my number, yeah? Our number,' he corrected himself, a kindly touch. 'Call me when you can.'

'You don't need it for work?'

'It's from my old job. Take it.'

'Thanks. You're a good friend.' Rick frowned. 'Hang on, is that my suit you're wearing?'

'Well, *I* don't own one, do I?' Rollo flashed him a smile, a dash of his old mischievous charm. 'I didn't think you'd mind.'

Rick laughed. 'I don't. Wear whatever you like.'

*

On the tube, he counted the prints – all present and correct – before examining the cuttings properly. The articles were short and offered little beyond the most basic court reporting of a clash between squatters and the authorities. Alongside one, however, was a column containing a first-person profile of one of the squatters, a nineteen-year-old woman. Her identity was represented by a schlocky silhouette, but she was instantly familiar to Rick as the girl he knew.

'*At the End of the Day, I'm On My Own*' read the heading, and he skimmed the account:

'I became homeless when I was seventeen ... parents said I was out of control ... a friend of my dad's

assaulted me ... devastated when they believed his story over mine ... I did cash-in-hand work in clubs ... a blurred line in those hostess jobs ... times when I've taken money for sex ...'

The heartbreaking part was she hadn't hidden her past from him, at least not the bones of it; she'd told him far more about herself than she'd ever presumed to know about Marina Stanley. He hadn't fallen in love with her impersonation of Marina, he'd fallen in love with *her*, with Kirsten.

And, unless Rollo's doubts proved justified, he was about to visit her home – the home he'd never known existed, much less been invited to enter – for the first time.

38

Alex

September, present

'Alex!' Beth called, ominously, artificially upbeat. 'In here!'

He was justified, surely, in judging it a callously brief period between her having dropped her DNA bombshell and choosing now to subject him to one of the most anxiety-inducing episodes in an already hyper-stressful period.

Zara wasn't present on this occasion, but you could bet your bottom dollar she was behind it, convincing Beth to act against her instincts, to disrupt and pivot and all the other things Zara was so keen to advocate at home now she no longer could in the office because she'd proved so impossible for decent people to work with that the two sides were now engaged in a legal dispute.

It was a Friday evening and, following an arduous week on his presentation ('his' now, not the team's), he was approaching his front door when he caught sight of his wife and another woman through the window, a tray of tea things on the table between them. A friend or neighbour, he assumed, but when he let himself in and she called out to him with that tell-tale artificial cheer, instinct propelled him past the living-room door and into the kitchen. As he opened a lager and let the cold liquid gush down his throat, Olive dashed in, nose to his groin, and he crouched to pet her.

'Good girl. What's going on in there, eh?'

Beth now came scampering after, discreetly toeing the door shut behind her. 'Did you not hear me?' Her eyes sparkled with a strange vivacity. 'We've got a guest.'

'We?'

'Yes. She's the girl I told you about.'

'Which girl?' Of course, by then, he was beginning to understand, but he was damned if he was going to save Beth from spelling it out. Owning it. This was an ambush, no more, no less.

'We connected through the ancestry website, remember,' she said, her tone warning him that it was possible they were being overheard. 'Bring your beer and join us.'

'Why would I do that?' It beggared belief that she actually looked taken aback by his refusal. In feigning good cheer for the benefit of her guest, she seemed to have convinced herself. The blood was hot in his veins, his breath short. 'You *promised* you wouldn't act on my behalf, Beth!'

'I know, but when you didn't follow it up yourself, she got in touch with me direct.'

It was true that his wife had forwarded earlier

communications with the site to him, a quick scan of which identified his genetic match as 'Miss S. Griffiths', born 28 May 1996, but he'd never for a moment intended 'following up' with this person. Even a polite rejection constituted a building block he wasn't yet ready to set in place. (He had, however, googled 'Kirsten Griffiths' – he was only human – fascinated to know who she'd married, but had been deterred by the sight of the million-plus results.)

'What was I supposed to do?' Beth added, more imploring now. As if conducting a secret correspondence had been her only reasonable option. And at speed; she'd had only a matter of weeks to set this trap.

'You should have explained you'd made a mistake and shut the whole thing down.'

'Fine, but it's too late now, isn't it? She's here. Your own flesh and blood, Alex! Aren't you a *little bit* curious?'

He'd had enough of this. He whipped open the door, half-expecting to find their visitor right there. At the sight of the empty hallway, he paced into the living room, where he found her standing at the window overlooking Long Lane, her back to the room. At the sound of his footsteps, she spun gracefully to greet him. She was slightly built, blonde, heavily made up. 'Hi! Are you Alex? I'm—'

He cut her off. 'Please don't tell me your name.'

Her mouth hung open in astonishment. Standing face to face with her like this, he had no choice but to register the details of her features: was there anything to suggest a likeness? She was dark-eyed, strong-jawed, with a long, fine-tipped nose, not at all like him, *or* Kirsten for that matter, though it was hard to tell through the mask of make-up. Who knew, maybe under all that crap she was his double.

'I'm very sorry, but my wife has invited you here without consulting me. I'm going to have to ask you to leave.'

Vexation crossed her face. Hurt, too. 'Leave? But Beth said—'

'She wasn't aware how I felt.' He thought he'd detected an accent and it struck him the girl may have travelled some distance to get here. He was aware of Beth hovering behind him, no doubt anxious to get this onto a friendlier footing, and he lost his patience. 'Actually, you know what, *I'll* go. You two finish your conversation. I'm sorry there's been this misunderstanding, but I haven't actually decided yet whether I want to be in contact with any matches. This whole thing was initiated without my consent.'

'Can't we just have five minutes?' the girl pleaded, and Beth echoed the proposal, asking what harm it could do.

'Please. I don't want to get into an argument. This is the worst possible time for me,' he added, addressing the girl. 'Believe me, you don't want to get involved with me. You really don't.'

He left without looking back and spent an antsy couple of hours in the pub by the station. The Plough was convivial enough, but he'd never settled into it the way he had his local in previous homes, never become part of the cohort of Silver Vale husbands and dads who gathered there after getting off the commuter train, delaying re-entry into domesticity with their faithful pint. He imagined Beth and Ms S. Griffiths discussing his churlishness, agreeing it might be best to leave it for now. Beth would see her to the door, forlorn. *He'll come around*: would she be extravagant enough to promise that, after all his objections? And the rejected visitor would depart, walking down Exmoor Gardens, trying to make sense of what had just occurred. It would be just his luck if she came in here for a consolatory drink, and so he relocated to the far corner from where he could see incomers before they saw him.

He would have preferred to think he didn't recognize himself, acting like this, but he did.

*

When he returned to the cottage, Beth was alone. She greeted him with a thunderous expression, her body language combative.

'How could you, Alex? That was unbelievably cruel!'

He'd had a skinful and the row erupted immediately. 'What was cruel was you springing this crap on me when I said I would make my decision in my own time.'

Her voice rose an octave: 'We'll all be dead by then! Why wouldn't you want to meet her? Who wouldn't want to connect with their own daughter? *I* would.'

'So you keep saying. But she's not your daughter, is she? Much as you'd like to think that. She's mine.'

Beth began crying then, but the sight of her distress moved him only enough to prepare what he ought to say as opposed to saying it instinctively because he loved her. 'Look, I know this is emotional. Everything we've been through, *you've* been through. I do get that. But this isn't a Disney movie, Beth. This girl is either lying and wants something or she's not lying and wants something. Either way, she wants something. And I have nothing to give. *Nothing*.'

Beth wiped her eyes with her sleeve. 'No one's asking you to *give*. Why do you have to be so cynical? She just wants to reach out to family. She didn't know who her birth father was until last month, when she was told about the match. Her mother doesn't even know she knows yet, she obviously had her own reasons for keeping your identity to herself all these years. And to be honest, I'm starting to understand why she chose to do that.' Her tone had an edge of defiance to it now. 'I'm starting to feel a bit relieved it's not *me* who had your child.'

Shocked, the two of them stared at each other. The silence was horrible but Alex had no idea how to break it. Finally, Beth fished in her jeans pocket for a tissue and blew her nose. 'Can you *really* not imagine how it must feel to have had that gap in your identity for over two decades? To live every day with the knowledge that someone so fundamental to you is missing from your life?'

Alex stared, horrified. *Yes*, he wanted to cry. *Yes, I can imagine how that feels!*

'You *really* don't want to know who her mother is?' she said.

I already know!

Speaking with frigid control, he pulled himself back from the precipice. 'No, I *really* don't. How many more times do I have to tell you?'

Beth tucked the ragged tissue back in her pocket and shouldered past him. 'No more times.'

39

Rick

September 1995

Moss Road, Tooting, was the kind of low-grade South London street most Londoners would judge squalid, with peeling paint, cracked roof tiles, overturned bins – maybe even the odd surviving outside loo out the back – but it was remarkable how his standards had slipped in the last couple of weeks. Now it looked like just the sort of forgotten place he might like to live when all of this was over.

At the door of number 21, as he clocked the scrawled name 'McKenzie' next to the buzzer for Flat C, his finger hovered over it as if there really were a chance that he would decide not to press it. Having finally reached this moment, he felt an odd vulnerability where surely white-hot fury should have resided, and yet, even if he *were* angry, it wouldn't help him to show it. He needed Kirsten's help and he would secure it whatever it took.

At last, he stabbed the bell.

The response was fast. 'Who is it?' Her voice, definitely hers: it raised the hairs on his arms.

He cleared his throat, raw from chain-smoking on the long walk from the tube station. 'It's me. Rick.'

The long silence that followed brought to mind his and Rollo's panic when they'd thought Drew's thug was at the door, their hissed debate about escaping via the roof. Was that what she was doing, calculating whether or not it would be possible to bolt?

'Hello?' he said. 'Are you still there?'

Finally, her voice came again – 'Come up. Top floor' – and, as the door released, he felt an illogical sense of relief that she was at the top of the house, that she'd be safer up there, safer from Drew.

Or, perhaps, cornered.

She was waiting at the door. He'd expected her to be different: unmasked, de-costumed, but she was just the same, even wearing the pink vest top he recognized, with jeans and a long grunge-style man's cardigan; so obviously herself it was disorientating. She was also quite unflustered – but, then, if he knew anything at all about her it was that she was adept at thinking on her feet.

They did not hug or touch, of course, and this most fundamental of alterations between them sent involuntary pain up his spine.

'How did you find me?' she asked.

What did it matter if she knew? 'I got someone to break into the personnel files at Culkins. I was worried you might have moved on, mind.'

'Where to?' she said simply. Then, 'How did you know my name?'

'I saw it on your passport, remember?'

She nodded, a quiet little *oh yes*. 'Come in. I'll make some tea. There's no trap,' she added, as if he had anything to fear on that score. If the police were somehow alerted, they'd find the very person he wanted them to find. And if Drew came bruising in – well, Rick would just have to take him on. Someone had to.

Her flat was the original attic – he'd seen a small shower room and loo on the half-landing below – with a single skylight. The pitch of the roof made for very little livable space and clothes were draped over wooden fold-out chairs in the eaves, shoes gathered in a heap in the corner, including her sandals with the plastic daisies at the toe. The sight of the wall hanging he'd given her, tacked next to a print of a bee-hived Dusty Springfield, caused particular pain. There was a smell of cigarette smoke and something savoury, like Bovril or Cup-a-Soup.

'Still waiting for your fee?' he said.

'I'm not working at the moment,' she said, with that natural talent for evasion.

'You're lying low, right? Your old manager thinks you're travelling. India, was it? Where did you get *that* idea?'

She didn't answer, but reached for the kettle on the tiny kitchen worktop. 'Tea?'

'Only if it's not spiked.' This, at least, caused a guilty flicker. 'I've worked a lot out,' he added.

'It looks like you have.'

She made the tea. He wondered if she'd apologize, but she just returned with the mugs and they sat on her sofa, which he presently realized must double as her bed. Had Drew had sex with her here? Had he sat where Rick did now, plotting the very downfall that had drawn Rick here this evening in search of salvation?

'Please can we not waste any time denying what's happened,' he began. 'It's taken me a long time to find you and I need information. Facts. There's been enough deception.'

She nodded. 'You almost had me one time, you know.' She spoke quite conversationally. 'When you saw them together at the house. I thought it was all over.'

'That was her, I assume? His wife?'

'Of course. I mean, God knows how many women he's fucked during his marriage, he'll sleep with anything with a pulse, but none like that, in her house.'

'You recovered quickly,' Rick said. 'Quite the gift.'

'I've had to develop it.'

He sipped his tea; it was black and lethally hot. 'The girl in the pub that time – Jessie, was it? I'm guessing she knew you by your real name?'

'Yes, I couldn't have her meeting you. She knew I wasn't married.'

How cleverly she'd made it seem as if the problem lay in the fact that she *was* married.

'That was the night you told me. You didn't plan that then?'

'No,' she said. 'The timing of that revelation was at my discretion.'

'You mean that *lie*.'

Her gaze dipped. 'Yes.' It was a struggle not to stare, not to be mesmerized, as he'd always been. She was so precisely the same. Just as he'd surmised, she'd been able to play the part of Marina as convincingly as she had by being herself. All that differed from before was her tone, which had a new deadness to it.

That was what she'd feigned, perhaps: hope. The thought would be heartbreaking if she hadn't been such a fucking Judas.

'How did he get you to do it?' he asked.

'Long story or short?'

Rick shrugged. 'Either, so long as it's the truth. I think we've already established I can't tell when you're lying.' He drew the cuttings from his jacket pocket. 'I know some of the back story.'

She peered with wonder at the copies of the smudged originals. 'I completely forgot about that journalist. She took me to a café and bought me a sandwich. She was nice. I didn't know it had ever been written up.' She placed the papers on the sofa between them. It was pathetic to think this was her entire published record, but, then, he'd swap it with his own in a heartbeat.

'You met Drew when you were working in one of these clubs, did you? Did he pay you for sex?'

There was only the faintest flinch at this directness. 'Not exactly, but he used to help me out. He got me out of the squats and into this place.'

'And you became his bit on the side. He can't have been married very long at that point. Did Marina know he was being unfaithful?'

'I don't know what she knew, but she must have suspected. She wasn't stupid.' Kirsten shrugged. 'But the big problem between them was money. His business was in debt and she controlled the purse strings. She had some accountant who'd started questioning where his cash went. He was worried she was going to have him tailed and then she'd throw him out and divorce him.'

'So he decided to make a pre-emptive strike,' Rick said, grimly. 'What I don't understand is how *you* got involved.'

'Because he's not the kind of person you say no to.' She passed a hand across her face, scratched the skin near her right ear with a sharp fingernail, leaving a red mark. 'When I got the temping job, I thought it would be over, I thought he'd find some other sap, but he kept coming back.'

'And he's paying you, presumably? You're getting a cut of the inheritance?'

She sighed. 'A bit. Enough to break free. If he lets me.'

Rick fell silent, pondering his chief difficulty here. If he succeeded in his aim, there'd be no payment coming her way, and he had nothing left to offer in its place, having spent his savings on his plans for *her*.

'How did it begin? With me, I mean.'

'I suppose it was when . . .' A flush crept over her cheeks. 'When I realized you liked me. He gets off on hearing me talk about other men, anyone who's got the hots for me. I just make it up sometimes, he's so into it.'

What had Rollo said, way back: *She sees you and then goes back and describes every sordid act ...* His instinct had been so much truer than Rick's, right from the start.

'Go on.'

'I'd seen you watching at me in the lobby at work. I told him you were stalking me, just exaggerating for a laugh, but he went all quiet. Then he went, "Does he know your name?" and I went, "No, we've not even spoken." He said, "Good. Next time you see him, talk to him. Tell him your name's Marina Stanley." I said, "You want me to pretend to be your wife? Why would I do that?"'

'We know why,' Rick said, bleakly.

She shook her head. 'I don't think he knew himself, to be honest. It took him a while to work out how he could use you. Obviously, he never told me the truth.'

Rick's gaze narrowed. 'Why obviously?'

'You think I knew he was going to do *that*?' Astoundingly, she looked as if her feelings were hurt. Could she not understand the horrific trouble he was in? 'I would *never* have done it if I'd thought he was framing you for murder.'

'What the fuck did you *think* he was framing me for then?'

'I thought it was just a burglary, that he was going to take her jewellery and watches and stuff. Sell it and claim the insurance. I just had to lure you there and he would take care of the rest. You have to believe me, Rick, that's what Drew said. I swear on my life.'

Rick digested this. She'd done a lot more than lure him there. 'Is that why you left Marina's watch in the car?'

'You found it? You know it's worth thousands?' She looked

pleased he'd received this unexpected windfall. Her naivety was staggering.

'So you were happy to have me go down for burglary, then?'

'Not happy, no. I was never happy. And, anyway, he said you'd just get community service or a fine.'

'That's bollocks, Marina.' He caught himself. '*Kirsten*. It would have been a prison sentence.' Though not as long as for murder, certainly. He tried the tea again, just about drinkable now. 'Did you not think it was all a bit elaborate for the sake of a few pieces of jewellery? We were seeing each other for almost four months. That's a long time to pretend you like someone.'

'I wasn't pretending.' There was a gulp in her throat. 'Not completely. Maybe at first, yes, but not later.'

'How much later?' he demanded, ashamed of himself for caring. 'When you said you loved me that night in Covent Garden, were you pretending then?'

She looked miserably at him – because of the inconvenient truth of her answer or her sudden inability to fib, he couldn't tell. He swallowed. 'It was prostitution, basically. Except I wasn't the one paying. Do you not think it's in incredibly bad taste to lie about being a victim of domestic abuse?'

'I'm not sure I *was* lying.' She gave the groan of someone who knew she could never win. 'You don't understand, Rick, I just did what I was told, one thing at a time. "Make him think you're in danger," he said. "Get him all fired up so he wants to rescue you from your monster of a husband." It kept getting weirder, more twisted, you know? He said he had to hurt me to make it look real, but I could tell he enjoyed it. That thing I told you about him saying he'd kill me if I left, that was true.

I was scared of him. That was real, I don't know how else to say it. It was real.'

She was trembling now and, in spite of everything she'd done, he found himself longing to comfort her. 'Okay, so maybe the feelings were real, but the way it played out, it was all staged, wasn't it? Like when he brought you to the flat that Sunday to break up with me?'

She dipped her gaze, but made no attempt to deny the obvious.

'Did you tell him about our plans? About the safe house?'

'No. The escape plan was only for you. For us.' Her voice grew wistful. 'You know, a part of me thought maybe I would do it. Maybe I'd meet you after work that day and say "Forget Silver Vale, let's go straight to the flat. I don't need anything." And we'd hole up, like we said we would. I had the watch, as well, I knew that could have funded us for a little while.'

Hearing this, despair filled every cavity of Rick's body. 'You could have told me. At any time, you could have told me it was all a set-up. I would still have gone through with the escape plan and looked after you.'

She gave a sad shake of the head. 'You'd have run a mile. You know you would.'

The truth was he *didn't* know this. If she proposed right now that they should reunite, flee together, do everything he'd thought they were going to do in the first place, wouldn't he be just a little tempted?

It made no difference now. And she saved him from the humiliation of having to comment by going to make more tea.

40

Rick

September 1995

'Tell me how it worked on the day,' he said, and her eyes
flared in alarm, as if she were only now comprehending the
magnitude of what she'd already disclosed. Twin columns of
vapour rose from the mugs in her hands.

'Wait, you're not recording this, are you?'

Rick stood, took the mugs from her and placed them safely
aside, then raised his arms. 'Frisk me if you like.'

Half-heartedly, she ran her hands over his chest and patted
the pockets of his clothes, causing a hideous collision of revulsion and desire in him, and then they both sat down again.

'So did you even go into the house yourself?' he asked.

'No. I've never been in there. He just wanted you to
come after me. He wanted you to come the front way, to
be seen by neighbours, but I told him you were going to
come down the track.' It was clear that she viewed this as

some sort of victory, but there was nothing to be gained from contradiction. 'I walked straight past the house and met him on the main road at that parade of shops. He had a minicab waiting.'

'Do you remember the name of the minicab firm?'

She said she did not, and nor had she noticed the make of the car.

'How did you know what to wear?' Rick said. 'You were wearing the same dress as her.'

'He rang me at work in the morning, told me to go out and buy it. It was from Hobbs.'

Rick tried to figure out how it might have worked. When Marina Stanley had got dressed in the morning, Drew had said how nice she looked, asked her where she'd bought the dress. What would he have done if it had been hard to find? It seemed awfully last-minute for such a well-plotted long game. Then again, an approximation would have done, he supposed. The plan was that Rick should find her dead. The exact style and colour of her clothing would not have been at the forefront of his mind.

'If you thought it was just a burglary, didn't you think it was weird that you needed to wear a specific dress?'

She gestured with her free hand, dismissive. 'Everything he does is weird, Rick. Everything. You learn not to question the details.' It was chilling the way she used the present tense. Still under his thumb. 'I assumed he wanted something colourful that people might remember when they were asked if they'd seen me.'

'What about *his* clothes? If you thought he was just staging a break-in, nicking a bit of jewellery or whatever, didn't you wonder why he was covered in blood?'

'He wasn't. There was a bit on his hands, but he said he'd cut himself on a glass.'

'The state Marina was in, I'd have expected it to be spattered all over him.'

She shuddered. 'He must have changed. Maybe he went back inside.'

'I wonder what he did with the clothes,' Rick said. 'He can't have left them anywhere near the house or the police would have found them.'

'He had a bag,' Kirsten said. 'He really was going away on a stag weekend, that part was true.'

'Maybe he got rid of them then.' He'd have planned exactly where; they'd be long gone now. He might have had a second, uncontaminated bag, in a locker at the station, ready to collect before hopping on the train. Perhaps there'd even been a quick shower in the station facilities.

And any blood he'd brought back into the house could be attributed to Rick.

He was starting to think like Drew now, he noted, wryly, even if it was a little late. 'So the cab took you to Victoria, did it?'

'Yes, well, a side street nearby. Drew wanted us to pass in front of some security camera by the tube entrance, you know, to be seen to say goodbye. Then he went to meet his friends for their train and I got on the tube to go home.'

'So you knew you were his alibi? He was supposedly interviewing you for a job?'

'We'd already agreed that. He said it was in case he had to give his whereabouts for the time of the burglary.'

He'd cut it fine, Rick thought. It couldn't have been earlier than 6.15pm by the time Kirsten got to the taxi in Silver Vale, plus a further forty-five minutes to get to Victoria. According to Drew's account in the *Standard*, their interview had been at 5.45pm; did the police really believe it had lasted for an hour and fifteen minutes? It wasn't so outlandish, he supposed. An attractive business owner, a gorgeous young hopeful. If he hadn't had a train to catch, they might have stayed drinking for hours.

'So you really had no idea he'd killed her? Did he not seem at all traumatized?'

'He just told me it had gone according to plan. He said he'd called the police anonymously from a phone box and told them he'd seen someone on the track with a crow bar.'

So there'd been an earlier 999 call. Rick had been lucky to flee in time; Drew had clearly intended him to be found at the scene, Marina's blood on his hands. It was brilliant, insane and sickening in one. The extended psychological grooming of Rick and then the brutally simple killing and getaway.

Had the crow bar the anonymous caller had 'seen' been the murder weapon?

'If I was supposed to be caught in the act of this burglary, why did you need to plant her watch in the car?' The question answered itself. 'Oh, I see. In case I got away.' Another anonymous tip at the right time, someone remembering the make of car, even the registration, supplied by Kirsten. A shame she hadn't also noted the registration of the minicab.

'What about the Coke can? I assume he gave you something to put in it?'

She nodded. 'He said it would be useful for the police to think you were a druggie. A motive for the theft or something. I just had to leave the can in the car.'

It beggared belief that she'd accepted such explanations without question. Was she really so stupid? So scared? Drew must have given the same thing to his wife – maybe in the morning – to flatten her responses, remove the possibility of her fighting back and getting away from him. 'When did you hear she was dead?'

Marina gave a shiver, wrapped her cardigan tighter. 'I heard it on the radio that night. As soon as they said Silver Vale, I knew what must have happened. I didn't know if he'd planned it like that or if she'd been there when she wasn't supposed to be and they got into a fight.'

'Oh, he planned it like that, don't you worry. What did you do when you realized?'

'I was sick. I ran into the bathroom and threw up.'

They'd existed in parallel, barely eight miles apart.

'He rang me late that night and asked if I'd heard the news. I said yes.'

'Did he admit he'd done it?'

'Not exactly. He said things had escalated a bit, but it didn't affect our situation and I should stick to the same story about the job interview after work. He'd given my details to the police, said they'd be wanting a statement, which they did.'

Rick drew a deep breath. 'You mean you've already given one?'

'Yes.'

Though it was only as he'd expected, he'd fervently hoped otherwise. Now he was going to have to persuade her not only to tell the truth but also to retract her previous version of events.

'I'm sorry, Rick,' she said. 'I'd never have got involved in this if I'd known. I know it's not the same, but he tricked me as well.' She took his hand then, a simple, childlike gesture that opened a tap in him, and all of a sudden he was filled with a terrible fatalism, the request he'd intended making with gravitas, even menace, suddenly spouting from him in the most artless way:

'Come to the police with me, Kirsten, will you, and explain all this to them? We'll both be in trouble, but at least they'll arrest the right man. He can't be allowed to get away with this. Think of Marina's family, her parents and brother. For all we know, she might have confided in them. They might have had their own suspicions about him if it weren't for this alibi you've given him. You've completely exonerated him.'

Kirsten said nothing, but her disconsolate expression encouraged him to press on. 'And what about the women he might hurt in the future? If we tell the truth, we'll be saving them from terrible experiences – while *we* get on with our lives.'

'*You* maybe, Rick. But he'd kill me.' For the first time, she lost her composure entirely, sinking her face into her hands.

'No, he wouldn't, that's just it! He couldn't, he'd be in jail. Once the police hear the truth, they'll lock him up straightaway and hold him on remand until the trial. Men on murder charges, violent ones like this, they don't get bail.'

Her hands dropped from her face, her gaze meeting his. 'Will they, though? Will they even arrest him? He's got them completely taken in.' She was shaking now. 'If there was any delay, even a day, he'd find me and that would be it. He's done it once, hasn't he?'

This was the repugnant truth.

'But he's the one who told the police about you, about the job interview,' Rick pointed out. 'If you ended up murdered, there's no way that could be a coincidence. But if you're really worried, come with me. The safe house I rented, that's where I've been all this time. It's completely secret, he couldn't possibly find you. Then once the police are involved, they'll protect us. It's their job. Please, Kirsten, I'm begging you.'

'Oh, Rick, I don't think I can . . .' And all at once she was in his arms, sobbing, and he was comforting her, stroking her back and her hair. He felt his hopes slide away. She wasn't going to do it. He was going to have to take what little he had and do this alone. At least he'd gleaned a few additional details of the deception. If he had an answer for every query, every doubt, he might just be given a fair hearing. Someone in Marina's family might support him. And maybe Rollo's posh family might know a good lawyer.

At last, Kirsten calmed and pulled away from him. 'If I do it, you have to promise to protect me. Not just now, but after he's out of prison as well. *For ever*, Rick, that's my condition.'

His spirits soared. He couldn't believe what he was hearing, the very words he'd longed for, words that possessed the solemnity of a marriage vow.

'I promise,' he said, and if there was the one thing in his

favour it was this: she knew he meant it, she knew she could trust him.

She exhaled. 'I'll need to pack a few things.'

'Do it now.' He sprang to his feet. 'I'll help you.'

But she remained seated, her expression pleading. 'I also have to be here for his call later.'

'Not this again, Mar—' He caught himself. 'Kirsten. Please don't speak to him.'

'No, I have to. He calls me every evening to update me and keep our stories straight. He'll know something's up if I don't answer. It's much better if he thinks nothing's changed.'

'What time?'

'Nine. Let me take his call, it will only be twenty minutes, then I'll come and meet you. We'll go to the police first thing tomorrow morning. What's your address?'

But there was no way he was going to hand over the address right before she was due to speak to Drew. Though he believed her in the here and now, who knew what coercive tactics Drew might use if during their phone call he sensed even the smallest withdrawal on her part.

'Meet me at Oxford Circus tube at eleven. The Argyll Street exit. If you speak to him at nine, that's plenty of time to get into town.'

Her eyes were huge, honest and trusting. 'Okay. I'll be there.'

'Thank you,' Rick said. 'Thank you so much.'

'Don't thank me. Please don't thank me.'

She was right. They both knew how tragic it was that he should feel such gratitude to the very person who'd plunged him into this nightmare in the first place.

If only it had been some other man beguiled by her and her blueberry yoghurt in the lobby café.

'Rick?'

'Yes?'

'I really cared about you. I know you won't believe that and I get it. But I did. Everyone else, they've taken from me, but not you. You were ready to give up everything for me.'

It looks as if I still am, Rick thought, as he departed.

*

By the time he got back to the West End it was nine o'clock, which meant he could get an hour and a half's kip before getting ready to meet Kirsten at Oxford Circus. Before returning to Newman Street, he phoned Rollo at the flat and told him the news. He hardly recognized his own voice, with its positive energy, its exhilaration. 'I think she's going to come clean, Rollo. I think I might actually be off the hook, or at least just get off on some minor charge.'

'Fucking outstanding,' Rollo said, more overtly triumphant than Rick dared be himself. 'But what about her? Won't she be done for whatever it's called, corroboration? Aiding and abetting?'

'I don't know. I'm hoping they'll understand that she was acting under duress. To be honest, I think she's only told me the bare bones, I think there's a lot more that went on, this whole history of men abusing her. I'm going to tell her to play that up. Maybe it could work in her favour, you know?'

'Let's hope so.' Rollo gave a low whistle. 'Wow, Rick, this is huge. Good luck. And I'm here if you need me, yeah?'

41

Alex

September, present

If he had to pin a date to his psychological collapse, his unmooring, it would be the Tuesday in September that he took the train into work for the stakeholders meeting – the meeting that involved Janice, Janice's boss, their minister and representatives from the Treasury and that had been convened, of course, for the presentation *he* was giving – but didn't ever reach the office. Instead, he continued up to Euston and boarded a service to the West Midlands.

Before then, he'd known he was paranoid, he'd known he was driving Beth to distraction, but he'd also been reasonably confident that his mental state had not yet jeopardized his working life. Nor had it sent him out of his . . . comfort zone wasn't quite the term, self-designated zone, perhaps. Yes, fine, he'd taken that impulsive tour of the old Albert Street flat, but this was something else, this was an urge in him that

351

was plainly never going to solve anything and might very well make matters worse.

To find the individual responsible for corrupting him, altering him, redefining him. To look him in the eye and see if he truly understood what a force for terror he had been.

His conversation with Eddie had been the trigger. Previously, he'd assumed that Googling Drew Stanley's name was a fruitless endeavour – like Kirsten, and Alex himself, the man would have kept a necessarily low profile if he'd known what was best for him. But, unlike Kirsten and Alex, he had a sister who he was close to, and whose married name, Gillian Woods, had appeared in the press reports of the trial. The flooring business, in which she'd been involved, had closed down at the time of his conviction, but a little digital diving hooked another business listing, a gourmet dog treat company in Burton upon Trent run by Mark and Gilly Woods, a portrait of whom showed a couple in their late fifties or early sixties, exactly the right age. Listed in its 'people' section was the name of the delivery manager: Drew Stanley.

Sitting on the train with his coffee, phone turned off, Alex pondered Drew's fidelity to his original, criminal name (he would *never* have used it had he been in Drew's position). Perhaps it had proved of assistance, that reputation, that notoriety; a case of *Mess with me and you know exactly what I'm capable of.* Or maybe it was simply that he'd done his time, paid the price, and if he had to explain himself to the occasional antagonist, some rogue moralist, then so be it.

And Lord knew it was preferable in the end, that

approach – crime, punishment, freedom – to the alternative. Which was, Alex knew all too well, purgatory.

There was no other word.

*

The premises were quite a trek from the station and, having dressed for a meeting in Central London, he felt the sting of the cold air through the inadequate layers. Kitchen, factory and warehouse were on the same site, protected by locked double gates, and he cleared his throat to address the intercom.

'Is your delivery manager available, please.'

'Drew's out with one of the drivers on a delivery down the M1, he should be back around five.' It was, by now, barely past midday. 'Can someone else help?'

'No, just Drew. I'm actually a friend. I've come from out of town and was hoping to catch him in person. Not to worry, there's other stuff I can do till five.'

'They usually go to the Nelson when they knock off, if you want to wait there?'

The Nelson turned out to be an old-style boozer a couple of minutes' walk back towards town. Tempting though it was to kill five hours getting sozzled, Alex resisted and set off instead for a stroll along the river, a pretty green trail with swans and other birdlife. But the slicing cold wind soon put paid to that and he found his way to the town's Cineplex, where he bought a ticket for the latest Stephen King adaptation and loaded up on junk food.

Then, just before five, he arrived at the Nelson.

He recognized Stanley as soon as he came through the door, in the company of two other men. His physique was notably bulkier now, his hair the full silver of a man older than sixty, but then twenty years of incarceration tended to age a person. His left eye was covered by a flesh-coloured patch, to conceal an old prison injury, perhaps.

In spite of having had a whole day to consider his intentions, Alex had rehearsed no lines with which to approach the man and, it seemed, was initially content to torture himself with whatever post-traumatic sensations might be stirred simply by looking. The overriding one was revulsion; a sense of motion sickness that took several minutes to subside.

After a while, a woman came in and joined the trio. She was in her fifties and fake-tanned, a fitted black coat streamlining her apple-shaped figure. Drew pecked her cheek before gesturing to the barman for her order. There was a bluntness to his movements that couldn't entirely be put down to weight gain or age; if Alex had to guess, he'd say he was on medication.

Two rounds later, Drew headed to the gents. Instinctively, Alex left his seat and followed. Drew was finishing up at the urinal when he entered, glancing without interest as he zipped himself up. Even stooped, he dwarfed Alex, and it came back to him in an awful surge, that Sunday in Albert Street, the way he'd stood in front of their house, a wall of muscle, his gaze brimming with violent intent, with that chilling wickedness. His senses heightened by adrenaline, Alex found the standard smell of urine and bleach nauseating and, when he opened his mouth, he almost expected to watch himself vomit. It was a surprise, therefore, to hear his own voice, sharp against the tiled walls:

'Does she know? That woman you're with, does she know?'

Drew turned to him with an unsettling sense of deliberation. 'Know what?'

'What you did. In Silver Vale. Does she know how you smashed your wife's head in, up on that track behind your house?'

'What the fuck . . . ?' The man's obvious bewilderment in the face of such brazen provocation suggested he'd experienced less outright confrontation from the community than Alex might have imagined. He made no move to leave, but stood, regarding Alex with a rough dislike, clearly unable to place him.

Alex brought a note of menace to his manner. 'Does she know how you set the whole thing up so someone else would do time for you? Does she know how you exploited a vulnerable girl to help you?'

At this, there was a change in Drew's energy, a sense of the bridled violence of a man with something to lose after all, and it was now that Alex understood why he was here: to get himself beaten – punished – by the one man who could reliably do it. He braced himself for a blow, but to his astonishment, Drew simply chuckled.

'Look, if you've got something to say to my woman, knock yourself out. She's heard it all before.'

'You destroyed other lives, as well, did you know that?' Alex swallowed a lump in his throat, heard the self-pity in his voice as he added, 'Mine, for one.'

Drew's gaze dropped to the good wool sweater under Alex's best blazer, his polished newish loafers; he'd dressed, after all, for a meeting with a minister. 'You look like you're doing okay to me, but if your life's been "destroyed", I'm guessing you've done that all by yourself.'

'Do you even know who I am?'

'Couldn't give a monkey's, mate. Now are you going to get out of my way and take a piss or not?'

And, as he shouldered past Alex, knocking him off balance and causing pain to shoot through his arm, it was clear that he really *didn't* give a monkey's. Beyond the immediate, superficial challenge, he was incurious, entirely removed from his past self; this was, Alex supposed, the difference between having received due punishment for your crime and having evaded it.

Lord knew no good had ever come of these lunatic impulsive missions of his, but at least this time he was sober, which gifted him the sense to turn on his heel and leave the pub via a side door. The evening air was more forgiving than earlier, the train station closer than he remembered.

*

On the train, he couldn't bear to turn on his phone and face the fallout of his missed day. Instead, he dozed, thinking of her.

He'd thought he'd seen her once, years ago, on the tube, between Charing Cross and Piccadilly Circus. It was in the evening, not late but after rush hour. Perishingly cold above ground, but stuffy enough down there to make you sweat into your coat within two minutes.

She'd slipped off her jacket – a chunky sheepskin thing – in concession to the heat. Her hair was much shorter, a pixie cut shorn close to the skull, lips pale, eyes heavily made up, like some hounded Sixties icon. She was quite still, her body language passive, even submissive, and he'd thought she was too old – in her mid-thirties by then – for the victim act. Except, it wasn't an act, was it? She'd always been the hunted, never quite able to protect herself.

Alex wasn't the only one whose eye she had caught in the carriage; others were sliding glances over the top of their evening papers and crime thrillers. He might have been the only one transfixed, though. Magnetized, even, for when she got off at Piccadilly Circus, he'd risen from his seat and followed her through the exit tunnels before he could even ask himself what he was doing. Only as he took a spot on the escalator fewer than ten steps behind her did he come to his senses. It was all very well for him to see her, but the last thing he needed was for her to see him.

What an idiot he was.

He'd done a one-eighty at the top and gone back down, arriving on the same platform he'd left just as the train behind hurtled in.

*

The window was greasy with his own breath as they blasted through the north London suburbs, and he succumbed, finally, to his phone. Instantly, it blew up with notifications of voicemails and messages about the meeting he'd failed to make.

'We need to talk,' Janice said, her voice vibrating with an indignation worthy of Zara. 'This is fatal now.' What a word to use, the self-importance of it, as if Alex's absence had caused open-heart surgery to go wrong or a military evacuation to flounder. For all she knew, something *fatal* could have happened to Alex to have caused his absence, and then how would she have felt?

Whatever.

Tomorrow, he would propose voluntary redundancy, try for a nice tidy ending.

42

Rick

September 1995

He was awakened by a strange intermittent buzzing and it took half a minute to locate its source in the pocket of his fleece, hanging on the back of the door.

Rollo's pager. The display showed their Camden number, alongside the word: *urgent!*

It was just after 10pm. Limbs still heavy with sleep, Rick donned the fleece and cap once more and headed out. The fleece was starting to smell of vagrant living – had Kirsten noticed that when he'd held her as she sobbed? Striding towards the phone box, dodging the punters outside a bar on the corner, he calculated there might just be time to shower and change before going to meet her at Oxford Circus.

His heart thudded as he breathed the brisk night air. Was there really a chance he would be exonerated as soon as tomorrow? That he might sit in a police interview room and be told he was free to leave, free to live his life? *Just mind who you fall in love with next time*, he imagined some friendly detective advising, and then he'd be back on the roof of his Albert Street flat, necking vodka and saying to Rollo, 'Did all of that *really* happen?'

'Best just to forget the whole thing,' Rollo would say. 'Drink through it, yeah.'

The phone box was free. He fed the coins into the slot and tapped out the digits. 'Rollo?'

'Thank God I gave you my pager!' His friend's voice was frantic, causing an instant surge of adrenaline through Rick's bloodstream.

'What's wrong?'

'It's Kirsten. He's grabbed her.'

'What d'you mean, grabbed her? I just saw her a couple of hours ago and she was fine.'

'He must have been watching her place and seen you there.'

Oh, God. Watching her place – or able to tell from her voice on the phone that she'd been turned?

'She says he's taken her to the house and he's holding her there. I'm not joking, she sounded fucking terrified, Rick.'

'She called you?' Rick demanded. His heart banged with a frightening ferocity. 'Why you?'

'She doesn't have a number for you, does she? But she's got one for here. She thought I'd know how to reach you and she was right. Seriously, Rick, I could hear him ranting in the background, it sounds like he's flipped his lid. We need to go to the police. We need—'

'Hang on a minute,' Rick interrupted. 'That might make

things worse.' *Worse for me*, he meant, battling to harness his speeding thoughts. 'As long as she's with him, she'll do whatever he says. We send the police round, he'll deny there's anything wrong, she'll go along with it. My only chance is to get her away from him.'

'How?'

'I'll have to go down to the house,' Rick said.

Where another man might have gasped, Rollo only paused. 'Mate,' he said, finally, 'that's not going to end well. How are you going to take him on, even if you manage to get in in the first place? After what happened, he'll have extra locks, maybe even a security guard.'

'Why? No one's after *him*. I'll find a way in,' Rick said. 'I'll go now.'

'You want me to come with you?' Rollo said.

Rick felt a lump in his throat. 'Really?'

'Of course. You'll get killed on your own. Might be better to arrive separately, though. Don't wait for me at Waterloo, just go ahead. I'll get the train after and meet you there.'

It wasn't hard to read between the lines of *that*. Rollo didn't want to risk being apprehended with a famous fugitive. Fair enough.

'Okay, but I'm not sure we should be seen out front.' It was reasonable to assume the Stanleys' neighbours would be in a state of high alert, each intimately familiar with the de facto mugshot of Rick pasted all over the papers.

'What then? Through the back way again?'

Again. How innocent that first expedition seemed now. Sneaking up to the window like schoolboys, a pair of

pranksters cheeking the nosy neighbour. Whereas this ...
This was dangerous. And Rollo had a point about security:
to all appearances, Drew had lost his wife in a home invasion,
he was hardly likely to leave the doors unlocked. They'd need
to break a window, find a brick or rock on the track.

'You remember how to access it? Just off Surrey Road.
That end of the track closer to the station. I'll wait for
you as close to the house as I can get. There might still be
police tape up.'

They hung up and, thoughts of a shower abandoned,
Rick headed straight to the tube. As the carriage rocked and
screeched through the black tunnels, he felt doubts start to
surface: could he trust Kirsten to have been straight with
Rollo or was she setting Rick up a second time, Drew still
her puppeteer? Was that what she'd done the moment Rick
left, got on the phone and started plotting his capture? She'd
certainly agreed to a joint confession far more readily than
he'd anticipated.

But by the time he'd walked across the concourse at
Waterloo from tube to train, he'd reverted to his original
conviction: the only way to end this nightmare was to go
together to the police and lay out the truth.

He no longer had a choice: to save himself, he had
to save her.

*

The train was full of commuters flushed with after-work
boozing, their breath warm and beery. Accustomed now to
making himself silent and unmemorable, Rick caught no eye,

exchanged no end-of-week fellow feeling. The service only ran every half-hour at this time of night, which meant Rollo should comfortably make the one after Rick's, even if he'd taken his time leaving Albert Street, and it was comforting to know his friend would soon be rattling along behind him.

At Silver Vale, several other passengers disembarked and turned right down Surrey Road, two or three detouring into the pub opposite the station. Spooked by a *Standard*-branded sandwich board bearing his own face propped against the station wall, Rick lingered until the last commuter was almost out of sight.

He reached the entrance to the track without incident. There was a new 'Do Not Enter' sign and the barriers had been reattached to their original posts, presumably by the police, but he was able to climb over without any great difficulty, just a twinge in his damaged knee. Though it was a clear, dry night, the overhanging branches made for a thick darkness on the track and he moved cautiously at first, not wanting to trip and cry out. Every so often, squares of yellow light from upstairs rooms could be glimpsed through the black foliage, even a silhouetted figure at a window – if he had to guess, he'd say they weren't sleeping so easily, these Silver Vale residents – and he caught the occasional snatch of music or television, the faint grind and bump of a sash window being closed. Otherwise, there was only the crunch of his own footsteps, the scrape of his breath in his windpipe. It was ridiculous to be frightened when he was the one the whole city was scared of – the women of the city, anyway – but that fear was manufactured, wasn't it? Rick had never laid a finger on a woman in anger. Only he, Rollo and Kirsten knew where the danger truly lay and surely, between them, they could prevail.

But as he approached number 54, the smell of freshly turned soil evident, an image of broken bone and blood-drenched hair flashed through his mind and he felt bile rise in his throat, a dizzying sense of nausea. After tonight, he would never come back to this wicked, wretched place again as long as he lived, but, for now, this last time, he needed to make a superhuman effort to manage his emotions.

First, he needed to make a practical assessment and, helpfully, any police cordons or tape there'd been had been removed and he was able to move freely over the site. It felt different spatially, and he quickly deduced that a tree had been removed, possibly two. It looked as if part of the bank had been dug up, too, perhaps to take out the roots of the trees, and several metres of chain fencing cut away – along with a chunk of the Stanleys' hedge – presumably to allow police access between garden and track. But they'd done a decent job of making good the site now that the crime scene was finished with. They had their evidence, after all.

They had their suspect.

And he clearly wasn't the first to visit, for bouquets of flowers had been tied to nearby trees, others laid on the edges of the clearing. Roses and hydrangeas, Marina Stanley's favourites, perhaps.

Not a sunflower among them.

He turned his attention to the house itself. There were no exterior lights on, so he could discern little beyond the narrow crack of light at the window of the same bedroom where he and Rollo had seen the Stanleys that time. Was Kirsten in there with Drew now, supplying the warped sexual kicks he demanded, or was he holding her in another room? That detail Rollo had given about hearing him ranting was worrying, for the man had to date proved himself a cold-blooded and meticulous planner, every word pitch-perfect, every variable neutralized or exploited. If he'd lost control of himself, then Rick was going to have to overcome a far more unpredictable force than he'd have preferred.

He was starting to shiver with cold and fortified himself by picturing his room high above Newman Street, safe and secret and still the only place he could be sure Drew Stanley didn't know about. If everything went well in the next hour or so, he'd take both Rollo and Marina back there with him to hole up overnight.

'Rick! That you?'

For a horrific moment he thought the voice belonged to Drew, but then the familiar lithe movements of his flatmate came into focus, the beam of a torch tracking the ground between them.

'Rollo. Thank God.'

Rollo slapped him lightly on the shoulder. 'It's fucking creepy up here. Looks different.'

'I think they've pulled up some trees. Careful near the bank, the earth's quite loose in places. And turn the torch off, someone might see.'

Rollo did as he was asked, creating a darkness so dense Rick could feel his other senses sharpening. Then particles of light began to register once more and he was able to make out his friend's features again, the grey of his unzipped jacket. 'I think they're upstairs, but I don't know for sure,' he whispered. 'What did she say on the phone? Has he tied her up or anything like that? How did she even manage to make the call?'

Rollo answered none of these questions, but, to Rick's surprise, gave a low chuckle. 'You really are a fucking tool, aren't you?'

There was something off about him; he wasn't sober, Rick could tell, and he hoped there'd been only a couple of vodkas or a can or two of lager involved. 'What do you mean?'

'I mean, she's not in there.'

'What? She managed to get out?' *Thank God*. The relief that they wouldn't have to tackle Drew after all caused a collapsing sensation that made him fear he might drop to his knees. 'Did she call you back after we spoke?'

'She was never there,' Rollo said.

Rick gaped, baffled. Rollo's gaze was so narrow, he could no longer catch the gleam of his eyes. 'Where is she then?'

'Wherever she told you she'd be, I imagine.'

'I don't understand.'

'I know you don't, Rick, I know you don't.' Rollo spoke with resignation, as if the matter were to be left there, any further explanation beyond Rick's intelligence.

Rick grabbed his arm. 'Why are we here if *she's* not? Let's get out of here. She was supposed to be coming to my place so we can go to the police first thing, but now I'll—'

'She's not going to the police,' Rollo said, speaking over him. 'You can forget about that.'

Still, Rick clung on. 'You mean Drew got to her?' Finally, agonizingly, his grip slipped. For a second, the only thing he could hear was his own tortured breathing, and then he heard himself whisper: '*You?*'

Rollo sighed. 'Sorry to have to break it to you, but you weren't the only one in Albert Street she was conspiring with. *Sleeping* with.'

Rick felt the air sucking from his lungs. 'I don't believe you.'

There was a cool nod of concession from his friend, who was somehow exactly as he always had been and yet also completely unrecognizable. 'Don't worry, she didn't want to be with me. I think she genuinely liked you, but with me she needed a bit of incentive.'

A howling started up in Rick's ears. 'You paid her?'

'Oh, the payment was all hers, mate.'

'What, you mean you *blackmailed* her?'

Rollo's shoulders twitched in a half-shrug. 'I just took advantage of her weaker negotiating position in this crazy power struggle of ours. I doubt Drew gave a shit, he was used to sharing her out, you of all people know that.'

'When?' Rick said. 'Where? At the flat?'

'Only once. The rest of the time at hers.'

'Hers?' The howling was threatening to split his skull. 'You've known all this time where she lived?'

A flicker of disdain crossed Rollo's face. 'Don't say I didn't warn you. I told you the first time I met her she was damaged goods. And that was before I knew anything myself.'

'Knew *what*?' Rick cried. 'I don't get what you're saying! None of this makes any sense.'

'Those cuttings. You were right, there *were* things that had to be removed. Pictures of Marina. As soon as I saw them, I knew our girl was a fake. She was up to something dodgy.'

Rick gaped. 'Why the hell didn't you tell me?'

'Because I wanted in. Whatever it was, I wanted a piece of it. I needed money.'

'Money? Why? You haven't been that badly off, no more than anyone else we know.'

'For fuck's sake, Rick, how naïve is it possible to be? I'm in seriously deep shit. That thug hanging around, he didn't want *you*, he wanted *me*. I owed over ten grand to the loan guys in Kentish Town. So, yeah, when it looked like your bird was on the make, I saw an opportunity to not get my arms broken.' All of this was said quite pragmatically, as if he were appealing to Rick's sense of logic.

'How much did you get from her?' *How much am I worth?* Rick thought, miserably.

'Not a lot as yet, though she did let me take the cash in your biscuit tin. But the big payoff comes when Drew gets his inheritance. She'll share her cut with me and I'll be able to clear my debts and get on with my life. So, you see, there's no way I can have her blabbing to the police. The family would contest the will, no executor is going to pay out to a murderer. Besides, I don't want her using me in some tactic to get herself off the hook. You said yourself, she could present herself as a victim. I can't have her spinning *me* as one of her abusers.'

The frenzied rhythm of Rick's heartbeat was starting to scare him: was he having some sort of an attack? At least the howling in his head had subsided, in its place an icy hush. 'You know that without her there's not a cat's chance in hell I'll be believed?'

Rollo gave a sad little nod. 'I know. It's really unfortunate how it's worked out.'

'Unfortunate? We're *friends*, Rollo.'

'We barely know each other. I rented a room in your crummy flat and we hung out now and then. We were hardly blood brothers.'

The realizations were coming so relentlessly, Rick couldn't separate them, until, at last, one broke free: if Rollo had shared what he'd known with Rick instead of manipulating Kirsten, they could have approached Marina Stanley and warned her. They could have saved her life! 'Don't you care what happened to that poor woman? Right here, right beneath our feet? Her injuries were horrific. She was trying to get away from him, she was completely defenceless.'

'We had no idea he was going to kill her,' Rollo said, not entirely devoid of regret.

'But you must have realized he was violent?' Rick cried. 'Those bruises Kirsten had, did you not see those?'

Rollo gave another casual twitch of the shoulder. 'How was I to know they were from him and not you?'

'*What?* Why would I hurt her? I was trying to rescue her! This is crazy, Rollo, it's *evil*. You're hardly any better than he is.'

For a moment neither spoke. There was the sound of a door slamming on the Pleasance Road side, a crackling high overhead as a brief gust of wind stirred the tops of the trees.

'Why are we here?' Rick demanded. 'Couldn't we have had this conversation at the flat?' With a sudden rush of clarity, he understood that he had to get out of here, he was in terrible danger, but the moment he took a step forward, Rollo mirrored it, blocking his way.

'We *could* have, but I thought it made more sense for you to return to the scene of the crime to do it.'

'To do what?'

'End it, Rick. End all the guilt and the misery.' There was a break in Rollo's voice, as if the thought truly pained him.

'How do you propose I do that?' Rick said.

'Bleed out, I thought. Like a sacrifice to her poor bereaved family.'

'You're insane. Seriously, you've completely lost your mind.' Abruptly, without conscious design, Rick snatched the torch from Rollo's left hand, hit the switch, and turned its beam on him. A square of silver glinted between the fingers of his right hand: a razor blade. He turned the torch off again, raised it high above his head, then brought it down sharply on Rollo's shoulder. It went flying into the undergrowth as Rollo moaned in pain and flung himself fiercely at Rick.

After that, all he experienced was the crack of bone on bone, the smash of flesh on flesh, the flash and dazzle and heat of the struggle, until, to his intense horror, he became aware of Rollo at his feet, immobile, unconscious, his face ground into the earth.

Rick stared, chest heaving, arms and legs paralysed. It was too dark to see any detail. When he was able to work his limbs again, he knelt and placed a palm on Rollo's back:

there was no evidence of breath in his chest, only the burn of his own inflamed fists.

It couldn't be true, could it? A second body in exactly the same spot as the first, and Rick, once again, right there, on his knees beside it, unable to claim his own senses, to trust his next actions.

He couldn't . . . He couldn't just turn and run a second time. *Could he?*

43

Alex

September, present

The end didn't always come in a single recognizable blow, he understood that; sometimes it happened incrementally, like the proverbial frog brought to a slow boil. Take his marriage. He'd begun as a fully voiced equal in a perfectly serviceable partnership – as serviceable as *he* was ever going to be able to manage – and ended up letting himself into his own house like an intruder, skulking at the living-room door, eavesdropping.

'That's exactly it!' Beth exclaimed, on the other side. 'I don't think I noticed before just how obsessive he is about it. He won't even join the street WhatsApp group.'

This was followed by a lengthy silence, a 'hmm' or two, and he gathered she must be on the phone.

'Yes, except that's how everyone else connects now, so it's more than withdrawing, it's completely opting out. He's resigned from work, now, as well. Mind you, I wouldn't be surprised if he's been pushed if he's been anything like he's been at home.'

Another pause.

'Yes, as far as I know. That's the thing, I don't know anything. Whatever I try, he gets annoyed.'

Pause.

'Couples therapy? Like Relate, you mean? Honestly, Colette, I think this is something outside of us. What happened with that poor girl, that can't be normal, can it?'

That 'poor girl' was presumably Alex's alleged daughter, information of the strictest confidentiality and yet casually bandied about to this Colette person.

'I suppose. Okay. Is there anyone you recommend?'

The call over, Beth still had pen and paper in hand when he flung open the door and confronted her. She clutched the items to her, glowering at him. 'Alex! You gave me a fright.'

'Who the hell is Colette?'

'I didn't hear you come in.' Doubt, perhaps a trace of guilt, crossed her face. 'Were you listening to my conversation?'

'I overheard,' he said curtly. 'There's a distinction. Who is she?'

'Just a therapist, someone Zara knows.'

He gave a snort of contempt. 'Say no more.'

'Why does it matter who put me in touch with her?' Beth demanded, exasperated. 'The point is I felt the need to talk to a professional because I'm worried about you.'

'Because I'm not in any WhatsApp groups? Because I decided to walk away from the world's dullest job? Or, wait, is it because I don't want to throw myself at the feet of a total stranger because some ropey DNA service claims we're father and daughter? Thanks for sharing that confidential information with this therapist, by the way. I bet she told you my reaction was actually quite normal, did she? More normal than your own decision to wade in, no questions asked – on behalf of someone else, I might add.'

Beth pressed her lips together; she was, he could see, determined not to cry this time. 'You're not just "someone else", Alex, you're my husband. And there's no "behalf" about it. She's my step-daughter and I intend to have a relationship with her, even if you don't.'

They stared at each other. Though dry-eyed, she was breathing heavily, he noticed; in a non-criminal, irreproachable existence like hers, this really did represent a crisis, probably the worst she'd ever faced. He should never have married her and exposed her to the risk of unimaginable horror; there was no way she was going to be able to weather it.

She broke the silence. 'You know, even from the start, I've always had this feeling that you're . . . No, it doesn't matter.'

Even from the start: this piqued his interest. He'd thought, until recently, he'd coped okay, passed as pretty normal. A bit on the sardonic side, sure, but normal enough. 'It does matter. What were you going to say?'

'Well, just this sense of disconnection. Like you're not able to empathize. I wondered if maybe it's a spectrum thing.'

'A spectrum thing?' Honestly, he despaired. 'Because I value privacy?'

'But it's more than that, isn't it? It's more a fear of anything too big, too public.' She hesitated, before committing herself. 'A fear of discovery.'

And there it was. Almost a decade of marriage it had taken, but here she was finally articulating the truth.

And, as ever, he had no choice but to deny it.

*

At least Zara was absent for the meeting they had the following Saturday morning at their kitchen table to bash out the details of their temporary separation. For Beth wanted them to live apart for the six-week duration of their marriage counselling.

Zara, it emerged, had argued for his staying. 'She thinks you need your safe space,' Beth said. 'Don't get me wrong, she also thinks you've been very rude to her, but she can see the root of it is to do with you, not her. She believes in supporting people through a breakdown, not blaming them.'

He mulled this. Was Zara speaking up for him now only because she knew she'd already won and it reflected well on her? Or was the optics problem his and his alone, the malice he'd ascribed to her simply a projection of his paranoia? Either way, her baby would be born within the hallowed six weeks of his absence; he was being ousted just in time for the house to become a maternity zone. Realistically, what were the chances he'd ever be allowed back in?

'Could you stay at your sister's, maybe?' Beth suggested.

'I'd rather pitch a tent on the roadside,' he said. He couldn't live with his sister for more than six days, let alone weeks.

And in any case, what therapist worth his or her salt signed people off after the minimum number of sessions? If it were *his* livelihood, he'd keep it going ad infinitum, even if there weren't issues galore to address, which presumably there mostly *were* because in the end wasn't every man his age, underneath the wisecracks and the bravado, little more than a kettle of pain, never quite sure what his boiling point was?

Beth was shaking her head. 'This is the problem, Alex. All the things you've said about Zara, like why she doesn't reach out to her family, you're no better. Maybe that's why you don't like her, because she reminds you too much of yourself.'

He did not dignify this particular theory with a response.

'Honestly,' she added, 'she's been so generous with sharing her pregnancy experience.'

'That's one way of looking at it.'

'Yes, it is! And you could have been a part of it, just like me, but for whatever reason you're not interested in connecting with the next generation. Maybe you never were, even when we were trying for a baby ourselves.'

'Come on,' he objected. 'I wasn't the one with the issue, was I?'

Grief passed over her face then and he knew he'd crossed a line. 'You think I haven't tortured myself about that every single day?' she said, voice cracking. 'Well, I have, Alex. I have.'

Knowing he should be stepping towards her, making love not war, he took a pace backwards. 'I'll find an Airbnb.'

She gave a heave of defeat. 'I thought you could come once a week to see Olive? Maybe Sundays?'

Hearing her name, Olive scampered over, pushed her damp nose into his hand.

'Yes, fine,' Alex said. Once a week wouldn't be enough. He'd have to come back without telling her. Not to be here in the house or anything sinister, but to check in on the trail.

Olive barked then, alerting them to approaching danger at the front of the house, which meant either the postman or someone else was at the door.

'That must be the cavalry,' he said to Beth, when, sure enough, the doorbell rang. 'Come to whisk you away.'

'I'm not the one who's leaving,' she said, sadly.

Olive accompanied him to the door, rigid with duty, and he opened up, a civilized smile for their caller already on his lips.

'Hello?' Immediately, he felt his face erupt with heat, his throat constrict. '*Oh.*' Even the measure of tension associated with marital crisis talks felt small compared with what he was now presented with. For on the doorstep stood a woman he was fairly sure was Marina – as he would always think of her.

In reality, Kirsten.

She was fleshier now, heavy dark clothes in place of the skimpy fabrics he remembered her wearing (but, then, it *had* been a heatwave and she *had* had the waif figure of a woman in her mid-twenties). Those amazing sea-glass eyes had an opacity he was certain hadn't been there years ago; the light within had dimmed. But she looked fine, a survivor rather than a victor, and maybe that was the best any of them could hope for.

She appeared to be grappling with conclusions of her own at the sight of him and there was a long moment of shared disorientation before she said, 'Yes, *oh*. It's really you. After all this time, it's really you.'

'Is *she* with you?' he asked.

'Who?'

'Your daughter.' He couldn't bring himself to say 'our'. 'She's the one who told you my address, I'm guessing?'

Bewilderment filled Kirsten's eyes, her pale eyebrows pulling together. 'I don't have a daughter. I don't have any children.'

'Oh,' he said again. There was no time to ponder his wrong assumption, to consider other candidates, other paths forwards or backwards. 'How did you know . . . ?' Then he remembered. 'That photo in the *Guardian*.' His fingers went to his naked scalp. He'd hoped baldness would conceal him, but he'd been as exposed as he'd feared.

She gestured over her shoulder. 'I can't believe you live right opposite those steps. Where that Range Rover's parked, that's where we parked that day. You've literally been here this whole time.'

'Only for the last decade,' he said. 'I really was lying low before that.'

'Wow.' She smiled, a smile that seemed neither for him nor herself, neither bitter nor sweet. 'When I think of all the places I've searched and here you were all along.'

She'd searched for him? The thought was both frightening and pleasurable. 'Why were you looking for me?'

'Why? Don't insult me. Not again. Not now.' She held

his eye, more disappointed than accusing, and took a step forward. 'So where is he, then? I know it must have been you who killed him, but where did you bury him? Does he even have a grave?'

And, as Alex gaped at her, the fear he had kept at bay for twenty-five years, even at times reducing to a pinpoint on the horizon, now spread across the sky, obliterating the last of the light.

'Where is he, Rollo?' she asked. 'Where's Rick?'

44

Rick

September 1995

He *would* run, he definitely would, but not yet. He was felled by exhaustion and finding it hard to breathe, so he'd rest for a while, just a minute or two, and then he'd run.

He lowered himself to the ground, lying with his head close to Rollo's. Brothers in arms, who'd turned their fists on one another. He was crying, but he didn't know who for. Rollo or Kirsten, false gods both, or maybe Marina Stanley, who'd breathed her last on this very spot, who'd fed the soil with her blood.

The crack of light at the Stanleys' window remained on. Had Drew really, as Rollo had claimed, hared over to Kirsten's place to prevent her from switching sides? Or had he got the job done on the phone and been up in that bedroom all this time, unaware that the man he'd condemned to suffer for his crime now lay on the track, a stone's throw away?

In a peculiar, perverse way, the pain in his body was soothing, the individual sites blurring to create one unified distraction from the problem of the lifeless body next to him. The darkness swamped his vision and he'd lost his sense of smell – a blow to the nose had blocked both nostrils with congealed blood – but his hearing still worked and he began to make out a low buzzing. An insect, perhaps, or a bird, tormenting him. He covered his ears with his hot, swollen hands, willed himself to think of Kirsten, to play his reel of key scenes that had both comforted and antagonized him during his long days in hiding.

The first time he saw her, in the lobby at Victoria Street, pale and beautiful, all alone with her dreams.

Their first conversation, white plastic spoon sliding from her mouth, down to the tip of her tongue.

The first time she came to the flat, a Thursday night, before Rollo moved in, before he knew there would only be Thursday nights, that she was to be shared, his portion rationed.

The fraught emotions of their drink in the wine bar on Litchfield Street and, later, of their wordless trudge through London in the heat.

And the sweet hours spent plotting their escape. This, more than anything else, had felt to him how a relationship was supposed to feel, when both of you wanted it, needed it, with the same intensity.

A part of me thought maybe I would do it, she'd confessed, but which part? The tiny piece of her heart that hadn't grown scar tissue?

It wasn't an insect causing the buzzing, he realized, suddenly, but Rollo's pager, no longer on his own person but somewhere in range. He must have dropped it during their struggle. He was too weary to reach out a hand; it would stop, anyway. He'd need to find it before he left, though; there'd be fingerprints on it. The torch, too. He'd smacked Rollo with it and it had flown from his hand. What about fingerprints on Rollo himself? Would the police be able to tell it was Rick he'd fought? Maybe . . . Maybe they would think it was Drew, given where they were? Or those loan sharks he'd got mixed up with, that big guy who'd roughed him up in the street.

Someone else, anyway.

Anyone else.

If not, he'd be on the run a second time, he'd have to find a way to sell the watch, move on from the Newman Street flat, start again, traumatized and beaten and isolated from everyone from his previous life.

His eyes closed.

Don't fall asleep, he thought.

*

He woke, half-woke really, unable to breathe. He couldn't see, couldn't open his eyes to try. More than that, he couldn't lift his head. It took a second to register the pressure coming from the back of his head, from below – except, no, he was on his front, he must have rolled over in his sleep, so the pressure was coming from above. Something was holding his head down, filling his nostrils and throat with soil and dust. His lungs were shrinking, burning.

'You fucking loser,' a voice said, close to his ear. Rollo's voice, which didn't make sense because Rollo was dead.

Instinct told him these might be the last words he'd ever hear, but he shut that down. It wasn't the will to survive so much as the right not to know. Better to believe you'd dropped, briefly, terrifyingly, into the abyss of hallucination and that none of this was really happening.

Just your brain too tired to tell the difference, your mind playing tricks.

Your blood slowing in your veins, but only for a moment.

45

Alex

October, present

'I'll show you,' he said, and Kirsten nodded. Already, there was a natural sense of deliberation to this, a ritual rather than a reckoning. Now that the initial shock had left him, he felt only shame, shame of the most profound kind, deep in the core of him, not detectable on the surface.

'I've got my car,' she said. 'I can drive us wherever. I don't care how far it is, I just need to see where he is, *be* where he is, just once.'

'We don't need a car,' Alex said. How mind-blowing it was, the notion that he had killed a man. Not a notion, a fact. And the absurdity of the woman in front of him knowing this while the one in the house behind him had no idea ... She'd married him, she'd loved him, and even now, when he'd become unendurable, she wanted to embark on marriage guidance and bring him back into the fold. Get his heart working again.

As if reading his mind, Beth now advanced towards them, clearly having waited long enough for him to return to their meeting.

'Hello there,' Kirsten said, pleasantly.

'Are you Julie?' Beth asked. 'From the ancestry site? Savannah's mum?'

Well, that answered *one* outstanding question, he thought. Not Flavia, whose name was the only one besides Kirsten's he might have dredged from buried memories, but Julie, the girl from the flat downstairs whom he hadn't given a second thought in all this time. But such was the shock of seeing Kirsten, the revelation scarcely had an impact and if Beth was expecting any reaction from *him*, she was going to be disappointed.

'No,' Kirsten said, with faint embarrassment. She'd come to initiate one showdown, hadn't expected to be caught in the crosshairs of another.

'Not everything's about the great *Who Do You Think You Are?* mystery,' Alex told his wife, in an amused tone she would certainly know to be fraudulent. If not funny, the situation was certainly surreal. 'I'm going out for a bit,' he added. Already in his trainers, he grabbed a jacket and closed the door on her baffled protests.

'Sorry about that,' he said to Kirsten. 'It's not the greatest time.'

'Still breaking hearts,' she said, with a more genuine smile than he deserved.

He led her the short distance across the street to the steps. 'Let's walk down the famous trail.'

'Really?'

'Really.' He took the steps two at a time and waited at the top for her to join him. Ignoring the eco community welcome board, the families by the pond, they set off down the path.

'I've never actually been down here,' she said, gently setting aside a spike of bramble so she could keep in step with him.

'It wasn't like this back then. It was skanky, really creepy. I mean, even before Marina's murder.'

She made no comment. Her lovely fine-spun profile was much the same, just a little droop at the eyelids, a softening of the jawline.

'Has life turned out okay for you?' he asked, curious.

'It could've been better, I'll be honest with you.'

'You married or anything?'

This time her smile was distinctly downturned. 'I've been married twice since I knew you. Divorced twice, as well. Never again.'

He whistled under his breath. Incredible that someone so abused by men had chosen to marry two of them; he hoped the fallout had become easier to manage. 'And you said no children?'

'None. What was all that about *Who Do You Think You Are?*?'

He had an urge then to confide in her, but that wasn't what she was interested in, not really; it wasn't why she was here. 'It's complicated. Sorry about the misunderstanding. You probably don't even remember Julie. She lived in the flat downstairs.'

'I think I met her at Rick's birthday party. Remember that?'

'Of course. I've got photos from it somewhere.'

Julie hadn't been important that summer, her company merely a way to pass the time when he'd been out of work. She'd split up with the boyfriend, that was right, and moved out of the capital. Had she known she was pregnant when she left, he wondered? Had they even said goodbye?

There was no one else on this stretch of the trail and they walked side by side, an early fall of leaves underfoot. In any other context it would have been pleasant, bucolic. 'What about work?' he asked.

'Oh, you know. I never really had any qualifications. I'm working for Bromley Council now.' Evidently, this exhausted her capacity to update him on her current status, because she rewound to where they'd been interrupted on the doorstep. 'Like I say, I looked for you. Not straightaway, but after Drew's conviction, when my situation was all sorted.'

'You got off with, what was it, a community order?'

'I was lucky. I had an amazing lawyer, all paid for by Legal Aid.'

He passed a hand over his head, his fingers finding the vertebra at the base of his skull. 'I know it's a bit late in the day, but thank you for keeping me out of it.'

Though he knew how offensively inadequate this must be, she remained quite dispassionate, again returning to her original thread. 'So, yeah, after a while I gave up. I thought you must have changed your name.'

'I did,' he said. 'At least I started using my middle names. Alex Parker. Parker was my mother's maiden name.'

'I remember. That's how I got your address, actually. After I saw the thing about the trail in the paper, I looked up the local streets on the electoral register. There was no Rollo Farnworth, but when I saw Alex Parker, I thought yes, that'll be him.'

He wouldn't have expected her to have such a good memory, but, then, he'd always underestimated her. 'I know I should have tried to find you. I did Google you, I mean once Google was a thing.'

'By then I would have been married and I took my husband's name. Not that I was ever in the press, they managed to keep my identity hidden, but I wanted a clean slate. You know, in case *he* had people coming after me. I've never done Facebook or Twitter or anything.'

'Same,' Alex said. 'I can't stand all that stuff. Sometimes I think, all these millions of people with completely clear consciences, nothing to hide, nothing whatsoever. They could be out there living their lives but instead they just stare at a screen, obsessing about other people's.' He could hear the passion rising in his voice as he spoke candidly for the first time: 'I'd give anything to have their freedom. Anything. I wouldn't piss it away on fucking Facebook.'

A woman came towards them then, holding hands with a toddler, and he and Kirsten adjusted to single file. He wondered what the passer-by might guess their relationship to be, what their body language suggested.

'Where are we headed exactly?' Kirsten said. She was so incredibly cool. But then she'd always had that ability, hadn't she? To take things in her stride. Even when she'd lied, she somehow retained a measure of integrity, some internal beat of honesty.

'We're here,' he said, drawing to a halt.

She turned to view the house on the Exmoor Gardens side. 'Is this . . . ?'

'Drew's house. Exactly.'

Frankie's boys had set up some sort of encampment behind their fence, long planks of wood tied with rope onto the larger of the silver birches, the sloping ground below semi-enclosed, but he wouldn't worry about that right now. He pointed to the section of bank adjacent to it. 'He's there, just below where they found Marina. I brought him here that night he came to your flat and we got into a fight. It could have been either one of us who died, that's the honest truth, he gave as good as he got. It was almost me, but it was him. I buried him right there.'

He'd never said these words aloud before.

Kirsten sank to her knees, touched the ground with her palms, fingers outstretched. The blood had drained from her face, now a ghastly ashen pale. 'How was that possible? How could you have dug a grave without any help? They say it takes hours.'

He nodded. 'The police had pulled up a couple of trees when they were investigating the site and the earth was still quite loose. I couldn't have done it otherwise. It turned out to be the best place it could have happened.'

46

Rollo

His initial plan, to fake Rick's suicide, had been conceived on the hoof, without proper thought – he'd had a few drinks, done a line or two of coke – and had to be abandoned the second they started scuffling. No detective or pathologist would have bought it, not with Rick covered in the kind of bruises you only got from a serious punch-up.

He'd played dead for what felt like hours but was likely only minutes, because time had ceased to make sense, face down, ears covered with his bent elbows to protect his head, waiting for his aching brain to do what it always did and figure out how to survive. When he'd fallen, he'd expected Rick to run and had a half-formed plan to tail him, all the way back to wherever it was he was hiding out, deal with him there, but Rick had confounded him by dropping to the ground himself. Rollo could feel the warmth of his body next to him on the cold ground, hear the asthmatic rasp of his breathing; also, a distant buzzing, which he ignored, focusing on the breathing, the interesting way it was slowing, steadying. Rick had passed out, he realized, from exhaustion or pain or maybe just the sheer wretched need for oblivion.

He'd taken some bad blows himself, not least the first, that whack with the torch – he'd be lucky if he didn't have a fractured collarbone.

He'd need to find the torch, he thought; it would be evidence.

When Rick had been unconscious for at least five minutes, he eased stealthily onto his elbows, doing his best not to cry out from the pain, and peered at the sleeping man's face. It was dark with dirt and blood, one eye already starting to swell. Careful not to make contact, Rollo struggled to his knees. Then, with a sudden lightning manoeuvre, he tipped Rick onto his front and used both hands to crush his face into the ground. By the time Rick woke and tried to resist, it was too late: Rollo had his knee in his back, bearing down on him with his full weight. Rick's arms were free but, with the shoulders pinned as they were, were too restricted to do much beyond a bit of feeble swiping. A couple of backwards kicks landed more heavily, but weakened as the oxygen supply failed.

He stayed in position for a long time, in case Rick was doing what *he* had just done, faking lifelessness as a last resort to avoid death, and only when it was irrevocably past the point that any man – let alone a badly beaten-up asthmatic – could hold his breath did he roll aside. His legs were cramping and he smacked them with his fists to reawaken the muscles, before crouching to check Rick's pockets, taking his wallet and keys. Then he heaved himself upright and set to work. First, he sifted the nearby undergrowth for his torch, found it quickly by pure luck. Next, he squeezed through the hedge of a nearby garden and helped himself to a shovel from the shed. Back on the track, he started displacing the looser soil on the bank where the trees had been removed, before going deeper into the compacted earth.

Unlike the killing itself, this *was* hard work. His entire body ached and protested, his clothes clinging to his skin with sweat. More than anything he was bothered by his eyes, sore with the strain of working for hours in the dark, grit and soil rubbed into them. When the hole was as deep as he dared dig without causing a section of the embankment to collapse, he dragged Rick into it and replaced the earth as compactly as possible, covered the area with loose bramble. He returned the shovel and picked his way back down the track in the dark, stumbling and sustaining the kind of scratches that would normally cause groans of pain but that he hardly registered.

He walked for miles, half-dead with exhaustion but not daring to break the journey with a night bus. After a safe interval, he tossed Rick's wallet (minus the cash) and keys into a bin outside a bookie's. When dawn broke and the tubes started, he went underground, alighting at Camden Town to streets empty of all but the most eager of early-bird workers, a low sun smothered by thick cloud.

At the end of Albert Street, he dropped his shoes in a bin and tottered the last stretch in stockinged feet. Letting himself into the flat, he found his flatmate Josh wasn't even up yet. It was just after 7am. The whole ghastly episode had taken place while the other man slept.

It was a Friday and he couldn't take the day off work. It would look suspicious later if the police cross-referenced it with a time of death. In the kitchen, barely able to stand from fatigue, he stripped off his clothes and stuffed every stitch into the washing machine, turned the dial to hot and hit go. Then, naked, he went up to the bathroom, turned on the shower and began cleaning his injuries. His shoulder was badly swollen, but he couldn't identify any crunching sensation under the muscle and he could, just about, rotate his arm. His face was surprisingly unscathed. His hands were the main problem, bruised and grazed from the fight, grotesquely blistered from digging. He'd tell his colleagues he'd been mugged, he decided, that he'd chased after the bastard and given as good as he got.

While it was a relatively simple matter to remove evidence of Rick from under his fingernails or on his hair and skin, he already understood that the problem would be the other way around. It would take months, maybe even years, before those skin cells of his trapped under Rick's fingernails, or even inside cuts in his skin, would disintegrate into nothingness. As for any fibres shed from Rollo's clothing, who knew, they might hang around for ever. As a precaution, he'd take his laundry with him when he left for work and dispose of it in a public bin.

*

Having lied to Rick about Drew snatching Kirsten from her flat, Rollo had expected her to call him. Who else could she contact for information when Rick failed to show up for their big confession?

He didn't relish the prospect of her distress, he never had. This was what she didn't understand, he didn't *want* to hurt her, he liked her; for a while there, he'd liked her to the point of obsession and it had baffled him that she preferred Rick, irked him that she seemed to regard him as some entertaining posh boy, the first girl in a long time to suffer him rather than desire him.

But he had bigger burdens, like his debt to the loan sharks, who'd stepped into the void vacated by his tight-fisted parents.

Then, with those cuttings, he'd been presented with a quick fix. Blackmail. Not only for money, but sex, too, whatever the fake Marina was willing to give when he felt like asking. She couldn't complain to Rick because it would blow the deception open, and she couldn't complain to Drew because he'd punish her.

She was damned if she did and damned if she didn't.

The call came as he was leaving for work, having somehow survived coffee and toast with Josh, who had, pleasingly, swallowed the mugging story without a trace of doubt, even offering him some sort of herbal salve to apply to his grazes. Herbal salve! Though Rollo had already ingested every pain-killer he could find in the flat, it had barely dented the agony that inhabited every cell of him – even his toes throbbed with pain, blistered from the marathon nocturnal trudge and two nails having peeled off. As for the mental anguish that came with the night's depravities, he was going to have to suppress that if he had any hope of surviving.

'Did I hear the phone go in the middle of the night?' he asked Josh in a casual, speculative tone. Josh hadn't mentioned taking any messages or – worse, far worse – knocking on Rollo's door and opening it, only to find the bed unoccupied, but it may have slipped his mind in light of Rollo's 'mugging' drama.

'Yeah, maybe. I was out for the count, though. Why, would it have been the police? You did report this, didn't you?'

'No point,' Rollo said. 'You know how useless they are.'

So if Kirsten *had* called, Josh hadn't picked up. Excellent.

Josh left for work first and so, when her next call came, he was able to speak freely.

'Rollo, I was supposed to meet Rick last night but he didn't turn up.' There was no missing the apprehension in Kirsten's voice; she feared the worst. 'Has he been in touch with you?'

'No, sorry. Where are you?'

'At home. I waited for ages, then I got the night bus back. I'm worried something bad's happened to him.'

Rollo made a tactical error then. He should have played ignorant, or cast suspicion on Drew, but he was dog-tired and not at his sharpest strategically and he said, instead, 'Well, if it has, that's probably for the best.'

He heard a sharp intake of breath. 'Why?' she demanded. 'What does *that* mean? Where is he? What's happened?' She was no fool, she understood straight away. 'You *have* heard from him, haven't you, and he told you we were planning to go to the police?' She began whimpering, a truly awful sound, like a baby animal in distress. 'I knew I forgot something. I should have warned him . . .'

'Not to trust me, you mean?' And his heart twisted at her suffering even as he sought to bring coldness to his tone. 'Yes, that *was* a mistake.'

Her groans faded. 'You thought I'd have no choice but to go crawling back to Drew, didn't you? To *you*.'

Bingo, darling.

'Well, your little plan has backfired, Rollo, because I'm still going to the police. I'm going right now, with or without Rick.'

'What?' He stiffened. This he had not anticipated. 'Then you'd bloody well better keep my name out of it,' he said, his tone meaner. Then, more persuasive, 'Keep me out of it, then when you need me, I'll help you. You can name your price.'

'You mean when I'm out of prison?' she cried in frustration. 'If Drew doesn't get to me before that.'

She started to sob then and he was closer to succumbing to the same response than she could possibly have imagined. He wished it didn't have to be this way, but they were already one down and he didn't intend to be next. It was a question of survival. 'If you want to take that risk, that's up to you. I'm just saying, I'll be a lot more useful to you later, when you might not have anyone else.'

Especially with Rick no longer around to help.

'I don't believe your promises,' she said. Then, 'How will I find you?'

'I'll be around,' he said. 'Seriously, Kirsten. I'm counting on you. And then *you* can count on *me*. You have my word.'

'You word is worth shit,' she said, and hung up.

She didn't phone again.

47

Rollo

The next few weeks were torment, pure and unsustainable. Not that he deserved any less, but still, there were nights when he got into bed and prayed for a fatal heart attack to intervene before he had to wake up and face more of the monstrous same.

He had pored over the papers since the whole Marina Stanley nightmare had begun, of course, keeping the guilt and trepidation at bay by the usual means of intoxication, but now he searched their pages with the kind of dread that minced the flesh from the inside. No longer was the liberty of a flatmate and casual friend at stake, but his own.

Setting aside the small matter of his having killed a man and buried him in the kind of amateurish conditions that would require a miracle for the grave to remain uninvestigated, his chief concern was whether Kirsten had made good on her threat to go the police. If so, had she reported his sorry part in all of this, using his blackmail as part of the abused-woman defence Rick had hypothesized?

And what about the sex? He didn't want to think about how *that* could be construed.

Meanwhile, finances remaining perilous, he had no choice but to turn up for work as normal, woozy with Nurofen and hands too swollen to hold a pen or use a keyboard properly. The mugging story was accepted by his colleagues with universal sympathy (it didn't harm the situation that his new boss openly fancied him) and he gained kudos for declining permission to take time off to recover.

Though he continued to help himself to Rick's office wardrobe and had latterly taken to spraying that cologne of his left in the bathroom, he didn't allow himself to indulge in the narcissistic notion that he sought some kind of *connection* to his dead friend.

During his lunchtime one day, he went to the library to look up the countries that had no extradition treaty with the UK. The Dominican Republic was a possibility and he even ventured into a travel agent to get a price for a flight.

One place he definitely wasn't ever going to again was Silver Vale, tempting though it was to sneak back up that abominable track and check that the offending section remained undisturbed. He lived in fear of the apocalyptic downpour that might wash away his handiwork.

It was a week or so before the media announced the explosive new development: Drew Stanley had appeared in court charged with the murder of his wife and had pleaded guilty.

A second person had been questioned under caution, but not yet charged. There was to be a separate hearing for Drew's sentencing, but there could be no doubt that he was going to jail for a very long time.

Which meant there'd be no money for Kirsten or Rollo. Rick had died for nothing.

And so had Marina, whose funeral finally took place and was reported in the *Standard* with due solemnity.

PRIVATE FUNERAL FOR
MARINA STANLEY

In a peaceful cemetery in Surrey, a sombre group congregated yesterday to bid farewell to 28-year-old Marina Stanley, who was killed near her home in Silver Vale on 15 September. It was an occasion cruelly delayed by the police investigation into her death and all but close family and friends were denied access to the grounds.

One family member conspicuous by his absence was the dead woman's husband, Drew Stanley, 35, now in prison awaiting sentencing for her murder. It emerges the couple had had a series of disputes over money in the months prior to her death.

A further charge of perverting the course of justice has yet to be heard.

The weeks between Marina's death and her husband's arrest bore witness to an extraordinary and ultimately futile police hunt for a different man, a

search followed by millions of Londoners in the pages
of this newspaper.

It now transpires that the original prime suspect,
Rick Ward, 26, an auditor from Camden Town, had
never actually met the victim. Mr Stanley admitted to
police that he had misled them into believing the two
had been having an affair.

Mr Ward remains missing.

Rollo read the piece twice, the pages splayed over the coffee
table. Drew charged, Marina buried, Rick lying undiscov-
ered in *his* grave. The rapidity with which the main players
had been dispatched, events tied up, felt almost glib, scarcely
to be trusted. And where was Kirsten? Her name was not
once included and the absence of reports of any third-party
charges suggested she'd somehow managed to get herself
exonerated or was in the process of doing so.

Crucially, she didn't seem to have implicated *him* in her
confession, for when the police got in touch again it was only
to ask him to come in and make a full statement about the
circumstances of Rick's disappearance.

He made himself presentable, even getting a haircut. By
then, of course, the bruises had faded. Just a residual soreness
in his shoulder, a cut on the middle knuckle of his right hand
that was slower to heal than the rest.

It was an awkward encounter. Previously, in the handful
of chats he'd had with officers on the phone and during their
one visit to the flat, it had suited him to co-operate with the
theory that Rick had fled because he was guilty. When shown

401

a photograph of Marina Stanley and asked if he'd ever seen his flatmate with her, Rollo had agreed he had, though, to be fair, he *had* faked a moment's uncertainty ('Yes, I'm sure – well, I *think* I'm sure . . .'). But now that Rick's innocence was established, Rollo sensed, beneath that professional neutrality, disapproval of his not having backed his mate from the beginning.

He told himself he was overthinking it. The police counted on friends snitching on each other, breaking confidences – look at Kirsten!

His formal statement echoed his previous verbal account, ending with that meal in the curry house and Rick's note on the kitchen table, which he'd handed to their colleagues when they'd come to the flat.

'What happens now?' he asked the officer, after reading the document through and signing it. 'I mean, if there's been some sort of mistaken identity, is it possible the husband killed Rick, as well? Found out where he was hiding and went after him,' he added, for it occurred to him that the last thing he wanted was to encourage them to take another look at the site where they'd found Marina.

'There's no evidence to suggest your friend is anything but alive,' the officer said. 'A missing persons file has been opened and we're hoping that when he's up to date with the news and realizes he's no longer a suspect, he'll return to his family.'

His family. Rollo swallowed, a gritty discomfort in his throat. He had thought nothing of Rick's family when he'd been forcing his body into that hole in the embankment.

Condemning them to a life of not knowing in exchange for his own freedom.

'Good,' he said. 'I hope that will be soon. We all miss him.'

He had a horrible intrusive thought then, imagined himself saying, 'Oh, one thing I forgot to say: he had my pager with him.' And the police saying, 'Why didn't you tell us this before?', before springing into action to examine phone records from the final night of its use.

It had been a day or two before he'd remembered hearing something drop during the early part of their scuffle, something he should have searched for besides the torch. He'd wracked his memory for everything he'd had in his possession that night, ticking the items off: wallet, cigarettes and lighter, a bit of loose change, all of which had returned with him to the flat the next morning.

Which meant it must have been something of Rick's.

Only later did he remember that buzzing he'd ignored as they'd lain side by side, half-dead after their fight. The pager: it had to be. Probably the loan sharks on his case again – they were great believers in round-the-clock harassment. While admittedly not his most disastrous mistake of that night, it was still a loose end worth losing sleep over and he itched to ring it, to discover if it was still functioning. But after a while, the anxiety faded. No one would hear it all the way up there, and, in any case, if the battery hadn't already died, it would soon.

He said nothing to the police, of course. There were more than enough self-inflicted wounds in this story already.

*

Later, he struggled to remember the exact chronology, but he was fairly sure Drew's sentencing came before the phone call from a man called Sam.

SILVER VALE MURDERER
GETS 20 YEARS

The Silver Vale businessman who admitted to killing his wife after a falling out over money was this morning sentenced to a minimum of twenty years behind bars.

The judge explained that Drew Stanley, 35, would receive only the minimum reduction for his early guilty plea in the murder of wife Marina, 28. 'Far from it being a spontaneous outburst of violence on your part, you laid the groundwork for your wife's murder in a wicked and repugnant act of premeditation,' the judge said, adding, 'You showed not an ounce of compassion or remorse.'

Marina's family declined to make any statement beyond saying that they welcomed the sentence.

48

Rollo

November 1995

Twice Josh had passed on phone messages from someone called Sam and twice Rollo had ignored them. He still got the odd call from journalists and other busybodies and had simply assumed Sam was one of those.

The third time, he happened to answer the phone himself.

'I manage a residential building on Newman Street and I've been trying to track down a short-term tenant called Gary,' the guy explained.

'I don't know anyone by that name,' Rollo said, amiably.

'Actually, I don't think it *is* his name. He was here with a girlfriend and, well, I understood they had reason to keep their real identities hidden. You *are* Rollo Farnworth?' he pressed. 'That's definitely the emergency contact he gave me, so . . .'

Rollo's heart began banging. This had to be Rick, the

building in question his famous hideout. Did this Sam know his erstwhile tenant was the man in the papers who the police had initially wanted for murder or had that somehow eluded him?

He put the guy out of his misery. There was nothing to be gained from leaving him to cast his net wider. 'I think you must mean Rick.' He offered a brief physical description, which was quickly accepted to be a match. 'I'm not sure where he is at the moment, but he used to live here. I'm a friend.'

'Right. Great. The thing is, his rent's overdue and I get the feeling he hasn't been in the unit for some time. I know his situation was fluid, so . . .'

Fluid was one word for it. 'You want to let it to someone else?' Rollo said, helpful, reasonable.

'Yes, that's it. Would it be possible to arrange for his things to be collected? We don't have the storage here and I don't want to get rid of them in case he comes back.'

'That's very kind of you,' Rollo said. To try three times *was* decent. 'I'll come down myself. How much stuff is there?'

'Not a huge amount by the looks. He's left a rucksack, so you can probably get it all in that.'

Rollo took down the address. It wasn't that far away, just off Oxford Street, you could walk it in forty minutes. Quicker to hop on the tube, though, in case this Sam character decided to go back in and take a closer look for himself.

*

He worried the experience would be haunting, but it was in fact banal. For starters, the place was actually okay. Having pictured Rick in some dripping hovel, shivering in a sleeping bag, it was a surprise to be let into a perfectly warm and secure studio flat, a step up from budget.

But then Rick always had been good with money.

It wasn't an elegant sight. A rumpled bed. A towel draped on the radiator. A jar of instant coffee. Two sets of plates, mugs, cutlery: one must have been intended for Marina – what a total and utter sap Rick had been. A collection of empty vodka bottles gave an indication of how he'd self-medicated in his final weeks. No TV, just a little travel radio and a couple of novels, *Tess of the d'Urbervilles* and *The Woman in White*. He must have been bored out of his brain, Rollo thought, before noticing a heap of *Evening Standard*s on the floor under the table. These he scooped into a Tesco carrier and sifted through the loose items on the table, adding anything that might link Rick to Silver Vale, including both sets of cuttings supplied by Sonia and a daily Travelcard from the day of his death, presumably used to go to and from Tooting.

There was Kirsten's Zippo and, to his surprise, an obviously valuable woman's watch. Cartier, no less, and possibly vintage. Rollo pocketed both, along with the photographs he'd had developed on the day of Rick's death. Everything else, he stuffed into Rick's backpack.

He checked in briefly with Sam in his office in the basement, before discarding the carrier bag in a bin on Goodge Street and flagging down a cab to take him and the backpack home to Albert Street.

*

One evening, a week or so later, he came home from work to find a bespectacled middle-aged woman in the living room with Josh, who looked up with relief at the sight of his flatmate. One glance at her face – ill-looking, caved in with worry – and Rollo knew who she must be.

'You're Rollo, are you?' she said in a tone that suggested a certain prejudice.

'I am. And you are?'

'Kathleen Ward. Rick's mother. We spoke on the phone a few times.'

'Of course, good to meet you.' Rollo stuck out a hand, aping Josh's solicitous expression. 'Has there been any news?'

Kathleen blinked behind her glasses. Her eyes were the same coffee-bean brown as Rick's. 'Not at our end, no.'

'Not here, either,' Rollo said, glancing to Josh as if *he* might pipe up with some crucial bit of intelligence.

'We thought it might be best if we take his belongings to the family home,' Kathleen said, as if expecting opposition to the idea.

'Sure,' Rollo said.

'I see you have a new flatmate already?'

Wise to this attempt to provoke him, Rollo maintained his scrupulous politeness. 'Rick told me he was working overseas and I was free to sublet. He boxed all his stuff up himself, I'll show you.'

'You don't seem very worried that he's been reported missing,' she said, more combative now, and he saw that her eyes had grown bright and filmy.

'I am worried,' he insisted. 'I honestly don't know what to think. The police haven't told me anything.'

'What do you know about this girl who tricked him into getting involved?'

He wasn't expecting *that*. 'What girl?'

'The police told us about her. She's the reason the husband had to come clean. She had recordings of him admitting to setting Rick up.'

Well, that was an interesting detail. 'Like I say, the police won't tell me anything. You're family, so it's different.'

'But you must have met her?'

God, she was persistent. 'Rick was quite secretive about his love life. I know there was someone called Vicky, could that be—?'

'No.' She cut him off, frustrated. 'She was after Vicky.'

Rollo regarded her with kindly bafflement. 'I'm sorry, I don't know what you want me to say. I'm sure he'll come back when he's ready.'

'You're sure, are you?' Dry-eyed once more, Kathleen subjected him to a cold scrutiny that reminded him of the woman in the gardening gloves. Odd how his charms had so little potency with this age group. 'Can I see his room, please?' she said, rising.

He showed her Rick's possessions, still stacked against the wall of the main bedroom, and offered to help carry them out to her car. Josh lent a hand too and it only took twenty minutes or so.

Kathleen said very little during this process, until asking, suddenly, 'Why's his backpack here?'

'What d'you mean?' Rollo had emptied it, of course, returning the kitchen items to the flat's own kitchen and redistributing Rick's clothes and other things among his boxes, but he hadn't considered there to be any reason to get rid of the pack.

'If he said he was going off travelling, wouldn't he have had it with him?'

'I didn't actually see him leave,' Rollo said, running a hand through his hair. 'I was out at a job interview that day. Maybe he bought a bigger one?'

She accepted this – or at least didn't bother arguing the point. 'I can't see his passport and driver's licence anywhere.'

'He must have them with him,' Rollo said, respectfully restoring the present tense.

He didn't say a word about Sam and the studio on Newman Street. He was damned if he was going to help her piece together the truth.

*

He agonized over the items he'd kept for himself: the watch, the Zippo, the photos and, a late acquisition, the Wilkie Collins novel. The last he added to his own bookshelf, keeping in its pages the one *Standard* article he'd been moved to cut out, the report of Marina's funeral. The photos he stored with others he'd compiled over the years; he could see no great danger in that. And the Zippo he eventually left in a bar near his office, releasing it back into circulation among the city's smokers.

But the watch was obviously of monetary value – far too

costly to have belonged to Kirsten, it must have been, if he were to guess, stolen from Marina Stanley – and as such presented a real dilemma. If he sold it, he could probably solve his financial problems, but for reasons connected indefinably to the news cutting about the funeral, he found he couldn't bear to part with it. He decided to squeeze his parents for money one last time, appealing to his sister to broker a deal.

She phoned with the offer: 'You can have a cheque for twenty thousand now and not a penny later, or nothing now and your half in their will. Obviously, that's going to be a lot more than twenty grand, so if I were you, I'd wait.'

He felt as if he were on a quiz show, the studio audience agog as to his choice.

'I'll take the cheque,' he said.

The funds were swallowed up by the debt to the loan sharks, by then over twice the amount he'd originally borrowed. Cunts. Still, it wasn't like he'd ever thought they were running a charity.

*

Not long after, Josh – rapidly becoming his personal assistant – alerted him to the article in the paper:

WHERE IS RICK WARD?

As residents of the idyllic suburb of Silver Vale come to terms with the dramatic conviction of Drew Stanley for the murder of his wife Marina, the mother of the original suspect in the case has made an emotional plea to the public to help in the search for her missing son.

'It's months since we spoke to Rick and the police have just been fobbing us off,' explains Kathleen Ward, who lives in Horsham. 'At first they said he was still in hiding and unaware that the real killer had been charged, but there's no way that can still be true.' Horrified now that she was led by police to believe her son was a killer, even allowing herself to be persuaded to make a television appeal broadcast to millions, Kathleen adds, 'We have serious doubts about their commitment to finding him.'

However, she reserves her harshest criticism for her son's flatmate, Rollo Farnworth, 26. 'The one person who could have helped Rick was Rollo. He must have known he was innocent and desperate for help, but he didn't do the first thing about it.' Recently visiting her son's flat to collect his belongings, she was shocked to discover that Farnworth was 'carrying on as if nothing had happened'.

'He's even taken our son's bedroom and moved in a new lodger. We've spoken to Rick's landlord and he told us that the lease is still in Rick's name and that he's paid months of rent in advance. If you ask me, it suits Rollo that Rick has just vanished into thin air. He doesn't want to get involved. He doesn't want to be associated with the scandal.

'I never trusted him,' Kathleen adds. 'From what other friends of Rick's have said, he was a bad influence, got Rick into drugs and all sorts. Now he's getting on with his life as if Rick never existed. Shame on him.'

Rollo was, absurdly, offended by her assessment of him – not to mention inconvenienced. The entire length of the original coverage he had avoided being mentioned by name, always the 'flatmate' or a 'close friend', and now, just when he was starting to relax, this.

When the heartless flatmate story was picked up by other papers, he left both the flat and his job, dispensing with his more memorable name for all future admin and using instead his blander middle names, Alex Parker. He intended the modification to be temporary, but found it suited him, and he eventually made it legal. Kathleen Ward turned out to be right: even as the scandal receded and digital news eroded the power of tabloid print – and even after he'd begun training to be an auditor in some bizarre, unfathomable tribute to his departed friend – he couldn't bear to be associated with it.

He couldn't bear to be Rollo.

49

Alex

October, present

Kirsten sat with her arms wrapped around her knees, staring at the kids' makeshift den but, judging by her expression of dazed horror, not actually seeing it. After a while, he settled next to her, careful not to make contact. He could feel the autumnal chill from the ground creeping through his jeans.

'This new nature trail,' she said, presently. 'How come he wasn't found when they did the construction work?'

'I don't know,' Alex said. 'Dumb luck, I think. They only excavated certain sections and this wasn't one of them. But I was expecting it the whole time. It's been terrible. Every day, I've expected to see the police. Those forensic investigators in their white suits.' Though he tried hard to keep the choke of self-pity from his voice, he must have failed because she flicked him a look of disgust.

'What would you have done? Confessed or denied?'

It was an excellent question and there was no reason not to answer truthfully. 'I've always thought I'd confess, but actually ... I've lasted this long, so I might as well hold out to the bitter end. By now, would they even be able to identify him?'

'I don't know.' Her shudder of distaste was replaced by acceptance and – dare he hope? – respect. 'I guess it's brave of you to confess to me. You're not going to kill me, too, are you?'

'No,' he said. What a perverse, black-hearted conversation this was. 'I know you can keep a secret.'

'I grassed on Drew,' she pointed out.

'That was the right thing to do.'

'That's not what you thought at the time.'

'I was just covering my own arse, making it up as I went along.'

They lapsed into silence again. In a nearby garden, a play-date was taking place, a young girl dictating rules about a game, telling another child off. He thought, briefly, of Zara and the victory he had handed her.

'I know what you mean about living with that dread,' Kirsten said. 'That was how I felt when I heard Drew had been released.'

'He hasn't ever come after you, though?'

'No. I mean, I've made myself hard to find, but even so, he could have done it if he wanted to. Private detectives can smoke anyone out.'

Alex thought of the man in the pub in Burton upon Trent; the firepower was still there, yes, the remorselessness, but it would be very reluctantly deployed, if ever. 'I saw him once and I don't think he's been looking for trouble. Not that you'd want to mess with him, but I think twenty years was enough. He was injured in prison, you know. He lost an eye.'

'I didn't know that.' As if cutting dead any feelings of sympathy before they could take root, she added, fiercely, 'He deserved everything he got. He took her life. Anyone who got in his way, he just stamped on them. I don't think you ever realized how awful he was. He was just so convincing, he made you doubt your own thoughts. It was gaslighting, I know that now. I honestly think Rick was the only person who ever believed me over him.'

'And the police,' he pointed out. 'To be honest, I never really understood why they did. Why was Drew so quick to plead guilty? I'd have expected him to convince them you were just some nutter.'

'The family had had doubts, apparently. They knew there'd been fights about money and he'd threatened her a few times. She'd told her brother she wanted to split but had ended up staying. So when they got wind that there was someone disputing his alibi, they put pressure on the police to take it seriously.' Drawing breath, Kirsten knitted her fingers together, one thumb nail picking at the cuticle of the other. 'It took a little while but they managed to track down the minicab we took to Victoria. Rick had asked me about it, what make of car it was, and I'd thought I couldn't remember anything, but when I was giving my statement, I remembered this sticker the guy had had on the windscreen. "I love the Eighties", you know, with the red heart? We were lucky he hadn't cleaned his car since the murder and there were specks of her blood in the back where Drew had been sitting.'

'I heard you'd made some recordings?'

'That's right. I had a Dictaphone I'd nicked from Culkins and I used it when he was at my place, talking about the burglary, what he was going to nick. It wouldn't have been admissible in court, but it rattled him and by then the cab driver had ID-ed him and it was pretty much game over.'

He watched as a sudden breeze lifted her hair, rattled the foliage. 'Kirsten?'

'Mmm?'

She didn't turn her head and so he spoke to her profile, watching the gentle sweep of her lashes as she blinked. 'I need to . . . I wanted to say I'm sorry. I mean for using you. Making you do what you probably wouldn't have done if you'd had a choice.'

'Probably?'

He conceded the distinction. At the time, it had been easy enough to interpret her surrender as consent, but in the two and a half decades since then, any last ambiguities on that score had been swept away.

She shrugged. 'I was used to it.'

'That makes it even worse.'

She bowed her head a little.

'Not Rick, though. He worshipped you.'

'He did.' She smiled a private smile. 'I loved him, you know. I didn't intend to develop feelings, but I did.'

'That can happen,' he agreed. As she'd been developing hers for Rick, he'd been developing them for her. Yes, the way he'd acted on them had been reprehensible, he'd been a self-serving twat, but the way he'd felt, those nobler emotions, *they* had had some merit, surely. It had endured too, his fixation, his love (he'd only named it that after she'd gone), or perhaps it was fairer to say it had been arrested, blocking the path of any successors. Years later, he used to dream of reconnecting with her, of it being her, not Beth, in his bed, in his marriage – and now here she was, telling him she'd loved the man he'd killed, whose remains lay beneath them.

They got to their feet and walked back to the Long Lane steps, passing a group of kids swarming the log pile. Then they were walking, apparently directionless, until he saw she'd extracted a car key from her pocket and was drawing up next to a decade-old Renault Clio.

'What happens now?' he said. He wanted her to stay and go with the same stomach-roiling intensity.

She met his gaze. 'I name my price. Like we agreed.'

'I might not be able to meet it,' he said, truthfully. 'But I promise I'll give you whatever I've got. Right down to the last penny.'

'Thank you,' she said. 'I'll take it.'

50

Alex

November, present

Later, he saw how it could have gone one of two ways — rather as at every other critical juncture in this sorry saga. This tragedy.

It could have been Kirsten and not Marina who was murdered.

It could have been Rick and not Drew who spent twenty years in jail.

It could have been Rollo and not Rick who perished in that ignominious last scrap up on the old track.

And this episode, too, how easily it could have condemned him rather than saved him. He could have walked down the trail this fresh-skied afternoon in November and found brawny men from the fire brigade thinking they were merely making the bank safe again, only to stumble on a ghastly discovery . . .

Or even the police forensics team of his nightmares, already in situ in their white space suits and masks, gloved hands searching and sifting and brushing.

An hour or two later and this could certainly have been the case. Instead, thanks to Zara of all people, he was in the right place at the right time.

They had split up, of course, he and Beth. If he'd had any intention of co-operating with the marriage counselling before Kirsten's visit, then it had dissolved by the time he'd returned to the cottage. Instead, he'd asked, candidly, irreversibly, 'Would you be able to buy me out?' and watched his wife's face sag with dismay and relief.

They'd had the place valued on the Monday and by the Wednesday Beth's family had agreed to loan her the portion of Alex's lump sum not covered by a re-mortgage. Since he had become co-owner, the place had soared in value (that *Guardian* feature had worked its magic too) and, give or take, he would get £200,000. He told Kirsten she could have it all. To start his new life – whatever that was, *wherever* that was – he would sell the Cartier watch. That was more than he deserved.

'If you even think about coming after me for more,' he told her, less in threat than in statement of fact, 'I promise you there'll be nothing left.'

'I won't,' she said.

Zara, meanwhile, would stay on as Beth's lodger. Unlike Alex, whose request for voluntary redundancy had been laughed out of town, she had every expectation of milking her employers for all they were worth via her constructive dismissal claim. Once the payout was awarded, she'd contribute financially to the household.

'If there's anything I can do, please just say,' she told Alex, and it was the last thing she said to him before he left. The expression in her eyes was sincere, too, the sentiment unfeigned. She *meant* it.

'Cool. Same here,' he managed in return. It was far too late to determine what he had fabricated of her malevolence and what had been real.

As for Beth, he was pleased for her that she was rid of him, to be frank, and, if anything *were* to come out, he would make sure his original name was used. That way, fewer, if any, of her friends and colleagues would be able to make the connection.

After all, it was Rollo who was guilty of murder, not Alex.

*

So, in the end, it was all down to luck. Really, he couldn't think of a better word. Maybe caprice. For, a week ahead of schedule, the baby was coming and Beth, as Zara's birthing partner, needed to drop everything and mobilize. She'd rung Alex at his new short-term rental two stops down the line: was there any possibility he could let himself into the house and take care of Olive?

'Of course,' he said. 'I can stay as long as you need me.'

He'd hurried from the station, muscle memory taking him past the turn onto Exmoor Gardens and to the Surrey Road entrance to the trail. And now, as he neared the stretch behind number 54, he heard a female voice, shrill, piercing, the cry of a mother at the end of her tether. 'Boys, what the *hell* have you done! *Look* at this!'

He drew to a halt and surveyed the scene. A section of the bank had collapsed. Not quite *the* section, but heart-stoppingly close, a couple of paces away. Standing by her gate, looking askance at the dust-caked chaos, was Frankie. Her sons stood in a line a short distance away, a trio of tiny suspects, electrified by the drama of it all.

'You need some help?' he said.

She swivelled at the sound of his voice. 'Oh, Alex. Thank God, another grown-up.'

'What've they been up to now?'

She gestured, eyes flaming. 'They had this den and I hadn't realized how big it had got. Now it's come crashing down and messed up this whole bit of the bank. I have *zero* idea how to make it safe again. I'm already in trouble with Cordelia across the way for letting them climb trees, I can't bear her to get wind and call the fire brigade or social services or God knows who.'

Alex gave an understanding smile. 'I'm not sure it's *that* serious. The main thing is no one was in the den when it came down.' Wasn't *that* the truth: the emergency services would have been on their way if there'd been a casualty, neighbours frantically summoned to help. 'Why don't we relocate the den to the bottom of your garden?' He winked at the kids. 'We can probably improve it while we're at it. I'll need your design input, mind.'

'What about all this?' Frankie said, indicating the gaping wound in the bank.

Alex did his best to impersonate a man who had not twenty-five years earlier buried a warm body alongside this very spot. 'I can sort that out for you, as well. It just needs patching up. It'll be as good as new, I promise. Just leave it to me.'

Thank *fuck* it wasn't raining, he thought, and turning the whole thing into a mudslide.

'Really? That would be fantastic!' Frankie gazed at him as if he were the Messiah. He wondered if the unfaithful husband had ever returned; he couldn't remember Beth's and Zara's appraisal ever veering from the 'better off without the bastard' rule to which he too had now fallen victim.

'You got some tools I can use?' he asked.

'Of course, come and see what's in my shed.'

'*Daddy's* shed,' piped up one of the kids in a show of loyalty and Frankie silenced him with a deathly glare.

'*You've* done quite enough for one day, thank you. Are you really sure you don't mind?' she asked Alex in a far sweeter tone.

'I'm sure,' he said. 'But after that I need to go and walk my dog. My ex-wife's friend's gone into labour and she's gone to the hospital with her.'

'I know your dog,' she said, as he joined her at the foot of the bank and followed her into the garden. 'Olive, isn't it? She's such a sweetie, the boys love her. Why don't you bring her here after your walk? Have a drink? It's the least I can do.'

'Maybe,' Alex said. Then, 'Sure, that would be nice.'

He pictured it then, startlingly fully formed, an image of the near future – too grand to call it a *prophecy*, but certainly an alternative to his planned life in hiding in a friendless territory where his only grasp of the language was to order the booze that would slowly kill him.

Instead, two recently separated people coming together. The easy blessing of his ex up the road and, harder-won perhaps, of hers too (there were kids involved after all). A view of his old friend's resting place from the bedroom window and round-the-clock surveillance of any further attempts to disarrange it. The only knock at the door a visit from his grown-up daughter with whom he'd chosen to connect, after all – tentatively, discreetly, for both their sakes – and who'd naturally inherited all of his best qualities and none of his worst.

Savannah, that was her name. Sweet Savannah.

But he was getting ahead of himself. First things first. As the shed door swung open to reveal a pleasingly well-ordered collection of implements, he stepped forward and reached for a shovel.

Acknowledgements

My heartfelt thanks to the team at Simon & Schuster UK, especially Suzanne Baboneau and Ian Chapman, who have been incredibly kind and supportive to me over the years. Also to Katherine Armstrong, Louise Davies, Jess Barratt, Hayley McMullan, Hannah Paget, Sara-Jade Virtue, Dom Brendon, Gill Richardson, Maddie Allan, Matt Johnson, Dan Ruffino, Heather Hogan, Susan Opie and Jane Selley. A huge thank you, too, to Laura Sherlock for PR.

Thank you, as ever, to the incomparable Curtis Brown crew, led by the best in the business, Sheila Crowley: Emily Harris, Sabhbh Curran, Katie McGowan, Grace Robinson. And, of course, the dynamo that is Luke Speed, brilliantly supported by Anna Weguelin and Theo Roberts.

I'm very grateful to all the booksellers, librarians, reviewers and bloggers who recommend my books, and to the overseas publishers and translators who help cast my stories far and wide.

Thank you to the TV teams developing my books for the screen. A special cheer for Red Planet Pictures, screenwriter

Simon Ashdown and ITV, the dream team that brought *Our House* to an audience of millions.

And thank you, of course, to my readers – some brand new, some who've read every word I've written: I await your verdict with chewed fingernails!

This is my sixteenth novel and I think was the most enjoyable to write, partly because of the 1990s strand, which was a thrill to revisit (even in the context of crime) in this more anxious era. Even so, I couldn't have managed it without research by Into the Breach – there were so many details from the summer of 1995 that I should have remembered and yet, thanks to a lifestyle not unlike that of Rick and Rollo, could not!

Finally, a word about inspiration. I remember very clearly listening to the BBC Radio 4 dramatization of Barbara Vine's classic novel *A Fatal Inversion* and thinking how heart-stoppingly powerful it is – that moment when misadventures from our younger, more reckless days come back to bite us. I thought, 'Ooh, I might try something like this'.

Well, I did try and here it is.

Enjoyed *The Only Suspect*?
Discover more edge-of-your-seat thrillers
from bestselling author Louise Candlish . . .

The Heights

'I didn't read *The Heights*, I inhaled it' LISA JEWELL

Ellen Saint is just your average mum. Devoted to her family, she's no different from any other mother who wants the best for her kids. But when her teenage son Lucas brings a new friend home, cracks start to appear in Ellen's perfect family life.

Kieran Watts isn't like Lucas. He's rude, obnoxious and reckless, and Ellen can only watch in despair as her son falls deeper under his influence.

Then Ellen's whole world implodes and she embarks on an obsessive need to get revenge.

There is nothing you won't do for your children – even murder . . .

AVAILABLE NOW IN PAPERBACK AND EBOOK

**SIMON &
SCHUSTER**

Our House

NOW A MAJOR ITV SERIES

When Fi Lawson arrives home to find strangers moving into her house, she is plunged into terror and confusion. She and her husband Bram have owned their home on Trinity Avenue for years and have no intention of selling. How can this other family possibly think the house is theirs?

Then, just as Fi needs him most, Bram disappears. Having made a catastrophic mistake, he is now paying the price and has nothing left but to try and settle old scores.

As the nightmare takes hold, both Bram and Fi attempt to make sense of the events that led to a devastating crime. What has he hidden from her – and what has she hidden from him?

And will either survive the chilling truth – that there are far worse things you can lose than your house?

AVAILABLE NOW IN PAPERBACK AND EBOOK

**SIMON &
SCHUSTER**

The Skylight

QUICK READS 2021

They can't see her, but she can see them . . .

Simone has a secret. She likes to stand at her bathroom
window and spy on the couple downstairs through their
kitchen skylight. She knows what they eat for breakfast
and who they've got over for dinner. She knows what
mood they're in before they even step out the door.
There's nothing wrong with looking, is there?

Until one day Simone sees something through the
skylight that she is not expecting. Something that upsets
her so much she begins to plot a terrible crime . . .

AVAILABLE NOW IN EBOOK

**SIMON &
SCHUSTER**

The Other Passenger

It all happens so quickly. One day you're living the dream,
commuting to work by riverbus with your charismatic
neighbour Kit in the seat beside you. The next, Kit hasn't turned
up for the boat and his wife Melia has reported him missing.

When you get off at your stop, the police are waiting. Another
passenger saw you and Kit arguing on the boat home the
night before and the police say that you had a reason to want
him dead. You protest. You and Kit are friends – ask Melia,
she'll vouch for you. And who exactly is this other passenger
pointing the finger? What do they know about your lives?

No, whatever danger followed you home last
night, you are innocent, totally innocent.

Aren't you?

Those People

'Nail-bitingly tense from the first page to the
last. Louise Candlish shows us the dark side of
suburbia – and of ourselves' ERIN KELLY

Until Darren and Jodie move in, Lowland Way is a
suburban paradise. Beautiful homes. Friendly neighbours.
Kids playing out in the street. But Darren and Jodie
don't follow the rules, and soon disputes over loud music
and parking rights escalate to threats of violence.

Then, early one Sunday, a horrific crime shocks the
street. As the police go house-to-house, the residents close
ranks and everyone's story is the same: They did it.

But there's a problem. The police don't agree.

And the door they're knocking on next is yours.

AVAILABLE NOW IN PAPERBACK AND EBOOK

**SIMON &
SCHUSTER**